W9-CMU-390

"A potent novel. . . . Best of all . . . is the complex and charismatic heroine. . . . Lovett offers an exceptional plot, unusual characters . . . and vivid forensic details."
—*Booklist*

PRAISE FOR SARAH LOVETT'S SHATTERING FORENSIC THRILLERS FEATURING DR. SYLVIA STRANGE

A DESPERATE SILENCE

"This is a spirited thriller that will keep the reader guessing and careening at the same time. . . . Lovett builds her yarn well, carefully placing her explosive climaxes and revelations throughout, which culminate in a huge border-crossing chase, complete with helicopters, traitors, and sudden reversals. You won't be able to put it down."
—*Providence Sunday Journal*

"[A] compelling read."
—*Milwaukee Journal Sentinel*

"The slam-bang opening of *A DESPERATE SILENCE* . . . sets the tone for a thriller that's a page-turner. . . . Lovett handles all the storylines with aplomb."
—*Albuquerque Sunday Journal*

"Tense and absorbing."
—*Publishers Weekly*

"The book opens with a bang. . . . Fast-paced, taut. . . . Serves up a nice plate of plot twists. . . . It's a compelling page-turner, and they do keep turning right up to the end."
—*The Capital Times* (Madison, WI)

"Should appeal to readers who like their thrillers . . . complex, and at a breakneck pace."

—*Library Journal*

DANGEROUS ATTACHMENTS

"[A] suspense-soaked thriller. . . . A welcome addition to Patricia Cornwell territory."

—*West Coast Review of Books*

"[A] chilling tale, peppered with continuous plot turns."

—*San Francisco Examiner*

"*Dangerous Attachments* continues to surprise and excite to the very end. An emotional, vivid thriller."

—Vincent Bugliosi, author of *Helter Skelter*

"If you're looking for electrifying, heart-pounding excitement, you can bungee jump into the Grand Canyon or you can pick up *Dangerous Attachments*. . . . Forensic psychologist Sylvia Strange is surely one of the most unforgettable characters in mystery fiction today."

—Douglas Preston, author of *Relic* and *Talking to the Ground*

"What drives *Dangerous Attachments* is not only its relentless plot and ruthless depictions of aberrant behavior, but the verisimilitude of character and place on each page."

—*Santa Fe Reporter*

"*Dangerous Attachments* introduces a likeable character in forensic psychiatrist Dr. Sylvia Strange, and a twisted-enough bad guy to ensure both a fun and fast beach read."

—*Entertainment Weekly*

"A well-written, cleverly plotted book about real characters. . . . It's about politics and power, paranoia and lunacy, terrifying situations, and missing body parts."

—*Arizona Republic*

ACQUIRED MOTIVES

"Lovett is a talented writer of the Patricia Cornwell genre."

—*Albuquerque Journal*

"A rip-roaring story."

—*Kirkus Reviews*

DANTES' INFERNO

"Lovett . . . is harder edged, higher tech, and cooler than ever."

—*Library Journal*

"WARNING: Don't start this book if you've got plans for the next day or so. I guarantee you'll cancel them to stay home and keep reading. *Dantes' Inferno* has everything readers crave: a full-throttle plot, top-notch psychological suspense."

—Jeffery Deaver, author of *The Stone Monkey*

"Should keep suspense fans turning the pages. . . . Skillfully wrought."

—*Publishers Weekly*

"[A] wild saga . . . [Lovett's] forte has always been a darkly fertile imagination untrammeled by the focus or discipline that could harness it."

—*Kirkus Reviews*

Books by Sarah Lovett

Dangerous Attachments
Acquired Motives
A Desperate Silence
Dantes' Inferno

Available from POCKET BOOKS

SARAH LOVETT

A DR. SYLVIA STRANGE NOVEL

A DESPERATE SILENCE

POCKET BOOKS
New York   London   Toronto   Sydney   Singapore

The sale of this book without its cover is unauthorized. If you purchased this book without a cover, you should be aware that it was reported to the publisher as "unsold and destroyed." Neither the author nor the publisher has received payment for the sale of this "stripped book."

This book is a work of fiction. Names, characters, places and incidents are products of the author's imagination or are used fictitiously. Any resemblance to actual events or locales or persons, living or dead, is entirely coincidental.

POCKET BOOKS, a division of Simon & Schuster, Inc.
1230 Avenue of the Americas, New York, NY 10020

Copyright © 1998 by Sarah Lovett

All rights reserved, including the right to reproduce this book or portions thereof in any form whatsoever. For information address Pocket Books, 1230 Avenue of the Americas, New York, NY 10020

ISBN: 978-1-4767-7980-5

First Pocket Books printing March 2003

10 9 8 7 6 5 4 3 2 1

POCKET and colophon are registered trademarks of Simon & Schuster, Inc.

For information regarding special discounts for bulk purchases, please contact Simon & Schuster Special Sales at 1-800-456-6798 or business@simonandschuster.com

Cover design by Tony Greco

Excerpts from: *Dangerous Attachments* © 1995 by Sarah Lovett; *Acquired Motives* © 1996 by Sarah Lovett; *Dantes' Inferno* © 2001 by Sarah Lovett; and *Dark Alchemy* © 2003 by Sarah Lovett

Printed in the U.S.A.

The angels are so enamoured of the language that is spoken in heaven, that they will not distort their lips with the hissing and unmusical dialects of men, but speak their own, whether there be any who understand it or not.

—RALPH WALDO EMERSON

this book is for three angels

ACKNOWLEDGMENTS

David Rosenthal and Leona Nevler
Louise Burke, Maggie Crawford, Christina Boys, and
    everyone at Pocket Books
Theresa Park, Julie Barer, and Peter McGuigan
Saul Cohen
Timothy Thompson
Miriam Sagan
The Edit Femmes
Steve Poland, Ph.D.
Jude Pardee, Ph.D.
Bernard Baca, Ph.D.
Susan Steinberg
Susan Cave, Ph.D.
Jacqueline West, Ph.D.
Layne Vickers Smith and Rick Smith
Alice Sealey
Peggy van Hulsteyn
Judge Bill Bivens
Connie Warren
Jim Burleson

Gloria McCary
Carrie Converse
Romaine Serna
Mark Donatelli
Carlos Ruiz
Richard Folkes
Officer Robert Gonzales
Rodger Armstrong
Lawrence Renner, P.A.
Shari Weinstein
Bruce Mann, M.D.
Suzanne Johnson and Brianna Johnson
March Kessler
Sally Sommer
Ana Matiella
Annik LaFarge
Zoe Wolff, Brian McLendon, Dennis Ambrose
Anne Williams and Victoria Routledge and, of course,
    Peter Miller and Jennifer Robinson

CHAPTER ONE

THE GIRL GRIPPED the steering wheel with both hands. Her fingers were pale where knuckles stretched skin, her arms were thin as sticks. Bones—not flesh—defined her body. Toes on toes, her bare feet pressed the accelerator flush against the Honda's floorboard. Her head scarcely topped the dashboard, but she saw the narrow horizon of blacktop change suddenly to desert and barbed wire. Raising a wake of dust, the car hurtled headlong off the highway toward a fence. Gravel smacked the windshield.

As the fence loomed closer, the world careened past the moving car—low trees, jutting rocks, rolling terrain. The child's chest heaved, but all sound of her breathing was smothered by a song blaring from the radio. The music rose tinnily above the rattle of loose metal and the high-pitched whine of hot engine.

The girl jerked the steering wheel to the left, straining her muscles, frantic when the vehicle didn't respond

the way Paco had taught her it would. She was sure the
car would crash and she would die in flames and
twisted metal. For an instant, she imagined giving in to
the black night. But she was a fighter, and so she focused
the last reserves of her energy on steering the car.
Finally, she felt the shudder of tires forced back onto the
hard surface of the road.

Dim yellow headlamps filled the rearview mirror, and
the child's heartbeat stuttered. It was *el demonio*, the
demon—with his dark hungry face. The lights glowed
like the eyes of a crazy animal. A sudden memory jolted
through her mind: fingernails scratching her neck just as
Paco's strong arms pulled her from the demon's reach.

But there were no grown-ups with her now—and no
safe place. Just the yellow glowing eyes of her pursuer
growing larger in the rearview mirror.

Blood smeared the girl's cheek and lip. Dried blood
where she had slammed her cheek against metal, fresh
blood where she bit her lip in fright. A deep blue-black
bruise darkened the inside of her left thigh. Beneath the
delicate chain and the silver medallion around her neck,
the skin was red and scratched where the demon had
torn at her with long cold fingers.

Suddenly, there was a new danger—bright flashing
lights in *front* of the Honda—coming at her! These
lights snaked across the road, blocking her path. The
child was trapped. Her eyes opened wide, and panic
stole her breath away.

What was it? A truck? A bridge? *A train!*

She swerved the Honda and hit the brakes again—
but too hard. The car went into a skid, across the road
toward barbed wire and tracks. She couldn't escape the
metal snout of the train engine.

A cry of terror escaped the child's mouth, just as a fat hunter's moon broke over the foothills of the Sangre de Cristos. The moon's glow suffused the night sky. She whispered the first words of the prayer.

Our Mother, Nuestra Madre—

And then she squeezed her eyes shut as a solid wall of moving metal caught the front end of the Honda. The noise of rending metal and a shower of sparks raked the night as the train pushed the car fifty yards along the track.

THE DARK GREEN CHEVROLET Suburban slowed on U.S. 285 just south of Lamy, New Mexico, and Lorenzo Santos Portrillo tried to make sense of what he'd just witnessed: the Honda had collided with a train. He peered out into the moonlit desert, straining to locate the ruined car, to gauge the seriousness of the accident. What he saw was an illuminated mess of smoke and dust and twisted metal roughly a quarter mile away. Directly ahead, the stalled train blocked the road.

His eyes were invisible in the unlit interior of the vehicle. His even white teeth were clenched. The scent of citrus cologne clashed with the uncharacteristic tang of nervous sweat and blood. Despite his agitation, Lorenzo's physical movements remained tightly controlled, but his mind refused to harness information with its usual discipline. He'd seen a ghost tonight; at first he believed she'd returned from the grave to do him evil.

But her terror had persuaded him she was merely human.

Renzo eased his foot off the accelerator, letting the Suburban coast. He was focused on the flashing lights of the train, and he almost failed to register a car, hazard lights blinking, pulling off to the side of the road opposite the scene of the accident.

The warning message squeezed through to his consciousness: *more people to deal with tonight.* They were crossing the road, shining flashlights over the terrain as they approached the crash.

Was the girl alive or dead?

Lorenzo drove slowly. In the time it took the Suburban to cover the last eighth of a mile, a man— lantern in hand—swung himself down from the train and darted toward the wrecked Honda. The car had been crushed by the train's massive engine.

Lorenzo's gloved fingers grazed his steering wheel; the gloves were cheap leather throwaways. On his left wrist, the thick silver bracelet—etched with the face of Serpent Skirt—was smeared with Paco's blood.

The blood had a dull sheen visible even in the darkness of the car. He remembered to check his face in the rearview mirror. When he briefly snapped on the overhead light, he saw the droplet of blood above his lip. He wiped the stain away.

The Suburban vibrated as its right tires ate soft shoulder less than a hundred feet from the wreck. The beams of the car's headlights illuminated weeds and a downed barbed-wire fence. A discarded plastic bag, caught on a barb, shivered in the evening breeze like a stranded octopus.

Lorenzo put the Suburban in park, engine idling. As he pushed his arms into his suit jacket, he slid a .22 semiautomatic into the right pocket. His briefcase was on the floor of the passenger side. His suitcase and his golf clubs were in the trunk.

A harsh sigh escaped his lips. It would be dangerous to deal with multiple witnesses. Not that he couldn't do it. Two nights ago he had killed four men—two of them trained bodyguards. But he needed all his wits, his resources—he couldn't deny he'd been shaken by the discovery of the child. He took a breath, exhaled slowly, and stepped out of the car.

Moving across the rough terrain toward the wreck, he quickly reviewed the possible scenarios. He discarded most of them. It would be best to deal with this particular situation quietly.

He prepared his face: overlaying concern with compassion, he became the essence of the Good Samaritan. When he was close enough to the men gathered around the driver's side of the Honda, he called out. "Can I help? Should I call someone?"

He saw several heads turn his way before the beam of a flashlight blinded him. He turned his face from the light. A male voice was ordering members of the group: "Let me through, see if I get a pulse."

Renzo moved around the far side of the Honda. He gazed in one window, but the vehicle's interior appeared empty. No luggage, no sacks, no bundles. This wasn't the time or place to complete his search.

He heard men murmuring worriedly. Fragments of conversation floated on the cold night air.

"Just a kid . . ."

". . . saw it happen . . ."

". . . one minute this white Honda was on the road . . ."

". . . why would a little girl be all alone out here . . ."

A minute passed, then two. Renzo's fingers slid over the grip of the semiautomatic. Covertly, he hefted its weight as he kept one ear on the conversation around him.

"Maybe she's illegal . . ."

". . . no I.D. . . ."

". . . called state police . . ."

His patience was waning. He stepped closer to the edge of the small group; shoulders parted to allow him a view. He stared impassively down at the child's inert body. Her head lolled back, and he saw that blood covered her eyes, her throat. One of her legs was twisted in a peculiar position. She looked dead.

Renzo thought each word as he pronounced it: "I know C.P.R.—"

"So do I." This man was hunched over the child's body, his fingers pressing for a pulse. "C.P.R. won't help this little one. She's gone."

Relieved, Renzo made what he thought were appropriate noises of distress. After a moment, he turned and walked back to the car. He guided the Suburban in a wide U-turn across the broken white line and into the southbound lane.

As he drove, he reached for his cellular phone, paged his associate, and entered Code 77. Divine wrath. Translation: kill complete.

Moonlight cut across his eyes for an instant, and Lorenzo Santos Portrillo—or Renzo as he was called by his few social contacts—blinked. What haunted him was the knowledge that he had killed this child already, ten years ago.

THE CHILD THOUGHT she heard a voice like music filled with unbearable joy. She stared up into eyes as deep as the ocean . . . sunbeams darted from a cloak of green . . . and stars sparkled everywhere like poor people's diamonds.

She reached out to touch this beautiful vision—

But a loud voice boomed like thunder. The child felt a whipsaw of pain, and she choked, gasping for air. Something warm trailed across her temple; her left eye was lost in a pool of darkness. From her right eye, she noticed the angels hovering over her body. They were big—surrounded by stars, *yes*—but they stank of gasoline and burning rubber. She hadn't known angels would make so much noise. They chattered like chickens. Heaven must be a confusing place.

It was a foreign place where the sky quickly remade itself—stars were washed away by white searing light only to be smothered out by thicker gray clouds. And then there was the screech of a huge bird—a cat—*no*, a siren.

Heaven? The child wouldn't be so easily fooled. This was no heaven. It was earth. She sighed, holding back tears. The shapes hovering over her were just people, not angels.

No one reaching out with loving arms . . .

At first the child heard fear in the strangers' voices. Then business. Then soft concern. Although she did not understand all the words they spoke, she knew that none of these was the demon.

She closed her good eye and let the soft sway of the world send her down into uneasy sleep. It came to her in a place of dreams that her friend Paco, *el viejo* Paco, must be badly hurt—or maybe even dead. He had always been like her grandfather, and he had protected her, even on this trip. He had fallen protecting her. She did not cry, nor was she surprised by this abandonment. Death came around plenty.

The child raised her hand to grasp the silver medallion around her neck; her fingers closed around warm metal.

The harsh lights buoyed her toward consciousness just long enough so she could breathe the smell of medicine, hear the distant howl of more sirens, and feel the fleeting panic of loss.

AT TWO-TWENTY A.M., the child was wheeled into the emergency room at St. Vincent's Hospital in Santa Fe. The triage nurse on duty spoke with the ambulance attendants, discovering only that the child had been thrown from a wrecked car. There were no other known occupants—no driver to be found—no victims except the girl. A train crew had witnessed the collision of automobile and iron horse.

One of the ambulance attendants pulled the nurse aside and handed her a plastic bag with the child's few possessions. "We got the call; first they told Dispatch the kid was dead," he said. "Frigging E.M.T. trainee and he couldn't even find a pulse. It's kind of a miracle she survived."

The nurse took a long look at the injured, semiconscious child. Hispanic. Preadolescent—nine or ten years old. About eighty-five pounds, not small but scrawny. Wide forehead, high cheekbones, she'd be a knockout when she grew into that face. Bruises, old and new. Scratches on her hands and knees. A large bruise on her thigh. Scalp injury. Maybe there'd been abuse. Triage priority: serious, but not life-threatening.

The first rescue worker on the scene had thought she was dead . . . in an accident that bad, she *should* have died. The nurse knew the little one was this week's miracle.

The child was moved to Cubicle 5, where one of the emergency-room doctors began a physical examination. Bent over the gurney, hands working expertly: abrasion on the forehead, blood pooled in the left eye but originating from the scalp wound. No other obvious external injuries. There were still internal injuries to rule out. For that they would need cervical spine film and a CT scan.

The child felt hands on her face, her skin. Some emotion flickered into her consciousness—fear, sorrow? Someone was tugging her back to the world—she didn't want to wake up, and she didn't like the hurt or the butterflies of terror in her stomach. She went down like a rock through water.

One hour and forty-two minutes later, Dolores Martin, a social worker from New Mexico Children, Youth, and Family's Child Protective Services Division arrived at the hospital to deal with the unidentified child.

Ms. Martin, a woman in her midtwenties, had neglected to comb her hair, and her clothes looked slightly rumpled. She briefly interviewed E.R. staff and was informed that the child had regained consciousness. Seated on a stool next to the bed in Cube 5, the social worker spoke in English. "Hello, little one. You don't have to be frightened; I'm here to help you. Can you tell me your name?"

After several seconds of silence, the social worker repeated her short speech in Spanish. Then she touched the child's arm gently, and whispered, *"Jita, estás sana y segura."*

If the child felt safe and sound, she did not say so. Her velvety brown eyes slid away from the woman. Her sigh was almost inaudible. She turned her face to the wall. She wished Paco were with her, holding her hand in his rough fingers, smelling nicely of pencils, paper money, and tobacco. These people were a sea of green, and their voices were big and jumbled. She clutched the silver medallion. Pictures flashed through her head— the hours of sleep and travel, noise and motion jarring her awake as the Honda was forced off the road, the demon's soft angry voice, Paco falling in his own blood.

Worst of all, the way the demon stared at her—never once blinking—as if he could kill her with his yellow eyes.

Without a sound, she bit through the skin on her knuckle.

Outside the curtained cubicle, Ms. Martin cornered the E.R. doctor, who was probably in his early thirties, with an athletic build and a brusque manner.

The doctor waved a chart and said, "Nothing abnormal showed up on the CT scan, and there was no evidence of spinal injuries on the film. She's mute because she has preexisting organic problems—or because she's scared out of her wits." As he spoke, his manner softened, becoming a mixture of fatigue and sympathy. "We can admit her to Pediatrics for a day, or you can use your department's resources. It's up to you."

At about that time, a reporter from the *New Mexican* gathered a basic description of the accident for a short column in the next day's edition; he recognized an eye-catching headline when he saw one—CHILD DRIVER SURVIVES CRASH WITH LAMY TRAIN.

The officer who had written up the single-vehicle accident arrived at the hospital. Ms. Martin asked the stolid officer to take custody of the unidentified minor and transfer custodianship to C.P.S. with a forty-eight-hour hold.

Ms. Martin sighed. *An unidentified child had run a car into a train on Highway 285. When that mute child was admitted to the hospital, no one claimed her.*

As she pulled aside the curtain of Cube 5 to gaze at the child, her words were barely audible. "Oh, *jita* . . . let's hope the gods are traveling with you."

When she had signed off on the custody paperwork, the social worker checked her watch: 3:59 A.M. She decided to request an emergency preliminary psychological evaluation for the child.

CHAPTER TWO

THE PRIEST OPENED his huge black mouth and squawked. Sylvia Strange was about to tell him to go to hell—he was hurting her ears—but he waggled one long, scolding finger at her and pointed to the telephone.

Shit, the priest in her dream was right—it *was* the phone.

Sylvia tried to sit up in bed, but something held her down. As she elbowed her way toward consciousness, she registered the fur tickling her mouth and the hot weight crushing her chest.

Both her dogs had sneaked into bed again.

She was fairly certain she managed to groan, "Off!"

Nobody moved, but a voice mumbled, "Phone."

Except for a thatch of dark hair, Matt England, the man in Sylvia's bed, was obscured by duvet and dogs. He had been asleep for less than twenty minutes, and he was already exhausted by a run of fourteen-hour days courtesy of the New Mexico State Police.

Sylvia mouthed, "I got it." She managed to free her numb right arm from the combined dog weight of 110 pounds. Nikki, the big animal, gazed at her with rueful eyes. Rocko, her terrier mutt, yawned. Sylvia slid off the side of the bed, her baggy pajamas tangling around her legs. From a squatting position on the floor, she managed to reach the telephone receiver. As she placed it to her ear, she caught a glimpse of the digital clock: 4:21 A.M.

"This better be good."

"C.P.S. has a kid at St. Vincent's who needs a psych eval. You're it."

"Wrong." Not for the first time it occurred to Sylvia that her colleague, Dr. Albert Kove, had a truly irritating habit of sounding professional—and awake—at any hour of the day or night. She shook her head, failed to clear the fog of R.E.M. sleep, and mumbled, "Call Roberto, he does kids."

Details of her waking life were starting to seep through the haze. She had stayed up past one o'clock working on a chapter of her book. She was on deadline. She was on sabbatical. She needed sleep.

And Roberto Casias was the Forensic Evaluation Unit's child expert, for Christsake.

As she was about to let the phone slip through her fingers, she heard Albert Kove's command—for an instant his image merged with that of the finger-wagging priest.

"Wake up, Sylvia. In case you don't remember, Roberto is away, and you're on call for his emergencies."

"But—" She blinked rapidly.

"And your sabbatical ended at midnight. Get your butt to the hospital."

Synapses weren't working correctly in her brain; she was sure she had a valid reason to protest this emergency call, but in her groggy state she couldn't remember what it was. Reluctantly, Sylvia asked, "What's the kid's name?"

"She doesn't have a name. She's got the clothes on her back, a coloring book, a necklace, and a stick of bubble gum." Albert's voice softened. "She's ex parte. She's not talking. That's why they want you."

"Did you tell me which hospital?"

"St. V.'s. The social worker says she's got puppy-dog eyes."

Sylvia sighed. "Does your mother know how you behave when she's not around?" She heard Albert's rumbling laugh just before she hung up the phone.

Someone whimpered, and Sylvia tipped her head back, mouth open. Dog eyes were staring down at her, brimming with reproof.

She shook her head. "Have pity, guys."

Matt's sleepy voice drifted out from under the covers. "Take Nikki with you." The Belgian Malinois was all business. Not trained as an attack dog but the closest thing to it.

Sylvia left for the hospital fifteen minutes later with the alert shepherd by her side. Her lover and her terrier stayed behind, soundly and snugly asleep in her bed.

THE CHILD CRIED out in the darkness. The demon was coming for her again—a thin shadow, wearing his pale face and the silver bracelet on his arm. He was far away at first, but always plunging closer with a soft growl more terrifying than any roar.

And for the thousandth time, she froze—unable to

fight, unable to run. She was a helpless bundle on the bed, arms and legs as useless as wood. Because she couldn't move, she was afraid to make another sound—perhaps she could hide.

He stank of medicine and blood. And he brought a hot dusty wind wherever he went. His face appeared above her own—his unblinking yellow eyes staring down at her, burning into her skin. His lips curled over thick white teeth. As the child stared up in horror, a drop of blood slid from his mouth over his lower lip; it fell, ever so slowly, to land on her cheek. She wanted to scratch and bite, but she couldn't move.

She heard Paco's voice from such a great distance that it was only a faint, sad whisper. "How did you find us?" And then he pleaded in Spanish: "Don't hurt her! She doesn't know—"

The child moaned. Couldn't she save Paco from *el demonio?* She tried to jump up, but the demon was on her throat, holding her down—

Suddenly she remembered Paco's secret prize, which he had entrusted to her. Her breathing raced, she trembled. *Where was Paco's secret now?*

Then the image played in her memory, so bright it seared her mind: the demon hovering over Paco, the sudden spurt of blood.

Turn. Run. Fight!

She woke with a start. She yelled. Her right arm lashed out at the demon's face.

SYLVIA HEARD THE yell but pulled away too late—the child's fist caught her square on the cheek. Thunk.

Safely out of range, she touched her fingers to the skin immediately below her left eye, gingerly inspecting for damage. The area was numb, just beginning to sting; from experience, Sylvia imagined she was going to end up with a respectable shiner.

Roberto Casias would owe her big-time when he returned from his forensic psych conference.

She considered the child. Dwarfed by the hospital room, she looked as young as eight years old. At the moment, she was no longer punching. Instead, she had made herself even smaller by curling up in a fetal position on the bed.

"So we know your vocal cords work," Sylvia said. Her cheek had begun to throb. "And you've got a mean right hook." She knew the social worker had tried speaking to the child in Spanish without results, but Sylvia was looking for any reaction, for the barest flicker of comprehension. "*¿Cómo se dice* 'fighter' *en español?*" She wasn't worried about grammatical errors, and she settled on the first nonword that came to mind: "*¿Boxador?*"

The child turned her face away, and her thumb slipped into her mouth.

The thumb sucking and the fetal position were regressive behavior for an eight-, nine-, or ten-year-old. Sylvia's voice dropped for her version of a movie tough guy—rendered in truly awful Spanglish. "*Tienes un* mean *derecho* hook." She stepped five paces from the bed and slapped her hands together.

The child flinched at the sharp clap of sound.

"And your ears seem to be working. *Muy bien,* we're off to a swell start."

Until they heard from Dr. Strange, the staff at St. Vincent's would defer their decision on whether to transfer the child to a room in Pediatrics. In the meantime, E.R. bays offered opportunities for exploration that might arouse a child's curiosity. Sylvia turned her back on the child and made a show of peering into a cabinet filled with hospital gowns, then searching through a drawer packed with tongue depressors.

Her eyes were drawn to a small pile of clothes strewn on a chair. The child's possessions had been forgotten in the face of pressing medical questions. Sylvia gently folded yellow cotton slacks and set them on top of a faded pink T-shirt. A hospital admissions clerk had provided a plastic Ziploc bag for small items. Albert Kove had confused the facts—there were *three* sticks of bubble gum. In addition, the baggie contained two broken crayons, three dimes, and a supple plastic coin case, the same kind Sylvia had carried as a kid.

Hadn't Albert mentioned something else? A kid's coloring book? She found it pinned to the inside vest of the child's pink sweater; it was made of cheap, well-worn vinyl, blue background patterned with black-and-white Snoopy dogs, and it was small enough to rest in Sylvia's palm.

Inside, a very childish hand had practiced the alphabet and numbers—on the first page, painstakingly printed capital letters wandered across the page, followed by a line of numbers including a backward 3. The printing was made even more illegible by overlapping colored images: rainbows, suns, flowers . . . drawings made by a little girl. On succeeding pages, the drawings became more adept, demonstrating practice and budding creativity.

Tucked back along the seam of the chair, Sylvia found a necklace—a small silver medallion with an unusual design face; it looked Indian, perhaps Mayan . . . a jaguar?

When she turned, the child was staring directly at her with an intensity so acute it was shocking. Her eyes were tiny dark vortexes alive with fear, intelligence, and fierce longing.

Slowly, Sylvia walked to the edge of the bed. She curved toward the child, and her gaze softened. "Are you going to let me touch you without a one-two punch?"

But she didn't get the chance.

Instead, the child reached out her scraped and battered hand and stroked Sylvia's cheek. Just once. Then she closed her eyes and curled her body up like a leaf.

WITH ONE CLEAN slice, Renzo Santos brought his knife across the pale crest of eggshell. He was rewarded by the sight of gelatinous orange yolk nestled in rubbery egg white. Flecks of yolk spattered the hotel's linen tablecloth, and Renzo's mouth pursed in distaste. Without looking at the waiter, he said, "I asked for a three-minute egg."

"I'm sorry, sir. I'll have the kitchen make you another one—"

Renzo shook his head. "Have them broil me a steak, rare. And I want a large orange juice, fresh-squeezed." He wondered if the waiter was staring at the pock scars on his face. Automatically, he dabbed at the corners of his mouth with his napkin, narrowing his attention to the front page of *The Wall Street Journal.*

He would not let a hotel kitchen in Santa Fe disturb his morning. He'd completed a grueling ninety-minute workout in the facility's gym; he'd allowed himself fifteen minutes in a very hot Jacuzzi while his muscles loosened up like butter. The salon had managed a decent manicure; when he tipped the girl, she'd told him he looked like Antonio Banderas, only taller and thinner and much more interesting.

Perhaps he'd fuck the manicurist tonight. If he felt like it, he would have her. And then he would finish his last errand in *el norte*. He would track down the Honda, tear it wide open, find the package.

The waiter arrived with a pot of steaming coffee and a tall orange juice. While the man was attending to cups and glasses, Renzo slid *The Wall Street Journal* off the table. A second newspaper, the local daily, was exposed, and a headline caught his eye: CHILD DRIVER SURVIVES CRASH WITH LAMY TRAIN.

RENZO SANTOS PRESSED the telephone receiver to his ear and waited. Two hours earlier, he had returned to his casita at La Posada hotel—a casita registered to a quiet and respectable Arizona businessman named Eric Sandoval. There he had begun his research, a series of phone calls that eventually led him to an office at Child Protective Services.

Now a C.P.S. secretary had him on hold; thirty seconds passed, then forty. Renzo had a working rule: he never remained on hold for a full minute. Perhaps, in the particular circumstances, his rule bordered on paranoia. He had placed all the morning's calls from his cell phone, a unit equipped with a built-in scanner/EIN decoder. With each new call, the unit was programmed to search out and clone an active number that was not currently in use. The unit made him virtually untraceable. It was all part of his uniform: three passports under three different names (two of which were hidden in a panel of his Vuitton luggage), matching credit cards, and cash. In his business, there was always too much cash.

He glanced at his Rolex—the sixty-second rule still stood—and prepared to hang up. He resolved to try again later, just as a woman came on the line.

"This is Mrs. Delgado. May I help you?"

She was mature, insecure, and felt her position of limited power within the state bureaucracy was beneath her capabilities—Renzo heard that much in her voice. Further information had come from his research: Mrs. Delgado was recently married; she was a fan of the new boss at the state's Department of Children, Youth, and Family; she had been guest speaker at a New Mexico Bar Association child-advocacy dinner just last week.

Renzo set his notes and the clipping from Thursday's *New Mexican* on the hotel's rust-and-cream-colored bedspread.

He lied smoothly, with a trace of a northern New Mexican accent: "This is Roberto Martinez from the I.N.S. legal department. We've had a query about that female minor who wrecked the vehicle out on Two eighty-five." His manicured fingernails skimmed the text of the newspaper article: ". . . unidentified minor was transported to St. Vincent's Hospital . . ."

"Yes?" The woman didn't hide her impatience.

Renzo pictured her in his imagination: dyed hair cut to the earlobe, sparse makeup except for lipstick, which would be too red. Clip-on earrings. Wedding ring, faux gold chain and locket. She was seated behind a large metal state-issue desk, and the stack of papers by her elbow seemed to pulse before her eyes. It was ten minutes to twelve, and undoubtedly she had a luncheon meeting with an anal-retentive supervisor.

He slowed down. "Chris Palmer, one of our case agents, was at the Bernalillo Detention Center this morning, and he talked to an undocumented woman who claims her daughter ran away three days ago. Says the girl's ten years old—"

"Is the child mute?"

"Mute?" Renzo's body stiffened slightly, and an almost imperceptible flutter of excitement spurred his muscles. It was possible that Paco had told the truth before he died; he'd begged for the girl's life, swearing she couldn't reveal any secrets.

"This one isn't talking." There was a sharp sound as the woman snapped the cover on a tube of lipstick. "But maybe it's worth checking out."

"You never know." Renzo glanced down at the telephone book on the floor. Three of his earlier calls had been made to the offices of Immigration and Naturalization Services; he'd followed a trail of appropriate federal employees. Then it had been just a matter of waiting until it was time for state workers to go to lunch.

He said, "She's on a forty-eight-hour hold. And her court hearing is scheduled for . . ." He rustled papers. "Monday?"

"Tomorrow at ten." She was crisp.

"We've got Roybal listed as the temp foster family."

"As far as I know she's not assigned to a family yet." Suspicion slowed her speech. "And you know I couldn't give you that information—"

"Maybe Chris Palmer should deal with this." Renzo allowed just a hint of intimacy to enter the space between his words. "By the way, I really enjoyed your speech at the bar fund-raiser last week."

"Oh. Thanks. Did we . . . ?"

"I wish we'd had a few more minutes to talk; you

were the most intelligent speaker on the roster." Renzo glanced at his watch. "Hey, it's almost noon. I should let you go."

"By *my* clock it's one minute after twelve." There was a pause while the woman softened up. "Why don't you tell your caseworker to call . . ." She faded away, came back, and recited the name and the phone number of a C.P.S. social worker. Renzo wrote the information neatly on the margin of the newspaper clipping about the girl.

". . . authorities are seeking information from anyone who has knowledge . . ."

He thanked Mrs. Delgado and hung up softly. He had knowledge of the child—he knew her name, her age, and he knew she possessed the power to destroy his world.

He lay back on the hotel bed, resting his head on the pillow. Dancing his fingers across his high cheekbones, he felt the slight indentation of acne scars that were never totally erased, even with repeated injections of collagen. The scars spoiled a face that was otherwise perfect for the camera. He'd been told by more than one woman that he resembled a matinee idol. Bitterly, he blamed his acne-ravaged skin on childhood malnutrition and deprivation.

He let his fingers skim down to his mouth, which was unremarkable except for the small scar that indented the center of his lower lip. The stubble on his chin bothered him. Schedule permitting, he would shave a second time that day. His very straight nose, narrow, then flaring slightly at the nostrils, was a genetic marker of the *puta*'s Nahuatl origins—origins that Renzo considered his pure identity. But he could never quite forgive his Aztec forebears: they had relinquished their birthright, their gods and goddesses, when the brutal Spanish conquerors invaded their lands, stole their riches, and burned their temples.

The Aztecs had given up *his* birthright.

He knew that his face was impassive; calm was his imprint. He was unaware that the impression of composure he gave was intensified by his pitch-black eyes—eyes that rarely blinked.

It was a face no woman had ever loved. Not even his whoring mother-the-*puta*.

Renzo stood, stretched his lithe muscles, and walked past the television, which was muted and tuned to CNN. Inside the small bathroom he opened his alligator shaving bag and selected a small velvet case from which he plucked a tiny gold cross. It belonged to a young woman. He knew her features by heart: the proud tilt of her chin, the bright, wide-set eyes, the sensual mouth. And he knew things that were not part of anyone else's memory. Things a man knew about his woman. *Elena.*

He pictured her as she had looked on her fifteenth birthday. In Renzo's mind, she was never any other age. Her skin was flawless, the color of coffee rich with cream, the blush of rose on her cheeks and a darker crimson on her lips.

The daughter was pale heir to her mother's Indio-Spanish purity.

Renzo would have to murder Elena's child. *Again.*

With reverence, he returned the cross to its velvet case. He knew he must be patient even though time was running out. It was the careful hunter who caught his prey.

Renzo's eyes focused on the contents of his bag. In

addition to aspirin, codeine, and penicillin, a half dozen pill containers filled small sleeves. Scissors, tweezers, file, and small surgical knife were enclosed in separate plastic cases. Several brushes and a comb made of tortoiseshell rested in the bottom of the bag.

Renzo rolled back the left sleeve of his Armani shirt. Impassively, he noted the myriad white scars that decorated his wrist and forearm. They were set at measured intervals, which could be halved again with new incisions. The scars were paper-thin and perfectly aligned along the median cubital vein.

He lifted out the fine brushes and felt for the smooth leather of a second kit, which fit neatly in the bottom of the case. Unzipped, it held disposable U-100 syringes, alcohol swabs, cotton balls, a specially made silver spoon, and several brown vials that contained very pure heroin, chunked and powdered.

The drug was pure enough to snort, but tonight he needed the intravenous rush. He rarely used his arms or hands to shoot up anymore, but he had already broken several of his rules during the last few days and he didn't want to wait until he had his pants, socks, and shoes off.

He cleaned the spoon with alcohol, then placed a chunk of heroin in its center, adding a measure of water from the syringe. He heated the spoon with his lighter. Cotton, dropped into the mixture, expanded like a tiny sponge. Renzo placed the needle in the center of the cotton, pulled up on the plunger, and guided the milky liquid into the syringe. Expertly he tapped the vein between first and second fingers, then nosed the needle under his skin.

The substance he was about to inject into his body had been born in the fields of Panama where poppies

were picked by hand and transported to an underground processing operation in Colombia. From
Colombia, the powdered heroin had been loaded onto
one of a fleet of 737s owned by Colombia's most powerful drug cartel. The jet had landed at night on a private
airstrip in the Mexican state of Chihuahua. A herd of
human mules had been waiting at the airstrip; they
were under the protection of federal judicial police who
had ensured a safe trip to a stash house in Juárez.
Renzo's personal supply came from that same border
town. But his was the highest grade possible, not street
shit. The rest of the shipment had already been smuggled across the Mexican-U.S. border for consumption
by *norteamericanos*.

Renzo had learned to control his body's hunger.
Always he rode the tension between craving and fulfill-
ment. But now it wasn't just the drug he craved; there
was this new hunger.

His own blood swirled up into the cloudy fluid in the
hypo, his eyes remaining open and glazed. As he anticipated the first rush, he realized that his hunger for the
child was even greater than his hunger for the drug.

CHAPTER THREE

THE DOG WAS tiny, minus one ear, almost hairless, a sore-infested, mangy hot dog on legs who knew everything there was to know about getting kicked around. He raised his nose from the pile of rotting tortillas and putrid grease. Hackles standing at attention, he caught something stronger than the smell of decay on the warm evening breeze. He smelled fear.

Curious, the dog picked his way over a mound of ripe trash to the edge of a dirt bluff. When he was inches from the drop-off, he set his paws wide and peered down. Even a dog knew that the dark, gleaming vehicle below did not belong at this dump within the miserable slum of Anapra on the western edge of Ciudad Juárez, Mexico. At first the dog did not see the man who stood so quiet and still. When he did, he growled.

Victor Vargas, investigator with the federal judicial police Juárez, was scared. His fear nested in a cold hollow behind his solar plexus. He gazed intently at the black Range Rover and its unfortunate cargo, and he inhaled deeply on his Negrito. When he was at home, off duty, he savored the occasional Cuban cigar. At a days-old crime scene, he sucked hard on crude Mexican smoke.

Victor had a headache gnawing like a rat at the base of his skull. It had nothing to do with piss-cured tobacco. It was directly related to the scene in front of his eyes: a Range Rover loaded with corpses. He exhaled a stream of rank smoke and sighed. The faint scream of sirens sounded in the distance. Why hadn't he listened to his mother and become a famous *mariachiador*?

Inside the Range Rover—no longer fighting against the duct tape that bound their hands and feet and covered their eyes—three dead men lolled against the bloodstained seats. Their features had been distorted by a severe beating; their cut and tortured bodies had bloated from three days' heat. A fourth man lay unbound, akimbo, oblivious to his bed of filth and dirt outside the vehicle.

Victor thought he knew the identities of the corpses. Rumors had flowed like tainted water down the information pipeline—there had been a big hit four nights earlier. Part of an ongoing war between factions: those who pledged allegiance to the ruling drug lord against those who did not. It was all very simple—and very, very complicated. A classic gangland tale of Chicago in the 1920s, only this was Mexico, this was the roaring nineties.

The rumors had named the victims of the hit: a district chief of Mexico's federal antinarcotics agency, his two bodyguards, and a formal federal police officer known to consort with narcotics traffickers. The quartet had been missing for five days, since arriving at the Juárez airport via a flight from Mexico City. Tonight they would be confirmed dead.

One of the corpses inside the Range Rover was almost certainly the district chief. The man on the ground at Victor Vargas's size-8 feet was the former *federale*.

Wearily, Vargas ran a hand through his close-cropped beard. Since the mid-1980s, when federal authorities closed down Florida as the Colombian-drug-cartel port of entry into the United States, Mexico had gained a reputation as the newest narco-state. There was no denying that tons of cocaine, marijuana, amphetamines, and heroin flowed across the border—much of it through the El Paso–Juárez gateway. Mexican drug lords had effectively divided the nation into feudal territories, buying the services of politicians and police, ruling with tyranny. Antidrug agencies had followed a trail of bribes to the toes of Mexico's president and a trail of money into the States, where it was sent around the world by the arbitrageurs.

The most powerful lords remained virtually inviolable.

And that scared Victor Vargas. The cop gazed up at the night sky; the reflection of the city's lights doused the stars, leaving only faint whispers of silver behind a dense polluted haze. He refilled his lungs with the Negrito's fumes. During the past six months, two dozen officials had been murdered in the drug wars. Victor sighed, expelling smoke. He had promised his wife he would not join the ranks of the dead; he had made the same promise to his mistress. For a street-smart cop, a veteran with *cojones* who walked the tightrope between warring factions, that was not an easy promise to keep.

Victor Vargas had heard another rumor: more antidrug agents were set to die, and his name topped the list.

He glanced at his watch; the illuminated dial fringed the hairs on his wrist in green shadow. It was almost midnight. The sirens were minutes away. He was first on the scene because his informants—his grimy, louse-infested street urchins, his junkies and his whores, his grand network of snitches, singers who would do the opera proud—worked overtime. But soon he would not be alone. He took one last hit of rank tobacco and gazed at the corpses.

He knew why they were dead. These men had been murdered because they came looking for Snow White. And now Victor Vargas was looking for Snow White, too.

CHAPTER FOUR

"YOU LIED TO me." Sylvia managed to direct an ominous look at Albert Kove before the force of her leashed terrier pulled her forward along Griffin Street; the Malinois heeled stiffly by her side. She was dressed in a linen pantsuit and leather pumps from a very recent appearance at children's court, and the narrow two-inch heels of her shoes caught in the sidewalk's seams.

Kove jogged a few paces to keep up with his associate. "¿Yo?" They were outside the Santa Fe Judicial Complex, and this was the first time he'd talked to Sylvia since their late-night phone conversation more than thirty hours earlier.

"Heel," Sylvia snapped, and the Malinois reluctantly abandoned the narrow metal post of a NO PARKING sign. At the same time, Rocko, the terrier, veered after a windblown scrap of paper.

Kove took Rocko's leash thinking that it might help

him get back in Sylvia's good graces, but she was already walking ahead with the Malinois.

Her words drifted back to Kove. "I was half asleep, and you told me my sabbatical was up when I actually had another week. My book is overdue, I've still got a hundred pages to revise, and my editors are threatening to come after me with a cattle prod."

"I had to get your attention." Kove's nose wrinkled as he caught a whiff of something that was very ripe, very dead, or both. "The child needed help."

"She still needs help, but that's no excuse. I'm not fond of cattle prods."

Eyebrows aslant, Kove said, "If you don't want to work with her, you don't have to."

"You are *so* obvious." As Sylvia waited for Nikki to finish peeing on the edge of a plastered wall, a sudden gust of air lifted her dark hair away from her shoulders. Overhead, a massive thunderhead threatened an abrupt change in the October weather. Gray light filtered through the branches of an elm tree and dappled the sidewalk.

Sylvia continued, "I just spent thirty minutes at the custody hearing—the state retains custody, the kid's been placed in a foster home, she's not talking, and I'm evaluating this afternoon."

"It's not autism?"

Sylvia shook her head. "It's not withdrawal. You and I have both seen enough autistic children to recognize the face they wear. This is different." She thought back, visualized the child. "I almost get the feeling her silence is a responsibility."

"To whom?"

"That's the question." Sylvia shivered as the thundercloud cut off sunlight and draped her shoulders in shadow. "The child wasn't in the courtroom today; she was too freaked out by the whole process."

"What's your read?"

Sylvia nudged her black sunglasses higher on her nose. "She's been through an ordeal, she's bright, and she's got plenty of chutzpah." She shrugged. "By the way, the foster mom's bilingual; she confirmed my feeling—the kid responds to English and Spanish."

Sylvia didn't say so, but she felt a kinship with a child she hardly knew; the feeling nagged at her insistently like a tiny yet formidable insect. She gave her head a small shake. "You know what interests me the most, Albert? Silence is not the normal response to trauma."

"Nobody says this kid is normal." Kove tweaked his eyebrows à la Groucho Marx.

Sylvia pressed her palms together, thumbs touching her chin. "The foster mom says the child prays a lot."

"She'll be a good influence on you." Kove frowned. "You think she was alone in that car?"

"I'd bet there was a driver—I'm guessing an illegal—who took off running after the crash. Maybe he or she figured the kid would be in good hands." Sylvia shrugged and glanced at her watch.

Albert Kove was in his midforties, with cropped hair, wire-rimmed glasses, and an almost completely unflappable demeanor. But not now. At the moment he seemed upset. Kove's sigh was a soft hiss of air. "You're right, I lied to you."

"Thanks for the confession."

Into the tiny opening of silence Kove wedged words. "I was afraid I'd never get you back to work at the unit if I didn't push."

Sylvia whirled around. "You were wrong," she said. "By the time I hung up the phone I'd figured out I had another week's sabbatical." She lowered her dark glasses and gave her friend a hard look; her left eye was ringed with a glorious purple-and-yellow bruise. "But I went to the hospital anyway."

Kove frowned. "Who gave you the shiner?"

"The kid."

Kove smiled. "Then you two hit it off?"

"Very funny. I'm great with children." Sylvia pushed her glasses back up her nose, suddenly self-conscious. "But I should have fucking ducked."

"You take your punches like a tough guy. You coulda been a contenda."

She shook her head and grudgingly returned Kove's smile. "I coulda been the champ." Abruptly, she snapped her fingers. "Sit!" Nikki sat.

Kove gave muffled applause. "I'm impressed. Four months ago you couldn't teach that dog to scratch a flea."

"We've been in training." Sylvia closed her bruised eye and made a show of assessing her colleague. "I'll consider forgiving you—on one condition."

"What?"

Sylvia clipped the lead to Nikki's collar, then slapped the leash into Kove's palm. "Finish their walk. I've got to meet with the kid and her foster mom in three minutes."

She was already striding back toward the offices of the Forensic Evaluation Unit when she heard Kove call out, "What do I do with them when we're done walking?"

"Give them water and put them in the back of my truck."

"What smells so bad?"

Sylvia held out both hands palms up. "The night I went to the hospital to see the kid? Rocko sneaked out his dog door."

Suddenly, the light dawned, and Albert inhaled sharply. *Skunk.*

BEHIND TINTED WINDOWS Renzo Santos was playing dead. Body resting against the seat back. Arms and legs immobile. Breath evaporated through the mind. From his parked Suburban, he watched the tall brunette wave good-bye to her friend. She'd left the *maricón* holding two dogs. Renzo didn't like dogs—not the mangy curs who roamed the barrios of Juárez, not the purebred guard dogs with their studded collars and shark eyes. Once he'd watched a rottweiler tear apart an ocelot—all for the enjoyment of a bored diamond-draped bitch who had a taste for blood.

Now the brunette turned into one of the old office complexes across from the courthouse. Renzo already knew that lawyers and psychologists worked in that building. The brunette was a psychologist. She was in her early thirties, well dressed, good body, dark eyes, dark hair—mixed descent ... part Italian or part Indian? He'd noticed her for the first time when she walked into the courthouse with the C.P.S. social worker. Renzo didn't like psychologists any more than he liked dogs. He'd dated one once—she'd told him he had issues with his mother-the-*puta.*

Where is the girl? When she didn't die, she'd changed his plans.

Without moving his head, he glanced down at the notepad tucked under his thigh. Four license-plate numbers were written on the page; the numbers belonged to the psychologist and the other people who had gathered for the custody hearing.

Renzo knew about the players—do-gooders, social workers, shrinks, court-appointed guardians, priests, nuns, doctors, nurses. He knew about the system—child protective services, welfare and food stamps, social services, shelters, Catholic charities. He analyzed the system out of professional necessity. He despised the system because he had survived it.

These people had all gathered to decide the immediate fate of the girl—Renzo's gloved fingers tightened into a fist—but the girl had been absent from the hearing.

Where would he find her?

Only Renzo's eyeballs shifted as he changed focus. The C.P.S. social worker was taking too long inside the courthouse. Maybe she'd exited through the other door. It was possible she'd gone to lunch on foot. Her parked car was in his sight lines.

Renzo had selected his surveillance location after driving these streets several times. He could see the courthouse clearly. He wasn't too close. He wasn't too far. His vehicle was parked in a small crowded lot on a corner. A map lay open on the car seat next to him. He had a Santa Fe phone book, a government directory, and a cell phone. All he needed—all he didn't have—was time.

He blinked once. The social worker had just walked out of the courthouse with a man. Renzo guessed the man was a public defender because his suit was so plain, so ugly. The pair walked to the woman's car. They talked for a few minutes, then the social worker patted the man's arm and climbed behind the steering wheel. The car's engine coughed and sputtered, then caught.

Roused from his meditation, Renzo turned to glance at the office building into which the shrink had disappeared. To the side of the building, the *maricón* was tangled in the big yellow shepherd's leash. The animal had mean eyes; Renzo had to shake the eerie feeling that it was watching him. It was the same breed the D.E.A. and I.N.S. used to patrol the Mexican-U.S. border—animals he both feared and admired for their brutal nature.

Now the *maricón* was loading the dogs into the back of the shrink's truck. More accurately, he was trying to load them; the little mutt was racing around the lot, pissing on tires.

Across the street, the social worker slowly guided her beat-up compact car around the courthouse toward an exit.

Follow her, or stay with the shrink?

He wasn't sure if the girl had been placed in foster care yet. Court hearings on juveniles were closed to spectators, but Renzo had paid close attention to the participants. The girl had never shown up at the courthouse; that wasn't the normal procedure. But maybe she was hurt more seriously than they'd admitted. Maybe she was still hospitalized.

Sooner or later the social worker would lead him to his quarry.

Girl, girl, girl, girl, girl . . .

Renzo turned the key in the ignition of the Suburban, shifted into reverse, and backed out of the parking lot. He knew where the shrink worked; it would be easy enough to find out where she lived. If necessary, he would follow up with her later.

He shifted the Suburban into drive and accelerated down the street.

Thirty seconds later, Nellie Trujillo, a licensed foster parent, led a small girl down the steps of the courthouse. The child moved stiffly, resisting the woman, resisting exposure. She had spent the last two hours hiding behind the couch in the children's waiting area in the recesses of the courthouse. The woman looked tired, perhaps overwhelmed. She spoke to the girl resolutely. "Honey, we've only got to cross the street. Hurry now—you're acting like you've seen a ghost."

THE CHILD ENTERED Sylvia's office like prey making one last dash from predator. She was a blur of red and white and brown, a specter of frantic energy who only came to earth to hide. Cornered behind the green couch, she curled around herself. The pulse of her quick, shallow breath jarred the room to life.

Sylvia felt the child's fear and experienced a sudden rush of anger at whoever had instilled such terror in this small person. The child appeared even more disturbed than she had seemed at either the hospital or the courthouse. Sylvia took a long breath, pressed her spine against the wall, then let her butt slide down to the floor. She sat with her arms around her knees at kid level. Children demanded patience—and enormous energy. An expanse of gray carpet separated her from the child; all she could see were two small feet in pink plastic shoes. The strap of one shoe straggled over the carpet.

After allowing a few moments to pass in silence, Sylvia spoke in a tone that was intentionally soft and easygoing. "We've met before. Do you remember me from the hospital? I'm the one with the black eye. My name is Sylvia. *Me llamo* Sylvia. I meet and talk with children like you. Sometimes we play."

A faint shuddering noise drifted from behind the couch. The pink shoes scooted back an inch or so until only two plastic toes were visible.

Sylvia was reluctant to move, afraid to spook the child, so she waited, only changing position to ease a cramp in her legs. The pocket on her jacket was starting to come unstitched; the heel of one of her pumps looked like it was breaking loose. She and the child were both unraveling at the seams—thread and glue would work for Sylvia, but the child would not mend so easily. From the way things had gone so far, they weren't going to accomplish anything resembling a traditional evaluation in this session.

She spoke to the pink shoes. "This room is a place where children can play . . . or talk about what's going on . . . or just hang out." She cupped her hands together, then produced what she hoped were the corresponding verbs in Spanish: "*Jugar, hablar, relajar.*"

There was no visible reaction.

Sylvia let the silence settle before she changed gears. She expelled air noisily from between her lips, then slipped off her shoes, exposing toenails polished to a gleaming fuchsia. She scooted on her butt toward a table covered with a tray of sand, toys, paper, and crayons. "Some kids like to use this tray of sand to make a world."

The first response was a whimper. But the pink shoes eventually began to move. Painfully slow baby steps, at first. Start and stop. It took those shoes a good two minutes to travel the length of the couch, finally emerging at one end.

She stood wide-eyed, her gaze darting around the room only to land repeatedly on Sylvia. The child appeared to be on the verge of bolting; Sylvia calculated the distance to the locked door. But instead of seeking escape, the girl took another tentative step forward with one hand clutching the arm of the couch. Her tongue flitted across her mouth before disappearing between trembling lips. She sighed, and her narrow chest rose and fell with a shudder. She hunched forward and reached out to touch one of Sylvia's polished toenails—then pulled her hand back abruptly.

Sylvia spoke softly. "Hello there." This was her first real view of the child outside the hospital setting.

She was wiry and tough, like a sunburnt weed. Fine bones and lack of weight made her look smaller than her actual size. In addition to the pink shoes, she wore a white cotton shirt trimmed in bright red. Her red pants were decorated with white racing stripes. The clothes were new, and Sylvia caught the faint but distinctive scent of fabric sizing. The knuckles of the child's right hand were scraped raw where scabs had been picked or torn away. Her skin was bronze, bruised and scraped above her left eye and on her chin—but the swelling had eased. Her lower lip was trapped between gapped white teeth. Dark hair reached midback, thick and tangled. She wasn't exactly pretty. Stray tendrils framed boyish features—nose a tad too big, mouth wide and supple, full brows dark as charcoal. But her dusky eyes held a hint of the woman's beauty that was to come. If she survived that long.

Now those expressive eyes spoke only of fear and exhaustion. The child's countenance was distorted by anxiety so intense it seemed to be a permanent feature. Her fear was contagious.

Sylvia had seen this level of terror in a few other children—like the six-year-old boy who witnessed his sister's decapitation. The killer had locked the boy in a closet with a warning that he would come back. The boy had been discovered four days after the murder, cowering silently in darkness, soiled and feverish with fright.

Sylvia felt a hollow dread work its way up her abdomen. What horrors had this child witnessed? She took several deep breaths before framing her next question: "Would you like to play with the toys?"

The child gave a shiver of a nod, barely perceptible. When at the same time her brown eyes cut to the sand tray, Sylvia knew her words were understood.

The child picked up a fabric doll from the lap of a wicker chair and moved warily toward the sand tray. The doll was pressed tight to her tummy like a baby trapped outside the womb; with her free hand the child fingered and discarded tiny plastic figurines, human and animal. Each movement was tightly contained; there was none of the easy exploration typical of children. Finally, she placed the doll in the far corner of the tray, where the plain cloth face gazed blankly out at the world—an eerie witness to the child's stifling distress.

Now she began a stilted sorting through the remaining toys. Plastic birds, horses, soldiers, and superheroes tumbled onto the floor. When the toy baskets were empty, the child picked up a piece of rough drawing paper from a stack on the table. She selected a box of crayons from a shelf. She pivoted suddenly toward Sylvia, her small arms held tightly at her sides. Then she walked away from the table, oddly stiff-gaited, disappearing again behind the couch.

From Sylvia's undergraduate classes she remembered the Sapir-Whorf hypothesis of "linguistic relativity": the language a person uses not only expresses but controls the way he or she thinks about the world. What if that language is silence?

For the next few minutes, the child's furious scribbling was audible, along with her breathing—the huff and puff of concentration.

Sylvia let her work in solitude until the session was almost over. When she was about to try to engage her again, the pink shoes abruptly reemerged from their hiding place. Empty-handed, the child crossed the room. Her small fingers closed around Sylvia's palm; the touch sent electricity through the psychologist's body. A faint alarm went off in her mind—*this isn't a child you can keep at a therapeutic distance.*

Minutes later the child left the office with her foster mother, and Sylvia looked behind the couch. She saw tiny bits of paper wrapping and broken crayons scattered everywhere, but there was no sign of a drawing.

She got down on her hands and knees and squeezed into the space between wall and sofa. She ran her fingers along the floor. Nothing.

Just when she was sure the child had taken away the drawing and some of the crayons, she noticed a white paper sliver visible in a seam of the couch. It was there, neatly folded and waiting, like a secret message.

The child had colored a sprawling village against a mountain. The rigidly narrow walls of one particular house stood above the others; its roofline was flat, the three small windows set high—and they were darkened and covered with vertical bars like a prison. The house had no door—no access, no "mouth." The sky in the picture hung low and ominous, as if threatening to envelop the solitary building.

The drawing reminded Sylvia of the work of the Mexican muralists—strong, sensuous, disturbing. The vivid colors and rich shapes of the swirling clouds over jagged hills took her breath away. The child wasn't just artistic—she was gifted.

Sylvia concentrated on analyzing the work's psychological presentation. The dark enclosures were consistent with a child who was disturbed, who had experienced trauma. The clash of sophisticated perspective and primitive imaging indicated regression. The "contained" message was clear: the four walls of the house encased family secrets.

Three *X*'s traversed the white space below the house—the letters were connected and seemed to represent a fence or barrier. On the crest of a jagged mountain peak rising up behind the house, a cruciform stabbed the sky.

At the bottom of the page, the child had drawn a tiny, dark crescent moon. Just below the moon, she'd signed her name.

S E r E n a.

CHAPTER FIVE

EL PASO POLICE Department narcotics cop William Robert Dowd punched in the last number on the pay telephone and waited for the short, high ring. His fingers trembled around the piece of dirty black plastic in his hand. Overhead, a neon taco flickered faintly—commas of yellow cheese spilling down a red-rimmed taco shell every few seconds. The lights gave off a steady hum that Dowd heard between rings in the sudden lull of traffic on Avenida Juárez. Exhaust fumes caught in his mouth and killed the taste of fast-food grease. From the alley next to the *taquería* Bobby Dowd scanned the street. Cars and trucks were backed up, headed for the bridge across the Río Bravo—a.k.a. the Rio Grande—into El Paso, Texas.

Impatiently Dowd counted six rings, seven. Then a deep voice said, "*¿Sí?*"

"I need to see you," Bobby Dowd said.

"If it ain't my old pal Wile E. Beep-beep, *'mano.*"

From the husky sound of the other man's voice, Dowd knew Victor Vargas was smoking one of his funky cigarettes—his Negritos or Delicados. And Vargas sounded tired. He sounded like he believed Bobby Dowd might be coked up. Bobby swallowed. "It's got to be today."

"*No puedo.* Not today."

Bobby Dowd slapped his thigh nervously. Across the street, a hooker was promoting her stuff to a punk in a Mustang; she kept pace with the car, strutting toward the bridge in cheap stiletto heels and sequins. At the opposite end of the alley, three street kids were squabbling over trash. Dowd said, "Big Tuna is hunting coyote."

Vargas made no effort to mask the anger in his voice. "No shit? You're a little late, *pendejo* coyote. I got my own *problemas con el* fish."

Bobby bit his tongue and let silence fill the next few spaces. He was afraid Vargas would cut him loose. Then the shaking would spread from his hands to his teeth— he wouldn't be able to stop the monkey chatter.

Help me. For a bad moment, Bobby thought he'd spoken his plea aloud, but the words echoed safely in his head. He knew he'd fallen too far into the abyss known as deep cover. He'd done one too many lines, taken one too many needles in the name of narco cop turned bad.

He'd never intended for it to go this way. When he'd started out, the boundaries had been clear. Still wet behind the ears, fresh from the academy, a training project with the feds, he'd taken to undercover work. *I can do this. I can stand on the line and never cross it. I can straddle the border between the good guys and the bad guys and never lose my balance.* What the hell had he been thinking?

Bobby spat on the sidewalk, then hunched low into his ribs as a Juárez city patrol unit cruised slowly past. When had he gone from being a straight-ahead cop to being a cop with a habit? A junkie. A freak. But still a cop who desperately needed to pass on information.

He played his card. "I heard something—about Snow White."

Somewhere, at the other end of this electromagnetic encounter, Vargas expelled smoke with a shudder.

Bobby pressed. "Snow White and a little dwarf in danger."

Vargas was silent a moment, absorbing information that carried heavy weight. Finally, he said, "I'll find you—two, maybe three hours."

Dowd tried to quell the panic that danced a tango in his stomach. He spoke softly, "TNT-time, Roadrunner. Don't forget your ole pal Wile E." He dropped the phone, letting it swing on its coiled wire cord. He glanced at the street, then he started down the alley. He had ten blocks to cover to his usual spot for a meeting with Vargas—but he had hours to kill. He moved with a casualness that belied his truly miserable state.

Unfamiliar fingers of self-pity stroked his skin. He needed a shot of tequila to loosen him up so he could function. One or two shots and he could truly refocus. His feet began to move faster, each step taking him closer to a bottle and that zone of higher consciousness.

He could still turn it all around. Bobby Dowd clung to that hope, he fanned it like a spark. It wasn't too late. He just had to talk to Victor Vargas. The funny thing was, of all the cops Dowd had known—on either

side of the border—Vargas was the one he trusted
most. When they'd first met, Vargas had mocked the
rookie's black-and-white world. The Mexican lived in
a realm that was solid gray, where you never knew if
you were crossing the line because the line shifted
every second.

No . . . Victor Vargas was no saint, but he had a kind
of wild honor. And he had something pumping in his
chest, something that closely resembled a heart.

It wasn't too late to save the life of Paco's little
dwarf . . .

A hazy picture wavered in front of Bobby's eyes like a
desert mirage: Paco sitting with another man at a back
table at Rosa's place . . . they were three quarters of the
way through a bottle of rough tequila and the bookkeeper was telling crazy stories that made the other man
laugh. Stories about treasure hidden in a straw house—
that made the other man joke about the three little pigs.
Stories about books with magic powers, and a little
girl—or was the little girl the one who was magic?

Paco had told wild stories to a lost man, to a narco
cop named Bobby Dowd.

And now Bobby had the horrible knowledge that
he'd failed Paco and his little girl. Failed them badly.

He stumbled as he crossed the street behind a low-
slung sedan. He heard the mellow tones of Conjunto
Bernal flowing from someone's radio. He glanced at a
sign as he turned the next corner. Five more blocks to a
safe haven. He was off the hard stuff for good. No more
crack, no more black.

Two hookers called to him in Spanish as he crossed
their territory; he knew by their voices they were
stoned—black tar, *chiva*, Mexican white, whatever their

pimp supplied. When Bobby didn't respond the hookers laughed and lazily peppered him with insults.

Three more blocks and a place to disappear.

He felt the tail before he recognized the low throb of a Mercedes engine. Without looking back, he automatically picked up pace, scanning for an escape route. From the corner of his eye he caught sight of a narrow opening between buildings. He had no idea if it was a dead end or a way out, but he cut sideways, out of options. Running flat out, he heard footsteps behind him. He ducked past a pile of trash, past a pair of street cats tangling. Their agonized yowls should have made his hair stand up, but all he heard was the sound of footsteps at his heels.

As he ran, Bobby Dowd braced himself for a bullet or a blade between his shoulders. But the end of the tunnel came first—the dead end. Nobody shot him. Instead, they slammed him into the filthy cinder-block wall. Pain electrified every nerve in his body—he flashed on Wile E. Coyote ramrod stiff and dynamite-charred but still breathing—and then darkness kissed him on both eyes.

CHAPTER SIX

AT TWO O'CLOCK, Sylvia finished a turkey sandwich in her office and thought about closing up for the day. She had fulfilled her obligations—the court custody hearing and the session with Serena. Nothing else was on her schedule, the open page in her appointment book was blank. It would stay that way. Albert Kove might have lured her prematurely from her sabbatical—she had allowed that to happen for the child's sake, but she still had a book to finish, a contract to fulfill.

In the hour since Serena's departure, Sylvia had organized files and made one phone call to her editor in New York for a long-distance discussion of a deadline extension. *Broken Bonds: The Search for the Lost Father*—the book was nonfiction like her first, but less academic, more personal. It was based on a series of case studies; the individuals included inmates, a teacher, a doctor, a few high-profile faces. Sylvia's personal story opened and closed the book—or would if the private investigator she'd hired to track down her long-missing father would get on the stick. It was difficult to write a last chapter when you didn't know how the story ended.

When it came to extending the book's deadline, Sylvia's editor had been sympathetic but uncooperative, offering only a ribald riddle in parting: "What did Little Red Riding Hood say to the Big Bad Wolf? Hurry up and eat me before Grandma gets home."

Sylvia sat back in her chair. The office was quiet. Kove was in a session with a client. Marjorie, the Forensic Evaluation Unit's secretary, had walked two blocks to the downtown post office to mail letters. Sylvia rested her feet on the desk, aiming scraps of wadded paper at the wastebasket. Absently, she studied the view of the Diego Building's courtyard. The apricot trees had lost most of their leaves, while the foliage of the Russian olive shimmered in the watery sunlight. But her mind wasn't on the shifting light or the fall colors. Her thoughts centered on Serena.

For the past hour, the child's drawing had lain on Sylvia's desk. Repeatedly, the grim, moody image had caught her eye and her imagination. Now she let her fingers play over the crayon colors, twisting the page, turning the world upside down ... her focus softened—and the cross, the house, the letters disappeared. Sylvia sat forward. The reversed image swam in her vision. Positive. Negative.

When she let the white background surge forward in her view, the X's resembled eyes, the house became a snout, the cross jutted out like the forked tongue of a beast. Consciously or not, the child had drawn the face of a demon.

Sylvia flipped through her Rolodex and reached for the telephone. She dialed an international exchange and listened to the short, quick rings. A sleepy-sounding woman answered, indignantly spouting French. Sylvia didn't understand one word of the tirade. She simply repeated, "Dr. Tompkins, *merci*," until her peer was summoned to the telephone.

Margaret Tompkins was a child psychiatrist who taught at the university in Albuquerque when she wasn't living in Paris.

After a quick greeting, Sylvia went straight to the point: "I'm working with a child—court-ordered. I may not have much time with her." She filled Margaret in on Serena's background—as much as they knew. The psychiatrist came back with a dozen questions. During a pause that seemed longer because of the miles between them, Sylvia said, "Margaret, last winter, when you presented your paper to the A.P.A. . . . two of the case studies were selectively mute children."

Margaret Tompkins sneezed and said something incomprehensible. It took Sylvia a moment to realize the psychiatrist was talking to someone in French. She waited and finally heard words she understood.

"You think this is selective mutism?" Another sneeze. "That will be interesting for you. I wish I was a bit closer so I could look at her myself." She sniffled. "You described abnormality in her physical movements—"

"She seems . . . stiff."

"A frozen gait? And she's not communicating verbally—we don't know if she was verbal in her home situation—and we don't have a *normal* situation for comparison. At the moment, no family background, no reports from school, no medical history." Dr. Tompkins blew her nose. "Well, my dear, you've got your work cut out for you."

"What about field research?"

"A few papers have been published, but there really aren't reams floating around out there. I am glad they stopped calling it *elective* mutism—everyone thinks these kids won't talk because they're just plain stubborn. Not true." She sniffled again. "Try the Internet. Chess and Thomas published something; it's more than ten years old, but it still holds water."

Selective mutism described children who were physically capable of speech and who might even be socially dominant *inside* the family setting—but they became "frozen" out in the world. If Sylvia remembered correctly, the rare childhood disorder had several basic parameters: a close-knit and often culturally alienated family situation; an overprotective mother figure and an overly attached child; identity and personality issues for a child who tended to be shy, withdrawn, and oversensitive from birth.

Dr. Tompkins gave an audible sigh. "If she's suffered abuse, or if she's witnessed traumatic events—"

"Then the normal response would be obsessive oral repetition—a verbal reliving of the trauma."

"Exactly." Margaret Tompkins continued: "Eventually she'll expel what she can't stand to keep inside." Pause. "The interesting question will be *how* she expels the experience . . . because it probably won't be verbal."

"Through her drawings?"

"You say she drew a demon. . . . Beware the interpretation of some demonic abuser; the demon may well be *inside* the child." She suppressed a sneeze. "Damn this cold. Let her know that silence is acceptable. Are you still doing that meditation of yours?"

"I try to sit every day, if that's what you mean."

"It will come in handy." Margaret Tompkins's smile was clear in her voice. "But don't be too patient, Sylvia. I don't want to be a doomsayer, but you know how intractable this disorder can be. Especially for children older than ten. It's crucial that the effects of additional trauma be identified and dealt with as quickly as possible—that is, if you want this child to have a fighting chance."

"If you're trying to alarm me, you're succeeding."

"Oh, dear." Dr. Tompkins lightened her tone. "What you need is a detective who can get to the bottom of the facts."

"I've got a detective. I sleep with him on a regular basis."

Sylvia was startled by an intrusive electronic beep that signaled a call on her other line. She gave a frustrated groan. "I'm sorry, Margaret, can you hold?"

A few seconds later, she was back. "I'm going to have to say good-bye; I've got an emergency—"

"Then go." Margaret Tompkins's voice grew faint. "Sylvia? Don't forget how infatuating wounded children can be."

Sylvia started to thank the psychiatrist, but Margaret had already hung up.

Nellie Trujillo, Serena's foster mother, was waiting on the second line. She spoke rapidly, her voice full of worry and frustration. "You need to get over here right away. She's driving me crazy—"

"Slow down." Sylvia heard the sound of keening in the background. "Is that Serena? What's happening?"

"She's throwing things around, dragging them outside, acting crazy. Crying and screaming—"

"Is there anything around that can hurt her—broken glass, scissors?"

"I don't think so. I can see her from here—" Nellie yelled suddenly, "Put that down!"

"What set her off?"

"Nothing. She was watching TV. Then she just went nuts. I thought she was a nice kid, but she's a little monster!"

"What was on the television?"

"Cartoons."

"Cartoons? Nothing else?"

"I don't know, I was in the kitchen." The high-pitched cries in the background turned to shrieks. "Dammit!" Nellie Trujillo whispered. "I never swear. Now look at me." She sounded like a woman who had used up all her emotional reserves.

"Did you call her social worker?"

"I called, but Dolores wasn't there. They took a message. I've had lots of kids in my home, some of them really screwed up, but they never acted like this. I mean it, you have to come now."

Sylvia's hand grazed Serena's drawing, and the impulse to tell Mrs. Trujillo to wait for Dolores Martin died on her tongue. As a court-appointed evaluating psychologist, her professional boundaries were wider than those of a clinical therapist. This situation qualified as a crisis, and a home visit would not compromise her ability to do her job; if anything, it would give her the chance to assess Nellie Trujillo's ability to continue as foster mother. All these thoughts raced through Sylvia's mind, but they didn't sway her—it was the child's distress that made her agree.

"Keep an eye on her until I get there. I'm leaving my

office now. Tell me exactly where you are on De Fouri Street so I don't get lost."

WHEN SYLVIA ARRIVED at the Trujillo home, she found Serena in the backyard on her hands and knees in a large sandbox. She was dressed only in underpants—with the medallion dangling around her neck. Her long hair had fallen forward across her young face, her skin shiny with sweat. She was digging in the sand with quick and methodical strokes.

All around Serena, isolated objects were scattered in the sand: articles of clothing, dolls, crayons, and other toys, even food. Her hands scraped sand from a deepening hole. When she reached solid clay, she snatched up a piece of clothing—the cotton T-shirt she had worn in Sylvia's office. She stuffed it into the hole and covered it with sand, obsessively patting and smoothing the surface particles. She scrambled on all fours, moving a few inches away to begin the process again. She buried the next item—a sock. And the next—a red ribbon. A piece of bread. A hairbrush.

As Sylvia stood watching the bizarre scene, she realized her mouth was open. She closed it and took a few steps toward the sandbox. Serena gave no sign of recognition or acknowledgment, but a high, thin hum seemed to come from the child.

Definitely Twilight Zone *time.*

"Serena," Sylvia murmured.

Serena lifted her gaze toward Sylvia. Her dirt-smeared face was blank—except for a tiny spark of rebellion in those charismatic eyes.

Sylvia walked across the lawn until she was a penny's toss from Serena. The neighborhood was quiet except for the sound of barking dogs. It took her a moment to realize the dogs were her own; they were shut in the back of her truck. She sat down, prepared to wait, willing to watch the show. Recognizing the stir of excitement in the pit of her stomach, she felt slightly uncomfortable. It was the excitement a psychologist feels when presented with an especially interesting case, an exotic psyche.

Sylvia found herself asking silent questions: Was this very bizarre behavior ritualistic? Repetitive? Were the gestures ceremonial? Practical? Had the child done this before—was the behavior studied?

She remembered Margaret Tompkins's words: "If she's suffered abuse, or if she's witnessed traumatic events . . . eventually she'll expel what she can't stand to keep inside."

Psychologist and child were the yard's only occupants. Nellie Trujillo was watching from her kitchen. Her blue-and-white apron was visible through the window; the soft chink of glass against glass drifted out from the house.

Sylvia kept the child in focus. Behind Serena, the rest of the world blurred into a soft backdrop. October's Indian-summer sun shone through tree branches, and the ground was dappled with light and shadow. Another rainstorm was blowing in from the Gulf of Mexico, its eventual arrival announced by intermittent thunder. At the moment, however, the sky was clear.

What would the child do when she ran out of things to bury? Was every possession—old and new—going to its grave? A stuffed animal disappeared beneath the sandy surface. A bar of soap was next. A few scraps of paper. When all the items were buried, Serena sat very still—for one minute, two . . .

Sylvia felt Serena's eyes. The child studied her for several seconds before breaking contact. Then Serena wrapped her arms around her knees and began sucking on the soft skin of her own wrist; her eyelids lowered, her lips pulled rhythmically. Sylvia had to admit it to herself—Serena unnerved her.

The sound of a screen door caught Sylvia's attention. She shifted her body to look at Nellie Trujillo just as a golden airborne blur flew over the backyard gate and raced into the yard.

Nikki had escaped from the truck. Now the dog charged toward the child, sand and dirt flying, and Nellie Trujillo screamed in horror. Sylvia lunged toward the animal, yelling out a command to sit.

She was sure she saw Serena's lips moving.

Nikki hesitated, kept coming. Sylvia bellowed. This time, the Malinois stopped, fur on scruff and tail erect, black lips stretched back from sharp canines. Drool glistened on the animal's teeth. Only eight feet separated child and growling dog.

Nellie Trujillo cried out again. The shepherd was inching forward.

Sylvia stopped breathing. "Nikki, stay!"

The dog refused to respond.

Serena sucked in her breath, and her small hand reached out to clutch one of the metal posts that anchored the swing set to the earth. Then she did something that astounded Sylvia. She took a step toward the threatening dog and dropped to her knees. Her face was raised, her arms extended, palms upward—as if she were praying.

Nikki sat, whining feverishly. Her bristly tail picked up tempo on the sand. *Thump thump thump.*

Sylvia began to breathe again when the Malinois inched forward to lick Serena's face. *Nikki almost ate her. Jesus.*

Nellie Trujillo made a small sound of amazement that couldn't quite mask the discomfort in her voice and said, "Look at that."

"Yeah." Sylvia nodded, trying to dredge up a relieved smile. She whistled, but Nikki was glued to Serena, fur flush against her new mistress. To top it off, Nikki growled at Sylvia when she approached. Her own dog was protecting a child. From her. Fabulous.

But Serena seemed oblivious to the animal—and to the world. Her deep-set eyes were still focused on some heavenward point, her entire being engaged in what could only be described as communion. In a moment of unguarded repose, the child's features softened and her expression filled with longing.

Abruptly, her body relaxed—and she nodded as if a question had been answered.

Serena made one more move. She scooted toward Sylvia and wrapped both her arms around the psychologist's legs. Her grip was hot and fast. Tight. Like she was never, ever going to let go.

WHEN THE TIME came to leave, Sylvia resigned herself to chaos. She explained to Serena that she had to go away. She cajoled. Soothed. Stood firm. But she was right. Chaos was inevitable.

Nellie Trujillo disappeared into her house dragging a furious child by the hand.

There was nothing wrong with Serena's lungs. She sounded like a kid screaming bloody murder because she was about to be thrown to the wolves.

Sylvia put Nikki in the back of her truck, where the shepherd settled down with Rocko amid the clutter of toolbox, blankets, and a bundle of clothes destined for the secondhand store. When she lifted the camper shell's rear window, she discovered Nikki's avenue of escape: Albert Kove had neglected to secure the latch.

She cracked the window open for air and returned to the Trujillo kitchen to make sure Nellie was coping with the distraught child. The room was empty. Following the sound of a woman's voice, Sylvia arrived at Serena's room. She stopped and stood quietly outside the partially closed door. Through the gap, she could see Nellie standing with her arms wrapped around herself; the woman looked weary. The child was curled up, tucked in bed, crying softly. One small fist enclosed the silver medallion.

Minutes later, Nellie joined Sylvia in the kitchen, where she begged her to stay for tea. Sylvia agreed— swayed by the desperation on the woman's face. While Nellie placed two mugs of water in the microwave, the telephone rang. She answered on the first ring, keeping her voice low so that Serena would not be disturbed. "This is Mrs. Trujillo."

Sylvia finished making the chamomile tea and sipped the hot liquid while Nellie carried on a brief conversation. Coming from the street, she heard the faint sound of barking dogs.

Nellie hung up the phone and turned to Sylvia. "They got in touch with the social worker. She may stop by later." Her expression shifted quickly to concern. "I wonder if you'd talk to her about this?"

Sylvia nodded. "I'll call her this afternoon." She held out her business card. "And I want you to call me if you have any questions. Or if anything changes. Anything. Especially if she starts talking!"

Nellie Trujillo nodded as she accepted the card, and her eyes swept over Sylvia's bare fingers.

"You don't have children of your own?" she asked.

"Not yet."

"But you specialize in kid psychology?"

"No."

The woman looked confused. "Then why . . . ?"

Sylvia frowned. *I'm here via a circuitous route that includes managed care and downsized government contracts in addition to an absentee colleague and a boss who won't leave well enough alone.* "Let's just blame it on the HMO's."

Nellie Trujillo's fingers tamped stray hairs behind one ear. She seemed to accept the explanation, which wasn't surprising, since she was a veteran of the state's foster-care system. She bit her lip, then said, "About Serena . . . that child's from another world."

When Sylvia didn't respond, Mrs. Trujillo continued. "I feel bad about this, but I really don't think I can handle her. My other kids . . ." She trailed off.

Sylvia nodded. After a moment, she said, "I think Serena may need special care. It's not your fault. We'll get it sorted out."

Relieved, Nellie smiled hesitantly, but her gaze was steadfast. "Foster kids—whether they mean to or not—sooner or later, they break your heart."

Sylvia walked silently to the kitchen door. She'd heard the warning in the woman's words, but she couldn't think of any response.

CHAPTER SEVEN

RENZO SANTOS PARKED his Suburban a hundred feet from the modest one-story house on De Fouri Street. The quiet neighborhood had a muted quality, as if it were covered with soft gray netting. The old Sanctuario was quiet, apparently deserted. Along the street, the half dozen houses seemed to fade with the late afternoon light. The stillness was broken only when a noisy jay called from one of the staunch old cottonwoods.

Renzo pulled the dark blue baseball cap low over his eyes and took a slow breath. As he'd anticipated, the social worker had led him to the child's foster home. He'd realized he was in the right place as soon as the lady answered her door, stepping onto the front porch. He'd seen her at the courthouse that morning. He'd mistaken her for a clerk, an assumption that had cost him most of a day. But finally, he had the child within his reach.

After the social worker's departure, Renzo had driven the neighborhood, restlessly preparing himself for work. The surrounding streets meandered without coherent design, and the result was a numbing maze that reminded him of Mexico. But it wasn't Mexico; it was smoother, cleaner, less desperate, less alive. It made him hunger for the border.

He stepped out of the Suburban and walked at a medium pace along the sidewalk toward the house. In a dark suit and white shirt, clean-shaven, Renzo Santos wasn't worried about being noticed. At an early age, he had learned the art of invisibility. More than once it had kept him from being slapped around by the *puta*'s men. It had even saved him from death. Always it left him with the excruciating wound of vulnerability: he was a man who would never truly be seen by anyone.

To disappear, Renzo touched a shadow deep inside his mind. Then he let that shadow filter through his body like music. Vaporizing bone. Erasing flesh. Until he was nothing but the purest essence of being. And could be remade. Into a utility repairman. Into a delivery man. Into a Bible convert. Into oxygen.

When he approached the small home on De Fouri Street, he adjusted the smile on his face, adjusted the light in his eyes. He could look benign. Before reaching the front walkway, he cut purposefully along the property's southern boundary. A narrow gate led from front yard to back, and it swung open easily. The small grassy area was empty of occupants. A sandbox and swing set, looking forlorn and abandoned in the shade, occupied one corner of the yard. Here he was shielded from the street and the neighboring homes by fence and trees. He stepped over a low hedge into a flower bed. The earth was soft and spongy, and it gave way slightly beneath his feet. He stood close enough to the plaster walls to feel the warmth left by the sun. Level with his shoulders, a window offered a view of the living room. The television set was on, and two boys were seated cross-legged in front of the screen, eyes glued to wildly energetic cartoon images. He could see another child's leg swinging in and out of view. He shifted position; the child was sprawled on a flowered couch. A girl. His heartbeat picked up for a half second until he registered her unfamiliar features and the fact that she was only three or four years old.

He moved quietly, skirting the side of the house. He passed a bedroom. The curtains on these windows were drawn, but through a one-inch margin the carpet and bedspread of the master bedroom were visible. Lamplight illuminated a wedding picture. Renzo had seen no sign of the woman's husband.

The next window revealed the kitchen, where the woman was cooking an early dinner. Steam rolled off a large aluminum pot. She held dried pasta in one fist and shook it into the pot, recoiling slightly when she was spattered with hot water.

She called out—there was no one else in the kitchen—probably to one of the children. Renzo eased himself quickly around the corner, past the back door, to the other side of the compact home. Three final windows lined the wall ahead, single-framed, simple hinges, break a pane and you're in. He sidled up to the first window. As his eyes adjusted to the dim interior light, he discovered he'd found her. A child's night-light illuminated a small room furnished with two bunk beds and a single twin bed. She was a soft shape asleep and hidden beneath a flannel blanket.

Renzo didn't need to break the glass—the window was unlatched.

NELLIE TRUJILLO RAN a wooden spoon through roiling spaghetti. She thought she should probably have added two packages of noodles to feed four children and two adults. She checked the clock on the kitchen wall and sighed; her husband repaired appliances from seven A.M. to four-thirty P.M. He was late as usual. For the third time, she called out to her oldest son. "Rudy, *jito*, wake Serena to eat!"

When there was still no response, Nellie murmured, "That boy." She wiped her hands on her apron and started toward the door just as her twelve-year-old appeared. His eyes were glazed from staring too long at the television.

"Did you hear me, *jito*?" Nellie snapped. "Check on Serena."

He shrugged, eyes on the stove, on food. "She's not my sister."

"Don't make me tell your father—"

"I'm going." He swung around and stomped down the hallway.

Nellie clucked her tongue as she lured a strand of spaghetti onto her spoon. She sampled it, then retrieved a colander from a high cabinet. She was about to call her second son when she heard something that gave her goose bumps. A child's piercing scream.

Nellie dropped the colander and dashed into the hall. She cried out when she saw something on the floor. Her eyes caught motion—then she realized what she was staring at. Her two boys were wrestling, the older had the younger in a headlock.

Both boys ignored her until she grabbed Rudy by the scruff of his neck.

"Ouch!" Rudy finally released his choke hold on his brother.

"Didn't I ask you to check on Serena?"

Rudy moaned when his brother kicked him in the shin. Then he shrugged and said, "I did."

Nellie frowned at the odd expression on her older son's face. "And?" His silence alarmed her. "What?"

"She ran away, Mom. She's not there."

AT HOME IN La Cieneguilla, Sylvia slipped out of running shoes, stripped off shorts and T-shirt, and showered. She was energized from a three-mile run. Her favorite route led up the ridge behind her adobe house, but she had acres of relatively open country to choose from. That was one advantage of living fifteen miles south of Santa Fe. Another was the quiet seclusion, and the incredible star-studded night skies.

She found a cigarette in a kitchen drawer, lit it, took three long hits, then stubbed it out in the sink. She'd cut her smoking down to almost nothing. She tried her best to sit and meditate each morning—always with less-than-perfect concentration. And she was drinking vodka only on special occasions. It was all part of the year's reorganization. Her new priority: less bullshit, more peace of mind, a lot more sex. She squeezed half a lemon into a glass of iced tea, mugged a smile, then caught sight of her reflection in the kitchen window; the shiner lent her a rakish air.

It was early yet; just past four-thirty. She found the newspaper on the counter where she'd left it on a stack of mail. She began sifting through the pile. A large manila envelope contained a series of her prison-inmate interviews, just transcribed. The new issue of *Corrections Alert!* had a piece on female inmates' mental health issues; she set it aside to read later. There was a letter from her mother, letters from colleagues. She stacked those with the others. She knew she was stalling, not ready to tackle the book.

She refilled her glass with iced tea. Resting her elbows on the counter, she perused the newspaper; the front page had stories on the governor and new prison construction; she clipped a recipe for fruit salsa; she pulled out the movie schedule from the entertainment section. There were three films she wanted to see.

A story caught her eye: an upcoming gala fund-raiser for the Children's Rescue Fund was being held at the Frank Lloyd Wright Pottery House. Sylvia had always wanted to see the inside of the east-side landmark. She scanned the story—*music by Los Mariachis Nachitos . . . dignitaries expected to attend include the governors of New Mexico and Texas . . . hostess Noelle Harding . . . $500 to $5,000 per person*. She sighed and stopped reading. Harding was Texas "Big Rich," and five hundred dollars was a tad rich for Sylvia's blood. She'd catch a garden tour one of these days.

She gave the dogs water, then carried the tea to her study and sat down at her desk to rework a section of her book. This particular chapter centered around an inmate whose mother had been a prostitute, father unknown but probably one of her johns.

Light bedtime reading.

When Sylvia's first book, *Attached to Violence*, was published a few years earlier, it had drawn professional criticism and praise. Her publishers hoped a second book would increase her visibility. Sylvia just prayed she wouldn't end up on some talk show with a hyperactive confrontational host. She knew her publishers prayed she would. And they kept threatening to trash her subtitles.

It was no mystery to Sylvia why she wrote about attachment or bonding disorders. Most children who experienced the loss of a parent spent some portion of their life trying to fill the void. It was one of those wounds that never quite healed. Sylvia turned thirteen the year Daniel Strange walked out of her life. Bonnie, Sylvia's mother, had always insisted her husband was dead: "Why else would he stay silent, hurt us this way?" Sylvia felt in her heart he was still alive . . . somewhere in the world. Even as a young child, she had sensed a fundamental change in her father after his return from military duty in Southeast Asia. Years before his physical disappearance, he had abandoned his family emotionally.

She tried to focus on the revision, but she lacked concentration. Emotionally drained from the day's events, she found herself at half-mast in her swivel chair. Serena's file and the accident report were on a shelf next to her desk; she scanned the few pages again. And when she picked up the *Diagnostic and Statistical Manual-IV* to verify a term, the pages of the tome just happened to fall open to the categories of disorders usually diagnosed in childhood: mental retardation, autistic disorder, learning disorders, expressive language disorder.

Sylvia scrawled notes on scratch paper: *cognitive disorders? definite vocal capacity! lack of language skills? stuttering? selective mutism? silence intermittent? for days, weeks, months? years?*

"God, let's hope not years."

Rocko, who was stretched out on the floor of the office near Sylvia's feet, opened one eye at the sound of a human voice and yawned. His mistress absentmindedly scratched the terrier's tummy with her bare toe.

Since, at the moment, Serena was minus almost all history, there was no way to know if her family dynamics matched the selective-mutism profile. On one hand, she wasn't a "frozen child," completely withdrawn from all social contacts. On the other hand, she wasn't your average kid. The image remained in Sylvia's mind—the child's luminous features raised skyward.

Sylvia poked Rocko's belly. "Whaddaya think, big guy? Is Serena a wee bit tetched?"

The terrier raised his head attentively as if he were about to answer the question. Sylvia was reaching forward to pat the animal when someone grabbed her from behind.

She let out a short yell and thrust her elbow backward.

"Hey! It's *me*."

She recognized the voice, turned, and saw a familiar face gazing at her from under the brim of a baseball cap. His skin was weathered and tanned, his gray-green eyes fringed by dark lashes, his nose had encountered obstacles, and his mouth was wide and expressive. Tall and solid at forty-three, Matt England had a cop's seen-the-world face.

"It's *you*," she said, breathless.

"Who'd you think it was? You almost injured my manhood." He gave her a speculative glance before he disappeared from the study. She followed him to the living room—he wasn't there—and stepped out the open sliding glass door onto the deck. When Matt reappeared through the backyard gate, his arms were weighed down by something black and heavy and wrapped in plastic. He let the load fall to the wooden deck.

Sylvia bent close to read the label. "Pond liner?"

"Ummmm." Matt grazed one hand along Sylvia's bare arm. He pushed his cap off his forehead and smiled. "This one's going to be big."

Sylvia set her hands on her hips. "Bigger than the two ponds you've already made?"

"This'll be the best. We can stock it with spadefoot tadpoles next July. And it's going over by the moss rock and the blue spruce." He glanced off toward the rear of the house and the ridge beyond. Sylvia knew the spot he was talking about. It was on the other side of the fence, maybe thirty feet from the house. A place where she'd seen rabbits, foxes, and very recently a corn snake. Matt moved toward the sliding glass door. "What are you drinking?"

"Iced tea." Sylvia followed. "But there's still some beer in the refrigerator." In the kitchen, she watched him line up bread, mayonnaise, sweet pickles, and a plastic bag of sliced ham on the counter. She pulled a cold bottle of Rio Grande Lager from a six-pack, popped the top, and took a long drink. She wiped the bottle's rim with the base of her palm and handed the beer to Matt, who was busily creating a massive sandwich.

She perched herself on the kitchen counter like a kid, bare heels gently slapping a cupboard door. She'd been working questions in her mind like worry beads, and she was impatient to get Matt's feedback. They each had a distinctly different reasoning process; when they worked a problem through to its logical end, they reached two very different conclusions.

At the moment, to drive her crazy, he took his time returning various bottles to the refrigerator. When he was finally seated at the small table, eating, she asked, "If you've got plates and an I.D. number on a vehicle, how long will it take to trace it?"

Matt shrugged, then swallowed a mouthful. "The VIN will tell you origin of manufacture. Are the plates stolen? Is the vehicle stolen?"

Sylvia pursed her lips. "Maybe."

Matt closed one eye and looked skeptical. "What are we talking about here?"

"My new client." She frowned. "Remember the child I saw at the hospital?"

"You said you were going to work on the book." Rocko had taken up position at Matt's feet.

Sylvia thought about the unrevised pages stacked on her desk. She ducked her head as if she could physically dodge her own deadline. "I worked this afternoon—"

"Can you get me another beer?" Matt gazed at her over his sandwich.

"You've still got some."

"I'll need another one." Matt set the last quarter of the sandwich on his plate. He pulled crust from the bread and tossed it to Rocko. The terrier caught it, then let it drop to the floor, where he nosed it unenthusiastically, all carnivore.

Matt said, "The reason I mentioned your book is because you made such a point about finishing the chapter before the party."

"Uh-huh. I'd like to do that." She was puzzled by his reaction. She knew he'd been relieved when she'd taken a break from prison and court evaluations to concentrate on writing and research. He didn't have to worry about a stay-at-home writer the way he had to worry about a woman who worked with sociopaths and psychotics on a daily basis. Even her trips to California to gather data with her friend and colleague Leo Carreras had found Matt's support.

He said, "The party's tomorrow. Can you get me that beer?"

"Get your own beer." Sylvia stood. Her dark gold-brown eyes flashed, displaying temper. "If I don't get the pages done, it's not the end of the world. I'm trying to tell you about this child."

"Fine. Tell me." Matt shrugged as he rose from the table and carried his plate to the sink.

"Never mind."

"I'm listening." He ran water over the plate and squirted a dab of dish soap from a yellow bottle onto a sponge, scrubbing stoneware.

"All right." Sylvia's expression shifted as she concentrated on relating her experience. "Her name is Serena. She's nine or ten, probably ten years old, Hispanic, with a great face, and gawky the way kids are—"

"I know kids who aren't."

"—but she doesn't speak a word. I think she's capable of speech—" Sylvia refocused on Matt, saw his best poker face, and stopped speaking. "What?"

"Nothing."

"Something's going on." Sylvia watched Rocko slink out of the room. "You're upset I went back to work to see a traumatized kid?"

"No." Matt slapped his baseball hat on his head. He took a long breath. Paused heroically. Kept his voice very soft. "But I'm fuckin' pissed about that beer."

Sylvia eyed her lover suspiciously as she moved to the refrigerator and opened the door. She pulled a lager from the six-pack and closed the door. The quick intake of her breath was involuntary. Slowly, she opened the door again. There was a blue velvet ring box on the shelf between ketchup and beer.

"Oh." Sylvia's face broke into a smile. "Gee."

Matt looked pleased and embarrassed. "You're supposed to open it."

She lifted the lid and smiled at the delicate gold ring with its flower of shimmering rubies and tiny pearls.

"It belonged to my great-grandma Etty."

"It's beautiful." She catapulted herself toward Matt, grabbed him around the waist, and kissed him.

When he pulled back for air, his lopsided grin made him look twelve years old. He took the ring from the box and started to slip it onto Sylvia's left ring finger. "Let's see if it fits."

She protested, "My fingers are too fat—"

"Your fingers are lovely"—the ring hit her knuckle and stuck—"but fat."

"Thanks."

The gold band wouldn't budge. "*Really* fat." Matt dodged her punch. "Do you have any butter?"

"Wait." Sylvia licked her finger and worked the metal band until her knuckle felt raw. Just when she was about to give up, the ring slid into place.

"So . . ." Matt removed his baseball hat from his head and crumpled it between nervous hands. "Now it's official."

She forced herself to respond before the silence became uncomfortable. "Absolutely," she said lightly, swatting him on the nose with one finger.

They kissed. Matt's hands were moving up under her shirt when a high-pitched bleat sounded from the pager on his belt. "Damn." He glanced down. "Rosie."

"At the pen?" Sylvia frowned. Rosie Sanchez, penitentiary investigator, would only be working overtime if there had been an incident. There were plenty of incidents at the Penitentiary of New Mexico, an institution that was the center of constant political, judicial, and social controversy.

Matt nodded, even as he was reaching for the telephone.

Sylvia prepared the dog's dinner while eavesdropping on the monosyllabic phone conversation. "Matt. . . . Yeah. . . . Uh-huh. . . . Uh-huh. . . . Yeah." A glance at his wristwatch. "I'll be there in fifteen." He hung up and caught Sylvia's questioning glance. He said, "An OD at the joint. Some of that stuff coming up from Mexico."

She nodded, following him to the door. She knew the Rio Grande corridor was a major conduit for marijuana, cocaine, and the newest "super" heroin traveling from the Colombian-cartel drug labs through Mexico into the northern states. The D.E.A. clampdown on Miami had created a wealth of opportunity for Mexico's border towns.

And New Mexico State Police got their share of Mexico's drug crime; there was more than enough to go around.

In the doorway, Matt paused and cleared his throat. He had an odd expression on his face. He said, "By the way, that car your girl was driving? Dispatch ran a ten twenty-nine and—"

"Whoa, translation."

"You better bone up on your ten codes, ma'am. Ten

twenty-nine—wants, warrants, stolen; ten twenty-eight—registration."

Sylvia set her hands on her hips and took a breath. "The car's from Mexico, right?"

"Wrong. The vehicle had plates from a dealer in El Paso, Texas, so E.P.I.C.—" He caught himself before she could protest, and then slowed down. "El Paso Intelligence Center; it's law enforcement and military, they do the U.S.-Mexico border checks. They ran it on their computer and came up with a company in El Paso."

"You knew this and you didn't tell me?"

"I found it out this morning. I'm telling you right now. The biz, Hat-Trick Incorporated, turns out to be a drop box. The car wasn't reported stolen, and nobody answers the phone at Hat-Trick."

"That doesn't sound very promising."

"It sounds like a front for contraband, and the most likely contraband is drugs. So what's your kid's connection to sleazy drug deals?"

"She could be the daughter of a mule."

Matt nodded slowly.

Sylvia let out the air from her lungs with a huff. "Sometimes you're a real shit."

"Thanks for the compliment."

"Thanks for the research."

As Sylvia watched Matt's Caprice pull out of the drive, she felt a tinge of envy. For the first time in months, she actually wished she was going to prison.

CHAPTER EIGHT

GHOSTLY IN FADING daylight, a handful of protesters stood vigil outside the entrance to the Penitentiary of New Mexico. One protester held up a black-and-white placard as Matt England downshifted for the turn off Highway 14. The sign read EXECUTION IS MURDER.

Matt caught a glimpse of the protester's pale and drawn face. Why did professional crusaders always look as though they were allergic to sunshine? Didn't these people have lives of their own? In Matt's experience, they attached like leeches to the cause of the moment.

He glanced in his rearview mirror and saw the figure receding, now the size of a child's puppet. The state's "murder" was going to take place in less than a month. Death by lethal injection for a torture-killer named Cash Wheeler. The first execution in New Mexico since 1960, when David Cooper Nelson was put to death in the gas chamber for the murder of a hitchhiker. The chamber was still in the basement of the pen's old facility. Collecting dust. The new "death house" was a small, sterile concrete-block building constructed in 1990. It sat just outside Housing Unit 3-B at North, the maximum-security facility, where Matt was headed now.

He parked next to a hot cherry-red Camaro, climbed out of his Chevy, and walked around to greet Rosie Sanchez. He smiled to himself; Rosie didn't look like a penitentiary investigator—maraschino nails, copper curls almost touching her round butt, five-feet-two and given to wearing spike heels. At the moment, she was balanced on the trunk of her Camaro, filing a polished red fingernail that was brighter than the car.

Rosie tucked the file into her suit pocket and cocked her head at the state police criminal agent. "Took you long enough."

"Eleven minutes." Matt popped the Chevy's trunk and removed camera and crime-scene kit.

"More like twenty-five." She slid gracefully from the Camaro and dusted herself off. "Did I interrupt the lovebirds?"

"Yeah, actually—"

But Rosie was already leading the way across the parking lot to the maximum unit's main entrance. The multibuilding facility dated to the mideighties; all slab concrete, riot glass, high-voltage T-line edging the roof, perimeter fence, and razor ribbon.

"On the phone you said OD. What've we got?"

"Looks like heroin. Paramedics were here before you. Body's at St. Vincent's because they tried to resuscitate. No luck. His cell's cordoned off." As an investigator, Rosie knew how to process a crime scene, but serious offenses at the pen fell under the jurisdiction of the New Mexico State Police. She continued, "It's straightforward."

They were almost to the glass doors, and Matt slowed. He knew that every afternoon, on any yard in the joint, drugs were changing hands as easily as cigarettes and bullshit. "But something's bugging you."

Rosie shook her head and grabbed the lock bar on the first of the glass doors. She stood stock-still. "The dead guy wasn't just a max inmate. He was on death row."

Matt whistled softly. At New Mexico's penitentiary, death row was not a physical location but an administrative designation. The state's four death row inmates were housed in a segregation pod in Unit 3-B. All three dozen prisoners in that pod were kept under twenty-three-hour lockdown. For one hour of every day, each of the inmates exercised in a completely enclosed cage that measured approximately twelve by twenty feet. Alone. And each inmate came into contact with only a small, select group of correctional officers.

It was an accepted fact of prison life that drugs came in with staff. There weren't enough girlfriends, wives, mothers, or buddies to account for the volume of flow. Rumors ran fast, and Matt thought he could name at least three longtime employees who were trafficking. But proving it was another matter. Snitches didn't last long in the joint.

As if she read his mind, Rosie said, "I know every C.O. on that duty roster."

"One of them's dirty."

Rosie looked grim. "And I've got a dead man in Ad Seg."

Matt flashed on the protesters outside the pen. He asked, "So it's Cash Wheeler?"

"No. Wheeler's alive. The overdose was Darryl

Bowan, Wheeler's next-door neighbor." She pushed open the first door, and Matt followed her into the entryway.

The C.O. on duty at the admitting desk stood, recognized Rosie through the glass, and buzzed the locked security door. Rosie pushed down on the bars, and she and Matt entered North's small lobby and then the stairwell that accessed the gym, yards, and housing units.

While they were wending their way past Medical Services and then outside through Medical's asphalt-and-wire sally port, neither of them spoke. But as they stood waiting for a massive gate to roll open allowing entry into 3-B's perimeter yard, Rosie said, "It hasn't reached the press yet, but Cash Wheeler's started a hunger strike."

"Protesting his innocence?" Matt asked dryly.

"He got a raw deal, if you think about it." Rosie waved her fingers in the air. "The prosecuting attorney made his career on Wheeler's conviction. And now the governor won't commute to *life* because he's afraid it would brand him as liberal."

"He's right." Matt gave a curt nod. "People still remember a certain unnamed governor as the one who set the baby-killers free." After a moment, he asked, "If Wheeler's on a hunger strike, won't he be moved to the hospital?"

"Absolutely—if his lawyer ever eases up." Rosie nodded. "Anyway, the upcoming execution, the hunger strike—it's making the guys in the pod crazy."

"Crazy enough to overdose?"

"Bowan and Wheeler were buddies." She sighed.

"Tell me what you found." The gate clanged open with a shudder.

"He shot up in the thigh. He used a couple of condoms as a tourniquet to raise a vein." Rosie walked quickly, heels clicking out a two-four rhythm. Her legs were half the length of Matt's, but he always had to work to keep pace with her. One of these days he planned to sit down, do the math, and figure out how she moved so damn fast.

Rosie's mouth was moving quickly, too. ". . . a shake-down two days ago, but no drugs. Now Bowan's dead and there's a vial of whatever killed him in the sink."

Matt asked, "You remember that heavy-duty heroin coming up from Mexico last year?"

"¿Chiva?" Rosie spat out the local slang for heroin. "How could I forget? First it made the junkies psy-chotic, then it whacked them. We had six overdoses in one week."

"Didn't they call it Death Ride?"

"And Mexican Dog and Lone Ranger." Rosie nodded, looking unhappy.

Beyond the prison perimeter to the northeast, the land rose steeply for forty miles to Santa Fe Baldy in the Sangre de Cristo Mountains. To the northwest, the Jemez range jabbed against blue sky, while the Ortiz Mountains stood due south. Man-made boundaries seemed small and mean in comparison.

At the metal entry door to Housing Unit 3-B, Rosie spoke into the intercom. Moments later a C.O. buzzed them through. Matt took in the familiar beige severity of the hall that connected the overhead control booth with each of the three separate pods in the unit. They passed the strip-search cell, and then Rosie stopped out-side the door to the middle pod. Again, they were buzzed through. Officers in the control booth had visual access to all three pods.

Inmate Bowan's cell—second tier, last on the right—was cordoned off with bright yellow tape. Even without the tape barrier, none of the eleven other occupants in the pod were likely to set foot inside that cell. They were all locked down tight behind four-inch steel doors.

Matt could feel their eyes as he climbed the stairs ahead of Rosie. Someone hissed. Someone else whistled. It was a very quiet evening in 3-B. Maybe they were just warming up. The scent of blood, the proximity of death, should have revved them into hysteria. The silence was more eerie than any cacophony.

At the doorway to Bowan's cell, Matt gazed impassively at the mess. The concrete walls were spattered with dark fluid. The bed had been stripped, the bedding shredded, and the mattress was marked by gaping holes as though something had tried to dig its way out. The toilet in the cell had overflowed; Matt smelled it before he saw the human waste staining the floor.

He stooped under the crime-scene tape, stepped forward, and began to sift gingerly through the rubble.

Rosie spoke quietly from the door. "Bowan was discovered by C.O. Dewey on a routine body count. I was here before the paramedics."

"Where was Bowan?"

"Right where you're standing. On his back, having a seizure, foaming at the mouth." Rosie ducked under the tape and stepped inside the cell just far enough so her words didn't carry beyond the door.

Matt considered the scene and the questions it raised. Was it suicide or unintentional overdose? Did it really matter in the scheme of things? The man had been the self-confessed killer of a twelve-year-old girl. He'd also been borderline retarded—slow enough to get into trouble but not slow enough to be noticed by the system—until a tragedy had occurred.

From what Matt knew of Bowan's past, the man had lived a sad, destructive life. He wouldn't be missed. And he'd saved the state some money. Nevertheless, in the Land of Enchantment, death row inmates were not supposed to kill themselves. They were supposed to wait and let the state take their lives.

Matt glanced at Rosie Sanchez. "When was Bowan last seen alive? Or heard?"

Both investigators looked at the wall that separated the dead inmate's cell from the cell of his only neighbor, Cash Wheeler. Rosie twined two fingers and mouthed, "They were tight." With a shake of her head, she turned the same two fingers at herself: *Less than an hour earlier, Wheeler had refused to answer any questions.*

Rosie asked, "Are you going to need about thirty minutes up here?" When he nodded, she stooped under the tape and out of the cell, heading for the stairs. Matt followed, slower, stopping outside the door to gaze back at the ruined cell.

"You shoulda heard that asshole tear himself up." The words came from across the tier, where Matt saw a black face staring out through the grate.

Another inmate called out: "Bowan cryin' to the world when he did hisself."

A third man whispered, "Wen' offa his mind."

"Wheeler dyin', so Bowan gotta die, too."

The voices began to fly around the pod, echoing off the concrete walls, disintegrating to rough vowels and consonants. The words turned to hissing laughter and catcalls, reverberating to a painful crescendo.

Matt felt the hairs on the back of his neck stiffen. There

was only one cell in the entire pod with an occupant who wasn't making noise. The silence was conspicuous.

Slowly, Matt moved a few paces from Bowan's cell; he turned to look past the next grill.

At twenty-nine, Cash Wheeler had the face of an overgrown boy, with neatly symmetrical features, pouting lips, and prominent cheeks. His brown hair was cut short and tossed around by a cowlick at the apex of his forehead; a russet stubble dotted his small chin. His body was wiry, but beneath pale skin he was turning soft from inertia. His keen astringent gaze belonged to another man, one who was much older, much wiser, and world-weary.

He didn't look mean enough to stab the woman he loved and cut her throat. He didn't look cruel enough to drop his own infant child into the muddy, fast-flowing water of the Pecos. But evil often hides behind the mask of normalcy, and a jury had decided he should die for those crimes.

Now, more than a decade later, after all the appeals had been exhausted, Cash Wheeler had finally been given his date with death. Barring a miracle—or judicial prerogative—Wheeler would die before he saw his thirtieth birthday.

As Matt eyed the condemned inmate, he took a quick inventory of his own emotions, expecting he would feel nothing in the way of pity or compassion. All four inmates on the row had killed women, children, or both. And for most of those killers, murder was not their cruelest act. That didn't sit well with a cop, especially not with a man who had lost his wife and son. But there was something about Wheeler that didn't allow Matt's thoughts to settle comfortably.

Wheeler turned away from the grill, but his gaze slid back toward Matt. The two men stared at each other. Sniffing the air. Hackles up. For that minute they were two animals, one caged, one free. Then, abruptly, the inmate seemed to lose energy.

Matt's voice was barely a whisper. "You heard it happen, Wheeler. He was your friend." When the inmate didn't respond, Matt pressed. "Why did Bowan kill himself?"

Remaining silent, Wheeler shook his head.

"Don't you think it would be a comfort to his family to know what happened?"

"Darryl's family disowned him years ago."

"Then tell me. I'd like to know."

Wheeler smiled, but the skin around his eyes tightened. Slowly, he said, "I think Darryl couldn't wait any longer. He wanted rain and sunshine."

ROSIE WAS WAITING for Matt in the main lobby of North Facility.

When the investigators were outside in the illuminated parking lot, she asked, "How do you want to play this out?"

Matt slowed his pace for a moment, watching Rosie stride, shoulders back, head high, and then he caught up with her again. He leaned against her Camaro while she unlocked the driver's door.

He said, "Can you meet on Monday? I'll need the usual: active investigations, transmission logs, access to books and mail, staff—you know the drill."

"Monday's fine." She gave a quick nod and began to duck into the car.

They both knew the investigation wouldn't solve

much in the end. Drugs would still flow across the border and into the veins of addicts, whether on the streets or in prison. It was too late for people like Bowan.

"Will you call me with the lab results?" Rosie snapped her fingers. "Matthew? You're a hundred miles away. Are you thinking about Bowan?"

Matt's eyes slowly found hers. "I'm thinking about rain. . . ."

Rosie shot him a puzzled glance. As she slid her key into the ignition, Matt seemed to come back to earth. He asked, "What time do you want us at the party?"

"Eleven o'clock sharp." The Camaro's 305 horsepower purred to life.

"*En punto*. That's how it will be." Matt lost track of the Camaro's taillights somewhere near the old Main Facility, where Rosie had her office. He followed, driving slowly from the prison grounds, reversing his earlier route.

At the intersection with State Road 14, he was greeted by a small mob gathered under the harsh glare of television lights. At least two local-affiliate television crews wielded Minicams. A blond woman held center stage—Matt caught a glimpse of her before his attention was drawn to a black stretch limousine parked twenty feet from the crowd.

The illuminated license plate read RESCUE.

Matt slowed to a stop. With the Caprice engine idling, he watched the scene. The blonde was talking into a bouquet of microphones. Slender, good-looking, early thirties, hair tucked under a cowboy hat. She was dressed in Levi's, a white tailored shirt, and an embroidered jacket that had probably cost more than Matt's monthly paycheck. Her delicate features were familiar.

He called out to a member of the television crew, a girl of about nineteen, who was packing up some equipment. "What's going on?"

The girl grinned. "Hey, I just get paid to schlep, not think." She walked over to the Caprice, leaned one hip against the door. "You're a cop, aren't you? Nine-one-one. What's going on inside the joint?" She waved toward the penitentiary.

He shrugged. "You show me yours, I'll show you mine."

The girl jerked her head toward the blonde. "Press conference—but you missed the fun. About that guy who's gonna get fried next month."

Matt had seen the coverage of the anti–death-penalty protesters on local news. They had vowed to be on hand twenty-four hours a day until the execution. That was fine by Matt, but he knew it wasn't necessarily fine by the locals in the area. A lot of prison employees lived nearby. Small farmers, trailer-park residents, and leave-me-alone types tended to settle out on 14. There'd been trouble a few nights ago; Matt had heard about it on the scanner.

The girl said, "So, is there gonna be another riot?" She looked excited by the prospect.

"Not tonight." Matt stared beyond her to the blonde; he watched her deftly dismissing the reporters now that she'd gotten all the coverage she wanted. He said, "They don't fry anybody anymore. It's lethal injection."

The girl licked her lips. "No shit, it's lethal. Hey, I heard there's gonna be a riot 'cause they're shipping guys out—"

"That woman really thinks Cash Wheeler's worth her time?"

"Yeah, I guess she does." The girl laughed. "That's Noelle Harding. The guy they're gonna fry is her brother."

THE EVENING NEWS featured stories on a shooting in Albuquerque, an I.N.S. bust in Santa Fe, and the upcoming execution at the penitentiary. Sylvia downed a cheese sandwich while she stood in the living room staring at the television. The condemned inmate's sister, Noelle Harding, had staged a live press conference—the same Noelle Harding who was hosting a gala at the Frank Lloyd Wright house. The world was an interesting place.

Sylvia clicked off the television and returned to work. It took discipline—she felt chained to her laptop—but she managed to lose herself in the revision process. By seven-thirty P.M. she'd reworked five pages of the book to her satisfaction. Then weather broke her concentration.

With the windows open, gusts of air knocked the blinds about, and they were clicking loudly against the screens. Another thunderstorm was blowing up, but the air felt bone dry and electrically charged. It was part of a pattern that had been south of normal since the recent drought. Maybe the turbulence was making the dogs crazy; they were riled up, whining at the door every few minutes.

Their nervousness was contagious. She was feeling spooked. She thought she saw headlights flashing across the front of the house. Was that the low hum of a car engine? But when she stood by the window, blinds parted, all she saw was a dark sheet of land—fields and meadows—across the road, stretching into nothingness. And all she heard was the rustle of lilac bushes, the louder crackle of cottonwood branches shadowboxing the wind.

She closed out her file on the laptop and was about to switch off the computer. She changed her mind. She hadn't checked her E-mail for four days. She entered her password and logged on-line. As she had anticipated, there was mail. She scanned the various subjects and clicked on "reporting in."

Sylvia: I've made some progress. Got a hard lead on your dad at the VA Hospital in West L.A. Looks like he was there in 1980 under the name of Raymond Fremont. "Fremont" had psychiatric problems. Want you to know I'm going to talk to your mother tomorrow. She's serving tea and biscuits.

Harry.

Sylvia left the message on the screen, then walked to the kitchen to add a splash of Absolut and more ice to her glass. Joshua Harold—Harry—was the private investigator she'd hired to track down her missing father.

Actually, she hoped he was dead. It would make things so much easier after all these years. She'd read about a man recently—a Vietnam vet who had "died" during the war. A quarter-century later he turned up to apologize. *Big fucking deal.* She had tried to figure out what she'd say in those circumstances: "Welcome home, Pop?"

Without moving from the room, the house, Sylvia was a child again, remembering. Her father's dark moods, his extended silences, had been powerful weapons of passivity and withdrawal. They had served their purpose: control and punishment of those closest to him.

What about Serena? Was she using silence as punishment? Sylvia didn't buy it. She drained her glass and began to chew on an ice cube. Back in her office, she typed a quick E-mail response:

Dear Harry, What type of psychiatric problems are we talking about? Is my father alive or dead? I need an end to my damn book! By the way, my mother does a great tea—makes her own scones. Say hi for me.

                                                                    SS.

She logged off.

She felt a shadow of dread as she considered her next move: a fifteen-minute meditation. She readily admitted that the stillness of sitting had a fingernails-on-chalkboard quality. As soon as she readied herself and tried to concentrate on her breathing, her thoughts began to gnaw at her like an animal in a trap.

Sylvia sighed, turned the lights low, and sat on a small round pillow, her back against the bedroom wall. The minutes ticked by; she could hear the digital cards on the clock flip down every sixty seconds. Breathe in . . . the cycling water heater seemed louder than usual. Breathe out . . . was that the crunch of gravel under car wheels? Breathe in . . . her neck hurt. Breathe out . . . the Trujillo foster home wasn't working out . . . so where would Serena end up?

In the end, she cut her meditation time in half; her

thoughts were whirling like mad dervishes. The dogs provided a good excuse—Nikki was whining, scratching at the sliding glass door. Sylvia padded into the living room.

The shepherd had been a "gift." Of a dubious sort. More than a year ago, Sylvia's closest friends had presented her with the Malinois, a dropout from the Penitentiary of New Mexico's canine/contraband program. Nikki had spent her first night *chez* Sylvia growling at the world from a kitchen corner. A hundred dog-obedience hours later, Sylvia and Nikki maintained an uneasy truce. There were days when Sylvia still believed Nikki was too aggressive to keep—she'd come *this* close to calling the trainer. But the shepherd was loyal and smart, and Rocko the terrier was sweet on her.

"All right, go out and stay out. Sleep in your doghouse and see if I care." She opened the door and watched both dogs disappear into the darkness of the side yard.

Something drew her outside. It wasn't the taste of winter on the night air, or the sprinkling of stars in the sky. It was the incredible stillness. The wind had stopped, no sign of lightning, and yet the air felt charged. Sylvia felt it. The dogs did, too.

CHAPTER NINE

AT THE FENCE, Nikki planted her feet and began to bark. Within seconds, Rocko was at the shepherd's side, growling, fur erect. Just outside the gate, the motion-sensor light flashed on. Nikki bared sharp teeth—ninety pounds of dog in attack mode. Sylvia's body reacted, tightening with fear. Had someone been in her yard? She froze, then forced herself to take two steps away from the light.

Seconds passed. The frenzied barking shattered the night's stillness.

And just below the animal sounds, there might have been the soft whine of a car engine.

Now Nikki was racing back and forth along the coyote fence, sniffing, searching for access. Rocko followed like a small, dark shadow. There was no way for either dog to escape. Abruptly, the light went black, responding to an automatic timer.

Sylvia ordered Nikki to her side. The dog ignored the

command. Sylvia called again; this time Nikki obeyed, bounding across the yard, sitting alert and trembling with energy. A low growl rumbled from her throat.

Rocko would have no part of discipline. He changed focus and began to prance near the doghouse. The ruff on his neck bristled. His short, high-pitched yips signaled quarry; the terrier had cornered something *inside* the yard.

Sylvia glanced around for a weapon to wield and grabbed the closest object at hand—a rake. She pictured the skunk that had doused Rocko days earlier. She stepped forward, wary, in case her dogs had ferreted out a rabid animal.

A sudden gust of wind stirred the salt cedar's branches. A raindrop hit Sylvia's cheek. She stepped down from the deck and started across the yard. Nikki heeled at her side, whining but controlled.

The doghouse cast a shadow along the coyote fence and the chamiso that grew at the foot of the posts. Sylvia didn't see any sign of a cornered animal, but now both her dogs were intent on the small shelter. Whatever it was must be inside. She said a quick prayer that it wasn't a porcupine— that would be worse than a skunk.

Nikki sat down suddenly, threw back her head, and howled. Clearly, the shepherd was no longer in attack mode. Her tail was wagging. Sylvia squatted down beside her dogs. She saw pale fingers curled around the opening of the doghouse.

She let out a yelp of surprise, and the fingers disappeared inside the plastic shelter like a turtle into its shell. Realization hit—a hand, an arm, the outline of a face. Relieved, Sylvia held out her arms to the huddled child and said, "It's okay, Serena."

While she waited to see if the child would appear, she

tried to make sense of events. *Somehow the child had managed to end up here, hiding inside the dog's*—Sylvia's chain of thought broke as Nikki knocked against her and she fell back on her butt abruptly. She wrapped her arms around her dogs. She could feel Serena's fear. She knew the child was watching from the darkness like a small, frightened ghost.

Sylvia kept still, trying to read her next move. After a minute of puzzling, she lay back on the grass and stared up at the stars. Another raindrop hit her cheek, and another. Rocko immediately scrambled onto his mistress's belly. Worried, Nikki pushed a cool nose against Sylvia's cheek but kept her attention focused on the child.

Sylvia listened for any sign that the child was going to come out into the open. She knew Serena must be starving, thirsty, dusty, and scared to death. At the appropriate time, Sylvia would call the C.P.S. hotline to let them know the child was safe.

But she wasn't going to move until Serena showed herself.

She didn't have to wait long. Over the soft and steady touch of rain, a furtive rustling signaled that the child was moving. Nikki whined. Then Sylvia felt a small, warm body curl up next to hers.

RENZO SANTOS STARED at the small slip of paper for such a long time, the red letters and numbers blurred to a soft gray haze. The name and phone number belonged to the psychologist he'd seen at the courthouse, the tall brunette with the dogs. Where had the tiny stain of blood come from? He focused on the blood, let it blear, then, with effort, brought it back within its boundaries.

Had he tried to find the girl?

The windshield of the Suburban was beaded with water; the road was wet. Renzo had no memory of rain. He peered out at the dark, shining road. A hundred feet away lights reflected off the asphalt of another road—the interstate. So where was he? Parked along a frontage road; that was stupid and dangerous; a cruising cop would pull over to check out a stranded vehicle.

He flicked on his high beams; they illuminated a white highway sign—LA CIENEGUILLA—and an arrow directing traffic west. Had he driven there?

He'd lost himself, but for how long? Minutes? Hours? How long had his mind been gone this time? To regain control of his body, he began to make small movements, testing his senses. He flexed a finger, he stretched his jaw. When he peered in the rearview mirror, he saw dust around his nostrils. He had a foggy memory of snorting a line—hadn't he used the new drug? Yes, he'd opened one of the new vials . . .

And then he'd wandered deep into nightmares.

Renzo was not used to nightmares. As a boy, he'd learned *not* to dream. The same way he'd learned to deny his mother-the-*puta*'s drunk ravings. She would wake him late at night, after she'd come home from the streets to their plywood shack on the edge of town. She would climb under the blanket with her son and cry; about the first time she was raped—at seven years old. On those nights, he had hated his mother most of all because she was weak—a victim. On those nights, he banished all thoughts of her from his mind.

Banishment didn't work tonight. For that, Renzo blamed Paco's betrayal and, mostly, the shock of discovery just days ago. The news that Paco had crossed the border and was running north hadn't surprised Renzo. Paco was weak—Renzo had always said as much. How could you trust a man who didn't want to bloody his hands? Paco had always been different—he'd kept himself separate from the others—and that fact alone made him suspect.

When Paco ran, Renzo followed. He'd picked up the bookkeeper's trail almost instantly, and he'd tracked him almost as far as Santa Fe. In the middle of nowhere, he'd cornered his prey.

But then a ghost had walked toward him out of the darkness, so small, a child . . . with her mother's face. A child who refused to die.

Renzo stirred when he felt a tremor. Was that fear? No. Something was vibrating—the car or the earth? Then it became clear: the pager on his belt. He knew who would be paging him: Amado Fortuna. Tuna. The Big Fish.

Ah . . . Renzo nodded. He moved his mouth, waiting for words to formulate, rehearsing what he would recite for Tuna. *Found our friend . . . how many nights ago? Another issue to deal with . . . another problem. . . . No, I have not found your property. Not yet.*

While his eyes strayed around the dark interior of the vehicle, he saw something that revved his heartbeat and shot adrenaline into his bloodstream. The needle of the gas tank showed a quarter tank. He had filled up at noon. And then he'd driven thirty, maybe forty miles maximum. Where the hell had he been?

Abruptly, a face appeared on the other side of the windshield. Renzo was reaching for a weapon when he realized it was just his own reflection in the glass—but for an instant he'd seen the lean muzzle and the mean fangs of a dog, a yellow shepherd.

To clear his head, he lowered the window for air. As he pulled his arm away from the power button, he saw blood tracing a miniature river over his skin. It had stained his silver bracelet, obscuring the face of the Nahuatl goddess Coatlicue.

He had no memory of cutting himself. He sucked the liquid, drawing solace from its warmth.

WITH ONE HAND, Sylvia held the portable phone set to her ear; she listened to a low hum and waited while the state police dispatcher tracked down Matt. With the other hand, she searched her kitchen cupboard for something to feed a child.

Serena was seated at the kitchen table, watching every move Sylvia made. Her luminous brown eyes traveled right and left while Sylvia roved anxiously around the small room. Sylvia's free hand settled on a box of Cheerios just as Matt came on the line.

She turned away from the child and spoke in a low voice. "Can you stay at your place tonight? I've got Serena here." She walked out of the kitchen, into the living room—safely out of the child's earshot.

It took a moment for the name to register with Matt. "The kid? Why?"

"She hitched a ride in the back of my truck when I was visiting her foster home, she must have smuggled herself in with the dogs." Quickly, Sylvia related her take on the afternoon's events. "I tried the foster home, but there was no answer, so I left a message on the machine. The husband called me back two minutes ago. The whole family's been out searching the neighborhood."

Matt was silent for several seconds before he said, "You've notified Protective Services?"

"I called the hotline and left a message for the social worker, said I'd meet her first thing tomorrow morning."

"Can't you take the kid back tonight—"

Sylvia cut off Matt's protest with a flood of words. "I'm feeding her, I'll put her to bed, she needs rest. She does *not* need to spend the night in the back of a cruiser."

Matt sighed. "Just don't start acting like Ripley in *Aliens*."

"Hey, the alien's a piece of cake compared to Social Services." Sylvia glanced over her shoulder to make certain she was still out of the child's hearing. "Listen, this kid spilled a quart of milk, a half gallon of juice, a box of cookies—and that's just in the last thirty minutes. We're down to a bowl of Cheerios with chocolate milk. Next she'll probably blow up the house."

As she paced, Sylvia automatically straightened Serena's sweater—the coloring book was still pinned to the inside. She flipped the pages, catching a glimpse of the multi-colored drawings, and continued. "Serena will go back to C.P.S. tomorrow. I'm going to recommend she be placed in a private hospital until we can get things sorted out."

She heard Matt blow air softly between his teeth. "It might be better—"

"It would be better if she had a foster home to go to, but she doesn't. This afternoon Nellie Trujillo told me she couldn't handle Serena. Whether I like it or not, I've got a connection with this child. At the moment I'm the only person who does."

The silence lasted a few seconds, but it was enough to alert Sylvia to a problem. Matt said, "I heard something from an old buddy at the A.G. investigations office. Something about your kid."

"She's not *my* kid," Sylvia corrected him automatically.

"The A.G.'s office got a call from the *federales* in Juárez. The Mexican cops had a description of a missing child. Apparently, it matches the girl."

Sylvia's muscles went slack. "What will that mean?"

"She may get sent back. She's a temporary ward of the court; there'll be some red tape, some back-and-forth—"

"But what about her family in Mexico?"

"I don't have the details—"

"Who are they? *Where* are they? If she matches this description, why aren't they here now?" Sylvia walked across the room away from the kitchen, lowering her voice so Serena wouldn't hear the conversation. "How do we know she'll get the treatment she needs if she goes back to Mexico?"

"We don't."

"Well, shit." Sylvia tensed, caught up in her thoughts. She wanted more time with the child. And the last thing Serena needed was to become the pawn of feuding state, federal, and international agencies. It could set her progress back weeks, even months. But something else nagged at her—she couldn't shake the growing sense of urgency she'd felt for the past twenty-four hours, the notion that Serena's time was running out. Now that sense had been confirmed by a query from Mexico.

The silence between them stretched until Sylvia asked, "How was it at the prison?"

Matt's grunt was noncommittal, a signal that he didn't want to elaborate. After a beat, he asked, "You know anything about Noelle Harding?"

Sylvia thought for a moment. "I know she's been on the news recently, pushing her brother's cause. And she's hosting a charity thing. Why?"

"On my way out, she was holding a press conference."

"I saw something about it on the news tonight."

"The woman knows how to get press coverage."

"She's trying to save her brother's life." Sylvia made a wry face. "I don't think she's just some empty person with a crusade. Harding heads up an international fund for homeless kids. She's connected. Big Texas money."

"Well, I guess money can't buy everything." Matt's tone was intentionally provocative. He and Sylvia differed in their opinions of the death penalty. He was satisfied to rid the world of *scumbags*—his word—while Sylvia believed in life imprisonment for hard-core criminals; for the less hard-core, she still believed in treatment. Maybe because she couldn't write off the million-plus inmates incarcerated in the U.S.

"We should go to her fund-raiser," she said. "You've got an extra five grand in your pocket, don't you?" To her surprise, Matt didn't laugh.

He asked, "When is it?"

"*Why?*"

"I met her brother today. Hey"—Matt sounded as if he'd just snapped awake—"don't forget you've got an engagement party tomorrow morning—eleven o'clock sharp."

"Of course not." But for a moment Sylvia had forgotten.

"I love you." Matt hung up softly.

She switched off the handset, aware for the first time that she had paced herself into the living room. She tiptoed back toward the kitchen, freezing at the sight of the ruined wall, the brutal face.

Serena had drawn a demon. She was still working feverishly, crayons in hand, nose inches from plaster. Small sighs of effort escaped her lips as she guided color over the wall's surface. Wild lines quickly formed details on the face: seeds for eyes, a beaklike nose, sharp cheekbones. The mouth was a hole, a gaping wound.

Sylvia started forward but stopped when she realized the child appeared oblivious to everything except her work. Within seconds, the demon's face had grown a body. The dark form was tall and lean, walking upright. His body was crisscrossed with slash marks.

As Serena drew the monster, her skin darkened with an infusion of blood—she was visibly distraught, breathing rapidly. She looked as if she had a tornado trapped inside her body.

Suddenly, she slapped her hand against the wall. Again and again her palm struck plaster, and then her hand curled into a fist. Sylvia lunged forward and caught the child's arm before impact. Serena collapsed. The only sound of her rage was the harsh staccato rhythm of her breath.

RENZO'S GLOVED HANDS glowed inside the telephone booth. Outside, car headlamps flashed off glass and asphalt. Red lights reflected in Renzo's eyes when he glanced up at the Circle K sign.

Patrons at the gas station passed the pay phone on their way in and out of the convenience store. They avoided eye contact, but Renzo could see that their skins were bleached by fluorescence; their faces were blank, soulless. These were people who could die tonight and they would leave no trace.

A young woman walked past the phone booth. Idly, Renzo imagined inserting a knife into her brain.

He slipped the twenty-dollar disposable phone card into the slot and dialed. The distant ringing went on for six, seven, eight repetitions, then there was a hollow electronic click; Renzo recognized that the call had been forwarded to a new number. That new routing was answered on the first ring.

Amado Fortuna offered his customary greeting: silence.

Renzo imagined language—wondering if his lips and tongue would form the complex mix of Spanish, Indio, and slang—watching his own eyes reflected in the metal surface of the pay phone. Perhaps those two unblinking eyes would tell him who he was tonight.

He spoke very slowly. *"I found our friend three nights ago. He did not offer an adequate explanation for his recent behavior. I severed our business relationship."*

With care, Amado posed a question.

Renzo answered. *"I can't come back yet. There's another, smaller problem I must address while I'm up north."*

In answer to Amado's next question: *"No, it will not take long. I think the issue will be settled permanently."*

He brought his thoughts back to the words traveling from Mexico; Amado had offered no protest. When he asked about Snow White, he did so without direct reference.

Renzo took a moment to answer; he found he'd left his body again—just for an instant. But he had to pull himself back into flesh and blood. *"I did not find the item we wanted."*

For a few moments Amado turned away from the phone. He did not hang up. He was talking to someone in the room, in his home in Juárez. A child laughed. Amado had a six-year-old son, a nine-year-old son, and a twelve-year-old daughter. Renzo decided the laughter belonged to the youngest child.

Renzo knew that Amado Fortuna was controlling his rage. To do so, he would focus on his children, on the treasures in his home, on the possessions unlimited money could buy. The elegance of Fortuna's surroundings helped to remind the *patrón* how far he'd come in this life. His surroundings convinced him that he had risen far above the rest of the world.

Renzo also knew that Amado Fortuna was very unhappy to hear that the item was still unaccounted for. The item was a reminder of life before wealth, before elegance, before privilege. The item was dangerous.

When Amado returned his attention to the phone conversation, he expressed polite—but quite serious— dissatisfaction.

"*I understand,*" Renzo said. "*I share your sentiments.*"

Amado was ready to end the conversation. In impeccable Spanish he said, "*There is someone, a mutual friend from El Paso, who is waiting for you when you return. This is someone you must talk to soon. Someone who needs your professional touch. Can we tell him that you will hurry back?*"

The mutual friend would be the cop Bobby Dowd— the last man to talk to Paco before he crossed the U.S. border. "*Of course. It will be a pleasure.*"

"*Bueno. Hasta mañana.*"

Renzo hung up the phone gently. He smiled to himself. He could see his teeth glistening, reflected in the silver metal; they looked perfect. He was beginning to feel better.

CHAPTER TEN

BOBBY DOWD THOUGHT he was looking at the inside of his eyelids. But in a remarkably short time he figured out that the darkness was too velvety—and minus the little red sparks that always exploded when he squeezed his eyes shut.

So, it wasn't eyelids, it was the inside of a trunk—and the trunk was part of a motor vehicle. Yeah . . . there'd been a black Mercedes following him down the street before the assault. As fragments of his memory returned, he felt a staggering sense of relief. His mind was functioning logically.

There were more reasons to be grateful. He was still breathing, which meant he was still alive—and this was no coffin. Sure, he was packed like luggage inside a car, but the Germans had designed a very roomy trunk for the Mercedes. Things could be worse.

Abruptly, nausea threatened to overwhelm him, and his heart tightened in his chest. Things *were* worse. He broke out in a sweat, recognizing his body's reaction to a foreign substance. They'd shot him up with something. *Christ!* With what?

Breathe. Get a grip.

Some drug was cruising inside his veins like a shark—a sand shark, a hammerhead, a great white? So far, the animal—the drug—was an unknown. Was it deadly? He told himself *no.* He told himself he would find out soon enough.

After a few minutes, the terror subsided with the pulse of the drug. Whatever it was, it was moving inside his body with a tidal flow all its own. At the moment, the tide was out. Only now did Bobby realize he could hear voices; they were muffled but clearly male, definitely Mexican.

He spoke fluent Spanish, but he couldn't quite catch the words as they filtered through leather and metal. He wished he could replay the conversation in the privacy of his own life; but he'd stopped wearing a wire after a small-time drug dealer had demanded a body search out of the blue, and he'd only just managed to flush the sucker—he'd come within a mosquito's ass of dying, bullet through the head, body dumped in a trash heap.

Not the fucking Cadillac of Last Reposes.

Bobby caught something about Amado. Amado Fortuna, patron saint of the El Paso–Juárez trafficking operation. The story went like this: Amado Fortuna, illiterate, dirt poor, and ambitious, had risen like a phoenix from the ashes of the Pacific drug cartels.

Befitting a man of his importance, he decided he would learn to read. One of the first sentences he actually understood was "The moving finger writes . . ."

Buzz was: the *pendejo* being so thrilled with his

ABC's had started his memoirs—goddamn journals complete with transactions, dates, and names.

When Bobby first heard the story, he'd pictured the Big Tuna writing: *"Mi querido diario, Today I sold 2 tons of Colombian heroin to my best friend the Panzini godfather in Detroit."*

Bobby had worked next to feds who joked that the Tuna Diaries had existed—until Fortuna destroyed them. Anything was possible. In 1985 the biggest bust in history had gone down in a warehouse in Sylmar, California; the booty included tons of cocaine and a stack of ledgers. Sometimes these guys were not very frigging bright.

Dear Diary. The journals could've taken Amado down like a rock, but the Fish finally wised up and burned them in his front yard.

If the diaries had ever existed, they were long gone by now. And so was Paco; he'd taken flight with all his wild stories.

So what was Bobby Dowd doing in the trunk of a Mercedes? As far as he knew, he hadn't done anything to piss off Amado Fortuna. There was no cover to blow; he made no secret of the fact he was a cop on the take. Besides, he'd been incommunicado for weeks.

Except for talking to Paco . . .

A monster wave slammed into Bobby—the drug was at high tide again, jarring loose some fragment of memory.

He and Paco sitting at a table . . .

There was a loud noise, and the car jiggled. A scraping sound alerted Bobby that a key had been inserted in the lock of the trunk. The lid flew open.

The first thing Bobby saw was a bright light in his

face. Big arms wrenched him out of the trunk. When he could focus again, he caught his bearings; he was outside the Buenas Noches, an hourly-rate motel somewhere on the oily fringe of Juárez.

Somebody muscled him headfirst into the bumper of the Mercedes. He moaned, head jammed against metal, his shirt reeking of sweat.

He shouted hoarsely—felt hands release his arms—and then he vomited on the gravel of the Buenas Noches parking lot.

Lying there in the dirt, a fat man of a moon laughing down at him, Bobby Dowd thought about his old man. Smoky Joe Dowd had been proud when his son became a cop in 1982. Said it was a step up the ladder for all the Dowds. What would the old man say this minute if he were looking down from the Big Ranch in the sky? Would he know that Bobby had never intended to shoot up? That he'd always tried to be the best cop he could be? Would he understand that the drugs and addiction had come with the territory?

Somewhere over him, Bobby heard whispered voices. It wasn't the moon, and it wasn't Smoky Joe. He swallowed, hoisted himself over onto his stomach, and managed half a push-up. One man was waiting, arm outstretched, to give him a boost. Bobby attained a fully upright position with some difficulty. He swayed in the muggy air, a boat of a man moored in a choppy sea of desert.

But not so far gone he missed the word: *madrinas.* "Godmothers."

Madrinas was slang for the elite secret killers on the payroll of Mexico's federal police—*assassins* was another name.

Bobby Dowd found that extremely alarming.

The same hand that had helped him off the dirt now held out an offering. A dirty syringe, dripping fluid, right in front of Bobby's face.

A voice spoke in English: "Get comfortable, friend. Let's talk about your girlfriend Paco and that Honda he was driving when he flew north."

A tiny man rang a tiny bell deep in Bobby's brain. *Snow White and the Seven . . .*

CHAPTER ELEVEN

MATT ENGLAND WAS looking for a ruined Honda.
He tapped chain link with the toe of his cowboy boot,
and the gate swung open a few inches. A lock hung
limply from metal; the clasp was no longer in one solid
piece. Either Mungia 24-Hour Towing kept the gate
open for midnight visitors or someone had cut the lock.

No one said boo when Matt entered the yard; he
didn't draw his weapon, but his fingers were itching. He
moved in shadow for twenty feet; the overhead security
lamp was dark.

The tow yard covered several acres north of Siler
Road. Most of the acreage was enclosed behind a ten-
foot-high fence, which was topped with double strands
of barbed wire and cuffed with broken glass—a stand-
in for junkyard dogs. Matt had known Joe for years; as
he prowled the yard, he looked for the short, barrel-
chested man. Mungia still worked the graveyard shift—
claimed it was the secret of his long, happy marriage.

Matt almost tripped over the entrails of a battered Pontiac. Metal carcasses were strewn everywhere, depressing monuments to Henry Ford's vision. He stepped around what had once been a Ford Mustang— nuts, bolts, and trim shed long ago. The sole of his boot picked up a nail, and he hopped on one leg and yanked out the rusted metal spike before it penetrated to his skin. Away from the gate, the yard was lit up by the glare of overhead lamps. Flying animals—either huge moths or small bats—hovered around the circles of light. Matt stayed in the shadows, a strategy he planned to maintain until he found Joe.

Thirty minutes earlier, when he'd called the tow yard from his office at the Department of Public Safety, he'd reached Mungia's answering machine with its terse message in English and Spanish. There was nothing unusual about that; Joe often wandered his acreage, even when his night-shift driver was out on a towing job. He probably considered it one of the small privileges of staying in business for more than thirty years.

Matt had another hundred feet to go before he reached Mungia's fair-weather office—a corrugated-steel shack. Behind the shack, a small trailer provided winter lodgings. A portable toilet served both shack and trailer—all the modern conveniences.

A half dozen vehicles had been deposited near the shack. Matt figured these were the yard's newest arrivals because the vehicles' assorted paint jobs weren't yet obscured by grime and dust. Mungia 24-Hour Towing handled law-enforcement calls—abandoned vehicles, accidents, D.W.I.'s, impounds. First in line was a dark-colored pickup truck. Second was a beige Honda, crumpled, hood gaping open, and missing two wheels.

The Honda fit the description of the car the girl was driving when she ran off the road. Matt had reviewed the accident report within the past hour. Between the vehicle's murky ownership—registration to a drop-box business called Hat-Trick in El Paso—and the inquiry by the Federal Judicial Police in Juárez, Matt's curiosity had been piqued. He'd decided to take a close look at the Honda.

He stepped forward to peer inside the small vehicle, noticing immediately that the interior had been trashed. The door panels were gone. The floor mats lay outside the vehicle, and the interior carpet had been cut and ripped up from the floor. The glove compartment hung open; the ashtray was missing. Front and back seats had been stripped of large squares of upholstery. The visors looked as though they'd been shredded by huge cat claws. One radio speaker lay stranded on the ground in a tangle of wires. The hatchback was up. The side storage panels in the baggage area were gone, the spare tire missing.

Matt walked around to the front of the vehicle and shone his flashlight into the exposed engine. The radiator was minus a cap. The windshield-wiper fluid tank had been knocked loose. The carburetor looked naked without its casing.

The hair on the back of Matt's neck stood up. He'd searched vehicles in the same methodical effort to expose contraband. The Honda had been torn apart rapidly but thoroughly—by a pro. Just maybe by a cop.

His right hand hovered above the pancake holster that held his Colt .45. Somebody was behind him; he caught a whiff of rank smoke and sweat. Perspiration broke out on his forehead. He was about to make a move when a voice said, "You looking for new wheels, *pendejo?*"

Slowly, Matt eased himself around. He nodded at Joe Mungia. "Don't tell me. It's got three thousand miles on the odometer and a little old lady kept it in her garage?"

"It's got less than two, and the old lady was *mi abuela.*" Joe spat in the dirt. His face lost its play. "You see anybody on your way in?"

"I saw your padlock after somebody cut it in half. They get into your office?"

Mungia shook his big head. "Just messed with my cars."

Matt nodded toward the Honda. "I saw this one. Which of the others?"

Mungia led Matt to a second light-colored Honda a row over. This car was powder blue instead of beige, but otherwise, the two cars closely resembled each other, especially in the dark. Both had been searched.

Matt asked, "Just these two?"

"That's all I found so far." Joe Mungia stood watching the state cop think. When Matt asked if there were any other Hondas on the lot, Joe shook his head. He answered Matt's questions: his driver had gone out on a call about an hour ago; he'd locked the gate after his driver left; the light had been working when he locked the gate; he'd been on the other side of the yard when he heard a noise; the noise had come from somewhere near this same blue Honda; when he checked it out, he realized he'd had a visitor.

Joe shook his head. "Thing is, I think somebody broke in last night, too."

"Persistent guy." Matt retrieved his crime-scene kit from the trunk of his Chevy Caprice. Joe Mungia whistled, highly impressed, when he saw the semiautomatic AR-15 secured in the trunk. He followed the investigator back to the first Honda, held the floodlight, and watched Matt go to work with notebook, camera, brushes, and fingerprint powder. There were prints—too many. Probably none of them belonged to the night's interloper.

By the time Matt was finished with both vehicles and ready to leave, it was after one in the morning. Joe walked him toward the Caprice. Both men stopped outside the yard gates. Joe lit a cigarette and dropped the match on asphalt. "So, what do you think, friend?"

"I think he messed your place up for nothing. He searched the beige Honda first, then he started on the light blue one before he realized it wasn't the right car. I don't think he found what he came for."

Joe wagged his head. "At least he was good enough to come and go without disturbing me." The portly man seemed to find that fact comforting.

Matt did not. He had a very bad feeling about this whole thing, and he didn't like the idea that Sylvia and the child were involved. He had double-checked the Honda's plate number against the plate in the accident report—it was definitely a match.

He was convinced the car had been torn up by someone who needed very badly to find something. Drugs? That was Matt's first guess. His second guess: whoever had done the damage would return.

He glanced at his watch. He would drive by Sylvia's, check on the property, make sure everything looked right. He wouldn't disturb woman or child, but he would talk to Sylvia first thing in the morning.

*   *   *

SYLVIA WOKE WHILE it was still dark. She was sweating, breathing hard from a nightmare. The oppressive heaviness of her dream lingered, but the imagery was shadowy and only half remembered. Serena had occupied the dream world. And so had Sylvia's father, Daniel Strange. His silent presence, however holographic and unconscious, disturbed her deeply.

She felt eyes on her skin. The moon was staring in the western window of the bedroom. Milk-white light spilled over the cotton duvet and the child's feet. Carefully, Sylvia shifted her body. On the other side of the king-sized bed where Matt usually slept, Serena lay curled up next to Rocko's bristled little shape. Dog and girl breathed fitfully, and the air was heavy with sleep.

It had not been easy to get the child to bed hours earlier. Sylvia had tried soothing words, hot cocoa, silence, and finally—after *she* was way beyond exhaustion—a story. She had pulled the well-worn copy of *Grimms' Fairy Tales* off a living room shelf. The book was leather-bound; it had belonged to her father and his father and grandfather.

Which surely accounted for her father's attendance in her dream.

Serena had thumbed through the book, gazing intently at each color illustration. Eventually, she had pointed to a picture of a nobleman, a princess, and a crone. The story was the Six Swans. Whether by chance or intuition, the heroine of that story was a young girl who did not speak or laugh for six years in order to restore her brothers from an evil spell.

As a girl, Sylvia had loved this particular tale for its dark, evocative imagery. She knew the research, the modern feminist admonitions of patriarchal bias.

Classically, old women were the tellers of tales, sharing stories with other women and their children, easing the grind of domestic life. Over the centuries, as the stories were written down and printed in books, the male characters evolved heroically while the female characters were more narrowly cast as witch-crones, predatory stepmothers, or ingenues. The young, sweet, and sometimes mute princesses represented wish models of female stoicism. Sylvia acknowledged the critiques, but the story's power had never dimmed.

A king who was a hunter pursued his wild prey deep into a forest where he became hopelessly lost. An old witch agreed to show him the way out of the woods on the condition he marry her daughter. Although the young woman was fair, she made the king shudder; still, he took her from the woods, married her, and made her his queen.

It so happened that the king was a widower with seven children from his first marriage. Fearing that his new wife would do his children mischief, the king hid the six boys and one young girl in a castle deep in the woods. Eventually, the jealous queen discovered where her husband spent so many happy days, and she used the witchcraft she had learned from her own mother to turn the children into swans—except for the young girl, who escaped the spell.

Serena listened so intently to the beginning of the narrative, Sylvia was sure the child was familiar with the ritual of bedtime stories; her body language and affect made that clear. Someone had loved this child deeply, which made the fairy tale—with its absent mother and loving but unavailing father—all the more poignant.

Tonight, Act I of the old story had accomplished a miracle—it lulled the child into slumber.

At the foot of the bed, Nikki stirred. Her golden muzzle crested the mattress, and her taupe eyes watched Sylvia. The digital clock showed 3:07. A familiar time for restless musing. This night her mind was focused on the haunting presence of the child; even in slumber Serena's anxiety was palpable, invading Sylvia's thoughts. As the minutes ticked by, Sylvia lay in limbo between waking and sleep. Once she thought she heard a car engine, but the sound quickly faded and she decided it had been an airplane. Her land was isolated, and stray vehicles weren't common this far from city limits. She rolled over, let her hand touch the child, and closed her eyes.

SERENA FELT THE demon's presence before she heard the deep throbbing noise, the crunch of gravel. She stiffened, and her breath caught in her throat. Her fingers flew to clasp the medallion.

Paco had come to her in a dream, whispering a warning that the demon would return. *I cannot help you now. Use prayer to keep you safe. Let Our Lady hide you in the folds of her mantle.*

Paco, with his sad lullabies and his scent of pencils. Paco, who had come back to the child after a day's or a week's absence, always walking like a very stiff old man. A million times he had whispered longingly to her, "*You are my soul, you are my heart.*"

Now Serena wanted him to stay and talk. She needed to ask him questions. How was he doing? Where was he? Did his wounds hurt him very much?

She was sleepy, and she told him so. But she knew he would only wake her if it was urgent. She didn't scold him. Instead she listened to him—just as she had so many times before.

The demon follows the scent of blood. He's looking for you—for something you hold. Remember what I gave you? Do you keep it in a safe place?

Before Serena could answer, Paco began to float away. He was so light, he couldn't walk on the ground. His brown pants billowed out with air, and his suit jacket danced on the soft breeze. His worries settled into familiar crinkled lines around his eyes and mouth. He touched one hand to his heart.

The child reached out, but his rough fingers slipped through hers. The last thing she saw was Paco's face, his sad eyes, his lips moving. Although she could no longer hear his voice, she knew what he was trying to tell her. *Lo siento.* I'm sorry. *El demonio viene.* He's coming for you now. *¡Cuidado!* Be careful!

Serena heard footsteps on the gravel outside the bedroom window, and her body tensed. He *was* coming. Why didn't the dogs growl? Why didn't the woman wake? Suddenly alert, she knew what she had to do.

THE NEXT TIME Sylvia woke, the room was misty with predawn light and the other side of the bed was empty. She lurched to her feet and groped her way along the hallway. There was no sign of Serena in the living room, where objects were still swathed in night shadow, or in the kitchen, where the drawing on the wall stood out like satanic graffiti.

Sylvia flipped on exterior lights and started toward the side door to the yard. A ripple of sound stopped her, caught her attention. The night air was soft with mur-mured voices that bobbed just below the watery surface of her comprehension. For an instant, she thought it must be the television, but the set, which filled one corner of the living room, was mute.

Awareness came slowly—the voice belonged to the child. Serena was speaking.

Suddenly alert, Sylvia turned and tiptoed quickly back toward the one room she had neglected. As she stood outside her study, the whispering tantalized her, but its meaning hovered beyond her grasp. Although the syllables never quite formed recognizable words, the overall impression was one of prayer—a litany.

The door stood ajar, and Sylvia pushed it open. The voice ceased abruptly. She took a breath—only then realizing she had been breathless for several seconds. The room appeared smaller in dim light. The child was huddled on the window ledge, her body lost inside the turquoise T-shirt that belonged to Sylvia. Her thin arms were wrapped around her legs, her chin resting on knobby knees. Her body was rigid with tension. Apparently unaware of anything else, she was gazing intently out at the moonlit landscape of cottonwoods, dirt road, and the softly sloping fields beyond.

When Sylvia put her arms around Serena to guide her from the ledge, the child gave a startled cry. There was a glint of light off metal. In one fist, Serena clutched a pair of scissors. When she recognized Sylvia, she stopped struggling and stumbled from the window ledge.

It was clear that Serena had been keeping watch. The child was holding vigil.

CHAPTER TWELVE

VICTOR VARGAS WAS driving a taxi across downtown Juárez. He'd hidden his face behind huge dark glasses. Half his head had disappeared under the brim of a black felt sombrero that had white pompoms hanging off the brim. The outfit had cost him *dos mil pesos* at the Mercado Pronto. He changed lanes on Avenida Tecnológico, cut a hard right onto Carretera Juárez-Porvenir, and almost ran down a fare.

For an instant he considered pulling into the Bamboo Palace for some takeout—his stomach was grumbling and *pollo moo goo* sounded great—but he remembered it wasn't even five-thirty in the morning. Too early for *puerco* B.B.Q. or *Camarón* Bamboo. Anyway, if he stopped, he might encounter some drunk trying to wave down a taxi. He wasn't in the mood to drive some *pendejo* across Juárez.

Avoiding fares was a minor problem. The taxi provided him with cover, wheels, and protection while he

figured out what to do with his life. Since yesterday—
and the panic call from Bobby Dowd—Victor hadn't
been back to his office at federal judicial police headquarters.

He didn't plan to go back to work until he heard
from Dowd. Or at least until he'd heard what had happened to him. Victor had managed to make it to the
usual spot for a meeting; Bobby Dowd had not. That
was enough to spook Victor. But there was more.

As Victor slowed for a traffic signal, he mentally
replayed his actions of the previous night. Outside the
hole-in-the-wall where he and Bobby Dowd always
met, he'd come across a "mouth" named Charlie-Sorry.

Out on the streets of Juárez, Charlie-Sorry kept in
motion thanks to a rebuilt skateboard. Years earlier, he'd
lost both his legs in a collision with a bus. But last night,
there was Charlie-Sorry scooting out of a bar with a
tourist's sequined purse over his left arm. Victor had
taken up pursuit—running two full blocks to catch up
with the man—only managing to tackle him because one
of Charlie-Sorry's ball bearings went bust.

In exchange for not being rousted, Charlie-Sorry—
all the while loudly protesting his innocence—had
turned over the purse. As a bonus, he'd given Victor a
quick news break on the latest street buzz.

A whorehouse had opened above the Disco-Baile; El
Cero was running numbers for the fat man; a cop had
been popped by some of Amado Fortuna's boys—

Victor jerked the taxi into first gear. Horns honked
all around him. The light was already turning yellow;
he'd missed the green. He gunned the taxi through the
intersection and then pulled off to the roadside, his
heart beating a mile a minute.

Bobby Dowd had been popped by Amado Fortuna's boys. "Popped" could mean shot. It could very easily mean dead. Or it could mean *kidnapped*, tortured—and you *wished* you were dead.

Like Enrique "Kiki" Camarena, the D.E.A. agent who'd been brutally tortured by the bad guys in 1994. A nightmare nobody in law enforcement could ever forget—especially if they'd heard the tape recording of Camarena's death.

Last night Victor had slammed Charlie-Sorry into a urine-soaked doorway. He'd leaned in close, keeping his gun in the street snitch's face. Victor wasn't proud that he'd raised fear in Charlie-Sorry's eyes—but it had worked. Charlie-Sorry had added a postscript to his story.

Word on the street had a *madrina*—one of the godmothers—after Bobby Dowd. And this particular godmother had a nickname: The Chupacabra. People called him that because he had a taste for blood.

CHAPTER THIRTEEN

AT FIVE A.M., when Sylvia realized that Serena was not going back to sleep, she filled the bathtub with hot water and bubble bath and produced a new toothbrush from its cellophane wrapper. She wasn't experienced with kids; she'd grown up without siblings, but she'd learned a few tricks from the offspring of her friends. She kept watch while Serena brushed her teeth, wielding the toothbrush with great reluctance. And when the girl finally plopped herself down in the bathtub, Sylvia perched on the rim with a soapy washcloth. She felt like a hygiene cop as she worked over the child's ears, toes, and elbows, scrubbing fiercely.

While she supervised the morning bathroom session, she contemplated the possibilities for Serena's continued therapeutic treatment. She had already considered working with Serena within a scripted verbal format—her reaction to the Grimms' tale had been encouraging. One form of therapy for mute children involved working with songs, poems, stories, or games where verbalizing was scripted and demanded no spontaneity. In many cases—with patience—these children learned to speak outside the home. But Sylvia also knew that Margaret Tompkins had worked with children who would dictate lengthy stories but would not answer free-form questions—not even after months or years of treatment. She prayed that would not be Serena's future.

Although Sylvia couldn't yet express the idea clearly or even consciously, she was beginning to sense an undercurrent to the child's silence that might have something to do with extreme archetypal—

A bar of soap flew from Serena's hands and ricocheted off the bathroom sink. Jarred from her thoughts, Sylvia caught the soap one-handed, on the fly. She retrieved a plush terrycloth bath towel from a shelf, reminding herself that deliberation was probably a waste of time. At the very least the child would be placed with another foster family, and Sylvia's therapeutic role might be limited. At the most extreme, Serena might be sent back to Mexico.

Serena stepped from the tub, shivering and dripping suds, and Sylvia bundled her in the towel. While Serena dressed herself, Sylvia focused on the job of producing a pot of drinkable coffee. On her way to the kitchen, she switched on the television, volume low, listening for the early-morning news.

Framed by the kitchen window, the cloudless sky shone a brilliant blue. At the edge of the patio deck, finches were busy collecting seeds from a red-and-white feeder. It was already promising to be a perfect fall day. She measured coffee grounds into the filter, pushed the filter tray into the Mr. Coffee slot, and set the Pyrex pot

on the warmer, flicking the switch to ON. Almost immediately, the machine produced sounds of exertion. When
it began to gurgle, Sylvia went to check on the child.

She didn't have to go far. Serena was in the living
room, standing with her chin pressed flush against the
glass of the television. A replay of last night's news
report was flashing across the screen: coverage of the
upcoming execution at the Penitentiary of New Mexico
and footage of Noelle Harding, the inmate's sister, holding a press conference outside the institution. The pale,
drawn face of the death row inmate, Cash Wheeler, was
inset in the upper right-hand corner of the television.

Sylvia walked forward and gently touched the child.
Serena trembled, obviously bewildered and disori-
ented—eyes glazed, skin damp, her manner sluggish.
After a few moments, she pulled away and stood sucking her thumb.

SYLVIA ACCELERATED TOWARD the intersection of
Rodeo and Cerrillos. It should take less than fifteen
minutes to drive across town to the offices of Child
Protective Services. If only the traffic lights would stop
turning red just as she approached.

Serena leaned over and made a grab for the steering
wheel.

Startled, Sylvia pushed the child away with one hand.
"Serena! What are you—"

Serena clutched at the wheel again.

Inhaling sharply, Sylvia just managed to correct the
Toyota's course. She pulled into the right-turn lane.

Serena grunted and reached for the wheel; this time,
Sylvia was prepared for her interference. With one arm
extended, she fought to keep the child at a distance. But

it was impossible to drive. She swore under her breath and applied the brakes. Too hard. The truck jerked to a stop and stalled out.

Horns began to blare behind them. "Just let me get over to the side," Sylvia muttered. She started the truck again, this time waiting for an opening to cut across lanes to the shopping center on the northeast corner of the intersection.

As the truck accelerated, Serena lunged for the steering wheel.

"Goddammit, Serena—"

Panicked, Sylvia felt the child's fingernails dig deep into her arm. She managed to guide the Toyota into the parking lot, where she slammed on the brakes. Horns honked, and a driver waved a hand in disgust as he drove by.

Woman and child were so close, they could feel each other's breath. Serena's eyes burned into Sylvia; the black-green flecks in the pupil, the tiny webbed veins in the whites. Did the child sense that she might be beginning a long trip back to Mexico? Sylvia felt her skin flush with guilt.

Upon leaving the house ten minutes earlier, Sylvia had explained to Serena that she would have to spend some time with Dolores Martin, the C.P.S. social worker. The news had been received without visible reaction— until now.

Sylvia reached out to touch the child's warm skin. Serena pulled away.

Goddammit, why did she feel as if she were betraying this kid? The emotion wasn't rational; Sylvia knew she had no choice but to play by the child-welfare rules. But she also had to admit the truth: once she turned Serena over to C.P.S., she might never see her again.

Sylvia whispered the child's name. Except for a brief flicker in her dark eyes, there was no response. She dropped her head, trapping her small coloring book in a chin lock.

In the truck bed, Nikki began to bark. Serena had refused to leave Sylvia's home without the shepherd.

Abruptly, Serena slapped the dashboard hard. She began to rock, jerking back and forth in the small space. She grunted as she rocked, and her face turned pink.

Hoping to soothe her, Sylvia switched on the radio and then immediately selected another station to avoid news. Just as quickly, Serena's fingers punched down on the pushbuttons. The radio began jumping from frequency to frequency. Oldies, classical, gangsta rap, Top 40 all blared from the speakers. Small noises of effort escaped the child's lips, and her breath quickened. After a very long forty-five seconds, Sylvia guided Serena's fingers to the SCAN and SEEK buttons. Now the search began all over again. One station at a time. Until Spanish music filled the truck. Then Serena pulled her hands away from the radio. She pushed her shoulders back against the seat and closed her eyes. Her breathing slowed. Her head began to sway to the melodic ballad.

Although Serena seemed to find some moment of peace in the music, Sylvia was going crazy. But she ignored her own frustration and watched the child, assessing, gauging.

What had Margaret Tompkins said? *"The demon may well be inside the child."*

RENZO SANTOS WAS in a pensive mood. He'd had a successful meeting with the Child Protective Services social worker. She had explained quite thoroughly where C.P.S. stood on the issue of the girl, the psychologist, the future. If there was any confusion at all, it was not on Renzo's part.

He guided the Suburban down a quiet street past office buildings and vacant lots. By his watch, he had time to reconsider the situation; it was an interesting one.

He could eliminate the shrink. He could eliminate the girl. It would take him less than a minute to end two lives.

Here was the rub: once the child was dead, she couldn't tell him what he needed to know. And while she was alive, she couldn't tell him what he wanted to know. The social worker had confirmed that the girl was mute—at least temporarily.

Renzo thought she could be faking.

Of course, it was possible that the child knew nothing. But Renzo suspected that wasn't the case. In his work, Paco had been so self-contained, so uncommunicative that Renzo had always assumed the man kept a mistress hidden away. That was to be expected.

He had never suspected Paco's confidante would be a child. In fact, Renzo hadn't truly believed a child existed until he'd seen the hideaway in Anapra for himself— and by then Paco was already running north. Even while Renzo was in pursuit, it had never occurred to him that the child would be Elena's.

Renzo had badly underestimated Paco Fortuna. For ten years—ever since their terrible first meeting—he'd watched the rumpled, quiet man go about his business. *Ten years.* A decade. And all the while Paco had been hiding the child away in an adobe castle.

But now that Paco was a corpse and the girl was fair

game, how could Renzo get the information he so badly needed?

He closed his eyes, turning the puzzle in his mind like wine on the tongue. Tasting, absorbing, testing . . . like the Buddhist koans, the puzzles he'd heard about in martial-arts movies.

What is the sound of one hand clapping?

Tuna would answer quickly: That depends upon who it hits.

Renzo wasn't yet sure what his answer would be, but he was working on the solution.

He turned into the parking lot of a restaurant called Little Anita's. He parked near the door. He was hungry, so he would eat.

He had to follow his instinct; he had no alternative. Who would Paco trust? *The girl.* And who did the girl trust? *The shrink.*

SYLVIA PULLED INTO the parking lot of the low-slung tan building located on Vivigen Way just off St. Michael's Drive. A short distance behind the offices of Child Protective Services, the roof of the hospital cut oblique angles in the blue sky. The C.P.S. parking lot was deserted except for one battered Pinto. There was no traffic on Vivigen Way. Saturday was a slow day for area businesses. Sylvia parked next to the Pinto; she thought it might belong to Dolores Martin. She cut the engine and set the brake, leaving the keys in the ignition. She waited without moving for several seconds, then glanced at her watch: 8:38 A.M. The social worker had agreed to meet here at eight-thirty.

Serena was sitting with her hands folded in her lap. She refused to look at Sylvia. Her small body was an express statement of stubborn resistance—or resolute calm. Overhead, a jet thundered across the sky. It looked like a military craft from Alamogordo, flying low and loud. As the plane disappeared from view, the trail dispersed like cotton fluff.

Sylvia rolled down the window of the truck and glanced out at the C.P.S. offices. The front door was shut; the windows were dark. Nobody home, and no sign of the Pinto's driver.

Digging for her small notepad with the C.P.S. phone numbers, she reached for her cellular phone. It wasn't in her purse. *Serena!*

There was no phone booth in sight, even though common sense allowed that social-service offices were often the place where family dramas played out. Well, *they* could drive to a pay phone.

She knew better than to leave Serena alone in the truck.

She tapped her fingers on the steering wheel and watched a fat cloud lumber eastward across the sky. Serena eyed her and glanced away again; she was up to something.

Discreetly, Sylvia rechecked her watch. It was ten minutes before nine. She had dealt with Dolores Martin once before; she'd found her to be less than reliable. She sighed, opened the door of the truck, and jumped down. She walked around the front of the vehicle, her fingers grazing the warm hood, and when she reached the opposite door she patted the metal. Serena pulled up the lock and allowed the psychologist to lift her out and set her on solid ground.

A vacant field adjoined the parking lot. Developers were quickly using up the area, but a few acres remained for the use of prairie dogs, rabbits, and other durable animals. Sylvia took Serena's hand, and together they stepped over a concrete barrier into the field.

Sylvia stopped and glanced back when she heard a car engine. A dark four-wheel-drive vehicle passed slowly along Vivigen Way. The social worker? No, the car looked much too expensive for the salary of a government employee.

When Sylvia looked back, Serena was on her hands and knees—a small sharp twig in hand—scratching in the dirt. The child's mouth formed a moue around a tiny tip of pink tongue; her forehead was creased, her expression one of total concentration. She worked quickly, cutting a series of lines in the parched earth.

Sylvia crouched down to look more closely at the emerging pattern. As she watched, the child crisscrossed the lines, working along a two-foot measure of earth. Dirt flew, and granules stung Sylvia's cheek. But Serena seemed oblivious to dust and flying particles.

As she drew, the crosses linked to become a . . . fence line? A border?

Tracks.

Now Serena completed a series of rectangles on wheels directly above the tracks . . . in a line, connected. She stepped back suddenly, as if to allow Sylvia better access.

A train.

As she scrutinized the drawing, Sylvia pictured the police report detailing the child's accident; the Honda had collided with a local train on its way from Lamy to Santa Fe. The car had been pushed along the spur's metal tracks. Who had been driving the Honda? Had they managed to run away after the accident? Or could a young child possibly—

Sylvia heard the roar of a car's engine. *No, it was a truck.* She sprang to her feet and pivoted.

Her truck—with Serena behind the steering wheel!

As she raced across the field, she heard the clamor of grinding gears. The truck was moving, jerking backward. Sylvia dashed alongside it and yanked open the driver's door. Roughly, she jumped up on the runner, reaching inside to switch off the engine. It sputtered, then settled into silence.

Sylvia grabbed her keys from the ignition and set the emergency brake. She leaned her weight against the door and let her heart rate slow.

The child sat stiffly, gazing straight ahead out the windshield.

The little devil! Sylvia felt as if she'd been running a marathon for the past twenty-four hours just to keep up with Serena. Well, damn it, she was losing the race.

She shooed Serena into the passenger seat and climbed behind the steering wheel, slamming the door of the truck. Sunlight reflected sharply off the dashboard. The glare was intense. She could barely read her watch face. Twenty minutes to Lamy . . . twenty minutes back . . . that left twenty minutes free. She pulled a pen and a small notepad from her purse and scribbled a quick note—*Back by 10:30*—and signed her name.

If she kept to the schedule, she could arrive at her engagement party with time to spare. She made Serena come with her to tack the note to the door of C.P.S.

When they were back at the truck, Sylvia squatted down and grasped the child by the shoulders. "You drew train tracks. Was that where you crashed the car?"

Serena nodded.

"Were you driving—were you steering by yourself?"

She nodded again, stamping her foot as punctuation.

"Was someone else with you?"

Without moving, Serena closed her eyes.

"Do you want me to take you there?"

Serena expelled air from between pursed lips. She nodded a third time—an exaggerated up-and-down motion—and then she cupped Sylvia's face between the palms of both hands, as if she had to contend with a very slow learner.

Sylvia sighed. "Fine. Let's go."

SERENA HEARD PACO'S voice call out again, and she could barely sit still behind the seat belt. His voice was low and soft, but it was filled with need. He had come to her when she was sleeping, and he had looked so sad.

All morning, he had whispered in her ears.

Fresa, he called her—Strawberry.

¡Fresa, ven aquí! Come here!

Wherever she turned, she'd heard his low cries.

Te necesito. I need you.

¡Ayúdeme! Help me!

This was *her* Paco, *el viejo,* who must be lying cold and hurt in the desert. Maybe he had only broken a leg—from *el demonio*—maybe that's why he hadn't come to take her home. And why hadn't she gone to find him sooner?

His face had looked *so* sad.

Serena's eyes grew hot with tears, but she held them back. She knew that crying would not help. Tears were useless.

No, Serena would use all her power, and she would find her Paco.

CHAPTER FOURTEEN

SYLVIA REACHED OVER to lay a hand on Serena's forehead. She was warm to the touch. Her olive skin was unnaturally pale; her eyes shone overly bright. Was she crying? Keeping one hand on the steering wheel, Sylvia draped her linen jacket over the child's narrow shoulders.

She tried to focus on the drive. Sylvia had always loved this stretch of road; over the years, she'd watched it develop. Beyond a series of subdivisions, Lamy and Galisteo were the two true villages situated just south of Santa Fe. The former, an Atchison, Topeka & Santa Fe rail junction founded in the late 1800s, was named in honor of Archbishop John Lamy, missionary, pioneer, interloper. Galisteo began as an Indian pueblo that flourished for many years before it was first noticed by Europeans when Fray Rodriguez explored the area in the sixteenth century. Lamy was about seventeen miles southeast of Santa Fe, and the trains still rolled into the

AT&S depot. Roughly five miles further south on Highway 41, Galisteo's rustic adobes were interspersed with million-dollar homes. Still, against the vast geology of the Galisteo Basin, the sparsely set human dwellings seemed inconsequential.

The Galisteo Creek rose to the land's surface near Lamy, flowing west toward the Rio Grande. A mud-red snake of water slithering between high clay banks, the creek shimmered far in the distance as the truck crested a hill. Sylvia noticed a gray hawk scooping the sky above; she pointed the bird out to Serena. The child watched its flawless gliding progress. But it wasn't a hawk. Sylvia looked closer; it was a paper kite. There were two kites, three. Serena shivered as the tiny paper forms floated on distant air.

The truck was approaching the site of the crash. Even though the accident had occurred after dark, the terrain seemed to strike a responsive chord in Serena. She had grown more withdrawn with each mile. She hardly reacted when Nikki thrust her head through the connecting window, dog breath warm and rank. The shepherd whined, excited by the open space and the motion of the vehicle.

Sylvia found the truck's speed creeping up to sixty-five, seventy, seventy-five. She lifted her foot from the accelerator and forced herself—not just the pickup—to slow down. A semi roared by, leaving a wake of turbulence that vibrated the smaller vehicle. Sylvia noticed a handmade sign, then another, announcing the village of Lamy's FIRST ANNUAL OCTOBERFEST. That explained the kites dancing in the sky.

Now the child pressed her head to the window. She seemed to be searching for landmarks. A low moan escaped her throat. The pulse in her slender neck jumped, while her hands fluttered in her lap. Every few seconds she cast a quick glance at Sylvia, and then her eyes returned to the land skimming past like an earthen wake.

The truck topped another rise. Beyond the high point, directly south, the mesas and bluffs melted away from the vast blue sky, and the earth flattened to form the Galisteo Basin. To the east, a mile or so ahead, a small paved road turned off to Lamy. Just one hundred feet in front of the truck, the railroad tracks cut across the highway like a geologic vein.

In Serena's C.P.S. file, Sylvia had found police photographs of the accident; the Honda had crumpled under the force of the slow-moving train, had been pushed along the tracks, eventually ending up fifty yards west of the highway.

She tried to picture the scene that night—warning lights flashing, the small excursion train on its way from Lamy grinding slowly uphill toward the highway, the Honda racing along 285 to impact—

The Toyota shimmied as it rumbled across the steel tracks and wooden ties at the railroad crossing.

Sylvia pulled off on the shoulder, glancing in the rearview mirror as she braked to a stop. The two-lane highway was empty. It reminded her of the naked spine of a giant. She cut the engine. They were alone.

The land was remarkable for the thrust and pitch of hill and valley. Barbed wire edged the road, keeping cattle and motorized vehicles from violent encounters. At a distance of a few miles, the sedimentary rock of the Galisteo formation foreshadowed White Mountain and the Ortiz Stock. The sun's rays reflected off a solitary vehicle as it emerged along the Lamy cutoff. At the intersection, the vehicle headed south toward Galisteo or Clines Corners.

The sun was approaching ten o'clock, not yet directly overhead, but gaining strength. At a standstill, the truck's interior warmed rapidly. Realizing that Serena had unsnapped her seat belt and was now fumbling with the strap, Sylvia reached out a restraining hand, but the child suddenly broke free. Before Sylvia could stop her, Serena had unlocked the door and scrambled from the pickup truck.

Sylvia followed, almost colliding with the spiny arms of a cholla cactus. Tires had ripped through this delicate desert terrain; the scars would last for a century. Shards of glass and the glint of metal littered the ground. Even with that evidence, it was hard to believe Serena had survived a collision only three nights earlier.

Sylvia breathed a sigh of relief when she saw the child standing at the barbed-wire fence. The relief was short-lived; Serena took off at a trot, moving south at the fence line, downhill toward the Lamy cutoff. Sylvia dashed in pursuit, stumbling over rocks and prickly-pear cactuses. Within seconds she caught up, grabbing the child with both hands.

Serena was all flailing arms, and Sylvia narrowly avoided a second black eye. She did take a blow to the solar plexus. She knew her patience wouldn't survive another boxing match—she'd give this field experiment another fifteen minutes, then head back to Santa Fe and her engagement party at Rosie's house. By now, the social worker had probably called to apologize.

Sylvia swung the child around so they were face-to-face. "Where are you going?"

Serena opened her mouth, then shut it tight, yanking free one arm to point down the hill toward the Galisteo Creek bed and the floodplain where the main Atchison, Topeka & Santa Fe tracks ran under the highway.

Sylvia eyed the surrounding terrain; it had been rash to bring the child out here alone. This much wide-open space was intimidating, and she was going crazy following around this little sprite. Still, her curiosity was piqued: What was Serena after?

Sylvia sighed. "Get in the truck," she said finally. "I'll take you."

Serena considered her destination, then looked back at Sylvia and nodded.

When they were in the truck and on the highway, Serena seemed to settle into a trancelike stillness. Near the Lamy turnoff, there was a spurt of oncoming traffic: a sedan, a Jeep, and a rusty pickup passed them, probably headed for the tiny railroad town's Octoberfest.

Sylvia slowed to thirty-five miles per hour. At the rim of the dry floodplain, an overpass provided access to the opposite bank. She glanced out at the railroad tracks running under the overpass. She was waiting, watching for Serena to signal a stopping place.

Just beyond the floodplain, the child pointed straight ahead, directing the truck to continue along New Mexico 285 instead of turning west toward the village of Galisteo.

When the truck had traveled another hundred yards, Serena pulled up on the handle of the passenger door. Sylvia did two things simultaneously: she gripped the child with her right hand and steered the truck into a left-handed U-turn.

She didn't ease her grip on the child—*it was like*

holding onto a lizard!—until the brake was set and they were both out of the truck. A battered white Plymouth sped past them, and Sylvia caught a glimpse of the driver, a weathered rancher, glancing curiously at the child who tugged the woman. The car left behind an invisible track of exhaust.

Nikki was whining from the back of the pickup. Sylvia welcomed her presence; she wasn't sure where Serena would lead her. Beyond the fence line, there was no sign of humanity. Just land.

But the dog would be a liability, likely to race after rabbits, deer, or cattle—and then Sylvia would be dealing with an unpredictable child *and* an AWOL animal.

Just as Sylvia turned away from the truck, Serena pulled free and set off at a run. She scrambled through the barbed-wire fence and continued up a small slope.

Unmoving, Sylvia watched her go. She smoothed her hair back from her face, straightened her clothes, brushed burrs from her shoes. The canvas pumps weren't designed for outdoor sports. She followed at a leisurely pace.

As she ducked unceremoniously under wire, she noticed the fence was down just a few feet away. Some of the vegetation near the break was crushed. Adjacent to the injured plants and clearly visible, black skid marks stood out against gray, worn asphalt. At some point in the past, a vehicle had come to an abrupt stop.

Sylvia returned her attention to the path ahead. The earth was hard-packed and studded with gravel. Here and there, small junipers and low scrub marked the topography. She traveled beyond the fence, and the countryside took on new and surprising aspects. There was subtle variation in vegetation—native grasses, cholla, scrub, chamiso. Rock teeth jutted from the earth.

She gained on Serena as the child moved tentatively forward, toward a low outcropping of rock. Several large shapes loomed in the distance. Cows surveyed Sylvia disinterestedly; there wasn't a bull in the bunch.

Ahead, the child scrambled from patch to patch, rock to rock, circling back on her previous location. She was hunting for something. She would crouch down, stand, search the horizon. But landmarks were few, and each hillock looked much like its neighbors.

Sylvia followed Serena's movements from a distance of forty or fifty feet. She sat on a nicely rounded sandstone, stretched her muscles, and surreptitiously produced a cigarette from her pocket. She was hot and sticky. She lit the cigarette and inhaled gratefully.

By her watch, they had another five minutes. She took one more drag on the cigarette, exhaled smoke, tamped the butt between two fingers, and dropped it into her pocket.

Serena had come to a standstill at a rock outcropping. Sylvia was about to call out when she noticed a shoe lying a few feet away. It was leather, good quality, and it looked quite new. She bent and retrieved it from the dirt. She was dusting it off when her eye was drawn to something shiny embedded in dirt—a silver belt buckle. She was beginning to feel very uncomfortable when she heard the child's plaintive cry.

Sylvia stumbled on loose earth, racing to reach the child's side. Here the smell of decay was strong. Below the ledge, the outcrop gave way to the next lip of rock. Between the two rocks a shallow cutaway had eroded over centuries. It was roughly the size of a grave. It sheltered a corpse.

THE DEAD MAN was lying on his side, face bared; most of his features had been destroyed by predators and exposure. By the look of his physical form and his gray hair, he had been middle-aged. One arm was trapped between rock and earth. The other was flung casually across his chest. The fingers of his exposed hand had been eaten away. His shirt was stained with fluids—Sylvia didn't want to think about what type of fluids—but the tightly woven fabric had been high-quality. His trousers were nondescript. His legs were akimbo, one foot bare and toeless, the other covered in a sock. A single men's loafer lay askew nearby; the leather was smooth and supple. It was a match to the shoe she had discovered moments earlier.

The scent of death and decomposition was unbearable. Protectively, Sylvia gripped the child to her side, lifting her away from the rocky cleft—she had to restrain Serena from flinging herself upon the body.

"He's dead, Serena. You can't help him. He's dead."

Serena shook her head, then she stared at Sylvia, eyes wide with shock.

Sylvia managed to guide the child far enough away from the corpse so that its grim form was no longer fully visible.

She felt rather than saw the child's intense stare, and then a small finger touched her cheek. She pressed Serena's damp hair away from her reddened eyes, murmuring reassurances. The sound of her voice hovered on the air. Then she let the silence envelop them both.

She became aware of the ache in her own legs. Thigh

and calf muscles were cramped by her contorted posture. Gingerly, she straightened herself, clutching Serena
with one hand. But the child didn't respond. She was
crouched down—hands clasped, eyes closed. Her lips
were moving, mouthing words that were audible only as
the faintest of whispers. It was a good thirty seconds
before Serena allowed herself to be guided away from
the body and back toward the road.

They had almost reached the highway when a car
broke the small rise to the south. The thin whine of hot
engine grew louder. A nondescript sedan flew past,
quickly growing smaller with distance as Sylvia raised
her arms to flag it down.

Serena was tugging insistently on her hand. Sylvia
looked down, then followed Serena's gaze to see something that confused her; she was already functioning on
overload. A vehicle was parked in front of her truck—
dark green, four-wheel-drive. There was no sign of the
driver. There was no sign of another person in the
immediate area. She was maddened by the slowness of
her thoughts.

Abruptly, her imagination ran wild. Was it a motorist
with car trouble, a hiker, the rancher who owned the
land, a roadside rapist?

She shook off the free-falling panic. She was on a
public highway in broad daylight. The car must belong
to someone who had stopped to see if she needed assistance. She did. *They* did.

She suddenly became aware of Nikki; inside the pickup, she was barking ferociously. The camper shell
rocked and shook as the animal threw her weight
around.

Sylvia's skin formed gooseflesh. She knew the dog

could sense what she could not—the location of the car's driver. The awareness of danger sharpened her senses; her mind pulled back into a state of analytical calm.

Sylvia guessed she and the child were standing fifteen feet short of the barbed-wire fence. They were so close to the road, she could hear the *tick-tick-tick* of the other car's cooling engine. With her free hand, Sylvia searched for her keys in her pants pocket. She carried no weapon; the semiautomatic she usually kept locked in the glove compartment of the truck was at home on a high shelf—unloaded and hidden from Serena.

She imagined she could feel eyes touching her skin. Her brain was taking in everything at once—the car, proximity of escape, the child's reactions, her dog—and scrambling to process it all.

Very slowly, she half crouched and peered under both vehicles. No feet, no legs, no sign of a driver in view.

She whispered in Serena's ear. "I want you to stay right beside me. Don't let go of my hand unless I tell you to." The child's grip tightened painfully around Sylvia's fingers.

Woman and girl darted forward, dodging undergrowth and barbed wire. Sylvia grabbed the fence. She pushed Serena under the taut strand, then followed. She was only half conscious of tearing fabric. She figured the distance—eight, seven, six more feet. But what the hell was going on with Nikki? The dog's adrenalized cries were so intense it sounded as if she were being tortured.

Serena froze—she was facing the front end of the truck. Sylvia saw the toe of a shoe protruding just beyond the far tire. A man.

She became aware of the hum of an engine. From the corner of her eye, she saw another car approaching from the south. Instinctively, she rushed toward the road, waving her arm, intending to stop the passing car. As she moved, she lost her grip on the child's hand.

Out on the pavement, she could see the startled look on the faces of the car's driver and passenger, man and woman. She had a fleeting thought—the man resembled her father. And then they were gone.

Sylvia pivoted, reaching out again for Serena, but the world had shifted—the child wasn't there. She heard a scream, turned toward the sound.

The man was tall, thin, and dark-haired. He was dragging the struggling child between the two vehicles. With his left arm he held Serena possessively across the throat. He gripped a gun in his right hand.

He yelled a sharp command in Spanish—words that registered faintly in Sylvia's consciousness. She heard the report—understood he'd fired the weapon—and ducked as a bullet shattered the side window of her truck. She lunged alongside her vehicle, her hands sliding across paint and glass, toward the rear gate.

She was shaking as she slammed her palm down on the latch that would free her dog. Another bullet took the corner off the camper, and plastic shards stung her cheek. The bullet had torn the window's hinges, and sheeted plastic fell askew, making way for Nikki's escape.

A golden mass of fur and muscle flew through space. Nikki hit the ground running—disappearing in a blur around the truck—and a deep, primitive growl cut the air like a blade.

CHAPTER FIFTEEN

NIKKI SLAMMED INTO her prey with all the force of a ninety-pound body rocket. In full attack mode, the dog could tear a man's throat from his neck like a ribbon from a package; her massive teeth could cut skin from muscle, muscle and tendon from bone. For the first time in her short life, she intended to do what she'd been bred to do—kill.

The man was the target; the child was in the way. But the shepherd's instincts were taut; she caught the man on his right shoulder, her paws missing the girl by a half inch. The force of the blow was enough to send the man reeling backward onto his butt—he lost his grip on Serena but managed to lock his fingers around her arm before she scrambled away. He still held the gun in his right hand; if he fired, chances were good he'd hit the animal—and blow a hole in his own gut. Instead, he used the weapon to bludgeon the shepherd as she strained to lock her teeth around his throat.

Sylvia scrambled around the truck. As she lunged for the child, she caught a glimpse of the man's face, his features contorted by pain and effort. She registered three things: he might be Mexican; his skin was pocked; his eyes were *yellow*. The rest of him was obscured by the dog's body.

Sylvia reached out for Serena and pulled, but the man would not release his grip. A horrible cacophony of grunting, growling, and guttural cries filled the air. Sylvia braced herself, using her reserve strength to wrench the man's fingers from the child's arm. As he let go, the gun in his other hand swung wildly in her direction. A bullet shot over Sylvia's head.

"Serena, get in the truck!"

On the ground, dog and man were a mass of furious energy. As far as Sylvia could tell from a quick backward glance, Nikki had the man stranded on his back. His left arm was wrenched around defensively—at an extreme angle; with his right, he was trying to press the muzzle of the gun to the dog's body. The shepherd's head seemed fused to his groin.

Sylvia knew she could never call her dog off. Nikki would never retreat. She had rescued them, and she would sacrifice herself for their safety.

Sylvia pressed Serena around the front of the truck where she strained at the passenger door. Praying the keys hadn't fallen, she fumbled deep in her pockets. Fabric bunched between her shaking fingers, but she found the familiar metal shapes.

Beside her, Serena was screaming. Sylvia heard a gunshot, a shriek of animal pain, the low harsh cries of the man. Then she heard the crunch of gravel, the sound of the man lurching to his feet.

Sylvia jumped into the truck, pulling Serena after her. The door slammed tight. She jammed down the locks and stared out the side window, trying to locate man and dog.

A low moan escaped her throat when she saw the man, bloodstained and battered, lunging toward the pickup. He raised his gun and fired. The bullet went wide, through the camper.

Before he gained a yard, Nikki attacked again. This time coming from behind, twisted, probably injured; the shepherd bit deep into his thigh, and the man's body jerked forward as if it were stuffed with rags or straw. He went down on one knee. While he was vulnerable, Nikki clamped her bloodied jaws deeper, positioning them further along the muscle.

Sylvia turned the ignition and the truck roared to life. When she hit the accelerator, she saw a human form rise from the ground. The man stumbled against the door of his own vehicle just as Sylvia wrenched the steering wheel and pulled too wide across the highway.

Serena was thrown across the seat as the truck's tires cut dirt on the opposite edge of the asphalt. Rigid lines of barbed wire took form. Sylvia heard the squeal of burning rubber and Serena's sharp intake of breath.

She was blinded by sunlight. What was that noise? An oncoming vehicle. Was it one or two? From a great distance, she thought she heard an ear-splitting horn. A prayer flashed through her mind that she and the child would not be killed in a crash after barely escaping a gun.

She heard screeching brakes. Serena screamed, and then Sylvia slammed the truck back across the road, landing twenty feet north of where she'd started. They'd missed a collision with an oncoming semi by a car length.

Renzo stared down at the red-golden eyes of the dog. He saw the animal's face and its body close to his—the dog's jaw had become part of his thigh—but his mind refused to acknowledge more dangerous information; he was not truly under life-threatening assault.

He felt an intimacy with the beast inspired by the inevitable intersection of their paths. His path had led him to the child; the dog's path had led it to protect the child. Now animal and man seemed to be dancing. If the dance was rough, an embrace that included the scrape of teeth against bone, that was simply what fate had decreed.

As a semi roared past, Renzo considered these things from his place on the ground. He could see the highway stretched out like a blanket—the Toyota pickup truck had swerved off to the side. Dust kicked up from the tires. He would have to follow soon, or he would lose their trail. But he couldn't move.

He felt the tepid sun on his shoulders, the joggling of his leg, the blood in his veins. But he felt no pain, only wetness and a very persistent tugging on his flesh. Renzo's other senses failed. His eyes outright lied to him; he did not see the striations of muscle and fat in his mutilated thigh; his ears denied the grinding of bone.

But he heard the insistent growl.

He was *cold*. So cold he thought he might be brittle and, in that case, in danger of breaking. While he watched, the dog seemed to gain another inch of thigh. Renzo found this distasteful but not upsetting. He was only conscious of need. The need to reach the child. For seconds, he'd held her in his arms—her life in his hands. Until the dog had crossed his path.

This shepherd—*el lobo*—had earned Renzo's respect. He identified with the wolf, with its wild strength; an animal that tracked its prey for hundreds of miles, for weeks, even months. This creature wasn't like the scavenging mutts, the ugly runts that roamed the gutters of Mexico. This beast was fierce and pure in its killing intention. He and the animal were one, merging, sharing blood and air.

Renzo's fingers hit metal; he turned his head and saw that he'd pushed his gun off the asphalt onto dirt. He tried to sit up, noting sadly that his suit was ruined. He had picked out the dark raw silk himself. He had selected the buttons.

If he could move the dog two more inches, reach the gun . . .

But he was too weak. He allowed himself to give in to the tug and drag of the dog's jaws. His body slid across gravel and dirt, inch by inch. The fingers of his left hand reached toward his ankle. He felt the resin handle of his knife snug against his leg. He pulled it free, hit the switch, and the blade shot open. A low moan came from the dog. Renzo took a breath—fought the black haze that was settling over his eyes—and forced the knife deep into the animal's flesh near the throat. He focused on *el lobo*'s life energy—this was the sacrifice of one wild animal to strengthen the soul of another.

The shepherd shuddered, her eyes rolled up until the whites showed, and finally, the great jaws released.

SYLVIA ACCELERATED TO sixty-five, and the truck raced back across the overpass. Her knuckles were white; a tight grip kept her hands from shaking. Serena was huddled in the seat, body twisted, gazing out the back.

The pickup was fast approaching the cutoff to Lamy when Sylvia saw the dark vehicle in her rearview mirror. A cold dread seeped through her muscles: *It couldn't be him.* Santa Fe was another twelve miles away. What else lay ahead? A landfill, a store, a subdivision set off the main road.

She had almost passed the Lamy turn when she saw the sign: OCTOBERFEST. She turned the steering wheel, and the truck swerved off to the right. It shimmied, scuttling over shiny asphalt, then recovered traction. Now Sylvia was following a narrow, winding two-lane leading to a tiny village that boasted a train depot, a restaurant and saloon, and some scattered homes set back on acreage. And kites. Lots of kites.

She saw cars parked in a field to her right. The truck jumped the pavement as it crested a small rise. Immediately, she had to negotiate an S-curve as the road passed the old Lamy church.

It was still another quarter mile to the center of town. Sylvia downshifted, then pushed the engine into third gear. Serena was pressed against the seat; soft cries escaped her throat.

When Sylvia glanced behind her, the dark vehicle was gone. The road was empty except for a floundering kite that scudded across hot pavement.

CHAPTER SIXTEEN

THE SUN BROKE through early-afternoon clouds, and the hot white rays stood out against a sky darkening by the instant. A localized storm system had settled over the basin like a bad mood. The air smelled of rain.

At the edge of the highway, four people huddled around a small heavy bundle of fur and flesh. Sylvia was crying, tears running down her cheeks as she cradled Nikki's head in her arms. Serena was hunched protectively over the shepherd's body. Matt motioned to the state cop; it was time to load the badly wounded animal into the back of the trooper's vehicle. The officer had offered to transport the dog to Santa Fe for emergency care. Sylvia helped the men move Nikki while a policewoman took Serena's hand, gently guiding her away.

Two reporters had already arrived at the scene, alerted to a story by police scanners. Matt shooed them away when they tried to question Sylvia. They prowled the area, watching, listening, scratching notes on small pads . . . waiting for someone to offer them information.

Beyond the reporters, two state police vehicles, lights flashing, were parked between the medical investigator's van and Matt's Caprice. A black minivan from the state police crime lab was lodged at an angle. Another vehicle—this one F.B.I. or D.E.A.—was parked directly across the highway; it had that intentionally nondescript federal-law-enforcement look.

On the asphalt for three hundred feet in either direction, flares glowed like fiery snakes. The crime-scene crew had set up camp. They would work here processing the scene for hours, perhaps even until well past nightfall.

Sylvia's pickup was angled off the highway; at the moment, a bald and burly cop was examining the driver-side door. Beyond her truck, Sylvia could see Serena slumped in the backseat of a state police car. A female officer was seated beside her.

Sylvia had taken possession of Matt's cell phone. She dialed, pacing along the edge of the highway while the call went through. When Albert Kove answered, she began talking manically. It was Matt England who interrupted the flow of words.

"Sylvia, will you please get off the phone?" The criminal investigator's voice was neutral and controlled, belying his intense expression. "You'll have to go over this again for the feds—"

Sylvia waved her free hand in a demand for time out. She'd already answered too many questions about her trip to the site with the child—about the attack. She was keeping an eye on Serena from a distance—she was sure the policewoman would take custody, isolating the child any minute now.

Impatiently, she repeated the question into the handset. "I want her admitted to Mesa Verde. Do you think that's a problem?"

Albert Kove's response was slow, his voice filled with concern. "She'll be taken to St. Vincent's. If she checks out, Mesa Verde might be an option—"

"I want to go with her."

"You'll have to work it out with the transport officers. At the moment, Child Protective Services isn't likely to support you on anything."

Sylvia felt the sting of Albert's words. "The social worker didn't show this morning."

"That meant you had to go looking for a corpse?" He sighed. "Why didn't you just bring her to the Sanchezes'?"

"Bad judgment call."

"It was *your* engagement party, Sylvia." Reproach made Kove sound whiny.

Sylvia shook her head, refusing to defend herself. "Albert, will you support me on this?"

Matt stared at the woman he intended to marry. She was standing a few feet away, her clothes wrinkled and coated with blood, her hair hanging in tangled strands. Tears had streaked the dirt on her skin, and an ugly bruise was turning blue-black under her jaw.

Through the phone, Kove's voice softened. "Sylvia, if you want to protect this child, let the experts do their job. They're good at it." He hung up.

Without a word Sylvia gave the small portable phone back to Matt. She walked a short distance off the road. The sun was dipping behind clouds again. When she glanced up at it, the cloud-covered sphere burned orange spots into her eyes.

"Sylvia?"

"What?"

"Give me something I can use to catch the bastard." Matt worked to keep impatience from his voice. "Last night somebody tore your kid's Honda to shreds. We're dealing with a really scary bad guy, so talk to me."

She shook her head, covering her eyes with her hands. She tried to clear her mind, reaching for the remnants of memory, but individual events had blurred into a confusing haze. She groaned in frustration.

"What did you hear?"

"His scream when Nikki hit him."

"What else?" Matt was watching her closely, and he thought he saw something register. "Don't think about it, just tell me."

"His voice. He spoke Spanish. He sounded . . . not exactly refined, but educated."

"Good. What else?"

"Tall, thin . . . maybe Mexican or Indian blood. His face was scarred—acne or smallpox."

Sylvia pressed both hands against her eyes. Her breathing caught. She said, "He drove a dark green four-wheel-drive." She swallowed. "He was a professional— but more than that . . . he went for the child, and he didn't give up even when Nikki had him down."

Her voice rose with excitement. "CZ . . . CZ three. That was on the license plate."

Matt wrote the symbols on a pad. Behind the criminal investigator a man in khakis approached from a distance. Sylvia knew a deputy medical investigator was attending to the corpse while detectives were preserving and processing the scene. She didn't recognize this man, but she saw that he carried something gingerly in one gloved hand.

Sylvia heard Matt ask, "What you got, Ed?"

Ed was wide, flat-faced, and earnest. He tipped his head toward Sylvia. "The buckle she found? It's real fancy silver work, and it goes on the dead guy's belt; one of those decorative jobs—like this one has P-A-C-O stamped into the leather."

Matt nodded, waiting. Ed whispered something in a low voice. Sylvia just heard the words "dust" and "smack."

Ed's voice rose. "You maybe should take another look, sir." The man held up his final offering. "This was jammed behind the body—like he fell back on top of it. It slid out easy. Really. I didn't mess up the rest of the scene."

Sylvia could see a small purse—a woman's clutch, inexpensive vinyl, long past its prime. She walked the few steps to stand beside both men. Matt asked Ed to open the bag. It contained only a few items. A delicate lacy handkerchief. A cheap ballpoint pen. Several coins—pesos, dimes, and nickels. A plastic comb. A snapshot.

The photograph was frayed at the edges and creased with age and handling, but the colors were still some-what true: two young faces gazed out at the camera. For an instant, Sylvia thought the woman was Serena. The eyes, the mouth, the cheekbones—all the child's fea-tures were duplicated. But this face was older, more sen-sual, already reaching its promise.

Serena's mother looked no older than sixteen. She was wrapped in the arms of a young man. Their cheeks were pressed together, their eyes shining. They smiled shyly, like first-time lovers.

Ed said, "The guy looks familiar."

Matt was studying the photograph intently. He low-ered his head until he was only a few inches from the images. Finally, he grunted and said, "He should. He's in the newspapers every day."

Both Sylvia and Ed stared at Matt. She spoke first. "You know who he is?"

"Yeah." Matt's voice was harsh. "So do you. That's Cash Wheeler."

"The Cash Wheeler who's gonna be executed?" Ed nodded in dawning recognition; he'd answered his own question.

Sylvia plucked the photograph from Matt's fingers. She swallowed, and her throat ached. "Can I take my truck, or do I need to beg a ride into town?"

"Slow down."

"I'm going with Serena."

"I don't think they're finished with your truck. They'll need to dust for prints."

"Fine. I'll beg a ride."

"Sylvia, that photograph is evidence—you can't take it. Dammit!"

TEARS STREAKED SERENA'S dirty face where she sat in the backseat of the police car. When she saw Sylvia at the door, she gave a small cry of excitement and relief.

The policewoman next to her tried her best to comfort Serena, but the child would have none of it. She struggled to escape the car and reach Sylvia. Finally, the officer gave in and let Sylvia slide into the backseat. After a few minutes, Serena quieted. Then she looked at the photograph.

Almost instantly, the word escaped her lips. It was ever so soft, almost inaudible, but Sylvia heard it, and so did the others. Serena said, "Dada."

CHAPTER SEVENTEEN

CASH WHEELER WAS cuffed and shackled—he'd been giving prison staff a hard time. The restraints intensified his gaunt appearance—a vivid reminder that he was on day five of a hunger strike. He stared at Matt England through narrowed eyes and shook his head. "I don't know any Mexicans."

"I heard you grew up in El Paso. Few years back, Juárez and El Paso were one town."

"I lived in the American part."

"Your wife was of Mexican descent." Matt leaned back in the hard plastic chair. He was puzzled by Wheeler's almost perfunctory resistance. The slight wedge of compassion he'd previously felt for the inmate was in danger of collapsing. He reminded himself that a guy on death row would be short on trust—and social graces.

"Never had a wife," Wheeler said.

"Your girlfriend, then."

"What girlfriend?"

The one they say you murdered, asshole. "Elena Cruz."

Wheeler put on the act, searching his memory for some clue to the lady's identity. The interview was off to a great start.

Wheeler had been waiting for Matt in a private visiting room in North Facility's administration building. The visiting rooms were all identical—plain, hard floor, beige walls, a grilled security window set in the steel door, one table, two chairs.

Matt found the room grim. Cash Wheeler probably found it agreeable; he had consented to this meeting on the condition that he be allowed to leave Housing Unit 3-B. Although the administration building and the housing unit were separated by only a yard and a sally port, the short walk meant fresh air and sunshine for the death row inmate.

Matt gazed directly at Wheeler's pasty face; to a man who had spent years locked in a north-facing cell, sunshine was more valuable than any type of contraband. He was reminded of Wheeler's cryptic comment from their previous meeting.

"Are you like your friend Bowan?" Matt asked quietly. "Are you tired of waiting for rain and sunshine?"

To Matt's surprise, Cash Wheeler's whole demeanor softened. "The state is calling the shots for me." The inmate paused to light a cigarette, then quoted softly, " 'He maketh his sun to rise on the evil and on the good. . . .' "

Matt kept his attention on Wheeler, but he was thinking about his earlier discussion with Rosie Sanchez, who had arranged this early-morning interview.

"Who's Wheeler close to?" he had asked.

"His sister. His lawyer. He used to talk to Bowan."

"Staff? Any of the C.O.'s? Anyone from the libraries? Medical?"

"A nurse practitioner got involved in his sister's protest; she quit her job. Most of the time, Wheeler finds very little social interaction—he's on twenty-three-hour lockdown. He's always welcomed visits from the chaplain and various missionary types."

"He's a born-again?"

"He's lonely and scared . . . a dying man—unless the court rules favorably on the final appeal."

"It must piss the hell out of Wheeler's sister—all that money, all those connections haven't saved her brother from a goddamn thing."

Cash Wheeler's ankle chains clanked against the legs of his chair. The sound refocused Matt's thoughts, bringing him back to the present.

The inmate inhaled deeply on the cigarette that dangled from his lips. He exhaled smoke and words, asking, "You got a family—any kids?" The raw pain in his voice echoed off hard surfaces.

"No." Matt regretted the word as soon as it flew out of his mouth. He knew he should tell some part of the truth—even make up a sympathetic lie—to reinforce rapport and keep Wheeler talking. But a barrier had slammed down inside him, shutting off memories of his dead wife and son, guarding thoughts of Sylvia.

Matt could feel the inmate watching him closely; Wheeler had sensed the sudden emotional shift. To cover the moment, Matt said, "Tell me about Paco."

"The Mexican?" Wheeler's voice had a new and understandably hostile edge. "He's dead." After a beat of silence, Wheeler shrugged. "I got a gut feeling about . . .

what's his name?" Smoke from his cigarette wafted into his nose and eyes, but he didn't seem to notice. He smiled, apparently enjoying the slow rhythm of half answers and nonanswers.

He said, "I know some guys named Paco."

Matt told himself he was in no hurry. At the same time, his sudden and unsettling reaction to Cash Wheeler had disturbed his sense of himself; he preferred to believe he was the master of his emotions.

"Yeah . . . I know a guy, Paco Montoya . . . but he's locked up." The inmate turned to stare down the correctional officer whose face filled the observation window.

Matt said, "This man probably died on Wednesday night. He was driving a car with El Paso plates."

"Yeah?"

"You ever heard of a business called Hat-Trick?"

"They make sombreros?"

The session went on for another fifteen minutes. At times the only sound in the room was the growl of Wheeler's empty stomach. As Matt asked questions, Wheeler smoked three more cigarettes. Matt's head began to ache from secondhand smoke and tension; he wasn't getting information he could use. Still, he took his time, inching toward a goal. There was this moment that happened in some investigations, the moment when you were holding pieces of separate puzzles in your hands and, suddenly, you knew all the pieces fit in the *same* puzzle—and together those pieces made a brand-new picture.

He seemed half asleep when he pulled a C.P.S. interoffice photograph from his pocket. Lazily, he set the photo on the table.

Wheeler exhaled smoke and glanced down. From the look on his face all he saw was a girl. No apparent curiosity, no particular puzzlement about why this photograph of a child would be brought to his attention. Well—*there*—Matt thought maybe Wheeler's mouth had tightened around the cigarette.

Finally, the inmate said, "That's not Paco, is it?"

"No, that's not Paco."

"But she was traveling with your guy?" He smiled. "I saw the news. About that kid who crashed her car into a train . . ."

"Do you know her?"

"Maybe." He shifted position, working around shackles. "Maybe not."

"Too bad."

"Should I?"

Matt didn't answer as he started for the door. He got so close he could hear the C.O.'s footsteps in the hallway. But then he turned, a finger raised to his temple—as if he'd forgotten one last unimportant detail—and he walked back to the table. He set down a second photograph—this one taken from the child's purse the night before: Cash Wheeler and Elena Cruz.

Cash Wheeler was good, but this time Matt knew he'd seen the slight, involuntary stiffening of muscle, the vein in the jaw. And then the blood drained from the inmate's already pale face.

The investigator asked, "Can you think of any reason why a little girl would have a ten-year-old photograph of you and Elena Cruz?"

ROSIE SANCHEZ SHOOK her head. "She's not his kid."

"We don't know that." Sylvia frowned.

"It's all too weird, is how I know. Anyway, she's Hispanic."

"She could be half Anglo."

"It's possible." Rosie Sanchez tapped the metal desk-top with scarlet fingernails and returned her attention to the phone in her hand. She asked, "Have Criminal Agent England give me a call when he's through with Wheeler."

Sylvia Strange was seated across the desk from the penitentiary investigator; she watched as Rosie nodded for her benefit and mouthed, *"He's still with Cash."*

Behind the investigator, grilled windows offered a grimy view of a guard tower. Voices drifted up from outside. The air was tinged with the faint, familiar aroma of wastewater from the prison's treatment plant. From here, the world seemed terminally gray. But Sylvia knew for a fact that the sky was a brilliant blue.

Rosie's fingernails tapped out a complex flamenco rhythm. "That's right . . . have him use my office exten-sion." She shifted in her chair, still speaking into the phone. *"Bueno,* Sally. Bye." She hung up the phone and raised both hands, palms exposed. The gesture was nat-urally dramatic.

Sylvia was halfway out of the chair when Rosie barked out a command: "Sit down, *jita.* You can't go barging over there, interrupting an investigation. What do you think this is, the movies?"

Sylvia dropped back into her seat, protesting. "I need answers to questions, and Matt's not going to get them."

"Neither are you. Not today." Rosie raised a placating hand. "At least not from Cash Wheeler." Her eyes nar-rowed. "What makes you think you'd do better than Matt?"

"I can tell Wheeler about Serena. I can make her real for him."

"You can't just waltz over to Max and play knock-knock on Wheeler's cell door." She settled back in her seat, clearly signaling a change of subject. "How is Serena?"

"Obviously, she's upset." Sylvia ran her hand through her unruly hair as if to calm herself. "But C.P.S. agreed to admit her into Mesa Verde Hospital. When I stopped by an hour ago, she was just waking up. I made sure she had her breakfast, and I sat with her for a while."

"Do they have good security at that hospital?"

"She's in a locked ward. The cops have been alerted to patrol the area regularly." Sylvia was quiet for a moment. When she voiced the next question, her delivery was slow. "Do you think Cash Wheeler murdered Elena Cruz?"

"I don't have my crystal ball with me today."

"Rosie, speak to me. Do you think he's a murderer?"

"*Tal vez*. Maybe." If Rosie was startled by the ferocity in her friend's face, she only shrugged. "A Hobbs jury heard the evidence and convicted."

"You know what sentiments are like in that part of the state. Steal a loaf of bread, you get ten to fifteen."

Rosie shrugged. "I also know that most of us are capable of terrible acts of violence at some point during our lifetime."

"What if he's innocent?"

"Then his execution will be a horrible sin." Rosie sighed. "I'm sure the governor would commute Wheeler's sentence to life in prison if the political climate were different—if people weren't so fed up with violence—"

"If . . ." Sylvia's voice faded and she shuddered.

Rosie set the palms of her hands firmly on the desktop. "One of my C.O.'s told me a story. He said he overheard Cash Wheeler bragging about being a stone-cold killer. He said Wheeler went into graphic detail." Rosie saw the look on Sylvia's face, and she shook her head. "Don't act so surprised, *jita*. Ninety-nine percent of these guys are guilty."

Sylvia didn't respond for several seconds. Then she spoke slowly. "You and I both know there are reasons these guys boast about violent crimes—sometimes they do it to act tough, to try and protect themselves from harassment."

"I think you don't want the child to be related to a killer."

To Rosie's surprise, her friend stood and pivoted abruptly toward the office door.

Sylvia blurted out, "I'm going to drive over to North Facility to see if I can find Matt." As she opened the door, she heard Rosie's sigh of surrender.

"Wait up. At least let me walk you out."

SYLVIA FOLLOWED THE penitentiary investigator down the dank prison hallway, stepping past a metal grill as it slid slowly home. It clanged shut behind her, locked—the mirror action of her trip inside just thirty minutes earlier. Welcome to the penitentiary—an archaic facility destined for the wrecking ball by federal decree. She tried to forget this was her first trip to Main in several months, just managing to quell an internal whisper of claustrophobia.

Rosie Sanchez didn't slow her stride as they passed a series of administrative offices in the north wing of the old facility. Sunday visitors—two priests and two plainly dressed men—were huddled in conversation outside the doorway of the deputy warden's office. An inmate porter pushed a dust mop over the worn tile floor. His route went wide around the clergymen, then wider still around the women, but he gave Sylvia a small wave.

She recognized him and said, "Hey, Spider, how's it going?"

A minute later, when Rosie and Sylvia reached the stairwell that eventually gave access to Main's front entrance, a whale of a man stepped out to block their path. Both women came to a standstill.

Rosie was the first to respond. "Sylvia, do you remember Jim Teague, Cash Wheeler's attorney?"

Teague was a hard man to forget. The Texan weighed in at more than three hundred pounds, he was six-feet-five, and his taste in clothes ran to fringed and beaded leather jackets and hand-tooled Stallion boots. Sylvia's eyes were still traveling upward from Teague's ample belly to his face when she heard his Irish-tenor voice sharpened by ire.

"A little bird told me a state police officer is questioning my client," the attorney said.

Sylvia watched Rosie weigh her dislike of pushy lawyers against their very real ability to bankrupt the Department of Corrections with lawsuits filed on behalf of criminal-procedure abuses.

"Cash *agreed* to meet with a criminal agent," Rosie said. "But I believe that meeting is finished."

"If not, I'm about to interrupt it." The lawyer glanced at his watch and then refocused on Sylvia. "You made the *Albuquerque Journal*, Dr. Strange." He lifted one eyebrow and cocked his head; he was huge, but his movements were contained, almost dainty.

Sylvia faced Teague and set her hands on her hips. "I read the same article. It didn't mention me by name."

"No." He gave a brusque shrug. "Your identity cost me one thirty-second phone call. It was more difficult to obtain valid information about the child. And about a certain photograph."

Sylvia studied the death-row lawyer's naturally impassive features and his improbably green eyes tucked between layers of flesh. She could easily believe he had a source who had revealed her name and her involvement with the child—but only a handful of people knew about the child's tenuous connection to Cash Wheeler. So where the hell had he gotten *that* part of the story? Who told him about the photograph of Cash and Elena? Did he have a source at state police? At the A.G.'s office? Information about the photograph had been kept from the press—

Teague chuckled, wagging his head as if he could read her mind—*and he probably could.* He said, "And now I've got confirmation from you, Ms. Strange. What an expressive face you have!"

"So I've been told." She grimaced.

Sylvia had seen Teague at work in the courtroom, and she knew he was good. He was also stringently anti–death penalty. His actions supported his beliefs— he was "death qualified," an expert at the appeals process. His services did not come cheap. Local and national press had made no secret of the fact that Cash Wheeler's sister had spent a small fortune on her brother's case—most of it for legal fees. At this moment, beneath the smooth veneer, Jim Teague looked as if he'd blown a fuse.

She smiled sweetly. Since the lawyer had dealt the

first hand, she decided to play a quick round of poker. "The A.G.'s keeping you well informed, counselor."

"It's my job to be informed. My client is a dead man, barring a governor's pardon or an appellate miracle."

"This *is* a miracle." With effort, Sylvia kept her expression flat. "These new events change things—"

"Are you practicing law these days, Doctor?" Jim Teague snorted, and a look of sharp impatience flashed in his eyes. "This situation has not produced new and material evidence—not in any way, shape, or form."

Anger tightened Sylvia's throat. "We're not talking about abstract material evidence—" It was stupid to play poker with a lawyer.

"No, *you're* talking about a child who is probably in this country illegally, and who is most likely a Mexican national." He raised a palm to ward off Sylvia's protest. "I've already spoken to federal investigators. An old photograph of a man who vaguely resembles Cash Wheeler doesn't prove a relationship. Frankly, I tend toward another theory. This is some cruel scam to take advantage of a condemned man and his family."

"I can't believe you'll ignore this child." She stared at the lawyer, baffled and curious. "I *know* you won't. That would be absurd."

Teague shook his head; there was an air of weariness about him. He said, "If you think you know more after one day's involvement in this case than I do after four years, then by all means, tell me my job." He shifted his briefcase from left hand to right—the leather case looked tiny in contrast to his massive body. "Cash was convicted of Elena Cruz's murder and the murder of a motel clerk, period. Evidence of the child's death was not admitted at the trial because there was no corpus delecti."

"But Serena's appearance raises new questions—it might even provide new answers." Sylvia respected Jim Teague, and she wanted him as an ally. Her voice softened when she said, "The child's in a private hospital without parents or family. And there is evidence that connects her to Wheeler. I'm only thinking about her best interests."

"And I'm only thinking about the best interests of my client. It's my job to remain impartial in a potentially charged situation." Teague held up a finger and shook his head. Suddenly, he looked almost human.

His voice warmed up ten degrees. "Sylvia, we won't ignore this child. This morning I spoke with the attorney general—I got that insomniac out of bed—and tomorrow morning I'll file a petition with the courts for a blood test to determine paternity. We'll be in touch."

As the lawyer walked briskly down the hallway, Rosie spoke under her breath: "He's slick as floor wax, isn't he?" She caught Sylvia's eye. The dozen keys on her belt jingled. Her face was alive with curiosity.

A woman's voice rang out sharply. "Dr. Strange?"

Sylvia and Rosie both turned. Someone had stepped from the deputy warden's office into the hallway. She looked vaguely familiar, a medium-tall woman with shoulder-length strawberry-blond hair and classically European features. As the blonde brushed past Jim Teague, Sylvia made the connection: Cash Wheeler's sister.

"I'm Noelle Harding."

"Noelle." Jim Teague's commanding voice rolled through the hallway. "Let's do this the way we discussed—" His mouth twisted into a frown when Noelle Harding waved him off.

The woman approached Sylvia, fixing her with an intensely direct gaze. Agitated, she asked, "Do you have a picture of this child?"

Sylvia reached into her briefcase and pulled out a C.P.S. Polaroid. Harding took the photograph and studied the image—the child's face, dark, wide-set eyes expressing vigilance, mouth compressed with tension. In the photo, Serena's skin was still bruised and slightly puffy above one eye.

Noelle Harding didn't speak for almost thirty seconds. She seemed to be absorbing the chemical image. Her body remained motionless, her posture turned brittle with suppressed emotion.

Finally, she reached out to clasp Sylvia's wrist between ringed fingers: "Let's talk."

SYLVIA GAZED WARILY at Noelle Harding. The women were seated on plush leather in the back of Harding's black limo-van. Harding reached for a phone and said, "Stan, we'll be a few minutes. Why don't you enjoy a smoke?" After a second, the driver's door opened, then closed quietly.

A single pale pink rose was tucked into a brass vase. The scent of the flower was unpleasantly intense in the small space. On the other side of tinted windows, forty feet up the road, a prison utility truck was idling, and three inmates were pulling weeds along an asphalt edge; every few seconds, one of the inmates glanced furtively at the limo-van. Beyond the men, the building that housed the prison's sewage-treatment plant blocked the brilliant blue sky with gray. For several moments, Harding appeared to be completely engrossed by the scene.

Sylvia bit back her impatience and tried to gain a sense of Noelle Harding in this incongruous setting. In person, Harding was smaller and her features more delicate than the television news clips suggested. The Minicams had been interested in catching the nouveau riche social activist who raised massive funds for charities, the one-woman crusade who had dedicated ten years of her life to saving her brother from execution.

But the cameras had failed to capture the vulnerable woman who finally turned her full attention to Sylvia. Noelle Harding spoke in a soft voice. "I want you to understand our lawyer's position. This is a horrible time for my brother and myself. And for Jim Teague, too; don't imagine for a moment he's not emotionally involved with my family. With the execution date so close—" She raised her palms as if to ward off time. She fumbled in her jacket pocket and produced a pack of cigarettes. She was already flicking one out as she asked, "Do you mind if I smoke?"

Sylvia shook her head as the other woman lit a Sherman's. Harding brushed a shred of tobacco from her lip and inhaled. Sylvia felt a strong pang for nicotine and told herself the craving would pass in a decade or two.

Harding said, "From what I've already gleaned, you are involved with this child on a personal level." Sylvia began to speak, but Harding dismissed her words with a wave of her cigarette. "You and I are not at all different, Sylvia. You care for an abandoned little girl; I care for my brother." The woman lowered her head and ran a hand through her hair. When she looked up again her eyes were predatory, a female lion ready to defend her cub. Her voice rose harshly. "I don't want my brother's hopes raised, then dashed because all this turns out to be bullshit."

"What do you want from me?"

"Cooperation."

"Fine. You've got it. We're not on opposite sides of the fence." She leaned toward Harding. "The fact is, the courts, several federal agencies, the state police, and the Mexican Consulate are all involved because Serena is a minor, possibly a Mexican national, and because she's connected to a murder." Sylvia's eyes darkened. "I won't let this child out of my reach until I know who she is, who she belongs to, and if she's in danger."

Harding studied Sylvia for several moments. Then she nodded, exhaling smoke. "If you can prove the child has a parent in the U.S., she stays." She flicked her cigarette in an ashtray, casually summing up the stakes—a child's welfare.

"If by some miracle this child is my niece, I will do anything to help her." She leaned closer to Sylvia. "And she'll need my protection, because a killer is free . . . while my brother is locked away for a crime he didn't commit."

"You've never doubted your brother's innocence?"

Harding stubbed her cigarette out in the ashtray. "Never." Her stare was direct. "Cash loved Elena."

"Men murder women every day—love is the perfect motive."

"My brother isn't like that." Harding took a breath, readjusting the veneer of control that had slipped just slightly. She was dressed in a simple suit that had cost at least five hundred dollars; her small sapphire earrings were a perfect match with her eyes. She shifted her body in the leather seat.

"I don't know what you've heard about the case . . . or about my brother and me. Cash was nine and I was eleven when our parents died. We were dirt poor. We had an aunt who couldn't decide if she . . . could be bothered to care for us. We spent eight years off-and-on at a school for unwanted kids. In El Paso. That's where Cash met Elena."

As she spoke with just the softest hint of a Texas twang, Noelle Harding fingered the diamond-studded band on the third finger of her left hand. She took a quick breath and smiled. "My brother was a gentle kid . . . the kind you have to look out for every minute." For an instant, she'd sounded like a weary mother. Then her eyes changed, her voice hardening. "I won't sit back and watch my brother die."

"Then help me. Help Serena."

Harding's response was to press a button at her elbow, causing the window to lower with a soft whirring sound. The chauffeur was standing a few yards from the limo talking quietly with one of the prison officers. Harding called out, "We're almost done, Stan."

Sylvia didn't hear the chauffeur's reply, but she knew when he'd started the engine because the vehicle vibrated gently. She felt a fleeting sense of panic that her time had run out—not just with Noelle Harding but with Serena as well.

Noelle's eyes searched Sylvia's face. "I want to see her," she said. She touched Sylvia's arm gently. "I want you to take me to her."

Sylvia frowned. "You realize there's concern about her safety—"

Harding waved one hand dismissively. "When I'm in New Mexico, I play golf with both your senators." She continued slowly, as if she might be addressing a simpleton. "If I want to see the child, I will. She's been placed in Mesa Verde Hospital under your supervision."

Sylvia considered Harding's impatient assertion, the arrogance and the truth of those words, then nodded. "I think I can set up a visit for tomorrow."

"Not tomorrow. Now."

Sylvia and Noelle locked eyes.

"My brother has no time left. If the girl is his daughter, I need to know."

RENZO SANTOS STOOD at the window of his La Posada casita. Through glass, he had a clear view of the parking area—and of the boy who was stealing his car. The thief popped the lock on the Suburban's door; daylight didn't faze him. Renzo grunted—the boy's methods were crude but effective.

When a vacationing couple wandered out of the room next to Renzo's, the boy leaned casually against the Suburban; he patted his pockets down, pulling out a pack of cigarettes.

"Forget your keys?" the man called out in a heavy Texas twang. The boy laughed noncommittally, and the couple walked on toward the main hotel building, probably headed for the dining room.

When they were halfway across the parking lot, the boy jumped into the Suburban, flipped the locks down, and disappeared behind smoked glass. It would take him less than five seconds to find the key under the seat.

Renzo had made one phone call, given one order: make a vehicle disappear. He was satisfied with the service and fairly certain the Suburban was on its way to Mexico, where it would be abandoned near the border.

Now that the car was dealt with, Renzo calmly embarked on his own course of action: he prepared to deal with his injuries, the resulting fever, the probable hallucinations.

Blood coated his body, staining the towels he'd wrapped around himself, droplets even dotting the hotel-room floor. He groaned, let the nausea roll over him, then tried moving. Messages flew instantly to his brain and back again to his nerve endings: *pain*.

One bloody towel fell away, and the ragged wound on his thigh gaped open in an obscene show of raw flesh. The dog's teeth had gone deep enough to rip out muscle. He was lucky *lobo loco* hadn't killed him. The bite was centimeters from the femoral artery. He pressed another towel against the wound. He had smaller lacerations on his shoulder, his arms, his hands. *Lobo loco* had left a medium-sized bite mark at his waist.

First, Renzo would deal with the massive thigh wound—the blood loss and danger of infection were high. If he passed out within the next twenty minutes, the smaller injuries could wait.

As Renzo took three more steps, he clamped his jaw against the brutal pain. The movement of his leg muscles stretched the wound wider; when he removed the towel, the show of viscera reminded him of a terrible mouth.

He made it to the television, where CNN financial news was on the screen. He turned up the volume—loud enough to distract him, but not to cause problems with his immediate neighbors.

His muscles quivered, and he almost fainted. Shakily, he walked to the bathroom, where he vomited into the toilet. The feeling of nausea took him back to child-hood. He lay down on the black-and-white tiled floor—

he had no choice, although the effort caused him terrific pain. Smears of blood stained the floor; he'd started bleeding heavily again. He hung his head over the edge of the toilet bowl. His mind began to play tricks. The white porcelain supporting his cheek became a Mexican gutter. He became a boy named Jesús who watched the legs and feet of passing pedestrians. Someone spat near his face. As he lay there—fourteen years old, filthy, and stoned—he wondered which of the shoes belonged to his father? These were the streets his mother-the-*puta* worked every night. His father could pass him each day. The old man might be a shopkeeper, he might be a dentist, he might be a criminal, a junkie, a soldier. Jesús had seen the kind of men who used the *putas*. He'd already made up his mind to escape this world; he would do whatever was necessary. He would lie, he would sell drugs to his own family, he would murder. Jesús turned his face away from the street.

When the sickness and its accompanying vision passed, Renzo crawled to the shower stall, pulled himself up, and turned the nozzle to cold. Gingerly, he eased himself under the stinging flow. Pain redefined his world. He tried to make his inner self invisible. When he came to, he was huddled on the floor of the shower, water and blood swirling beneath his feet and buttocks.

Somehow Renzo made it from the shower to the toilet. He sat, took out his leather kit, and opened it. He removed his knife, rolled catgut, Betadine wash, a surgical needle, and various vials. Without water, he chewed and swallowed four large painkillers. Even morphine would not kill the pain. He flushed the thigh wound with the iodine-based disinfectant.

It was an ugly, imprecise wound. *Lobo loco* had partaken of his flesh. Now his body was inside the dead wolf. Renzo felt respect for this bond. Instead of its flesh, he had partaken of the animal's spirit, its life force.

That was the ritual of blood sacrifice.

He reached over to the wall, turned a black knob so the heat lamp flooded the room with light and warmth. He dabbed at the frayed corners of his skin with a washcloth soaked in iodine. It took him more than a minute to thread the needle with catgut; he stared at it for several seconds. His hands were shaking, and his unblinking gaze never quite landed on the sharp steel.

His fuzzy thoughts tried to settle on the next move he would make to find the child. He had already picked his local contact—he had the number, a private line. It was good to have friends in high places.

He brought the needle up to his face. He took a breath. *Blood sacrifice . . . Serpent Skirt . . . Coatlicue . . . goddess of his ancestors.*

When he was ready, he stretched one hand across his thigh so his fingers spanned the canyon of the wound. With a grunt, he pulled the edges together. The needle pierced one flap, then the other—not cleanly, not neatly. It took surprising force to pull the thick catgut through his battered flesh. After only three stitches he was overcome by nausea, simply heaving a small quantity of foam and bile onto the floor by his feet. He was careful to miss the lesion.

He heard something, looked up, and saw Elena's child staring at him. She was pointing at the dangling, bloodied needle. She was laughing. He reached out to touch her, but she shook her head and dissolved.

CHAPTER EIGHTEEN

THE PREVIOUS NIGHT, Serena had been transported from the crime scene to St. Vincent's Hospital and, finally, to Mesa Verde Hospital. The private facility was located on Santa Fe's west side; it covered half a city block, a bland institutional vision of Pueblo-style architecture.

Sylvia had driven Noelle Harding in the Toyota pickup; Harding's chauffeur had agreed to follow thirty minutes later. She parked in the lot opposite a sign that read STAFF ONLY. Since joining the Forensic Evaluation Unit approximately two years earlier, she'd become affiliated with Mesa Verde as well as several other local institutions; her status as a staff member meant that she could continue therapy with clients admitted to those institutions. Mesa Verde specialized in the treatment of adults and teenagers with substance-abuse problems, eating disorders, and non-violent psychiatric disorders.

Serena did not fit the profile of the hospital's usual resident—but she had something in common with other patients: she was in residence for her personal safety.

Before Sylvia climbed out of the truck, she asked Noelle a question that had been on her mind. "Your brother's infant daughter, what was her name?"

For an instant, Harding appeared at a loss. Then she said, "Elena was murdered before she and Cash could name their baby."

Sylvia's eyes went wide with surprise. "But you said the child was almost two months old—"

"And my brother and Elena had been separated most of that time. Cash told me Elena wanted him to choose a formal name because he was the father." Noelle shook her head quickly as if she'd suddenly remembered something else. "Elena had a nickname for the baby. Angelina."

Little Angel. As Sylvia led the way up the narrow cement walkway, disquiet tugged at her consciousness—or perhaps it was the overload of so much new information. But she couldn't easily accept the idea that two lovers would go for weeks, even months, without choosing a formal name for their baby. She pushed open the hospital's double glass doors and entered the reception area.

A woman seated behind a desk smiled, and Sylvia greeted her with a crisp "Hello, Charlene." When she was almost past reception, she called out, "How was the Mud Ponies concert?"

Charlene grinned. "Hot."

Noelle kept pace with Sylvia along a main hallway where the walls were off-white and the rooms had no noticeable numbers. The sound of heels on tile was intensified in the hard, angular space. When they reached a reinforced door, Sylvia used a punch code to gain entry. But only after trial and error. Still, it was better than a key ring. The hospital was in the process of updating its security system, and some of the private rooms still had key locks.

The locked ward was different—the lights were dimmer and the tile was a soothing shade of pastel blue. Sylvia slowed, then stopped to glance through the window of Room 21. It was empty, and she motioned Noelle to follow once more. As they walked, Sylvia said, "I wanted Serena to participate in supervised activities. She's probably with Betsy, who's an intern and really good with kids."

They continued down the hall through another locked door. This new area consisted of offices and treatment rooms. Just beyond a small staff room that smelled of coffee, Sylvia ushered Noelle Harding into a cramped office. It contained a folding chair and a narrow desk. A notebook lay on the desk, directly in front of what appeared to be a wide mirror. Sylvia pushed aside the notebook, motioning for Noelle to step forward.

The mirror was actually an observation window. On the other side of the glass, inside a room that functioned as a play-therapy area, a young woman was seated at a low table. Just beyond the woman's easy reach, Serena was on the floor, hunched over scattered toys. The child seemed to be all knees and elbows, and her face was hidden beneath her mane of ebony hair, which had fallen loose from a ponytail.

Noelle leaned forward attentively, her composure

worn like her perfectly tailored suit. "She's holding herself in . . . she seems stiff." She glanced worriedly at
Sylvia, then returned her gaze to the scene beyond the
window. "She's not autistic—"

"You're right, she's not." Sylvia was reminded that
Noelle Harding, as founder of the Rescue Fund, would
have seen hundreds of children with diverse problems,
physical as well as psychological. This time, though, she
was watching a girl who might be family—a niece who
had been presumed dead for the last ten years.

Harding asked, "You mentioned that the hospital ran
a battery of tests on her after the accident. Did they rule
out all organic problems?"

"As far as we can tell, none of this is organically
based. We know she's experienced trauma . . . and I
believe she also exhibits aspects of a psychological disorder. It would affect her social skills, her ability to communicate with strangers." Sylvia shifted her gaze to
Noelle.

"It's some sort of communication disorder? Give me
a name."

Sylvia pushed a loose strand of hair from her cheek,
then adjusted her eyeglasses. With her hair clipped back
and the tortoiseshell rims, she resembled a young, very
serious professor. She frowned, and spoke with obvious
reluctance. "Selective mutism; it's rare—"

"How selective?"

"I can give you diagnostic criteria—failure to speak
in specific social settings despite a level of competence
with the spoken language, despite normal or above-
normal cognitive skills." Sylvia removed her glasses and
rubbed her nose gently. "But I don't think it's wise to
slap a label—"

Noelle interrupted. "All I want is information."

"Then we want the same thing. And at the moment, I have very little information about this child. From observation, I believe selective mutism is a probable factor, but there are others that may be even more relevant."

Sylvia watched the other woman closely. "Serena said one word when she saw the photograph of your brother."

The weight of Noelle Harding's body pressed against the desk. "I was told she identified Cash, but I had no idea she spoke—"

"She said, 'Dada.' *Da* is one of the first sounds preverbal children form." She didn't add that she believed Serena had spoken previously . . . two nights earlier, while keeping vigil at the house.

Sylvia hesitated just an instant, then she touched the other woman's arm reassuringly. "Are you all right?"

Noelle didn't answer. Instead, the soft voice of the intern was audible through glass. It had been Sylvia's idea to continue working with the story of the Six Swans; Betsy was reading from *Grimms' Fairy Tales*. She was in the middle of the story.

> *After watching her six brothers turn into swans, the young girl ventured deep into the forest where she found the large white birds in a rough wooden hut. The swans shook off their feathers, and for a very brief time, they regained their human form. The boys told their little sister that she could save them only by remaining mute—without giving voice to words or laughter—for six years. And that she would also be obliged to make six tiny shirts of*

wildflowers, one for each brother. "That would be much too difficult for a little girl like you." And then the girl's brothers turned back into swans once more and flew away. But the girl vowed she would free her brothers; she would remain silent for six years, and she would sew six tiny shirts of wildflowers. And without a word she climbed up into a tall tree deep in the forest, and she began to sew.

Much later, the king of that particular forest was hunting, and his huntsmen came upon the girl perched up in the tree. When they pestered her with questions, she tried to make them go away; she threw down her necklace, her belt, her stockings, everything but her dress. They would not be dissuaded; they climbed the tree and took her back to the king.

The king asked many questions. "Who are you? Why were you sitting so high up in a tree? Why won't you answer me?" He talked to her in different languages, hoping she would understand—but she refused to speak.

The king fell in love with the girl, and he took her to his castle, and he married—

"Her lips are moving! She's talking!"

Sylvia looked through the glass. Noelle was right, Serena's lips were moving—quickly, as if she were whispering urgently into some invisible ear. Was she following the story? Whatever she said was lost; her words—if indeed they were words—were inaudible.

Abruptly, Serena grabbed the picture book from the young woman's hand and flung it at the mirror. When the book thudded off the glass, Noelle Harding flinched and stepped back.

"She saw me." Noelle paused, then shook her head rapidly. "No—of course not . . . what's wrong with me? I know she can't see anything through the mirror."

Sylvia studied Noelle, but she couldn't read her expression. She was aware of the anxious ache in her own stomach, and the question looping through her mind—was the child related to Cash Wheeler? She could only imagine that Noelle was feeling the same anxiety, heightened even, by relationship and circumstance.

At that moment, Serena turned toward the observation glass. Her hair fell away from her heart-shaped face, and her features were plainly visible—wide mouth, broad nose, small chin. The charcoal-dark eyes opened wide as her gaze settled on the mirror. She stared as if she knew other eyes were watching. Not an eyelash flickered as she regarded them stonily. Then she turned away.

Noelle's shoulders slumped, and her chest barely moved beneath the pale silk fabric of her suit. Was her reaction caused by disappointment? Did Serena look like millions of other lost children in Juárez? Noelle walked quickly from the room. Uneasily Sylvia followed.

At the entrance to the hospital, Noelle thrust open the doors and strode outside. Sylvia called to her. When Noelle turned, her blue eyes glistened. The harsh sunlight bleached the warmth from her hair, turned it from blond to bone-white; her voice was low and taut as strung wire. "She doesn't look like Elena."

Sylvia felt her body contract with barely suppressed disappointment. Was the woman saying *yes* or *no*?

But Noelle spoke again. "She *is* Elena. She's my brother's little girl."

*   *   *

BY THE TIME Matt drove off the prison grounds, he had spent three hours dealing with business related to Cash Wheeler. His meetings with Rosie Sanchez had taken up most of two hours; he had been shut up with Wheeler inside a twelve-by-twelve space for another forty-five minutes; then Jim Teague, Wheeler's irritatingly flamboyant lawyer, had waylaid him outside North Facility.

As Matt guided the Caprice along Highway 14, he thought about his own response to the death row inmate. There were some sins the investigator believed pardonable—killing a child wasn't one of them. It had been more than two decades since Matt's wife and young son had died in a car crash. He still felt the loss—most days the pain was a faint ache. Had Cash Wheeler murdered his infant daughter? It seemed believable given the information Rosie had supplied via one of her correctional officers. Sure, some inmates bragged idly about crimes they didn't commit—these guys were cons, they lied about what they'd had for breakfast. Matt didn't believe Cash Wheeler was the "idle type."

But he might lie for other reasons—out of bitterness, as a defense against prison predators, to protect someone else.

Matt braked to avoid tailgaiting a slow driver on the rural road. It had been a very long day; prison always wore at him. He'd promised to catch up with Sylvia by late afternoon, but he had to stop by his office on the way. He followed Highway 14 the few miles to Cerrillos Road, turning off at the Department of Public Safety.

The main building was almost deserted. His office, part of his section's new addition, was pleasant enough. And, to his liking, it was sparsely furnished: a government-issue desk, his swivel chair, a hard metal chair for visitors—facing the window and bright southeastern sun—two filing cabinets, and a bookcase that supported a VCR and monitor.

He had bought a Coke from the vending machine, and he opened the can at his desk. Feet up, Rolodex at his fingertips, he placed a phone call to the Office of the Medical Investigator in Albuquerque; during the brief conversation he scratched notes with a fountain pen on a pad of graph paper. After he hung up, he called the El Paso Information Center.

Dale Pitkin was working on Sunday. Matt wasn't surprised. Pitkin had worked Sundays for the last dozen years; he'd worked them up in Santa Fe when he was with the governor's detail, and he worked them at E.P.I.C. in Texas. He'd always said it gave him two weekdays off when "a man can hunt and fish and spelunker without a goddamn crowd."

Now he answered his phone with his familiar drawl. "Pitkin here."

"Hey, Dale." The toes of Matt's cowboy boots pointed to ten past twelve. "Did you catch your limit last week?"

"Nope. Went caving. Just me, the wife, and the blind scorpions."

"Sounds kinky." The two men spent a few minutes catching up long-distance. Matt's segue to business was a statement. "We've got a homicide: Hispanic male, forty-five to fifty—"

"Good, you can keep him."

"We don't want him." Matt crumpled his empty Coke can accordion-style. "The postmortem's tomorrow—at this point, no match on the prints—but we do have a handmade leather belt, personalized: P-A-C-O.

Got a silver buckle." Matt tossed the can at a trash recep-
tacle by the door. The aluminum clattered as it hit
home. "I've seen all kinds of silver work . . . but I've
never seen this. Hammered silver, real ornate, maybe
some kind of Indian, maybe Aztec motif?"

Pitkin paused on the line for a moment. Matt imagined the man was cracking his knuckles, a chronic nervous habit. Dale's voice was low, teasing. "You say *Paco*?
Hell, I'll be frank." He chuckled to himself while Matt
rolled his eyes. In English, Paco translated to Frank.

Dryly, Pitkin continued. "Besides the fact he's Hispanic like five billion other guys—one billion of them
named Paco—why do you think he's one of ours?"

"He's connected to a vehicle, and your computer
tracked the El Paso license plates to a business: Hat-
Trick. A drop box."

"What do they sell, bunny rabbits?" Pitkin's throaty
laugh was beginning to irritate. "Describe that buckle
again."

Matt gazed at the Polaroid on his desk. "The grade
of silver is excellent. The technique is cutout, overlay.
The metal is beaten, pounded, but delicately shaped . . .
the design is distinctive . . . the clasp-hinge system is
unique."

"What you need is an expert on silversmithing."
Pitkin let a beat go by. "Anything else?"

"Yeah. My guess is Taxco. That's what, a hundred miles
southwest of Mexico City?" Matt tapped the edge of the
Polaroid against the phone. "You know there was a silver-
smith from Santa Fe—name of Parsons or Larson—he
went to Taxco in the 1950s, taught the locals his designs.
He had a big influence on the area's silver work."

"What happened to the guy?"

"He died, long time ago. But Taxco is famous. A couple of families have an international reputation. The designs are flavored with Indian, Aztec, Mexican motifs."

"What are you thinking?"

"The area down there—it's not far from Guadalajara."

"And Guadalajara's an infamous drug nest filled with nefarious criminals?" Pitkin cleared his throat. "The only Paco I know who might be missing . . . he's the *primo* of Amado Fortuna. You eat tuna, don't you, Matt?"

Matt sat up in his swivel chair, and his boots hit the floor. "You eat *shit*, Dale."

Pitkin snorted and let his voice ride sing-song. "The Holy Grail, Noah's Ark, the Tuna Diaries. You've heard of the Tuna Diaries, haven't you, *hombre*?"

"The next time you buy the Gold shots, I'll listen to that fusty old wives' tale again."

Dale Pitkin got serious. "You ever work with an El Paso narc named Dowd, Bobby?"

"Rings a bell. Why?"

"He's missing, too." Pitkin's voice dropped. "The thing about Paco Fortuna . . . if he happens to be your guy, he's Amado Fortuna's bookkeeper. If you caught the big *pescado*, maybe you better throw him back, call the feds. Hey, am I the information officer, or what?"

This time, Matt could actually hear knuckles cracking. Pitkin continued. "But there's someone you should talk to, one crazy *hombre*—a lone cowboy but a pretty good amigo. You ever met a Juárez fed named Vargas? Victor Vargas?"

CHAPTER NINETEEN

WITH A GRIMY baseball cap pulled low over his eyes, Victor Vargas sauntered along Avenida Paso del Norte toward the bullring. He moved with a sloping gait, hands shoved deep into his pockets, shoulders hunched beneath a grease-stained jacket.

Marking the entrance to the bullring, plastic confetti shimmied in the hot breeze. Twisting on rope ties, the brightly colored signs announced: ¡CORRIDA DE TOROS! ¡HOY! Bullfight today. But there were no crowds, there was no scheduled fight. The banners were optimistic.

He slumped another inch into his heels when he felt the touch of the street. He didn't turn to look but cut his eyes over and caught sight of a funky red van. He hoped it belonged to his associate.

Here the *avenida* widened to four lanes bordered by additional frontage routes; the complex scheme made motorized navigation almost completely impossible. Traffic merged, diverged, and collided.

Victor heard a quick honk—more accurately, a bleat—once, twice, three times. He tacked over toward the road, moving parallel to the red van, passing the passenger door just as a bag fell into his arms.

He swore violently, ready to explode. Clasping the bag under his arms, he kept moving as if nothing had happened. The clumsy exchange could cost him his life. He was almost beyond the entrance to the bullring now, but he turned sharply right, passing beneath the straining sign, into a parking area.

Victor kept walking, sending a flock of pigeons skyward. He moved between plaster arches, past food stands that were closed until the next fight.

He clutched the bag even tighter. For several anxious seconds, he thought he'd been followed. It turned out to be a dog, a mangy, parasite-ridden street hound desperate for a scrap of food. The animal was so ugly, Victor was tempted to kick it. He shook his head; he liked dogs. But some creatures seemed to beg for abuse.

He found a shaded arch, beyond the parking lot, well beyond the street. He sat, pulled his legs into the plaster lap, and opened the bag. A file was inside. It was thick, accordion-style, and bore the filing-system numbers of the M.F.J.P.—the Mexican Federal Judicial Police.

Inside the first manila folder, he found photographs. One of Amado Fortuna. Others of his associates. Of his staff.

He set the file on his lap, took a deep breath, and glanced around. What he saw was the street hound, crouched just out of kicking range. Pus drained from one of the animal's eyes. An open sore on its belly had attracted flies. Victor shook his head, searched his pockets. He found the last dregs of a bag of chile-dusted peanuts in the pocket of the greasy jacket. He emptied the sack, scattering the nuts in front of the animal, and watched them disappear. The dog offered him a wag of his tail in thanks.

Victor murmured, *"De nada."*

He found the surveillance photograph he was looking for buried deep in the folders. It pictured undercover narcotics cop Bobby Dowd walking almost shoulder to shoulder with a second man. It had been taken on a Juárez street. If you hadn't been looking for it, you would never know the two men had made contact.

Victor knew the identity of the second man. Out of habit, he turned the photograph over. It was numbered—132-w-95.

It took him fifteen minutes to find the corresponding legend. The number had two names typed carefully alongside: Dowd, E.P.P.D./Fortuna, Paco.

And to the right of the names someone had penciled three words in Spanish—*¿Proyecto Nieve Blanca???* Project Snow White???

CHAPTER TWENTY

AFTER NOELLE HARDING left Mesa Verde Hospital in the waiting limo-van, Sylvia had spent the rest of the day with Serena. The child seemed especially withdrawn, hunched over her worn coloring book, drawing intricate abstract patterns—stars and moons linked in ever-expanding chains.

Pale and distant—with dark eyes that had seen everything—Serena reminded Sylvia of an apparition, a child from a distant world. But *which* world? The question nagged at Sylvia.

Serena was no street urchin. She was thin, a waif, but she had not suffered from long-term malnourishment. If she was from a barrio in Mexico, she was one of its exceptions. If she was related to members of the drug trade, she had been educated, cared for. She was bilingual, and her artistic talents had been nurtured by someone.

The dead man they were calling Paco?

Sylvia would remember to ask Matt about plans for the man's funeral. When the body was released, would it be buried in Santa Fe?

She had pondered these things on her drive to Rosie's house. Now she pulled up and parked the truck on Hopi Street. She jumped when she caught sight of a man walking his dog—an old man with a harmless corgi tugging on the end of a leash.

She recognized her paranoia; in the circumstances it was a normal reaction to yesterday's violence. For several minutes, she watched the streets to see if someone had followed her, searched for any sign of a dark four-wheel-drive vehicle. When nothing and no one threatened, Sylvia drove two more blocks and parked directly in front of Ray and Rosie's house.

The sky was smeared with sunset colors: hot orange, turquoise blue, pink, gray. The truck radio was playing Sinead O'Connor singing "Nothing Compares 2 U." She sat back in her seat and closed her eyes, not quite ready to face people, not even friends.

The sky's palette was imprinted in her vision, the colors vibrating behind closed eyelids. Pieces of the day finally settled around her. She thought about her meeting with Noelle Harding and wondered how she was dealing with the day's revelations.

But just behind all her thoughts, like a translucent emotional scrim, she felt her longing to help Serena. It was arrogant to think that she had somehow been chosen to protect the child. Or maybe it wasn't arrogance after all; she felt as if Serena had picked her out. Circumstances continually brought people together from different worlds—the results were sometimes chaotic, occasionally even dangerous.

The sound of a child's laughter brought her out of her reverie. Down the street, a half dozen boys and girls were making the most of twilight, racing from yard to yard, dashing after a large red ball. A rowdy boy tumbled over a hedge; a smaller girl grabbed the ball and whooped. In front of one of the neat, adobe-style homes, a gray-haired man raked leaves into orderly piles. The houses in this small neighborhood had been built in the 1950s and 1960s. The lots were compact, but the tree-lined streets gave an added sense of space and comfort.

Sylvia smiled and sighed. It was time to face the Sanchez family and try to make amends for screwing up yesterday's party—*her* engagement party. A shrink would say she'd missed it because she was afraid of commitment; a shrink would be half right. She was fully committed to Matt, but the other *M* word scared the hell out of her.

As she reached over to lock the passenger door, her eyes caught a glint of silver on the floor. She grasped the child's medallion in her hand; the silver work was unusual for its careful detail and ornate overlay. A link in the chain had pulled loose. She pushed the open link over its partner and applied force with her fingers. Instant, if temporary, repair. Without thinking, she slipped the chain around her throat, the medallion settling in the cleft between her breasts. At some point yesterday in the pandemonium, Serena must have lost it.

She stepped out of the truck and heard whistling. The sound was coming from the garage. More precisely, from Ray Sanchez's lips. Sylvia found him on his back wedged beneath a battered gray Chevrolet Impala. Another set of legs, lying parallel to Ray's belonged to his eighteen-year-old son, Tomás. In Sylvia's eyes, the car was a wreck, but she knew that to the Sanchez males, it was a low-riding work of art in the making.

Ray's body appeared inch by inch from underneath the automobile, until finally his grease-smudged face was visible. "It's our hero!" With surprising agility, he was on his feet, wrapping her in a bear hug. When he finally released her, he made a show of dusting off her clothes.

"I'm sorry, Ray," Sylvia began, "I screwed up the party—"

"Sorry? You've got a fan club waiting inside."

"Yeah." Tomás had scooted out from under the Impala. He unfolded his lanky frame until he stood two inches taller than his father. "We heard he shot you!" His brown eyes glowed with admiration.

As father and son escorted her across the garage to the kitchen door Ray said, "Rosie and my *abuelita* are enjoying the sunset from the portal." A quizzical expression crossed his face. "Your party decorations are still up from yesterday."

Sylvia followed him into the kitchen. "I feel so badly—"

"Hey, we had more fun without you, *jita*." Rosie Sanchez pecked Sylvia's cheek. She was barefoot, on her way from the refrigerator, two beers in hand. "And you better watch out, Matthew almost got engaged to someone else. Remember Angelique from the lab? She just happened to invite herself over."

"You mean Angelique from latent prints? Bleached blonde, room-temperature I.Q.?" Sylvia smiled sweetly, and Rosie gave a throaty chuckle. The penitentiary investigator was one of Sylvia's oldest friends—Sylvia had gone to elementary school with Rosie's younger sister—and the women had renewed their friendship a few years back when Sylvia returned to Santa Fe from California.

Rosie raised dark eyebrows. "It's over and done, and everyone's just glad you and the little one are safe. Getting chased by a madman is a decent excuse."

"*I* don't think so."

Sylvia recognized Matt's voice coming from the portal. She accepted a beer from Rosie and stepped out the back door to find her fiancé seated next to Abuelita Sanchez. The wide, screened porch ran the length of the house. It faced west, offering a view of the sunset framed by a white wooden fence and a variety of trees.

Sylvia kissed Matt on top of his head, and she smiled down at the elegant eighty-one-year-old face of Abuelita Sanchez. Ray's grandmother occupied her garden chair like a queen on a throne. And why not? She was surrounded by generations of her family: her fifty-year-old grandson, Raymond, her great-grandson, Tomás, and his three-year-old cousin, who now utilized Matt's knee as a rocking horse.

Sylvia heard Abuelita Sanchez murmur. "Sylvia, *tienes una familia, necesites un esposo ahora.*" You have a family, now you need a husband. "*¿Matrimonio éste semana?*" The old woman's expression was serious, but she pinched Sylvia on the bottom with strong fingers.

"Did I hear someone say we're getting married this week?" Matt reached into a dish of tortilla chips. Sylvia smiled at the man she'd been involved with for the last . . . year and ten months. She shrugged.

He winked back at her, then cast a baleful eye at *la vieja.* "*¿Abuelita, comprende usted? Estoy desolado.* Sylvia's been stalling me for a year. She even goes out and gets attacked to avoid her engagement party. I think maybe I'll have to marry Angelique after all—an old flame never dies." The three-year-old squirmed his way off Matt's knee, propelling his tiny body away from the adults toward a pile of small metal race cars on the floor of the porch.

Abuelita Sanchez patted the empty chair by her side, and Sylvia sat as ordered. Through wrinkled eyelids, the grandmother studied the two lovers. After a few moments, she grunted. She produced a flask from the pocket of her floral-print dress and shook it. She unscrewed the cap, which doubled as a shot glass, poured out a full measure, and held the brew out to Sylvia. "*Salud*, Sylvia."

Gingerly, Sylvia sniffed the concoction; she caught the essence of rosemary, sage, vervain—and God knows what else. She was familiar with the old woman's herbal beverages, designed to cure rheumatism, grippe, and "female complaints." She put her lips to the shot glass and drank; she didn't dare refuse. The beverage was sticky sweet, then bitter with a zinging aftertaste, and it made her skin tingle. As she returned the small container to Abuelita Sanchez, she caught Matt watching her. His grin was cocky, insolent, and irritating as hell.

"*¡Jijito, ahora, tú!*" Abuelita Sanchez refilled the shot glass and held it out to Matt. Sylvia laughed at the old woman's familiar use of *tú*. As far as the *abuelita* was concerned, Matt was just an unruly kid.

He drank, wrinkled his nose, and wheezed dramatically. "Is this one of your love potions?" he asked.

Chortling silently, Abuelita Sanchez rattled off a response in Spanish. Matt answered, and Sylvia enjoyed the soft, sensual sounds of the language. Her own mastery of Spanish tenses was limited to present and simple past.

Matt reached across the woman's lap and pulled Sylvia close. He whispered in a deep voice: "She said she doesn't make love potions, but if I need something for arthritis, gout, or bunions, no problem."

Rosie plopped down in an empty chair. "If you're that much of a wreck, Matthew, I won't let Sylvia marry you."

"Hey, watch it—she's looking for an excuse to back out." Matt laughed, but his eyes stayed serious.

Sylvia eased her hand from Matt's grip and made a too casual show of stretching her long legs. He set his empty beer bottle on the floor, where it promptly toppled and rolled with a clatter.

He called out, "Ray! How about a quick game of one-on-one?" He tipped an imaginary hat—"Ladies"—and then disappeared into the kitchen.

Sylvia leaned forward, resting both arms on her knees. She expelled a puff of air. "He's pissed."

"Totally pissed—and only because you missed the engagement party he'd been planning for the last three months."

"Thanks for the support."

"You're welcome." Rosie's cheeks were flushed from beer, and she raised Sylvia's left hand so the *abuelita* could see the flash of metal and stone. "Did you see the ring Matt gave her?"

"Caro." Precious. The old woman lit a small candle with steady hands.

The women drank their beer in silence. Unconsciously, Sylvia pulled Serena's medallion from under her white cotton blouse. Her fingers played over the raised metal.

"What's that?" Rosie asked. Outside the screened porch, night had fallen. But the soft darkness was unsettled when a floodlight suddenly accented a rectangle of concrete behind the garage. The light was followed by the *flap-flap-flap* of a dribbled basketball and the rumble of male voices.

Sylvia lifted the chain from around her neck. "I can't keep my saints straight, but it belongs to Serena."

The *abuelita* took the necklace in her bony fingers, staring closely at the delicate carving. "*No es santo*—no saint."

Sylvia turned toward the old woman and found herself trapped by black eyes. "*Los cihuateteos.*" Abuelita clasped one withered hand over the pendant, the other over Sylvia's wrist. She said, "They walk at night, searching for children because they've lost their own."

The *viejita*'s grip was strong. "*Los cihua*—what?" Sylvia jumped when someone growled in her ear. She twisted in the chair and saw Tomás. The teenager straddled a bench and popped open a can of Coke. He gulped half its contents and wiped his lips with the back of his hand.

Tomás said, "I know a vampire." His tone was deep and extremely serious.

"Is that what they are? Los whatevers?" Sylvia asked.

"In Mexico, they call them *chupacabras*, goatsuckers." Tomás delivered this statement with academic largess.

And now Sylvia remembered. Recently, the story had been carried in the local papers and in *The Wall Street Journal*. The same vampirical-beast scare that had captivated much of Mexico a year earlier had occurred again in the Pacific-coast state of Sinaloa. Psychologists speculated that this recurrence of collective psychosis was connected to Mexico's political destabilization. But there was a twist on the most recent story: reported sightings of the bloodsucking beast had reached across the border into southern New Mexico and Texas.

Tomás said, "The vampires I know, there's this girl at school who wears black and she's real white. And I saw some on *America's Most Wanted*. They didn't have bat wings, or vampire teeth, or the horns of a goat. But they suck blood, and they murdered this girl's parents—"

"Enough, Tomás." Rosie shushed her son.

Sylvia took a swallow of beer, and the liquid foamed up, dripping down her chin. She said, "There *are* clinical vampires. The Hanover Vampire, beheaded in the early 1900s for biting and killing something like twenty-five victims. In the 1970s, the Sacramento Vampire murdered a pregnant woman, a baby, and three or four more people. Shot them, then drank their blood."

"You're as bad as Tomás," Rosie clucked.

"That's harsh," Tomás said, fascinated.

Sylvia continued. "Before the murders, he'd been in a psych hospital where he was known for biting the heads off birds. He even tried to inject rabbit blood into his veins."

Tomás leaned closer toward the flickering candle. "What happened to him?"

"F.B.I. caught him. He ended up committing suicide." Sylvia's body was completely in shadow, only her face illuminated by the glow of candlelight. "Psychoanalysts would tell you the"—she raised two fingers to the light and dipped them in quotes—"*vampire* suffers

oral-sadistic rage because of maternal rejection. Then
he banishes those impulses, splits them off to some dis-
sociated portion of his ego. Teeth and mouth are all
about the late oral stage—you've got sadistic biting,
controlled feeding, and, ultimately, merger because the
victim ends up a vampire."

"That's crazy." Rosie bit into a chip loaded with salsa.

"Go on!" Tomás said.

Sylvia gave Rosie a light jab to the leg. "The
Jungians have a different theory on vampires. They
talk about narcissism, self-obsession, moral self-
absorption. The vampire is the perfect reflection of
our culture—our obsession with ourselves. The vampire is the ultimate narcissist; he thirsts for himself in
others—relates to others only as they reflect his image
back to him. Remember, he has no image of his own in
the mirror."

Unconsciously, Sylvia had acquired a slight Lugosi
accent. "He exists in grandiose isolation, he's empty, and
in an effort to refill himself, he 'drains' those closest to
him—but he can't allow himself to acknowledge the
depth of his pathology, his destructive power, so he
'sleeps' in the day and walks at night."

"The living dead," Tomás intoned carefully. "But the
chupacabra is not just psychological stuff. I'm telling
you, it's *real*."

"Narcissists are definitely real." Sylvia laughed. "You
mean your *chupa*-thing rides around on a broom and
sucks the blood of innocent children?" She bit back the
urge to add something about Catholic hocus-pocus or
mumbo-jumbo and men in funny hats.

Abuelita Sanchez interrupted in her low, gruff voice.
"Sylvia, you don't believe because you're a faithless infi-

del. When I was a girl, I saw *el vampiro*. In the cornfield at night. He came out of the *acequia*.

"It was the year all the corn rotted and the *acequias* dried up. I came over for the first time to stay with *mi tío*. This girl Erlinda and her family lived near Ojo Sarco. One day, we were walking in the arroyo. We saw a big black dog run into the trees ahead. I followed, but my friend refused to go." Abuelita's head and hands shook very slightly—age or fear? "A few minutes later I heard my friend Erlinda scream. When I found her again, her leg was broken, the bone sticking out like a branch."

"Did she fall?" Sylvia asked. Her eyes had grown big in spite of her cynicism, her Ph.D.

Abuelita Sanchez turned to stare. "The dog had doubled back and jumped on her. She fought and screamed. But when she was down, he tore open her leg, licked her blood."

Sylvia said, "I have the same problem in my neighborhood; no one controls their dogs. They run wild and pack—they killed a burro. And they almost killed a little boy last year."

Tomás spoke up. "This is different, Sylvia."

The *abuelita* remained silent. Sylvia stared at her. "But what does the *chupacabra* have to do with the medallion?"

The old woman's raisin-sized pupils seemed to shimmer. "In Mexico—and in some parts of Latinoamerica—parents give these medals to their little ones, to keep them safe from the *vampiro, el demonio*. Without the medallion, a child is vulnerable."

Abuelita Sanchez nodded pendulously. Her gray hair seemed to cast a glow. "Someone cared very much about your little girl. And now you care for her, too. Give her back her protection. Keep her safe from the evil one."

By ELEVEN P.M., the fever from the infection was blistering Renzo Santos. His skin was on fire. His eyeballs shriveled and shrank in their sockets. His skin peeled back from his neck and face. He was sure his bones would pop from their ball joints.

Renzo bit down on the washcloth stuffed between his teeth. Even when he was caught in the delirious arms of fever, he knew he could not cry out; someone in the hotel would hear and call the police.

Past midnight, the Virgin de Guadalupe came to see him when the flame was at its hottest. She came as she had appeared to Juan Diego—Cuauhtlatóhuac—in Mexico three centuries earlier. But now she sat on the edge of the bed, and she pressed her palm to Renzo's forehead. Her touch was cool, soothing. He thought he saw tears stain her cheeks. Her eyes were an ocean of empathy—so much pity, so much sorrow. She was more beautiful than she had looked long ago when his mother took him to pray at her feet.

Before he could thank her, she disappeared.

Dirty, bloody Coatlicue made the bed shake when she sat in place of *La Virgen*. Her eyes were red. Her face was black. She stank of rotting flesh. When she opened her mouth, snakes crawled out from between her lips. They slithered between her withered breasts, they twined between her thighs. Into the world they carried slime from the goddess's viscera.

Renzo cried out, biting even harder on the towel, cutting his own tongue. He raised one hand to ward off the poisonous animals. Coatlicue kept screaming that she had been buried too young; buried in a closed casket because he had destroyed her face and her body. That's when he understood that it was not the angry goddess, but Elena who screamed at him. She wanted revenge. She cut out his beating heart with a knife, eating it in front of his eyes.

He wept as he watched his pulsing heart devoured. His mouth was so dry he thought his teeth would crumble. Through the early morning, he stayed rigid with pain until he finally fell into fitful sleep.

Before dawn, his eyes flew open. He sat up, his body still oddly stiff. He made it to the bathroom. For minutes he could not find himself in the mirror. But slowly, his reflection filled the glass. His battered and bruised face looked younger, newer, somehow fresh. Through thin hotel walls, he heard a toilet flushing. Someone else was awake, if only for a moment.

Someone was banging on his door. He waited—without answering—until it grew quiet once more. When he cracked the door and peered out, he saw that a tray of food had been left on the welcome mat. Had he ordered food? Yes, he remembered vaguely . . .

He set the tray on a table and returned to the bathroom. This time, when he cleaned and dressed his wounds— removing dead tissue and pus—the pain was bearable. He swallowed more painkillers and injected himself with penicillin.

He walked out of the bathroom feeling revitalized, reborn. He sat in front of the food tray, took the stainless steel covers from the plates, and gazed down at three rare steaks and a full loaf of bread. He poured himself a glass of Burgundy from a bottle he had saved.

He ate, drank, ate again. As food filled his stomach, he realized the extent of his hunger. He was ravenous. When he was finished with the meal, only a small portion of meat remained on the plate.

For almost an hour, Renzo sat stuporously. His stomach was full, his belly protruding, but the hunger was not gone.

He returned to the bathroom, where he swabbed one arm with iodine. With his gold straight-edged razor, he made an incision on the inside of his left elbow, cutting deep into the median cubital vein.

He lifted his arm to his mouth, and he drank from the wound.

CHAPTER TWENTY-ONE

MATT ENGLAND STOOD inches from a dozen vials filled with cloudy blue liquid, which were arranged in a small wooden stand in the chemistry section of the D.P.S. crime lab. Serologist Hansi Gausser was busy rinsing his gloved hands in a decontamination basin.

"If you break those, I'll kill you," Gausser said.

"I'm too young to die." Matt backed away from the glass vials and bumped into the edge of a computer monitor, nudging the keyboard but avoiding the rectangular body of the gas chromatograph/mass spectrometer.

Gausser made a face. "Trash the GC/MS while you're at it."

"Anything to make you happy." From street experience and basic forensic-science classes, Matt had learned the rudimentary chemistry of drug identification. For instance, he knew gas chromatography provided a tentative I.D. by separating a drug from its diluents. But chromatography, in combination with mass spectrometry, was a whole other ball game: GC/MS separated the components of a drug and provided positive identification of each substance in the mixture.

When a sample was injected into a heated port, a carrier gas swept it into the GC column, where it was separated into components; electrons caused the sample molecules to fragment, and those fragments were isolated according to mass and counted. The computer data system monitored the entire show, and a printer spat out a paper displaying a series of lines, graphs, and numbers. In a courtroom, in the hands of an expert witness, that printout could work miracles.

At the moment, Matt held a page in each fist; he stared at lines representing abundance and mass/charge. They might as well have been Greek. He said, "Both printouts look the same to me."

"You're a genius!" Hansi wiped his hands with a flourish and took possession of the pages. "They *are* the same. Or they may as well be. And they match *this*." He waved a third printout: "This is the residue you found in Bowan's cell. Take a wild guess—what do you think it was cut with?"

Matt propped his butt against a counter that was noticeably clear of obstacles. He said, "Quinine? Baking soda? Ajax? Shit? I don't know. If it would give them a buzz, the guys at the joint would shoot up kitty litter."

"Nothing."

"Nothing?"

"It wasn't cut."

Matt's spine straightened like a rod, and his mouth fell open. "What are you telling me? The shit Bowan overdosed was pure heroin?"

Gausser shook his head and tapped a finger against

one section of the printout. He said, "It's not heroin. At least not your growing-in-the-poppy-fields heroin. It's C-ring etheno Diels Alder adducts of thebaine."

"Say what?"

"Etorphine; it's not a true synthetic analgesic. Clandestine lab operators played around with it back in the early eighties after Shulgin's article on the future of synthetic drug abuse was published."

"So you're telling me Bowan overdosed on a synthetic drug that's like heroin?"

Gausser jutted his lower lip and wagged his head, considering his answer. "Etorphine has an analgesic potency about a thousand times that of heroin."

"Jesus." Matt whistled. "*Jesus.*" The usual cut for heroin at the joint was anywhere from 5 to 40 percent—maybe even 70 percent, if it was a primo load. He pictured Bowan in his cell, injecting himself with 911 or White Horse or Red Rum or whatever they currently called the most potent forms of heroin.

Turn "Red Rum" around and you got "murder." Just like Bowan. Only the inmate had injected something that would give him a thousand times the normal rush.

Matt asked, "What about the high—is it the same as the real stuff?"

"I can't tell you that. It depends on the synthesis process. Some of the synthetics have neurotoxic properties. Some of them have been proven to cause full-out Parkinsonian symptoms. That was a problem with MPTP. . . . Never mind."

Matt ran his hand over the top of his head. "So that might explain why Bowan worked himself over before he died."

"It might." Gausser had been watching the investigator, and he figured he knew what Matt was thinking. But the serologist wasn't finished with his presentation. He'd done some detective work that made him proud. He said, "Aren't you going to ask me about the other printouts?"

"Hell, Hansi, what about the other printouts?"

"They're identical to the first printout."

"You already told me that."

"But I didn't tell you where they're from." He waved a page. "This is a sample from a bust two weeks ago in Farmington. And this one"—he gestured toward the final printout—"it's the sample from your corpse—your Juan Doe—out on Two eighty-five."

Matt stared at Hansi Gausser as if he hadn't heard a word. His face didn't change expression; only his eyebrows moved. After three long beats, he said, "Run that by me again. The stuff we found in the dead guy's pockets and the shit that killed Bowan and a bag from Farmington—they're from the same batch?"

"I didn't say that. I can't say that. They're etorphine, on paper they match up like triplets. And that means you've got an extremely potent drug flooding the Land of Enchantment."

"And a bunch of junkies in for a nasty surprise." Matt closed his eyes.

Hansi nodded. "I'd say emergency rooms around the state are going to have their hands full."

"We already lost Bowan." Matt was beginning to feel extremely uncomfortable. Fragments of conversation ran through his mind—yesterday's call to Dale Pitkin in El Paso, and the implication that the dead man might be Paco Fortuna, cousin of drug kingpin Amado Fortuna. Dale was right: the Tuna was a very big fish, and Matt was one small cop.

Pitkin had called back this morning to pass on more disturbing news. His friend the Juárez cop, Victor Vargas, had gone missing. Pitkin was trying to track Vargas down via the snitch network.

Dale had gone quiet on the phone for a moment before adding, "This is not a good sign, amigo."

Matt agreed with Pitkin. Now he glommed on to Gausser with both eyes and said, "I witnessed the Juan Doe autopsy this morning." For the moment, he wasn't voicing the possibility that Juan Doe might be Paco Fortuna. He glanced at a workspace at the other end of the room just as a woman in a white lab coat pulled a bloody swatch of cloth from a paper bag.

Gausser grunted. "How's my buddy the fair M.I.? Did you learn anything worth the hundred miles to Albuquerque and back?"

"I learned Juan Doe looked like shit." Matt crushed a Life Saver between his molars. Lee Begay, the chief medical investigator, was an old friend. More times than Matt could count, she'd helped him out when he needed information.

"Funny how desiccation, decomposition, and decay rob a man of his youthful glow."

Matt shook his head. "Begay says it looked like he fought hard against the perp, but he wasn't healthy. She's betting on cancer."

Gausser gave a snort. "I wouldn't get too excited when the M.I. gives you her best bets. That's like getting astrological predictions." Gausser and Begay knew each other, but their relationship had been born with a streak of good-natured rivalry that grew over the years.

Matt smiled to himself, but his voice remained flat.

"Then I won't bother to give you her best bet on the C.O.D."

"All right, I'll bite."

"Try a long, sharp instrument inserted into the base of his brain." Matt pulled a pack of Life Savers from his shirt pocket and offered the candy to Gausser.

Gausser shook his head. "Those things will rot your teeth. If the vic was stabbed here"—he slapped Matt gently on the back of his head—"we're talking bleeding in the brain—a major headache."

"The orange ones are full of vitamin C." Matt held up a Life Saver between two fingers and then popped it between his lips. He held the same fingers to his neck. "His left carotid was severed *before* death—severed very neatly—and then the knife to the brain stem and—as a parting gesture—he was turned on his side and left to drain out."

Gausser said, "He bled out heavily into the dirt around the site."

"Heavily?" Matt pulled his gaze back to Gausser and said, "The body was almost completely drained of blood."

"I'LL NEED TO see the transcripts of the trial, the crime-scene reports, newspaper clippings, private-investigation results." Sylvia leaned forward in the chair and ticked off each item with a finger. "Basically I want access to every file on the investigation and the prosecution of the Elena Cruz murder."

"Is that all?" Jim Teague's eyebrows arched toward his scalp, and he expelled air in a derisive snort. His shoulders appeared even bigger when draped with the trademark fringed and beaded jacket, his bulk stressing his oak swivel chair to the breaking point. The lawyer's size and bearing made him an impressive sight behind his wide desk. His office was spacious and designed for practicality at the cost of elegance. Files were piled on either side of Teague's elbows. Stacks of books rose like stalagmites from the floor.

The lawyer leaned back in his chair. "Why should I show you even one file?"

Noelle Harding began to speak, but Teague raised a hand. "Noelle, please, you pay me well."

Sylvia waited a moment, then said, "Anything I learn about Serena's background will help with her treatment. If she is your client's daughter, then I've got something to work with, a place to begin . . . and Serena has a history." Sylvia was seated across the desk from Teague; Noelle Harding was at her back.

"Cash has agreed to a paternity test," Noelle said. "He wants the blood drawn at a private testing facility."

Teague's eyes were bright with ire. "Even if we prove paternity, Cash's daughter was an infant at the time of the murders."

"She was seven weeks old." Noelle Harding's voice was soft.

Sylvia kept her gaze on Teague. "A seven-week-old child is a preverbal witness. She experienced the loss of her mother, a loss that occurred through a violent act, and now, ten years later, she's probably witnessed a second murder."

Teague frowned. "You're not trying to dole out some psycho mumbo-jumbo that says this child would remember her mother's murder."

Sylvia shook her head impatiently. "If Serena was present at the time of the murder—even at seven weeks old—I'm telling you she was deeply affected by whatever occurred."

She didn't shrink under Teague's stare. Language was the most powerful human weapon of transmission, information, socialization. Studies of the origin of language had shown infants were extremely sophisticated in their ability to distinguish the phonemes of the planet's four thousand or so remaining tongues. It was possible for some five-month-old infants to distinguish between Hindi, Navajo, and Eskimo tongues. Why was it difficult for intelligent adults to accept the fact that any infant would recognize and be affected by the intimate proximity of violence?

Sylvia pressed the palms of her hands on the edge of the lawyer's desk, and her voice deepened. "Serena is physically capable of speech—silence is an extreme sacrifice. I want to know what's driven her to make that sacrifice. I want to know where she's been for the past ten years."

"My files won't provide those answers."

"I need a place to start." Sylvia shifted her body deep into the chair. "Ultimately," she said, "what helps Serena might also help Cash Wheeler."

Teague wiped a hand across his brow. "Even if it turns out this child is related to Cash, it's unlikely that fact will have any bearing on his murder conviction."

"The only thing that will free my brother is a detailed confession from the real killer." Noelle stepped to the edge of the lawyer's desk, picked up a fountain pen, and began to flick it between her fingers. The action seemed to irritate Teague, but he said nothing.

The silence stretched. Sylvia felt the stillness like electricity against her skin.

Finally Teague sighed. "There's a possibility the paternity issue could work in our favor. That depends on the A.G.'s office, if they'll play ball."

"A blood test will show within a ninety percent probability if the child was fathered by my brother," Noelle said.

She paced a few steps; even in the small space, her presence demanded attention. "The legal process is slow, and best left to lawyers. We're dealing with state agencies, federal agencies, even international interests. Until the paternity issue is settled, I'm going to assume this child is my blood relation. And I will offer her every resource I can. That includes allowing Dr. Strange access to case files."

Teague and Noelle locked eyes. They might as well have locked horns.

The lawyer cleared his throat, wiped a big hand across his big face. He spoke to a spot on the wall beyond Sylvia's head. He said, "You and I will settle the confidentiality issues before you have access to anything in my files. I'll have my paralegal draft a binding agreement."

Sylvia assumed she had been the object of his address. She nodded.

Harding dropped the pen into its holder. When it hit the desk and rolled to the carpeted floor, she ignored Teague's unhappy reaction and shifted her attention to Sylvia. "As far as I'm concerned, Serena's life begins today. I don't believe in focusing on the past—I've always moved forward in my life. The children under my care start fresh, and they thrive." She shrugged. "I don't expect any psychologist to agree with my viewpoint."

"Good," Sylvia said succinctly.

Noelle's mouth compressed into a small smile. "By

the way, Cash has agreed to meet with you." She noted Sylvia's obvious surprise. "I don't guarantee he'll be helpful, but you'll have your shot."

Sylvia nodded slowly. She kept her eyes on Noelle's face, but her thoughts turned inward to an image that was clear in her mind—the first time she had seen Serena. If Cash Wheeler was the child's father, what would it do for her to discover him a few days before he was scheduled to die? Wouldn't it be better if she were adopted by a new family? If she could start "fresh," as Noelle insisted? But Sylvia couldn't shake her belief that Serena's salvation lay in uncovering the truth about her past, whatever that truth might be.

"Cash is expecting you tomorrow morning at nine o'clock. I know you're never late." Noelle perched briefly on the chair next to Sylvia, flashed a smile, and glanced at her wristwatch. "Before you meet with my brother, you'll have questions for Jim about the case, so I'll leave you two alone." She stood and walked toward the door. Her stride was light and agile. She set one hand on the doorknob and said, "I want you to come up to the house tomorrow night; I'm having a get-together. A fund-raiser, but we'll find some time to talk. I want to hear how it goes with my brother."

Noelle raised her eyebrows, and her face held a hint of the coquette. "You're welcome to bring your friend—Matt England?" And then she was out the door, leaving a void in her wake.

Sylvia raised her eyebrows. A get-together? She'd just been invited to the Rescue Fund Gala—at the Frank Lloyd Wright house. She turned back to Jim Teague.

He was bent over a faded orange file folder, effectively masking any response to Harding's demand that he cooperate with Sylvia. He said, "For the most recent appeal my best paralegal produced an abstract of the entire case to date. You're welcome to look at it."

Behind the file and Teague's mass, a four-paned window offered a view of the Atchison, Topeka & Santa Fe Railway spur. At the moment, a shiny silver locomotive occupied the track. Sylvia recognized it as the American Orient Express, the local that carried tourists the twenty-odd miles to Lamy for dinner and drinks.

The same train that had collided with a Honda just a few nights ago.

She said, "I'd prefer a brief summary from you."

Teague lowered the file; his face looked slightly pink. He cleared his throat and said, "I don't think you appreciate how brutal the crimes were. Especially Elena's murder. From the forensic evidence, the stab wounds were inflicted in a manner that caused suffering." He coughed. "The pathologist reconstructed a rough chronology. She did not die quickly."

"She was tortured?"

"In the pathologist's opinion."

"What did the prosecution use for motive?"

"Cash was under extreme stress. Unmarried father of an unwanted child. A marital crisis."

"Was that true? Was the baby unwanted?"

"Cash Wheeler was nineteen years old," Teague said. "I think he experienced deep conflict over the child's birth, but I have never doubted his love of Elena Cruz."

"Now you're a shrink?"

Teague laughed, caught off guard. "I always put my client's needs first." He began again with a deep sigh. "Cash Wheeler and Elena Cruz met at St. Sebastian's School in El Paso. They grew up together, fell in love, and eventually, they became lovers. In the fall of 1984, when Cash was barely nineteen and Elena was sixteen, she got pregnant. She gave birth to a baby girl in a Catholic charity hospital; the nuns tried to convince her to give the child up for adoption. She insisted she wanted to marry Cash."

"Noelle says that Elena called the baby Angelina."

The lawyer nodded, fingering the fringe on his jacket sleeve. His voice settled into its honeyed stride. "Cash left Texas after the baby was born and ended up in Loving, New Mexico, looking for work. Loving's a town of roughly eight thousand; in 'eighty-five, the population was approximately half that number. Cash took a room at the Sunshine Motel. It's been torn down since, but at that time it was located about three miles outside of town. When they redid the interstate back in 'eighty, it was a motel for road workers. But times change, and on that particular Thursday, Cash was the only customer."

Sylvia realized she had shifted in the chair, tilting forward, and her back was uncomfortably stiff. She could hear the faint noise of the railroad and motor traffic coming from outside.

Teague didn't seem to notice, continuing with the story of the murders: "The motel owner's wife was at the desk that afternoon when Elena Cruz arrived, dusty and exhausted from buses and hitchhiking. She'd run away from the nuns, and she'd been traveling all day with a colicky baby."

"Was Cash at the motel when Elena arrived?"

"No. He'd started the day looking for work but ended up in a bar. Drank enough to get loaded, then the bartender threw him out." Teague took a breath. "Meanwhile, the owner's wife let Elena into the room, closed up the office, and drove into town to run errands. She left her husband napping in his room behind the office.

"Three hours later, she found his body in the parking lot. He'd been hacked to death." His voice wavered. "Elena had been stabbed thirteen times."

Sylvia was startled by the shrill blast of a whistle; outside, the train . . . Her concentration swayed for a moment, then settled again on the lawyer.

"The prosecution had a field day. Cash Wheeler was found in the motel room with Elena's body. He was covered in both victims' blood." Pause. "His prints were on the knife." Teague took another audible breath, and the silence stretched. "The baby's body was never found."

Sylvia said nothing, but the images were vivid in her mind. "Did Cash confess?" she asked.

"His story was this. He claimed he didn't know Elena was coming that day. After he was tossed out of the bar he wandered around by the river, fooled around, smoked some marijuana. He was depressed about not getting work. When he arrived at the motel, drunk and stoned, someone attacked him. He doesn't remember who—or anything else, until he heard the motel owner's wife screaming."

"What about the baby?"

"The Pecos River runs deep and fast about a quarter mile east of where that motel stood. It's actually a good fishing river. Two witnesses, fishermen, saw a man standing on the middle of a wooden bridge that spans the river. They said the man dropped a small bundle into the water. Later, searchers found a blanket but no body. They never found a body."

"So they couldn't accuse him of murdering the child."

"They didn't need to. They got him for Elena's murder and the murder of a witness. Under the state's new death-penalty statutes." Teague shrugged. "Public opinion branded Cash guilty of the baby's murder, too."

"The case was tried in Hubbs?"

"Cash had a public defender. He and his sister had no money—until she married 'oil' a few years later. That's when I got involved."

"Was it a fair trial?"

"The witnesses were reliable—as witnesses go. There were no obvious procedural errors. It was straightforward. That's made it difficult to gain a foothold on the appeals." Teague hesitated, seemed to be debating something, then apparently made up his mind to continue. "Due process was served—unless you don't like the idea that a district attorney made his career on the conviction."

Sylvia leaned back in the leather chair and allowed the story to settle into her bones; there was a lot to absorb. The silence didn't seem to bother Teague. He sat quietly with his own thoughts. On one wall, a fine old train clock ticked comfortably.

When Sylvia finally asked a question, Teague seemed to have forgotten she was still in the room. She said, "I've got plenty of questions, but let's start with one. If Cash Wheeler didn't murder Elena Cruz, who did?"

"Ah, that's the pickle, isn't it?" The lawyer twined his fingers and set his elbows on his massive desk. His small eyes sparkled with intelligence.

"We were never able to get far on our only other lead. It seems there was a weird kid named Jesús. He was in love with Elena and sick with jealousy—or so Cash has always claimed. There was some evidence that Jesús disappeared in Mexico." Teague sighed. "It didn't sit well with the jury."

*   *   *

MATT FLIPPED A chicken breast over the hot flames and said, "State police found a Chevy Suburban, license plate KCZ 310, bloodstains on the driver's seat."

Sylvia sat up abruptly in the lawn chair. "Where?"

"Outside Columbus, near the Santa Theresa border crossing into Mexico. It was abandoned."

"So he's gone?"

"Maybe." Matt was cautious.

"You think he's still around?"

"His vehicle is four hundred fifty miles from Santa Fe. He probably is, too. From your description—and the amount of blood in the vehicle—he was in bad shape. He'd have to be superhuman to present a threat in the near future."

"But if this is about drugs, there might be other guys—"

"There might. That's why the child is where she is. For the moment, she's safe."

Sylvia sighed. Ten minutes earlier, she'd arrived home from Jim Teague's office to find Matt tending the barbecue. Now Rocko pushed his cold, wet muzzle against the palm of her hand. She scratched the terrier's head, murmuring a half-truth, "The vet says Nikki might come home soon, Mr. Rock. You'll have your sweetheart back."

What the veterinarian had actually said could be interpreted in several ways: Nikki was still in critical condition, but she was an exceptionally strong animal. There was a good chance she would recover.

The wiry mutt grunted. His muzzle quivered and his nostrils flared as he picked up the scent of grilling chicken and green chiles. The smells were too tantalizing to resist; Rocko trotted over to sit beside Matt and the rusty, well-worn barbecue. One short bark, and Sylvia saw her lover slip the terrier a tiny scrap of meat. Matt's absolute rule for dogs: no rewards for begging. He broke it all the time.

Matt prodded the cooking chicken with the tip of a long fork. "How did it go with the kid today?"

"It's getting pretty interesting." Sylvia took a sip of a very pleasing cabernet. "I told you I'm working with the scripted narrative form, using the Grimms? I think Serena's responding." She saw his eyebrows raised in query, and she shook her head, anticipating the question. "She hasn't started speaking aloud. Not yet. But she will."

"Isn't Grimms too *grim*?" Without appearing to, Matt watched Sylvia transform—when she went into her abstract shrink-think mode, whatever *that* was, she came up with some amazing stuff.

"The Brothers are fabulously gruesome and perfect for kids. The tales deal with separation anxiety, death anxiety, all the mortal fears children experience so deeply—they deal with these fears directly, offer solutions, and they work on different levels."

"If I sit in your lap, will you read me a story?"

But Sylvia was on a roll; she held up fingers, listing facts: "Serena was kept in an enclosed space, some type of controlled environment—when she's outside, she hides, she buries, her actions are obsessive. Her internal mythic motif is highly developed—it's clear in her artwork and in her response to fairy tales and bedtime stories. She's religious, spiritual—even mystical.

"I'm wondering about Serena's primary caregiver. Was it the man? Serena responds easily to maternal attention—the bathtub routine, the milk and cookies, the story." Consternation twisted Sylvia's mouth. "What if she's completely alone—"

"Then she has you." He was matter-of-fact. "One thing about you, Sylvia. You won't let her down."

Sylvia's eyes were wide with worry, but she smiled, letting the weak rays of October sunshine soak into her skin. Ivory Joe Hunter's version of "Since I Met You Baby" began to play on the portable CD player. She closed her eyes, tapping her fingers to the lazy rhythms, and suddenly the tang of green chile drifted in front of her face. Opening her eyes, she saw Matt's hand—and an edible offering. She accepted, tasting the rich flavors of wood smoke, grilled meat, and the hot bite of Hatch chile. The very last of the fresh crop for another year. There would be snow and ice, holidays, rain, mud, and one-hundred-degree temperatures before New Mexico's chile was ready for another harvest.

"Can we forget about work for a few minutes?" Matt kept his eyes on her face.

She yawned, smiled, shrugged. "Already done. I was thinking how much I love you." The aftertaste of chile was beginning to burn on her lips.

"Liar." Matt grinned. "If I know anything, you were still thinking about the kid. Or food."

She stood slowly and stretched. "I'm lucky."

"I know." He watched suspiciously as she moved slowly toward him. "Why?"

"I've got a man who's a terrific cop, a fabulous fuck, and a gourmet cook."

"Grilled chicken and chile, that's gourmet?" Matt slid his arms around Sylvia.

"Absolutely."

"Whaddaya know." He let Sylvia take his right hand

in hers. She pressed against him and began to lead him in a slow dance. Matt groaned—embarrassed, secretly pleased—but he didn't resist.

For a minute, neither of them spoke. Just the two of them, alone and slow-dancing on the small wooden deck, sheltered by a coyote fence and isolation. Two lovers, a mutt, and some curious ravens on the power pole.

When the song was almost over, Matt began to talk in a soft voice that was almost a whisper. He was talking to the top of Sylvia's head, but she heard him. He said, "I want you to know something. I'm the lucky one. I know you love me." His fingers pressed against the ring she wore on her left hand—the ring that had belonged to his great-grandmother. "And you're committed to our relationship."

She started to look up at him, but he kept her pressed so close to his body she couldn't move. So she listened.

"I also know marriage scares you to death," he said. "Because of your father and all that. Marriage scares you so much I don't know if we'll ever make it to the altar." Matt gripped her even tighter. "It's supposed to be men who don't want to get married."

Now Sylvia did pull away. She lifted her chin, half defiant, half joking. "If we just live together, we'll save on taxes."

Matt gave her a gentle push, and she fell backward into the chaise. He brushed the palms of his hands together—*that's that*—and leaned in close. "I'm flying down to Juárez tomorrow. I'll be gone a night or two. Why don't you spend some time, think about what you want for a relationship."

She nodded, and she was quiet for a few moments. Finally she asked, "Why Juárez?"

"I've got a lead I need to follow up." Dale Pitkin had

left a cryptic message on Matt's home number: "Our friend will meet you tomorrow morning, Stanton Street bridge, Mexico side."

Sylvia swallowed her words of warning; Matt would take care of himself. "How long will you be gone?"

"That depends. I may turn around and fly back tomorrow. I may stay another day. I'll call, let you know what I find." He ran his hands under her T-shirt, along her belly.

Sylvia stretched lazily, guiding his fingers beneath the waistband of her boxer shorts, and even lower, to her thighs. The chile on his fingers stung her skin. The sensation was somewhere between pleasure and pain . . . mostly pleasure. "Since you're going to be in Mexico, can I borrow your truck?"

He nodded, his voice low, his hands busy. "Swear to me you will not speed. It's scheduled for a tune-up. And don't forget the gas gauge. . . ."

"No speedometer, no heater, no radio . . ." She bit his neck, then released him. "No defrost, and no car phone." She pressed the palm of her hand to his groin. Her eyes widened. "Whaddaya think, I'm soft?"

He raised his head just long enough to say, "Tough as nails, persistent as a hungry mosquito."

SYLVIA WATCHED CASH Wheeler's name swim in front of her eyes. She had inches of documents and transcripts on her study desk. She adjusted her reading glasses and massaged the narrow ridge of her nose. At midnight, she'd left Matt sleeping in bed next to Rocko. She needed the time to begin examining the case files on Wheeler's murder trial. Now sleep was threatening to catch up with her.

She jerked awake, only then aware she had nodded off. To refresh herself she made a pot of coffee. With a full mug of steaming French roast she sat down at her desk, tackling the pages once more. Yawning, she thumbed through the pile for something new. Her fingers settled on a worn and discolored manila file labeled: POSTMORTEM.

The autopsy photographs of Elena Cruz and the motel owner were grisly, but they weren't as disconcerting as the actual crime-scene photos. By the time a corpse had been placed on the autopsy table in the coroner's office—or the Office of the Medical Examiner, as it was called these days—there was something anonymous and sterile about the whole procedure. But crime-scene photographs displayed vivid touches of real life—personal articles, recognizable locations, human moments of a life or lives interrupted. Elena Cruz had multiple stab wounds. She'd been tortured before death. Jim Teague had been right when he said the crime had been brutal.

Without considering the hour, Sylvia picked up the phone and began to dial. Only then did she remember she needed the lawyer's phone number. She flipped through her files until she found Teague's business card. While the telephone rang, she composed the message she would leave.

Jim Teague answered with a sleepy grunt, definitely irritated.

Flustered, Sylvia identified herself.

Teague yawned. "Do you always call people in the middle of the night?"

"I wanted to leave a message. I thought I was dialing your office—"

"The call was forwarded. What do you want?"

"I need to know about Jesús."

"Who?"

"The boy you mentioned—the weird one who liked Elena."

"Oh." Teague's hand brushed the receiver's mouthpiece. Muffled voices were audible for several seconds, then Noelle Harding came on the line.

She didn't bother donning social graces but said, "Big Jim fell asleep on the couch again. He works twenty-three hours a day and forgets to go home."

Sylvia made embarrassed noises of agreement. *On the couch? Whose house was this?*

Noelle continued. "Jesús disappeared, vanished, and two very efficient private investigators couldn't track him down. Neither could the police."

"But there must be some information on him." There was silence, then another muffled exchange between Noelle and Jim Teague. Were they lovers? Sylvia found that unbidden thought bouncing around her brain. For some reason, she found the idea unnerving.

Noelle's voice softened. "Jesús went to school with Cash, and me, and Elena. Very briefly. The closest the investigators came to him was when they located the mother of a boy named Jesús Portrillo. She was a street whore."

"What about her son?"

"Dead. Overdosed on drugs, died in a gutter. Good night, Sylvia."

Sylvia stared at the phone, finally clicking it off. She switched on the screen of her laptop. For a long while she watched the flashing cursor against the blue screen of her computer. When that grew old, she played a round of solitaire and three games of Minesweeper. All the time, her mind was racing.

At a few minutes after one o'clock, Sylvia decided to check her E-mail, shut down the computer, and go back to bed. She logged on-line and pulled up new mail. There was a message from Harry in California.

Sylvia:
Did you inherit your mother's brown eyes? We hit it off. She was open about your dad. I'll bring you up to date when I've got a full report. Today's question: Do you ever remember him mentioning a girlfriend? Or a woman named Cora Tate? That would've been when you were twelve or thirteen.

Yours by the hour—Harry

Her response was short and to-the-point:

Dear Harry: Cora Tate? What was she, his lover or something? No, don't remember any Coras. But I do need to end this book, this saga. Find my ever-loving dad!

THROUGH ONE BARELY open eye, Matt watched Sylvia tiptoe back to bed. Her face was visible, though only for an instant, in the moonlight. Dark hair tousled around her face, pajamas rumpled. He thought she looked about ten years old—and sad. He wondered if her sadness was caused by the issue of marriage—or child? When she was settled under the cotton blanket, he sleepily flung one arm over her belly and snuggled close.

CHAPTER TWENTY-TWO

NARCO COP BOBBY Dowd crawled back to semiconsciousness from a deep ragged tear in the center of the earth. Manic monkeys and a woman with half a face had been chasing him around for hours. Then, for some short-lived eternity, he was caught in a video-game grid; he eventually figured out the grid was nothing remotely high-tech, just the filthy, smelly orange-and-brown plaid carpet directly under his nose.

Without moving a muscle, Bobby tried to reconstruct the last few hours of his life. A shadow hovered on his brain, something about fairy tales.

Snow White.

Oh, yeah . . .

The moment Bobby Dowd got a little bit pleased with himself for his recall abilities, one of Fortuna's gangsters gave him a swift kick in the butt. In the kidneys, was more like it. The Kicker had big feet, and he was hurling insults.

He kept repeating, *"¿Qué te ha dicho, Paco?"* Kick. *"¿Dónde están los libros?"* Kick. *"¡Dime el nombre!"* Kick. *"¿Quién compró los libros?"*

Bobby groaned. Damn, that hurt. He curled up into a tighter ball, bracing himself for the pain that came with even the slightest movement. After a few moments, he rolled over and stared up at the ceiling. Well, that was some kind of progress. One step at a time.

The fog drifted from his mind out his ears, just enough so he remembered: *Snow White—the feds' project.*

But these guys kept nagging him about the name. *Which* name? The name of one of the feds' snitches . . . the name of some undercover cop . . . the name of an arbitrageur?

Bobby had helped the feds on their arbitrage project two years back.

And what about Paco? Had they found him already? Did they have him in the room next door? Were they torturing both men at the same time? Or was he dead?

If so, only Bobby had heard Paco's last words in Mexico.

With his ear and cheek to the filthy carpet, Bobby took a shuddering breath. Amado Fortuna's creeps were huddled in a corner whispering again. He listened, straining to hear—and to comprehend. He translated the fragments: *move the cop . . . dump him at the warehouse . . . Amado says do him today.*

Bobby rubbed his eyes and saw the kid standing over him. Fortuna's gangster boy with a dirty hypo—the blood and the cloudy drug swirling together in the cylinder, a perfect bead of milky liquid pendulous on its point.

The boy murmured, *"Muera, chingado."*

Bobby Dowd felt terror, a sting much sharper than the filthy needle.

CHAPTER TWENTY-THREE

THE BORDER BETWEEN the United States and Mexico shifted every day. The river known as the Rio Grande and the Río Bravo simply did what rivers do—cut back and forth between its banks. The headwaters of the Rio Grande were in south-central Colorado; the river traversed the state of New Mexico, continuing on to divide Texas and Mexico. By the time it flowed between the border towns of El Paso and Ciudad Juárez, it was little more than a polluted, international trickle encased in concrete in a desperate attempt to contain it so neither side lost ground.

Across this concrete casing, four bridges spanned the Rio Grande/Río Bravo. The bridges on El Paso and Stanton streets connected the bellies of the sister cities, providing access to older, somewhat shabby downtown neighborhoods.

Matt England checked his wristwatch; he'd been standing on the corner of Avenida Calle Lerdo and

Avenida Riberena for fifty-nine minutes. His Southwest Airlines flight had landed promptly at eight-fifteen A.M. at the El Paso airport. From the terminal, he'd taken a taxi downtown to Stanton Street, then walked across the Santa Fe Bridge. Pedestrian traffic was heavy from Mexico; the stream of weekday workers trekking to day jobs seemed to stretch farther than the Rio Grande. In contrast, foot traffic from the U.S. into Mexico was moderate, customs minimal (especially for a man without luggage), and the toll was all of fifteen cents.

Such a deal.

But the decision to travel on foot had been made for reasons that had to do with anonymity and security. For vehicles crossing from the U.S. to Mexico, the border-checking system was as random as a traffic light. Green light, go ahead. Red light, pull over. Cars traveling from Mexico into the States—the usual direction for heroin, marijuana, cocaine, amphetamines—faced the possibility of stringent searches. Occasionally, those contraband searches also occurred in the north-to-south lanes—U.S. to Mexico. The main contraband moving in the southerly direction was laundered drug money, portions of the cash backlog that continued to pile up in Texas safe houses as the Department of Justice tightened its operations. Some drug lords had resorted to mobile couriers to transport loads of money across the border into Mexico. Although his chances of being stopped were slim, Matt needed to minimize the possibility of his crossing being documented.

He checked his wristwatch again: sixty-two minutes. The flight from Albuquerque to El Paso had taken less than fifty minutes. All around him, the streets were thick with people—shoppers, vendors, hustlers, and those with nothing better to do than hang out.

A cabdriver trolled past on Riberena. "*Hola, señor. Youwannarideconmigo?*"

Matt waved him off just like he'd waved away the last five taxis.

"*Muy barato.*" The taxi driver winked. "Very cheap for my taxi."

"No, gracias." Matt glanced at the driver, started to walk away, then stopped. Slowly, he stepped over to the battered red-and-white Taxi *Heroe*—noticed a string of bullet holes along the door—and leaned in the window.

The taxi driver was smiling, but his eyes were sharp as glass. He mumbled, "I give you the Pitkin tour, *señor.*"

Matt adjusted his sunglasses against the mean Mexican sun, tasted baked smog, and slid into the backseat. Dale Pitkin had finally managed to contact Vargas through the Mexican's street network. Vargas had agreed to meet with Matt—as long as it was done *his* way.

Matt noted that the bullet holes were not visible from the vehicle's interior. He knew the Mexican police had access to bulletproof delivery trucks, vans, buses; why not taxis? He leaned forward, said, "Nice wheels."

Victor Vargas was somewhere past thirty-five but shy of forty. He had a head of thick, dark hair and a trim mustache and a stubble of beard that went nicely with his bronze skin. He sat erect, dressed in a white polyester shirt and dark slacks, and he had a presence that belied his relatively slight physical stature. At the moment, he looked like a cabdriver who had already worked the graveyard shift, not a cop.

Vargas glanced in the rearview mirror, and a wide smile broke open his face, revealing white teeth. "I have a little something for you."

"I hope it's a Cuban cigar."

"Take a look." Vargas pulled the taxi into a heavy stream of traffic. Two traffic officers—Laurel and Hardy in uniform—directed him past a construction detour.

Matt saw a manila file on the floor of the car by his feet; he lifted it onto his lap and opened the cover. The contents included a half dozen photographs and a stack of typewritten reports in Spanish. He focused on the photographs; there was one man in the first picture.

Without looking back, Victor said, "The first photograph is Amado Fortuna—one of the few on file because the Big Tuna is allergic to cameras. The other five photos are of his *primo* Paco."

Matt studied the drug kingpin. The surveillance photo was grainy, its subject disappointingly mundane. The slight, middle-aged figure did not look like a man who had ordered a hundred-plus executions, a man who doled out death with his bare hands. No fangs, no horns. Only in kinetic energy had the photographer caught a hint of the international criminal's cocky machismo, his natural brutality.

Matt moved on to the photographs of Paco Fortuna. He appeared to be a soft man with nondescript fleshy features. On the street or in a crowd he would disappear behind a cloak of ordinariness. A witness would describe him as average, normal. Matt studied each photograph, taking in the narrow mouth, the deep-set eyes behind thick glasses, the unremarkable nose. Was there intelligence etched in the mocking curve of the lips? Did a hint of deftness escape through dark pupils? Matt was careful not to project keenness or cogency upon that two-dimensional image.

The photographs slid across Matt's lap when Victor was forced to jam on the taxi's brakes. They were inching through a jammed intersection. All around them, vehicles with Texan and Chihuahuan license plates played stop-and-go while car horns created a disharmonious symphony.

Victor gave a noncommittal snort as he glided the car to a stop.

Matt tried to roll down his window—it lowered most of four inches and stuck. Enough to register the smell of oil refineries, hot asphalt, anxiety, fast food, car exhaust— plain old urban burn-off at somewhere near ninety degrees. On the first day of November.

A hawker waved to Matt from between the rows of idling cars. A barefoot boy with mestizo features, no older than seven or eight but already hard at work, covered with plastic skeletons, skull maracas, paper coffins, and toy spiders with gleaming red eyes.

"*El Día de los Muertos,*" Victor murmured.

Day of the Dead. A major Mexican holiday and one that Matt had always been partial to. He motioned the kid over to the car. The child's dark skin was covered with a film of dust and grease. When Matt pressed his nose over the window, he could hardly breathe through the thick exhaust fumes; but this polluted strip of the world was the child's office. The boy wiped grimy fingers across his face and kept up a running pitch in mongrel Spanish.

Matt asked the kid how he split his take—the *policía* had been rumored to rent space to beggars and vendors. The boy shook his head, his broad smile revealing missing front teeth. His fingers clutched the door as the car inched forward in line.

He said, *"No problema, Señor Norteamericano."* But his accent was bad, and Victor explained that the boy was probably Indian, a traveler from somewhere deep in Mexico's interior, or farther south, Guatemala or Ecuador. He was a young member of the migrating masses—rivers of people who flowed across natural and man-made borders.

Matt bought two of the plastic skeletons—they turned out to be puppets—and gave the boy two dollars.

He dropped the skeletons into the front seat. "Happy birthday, Vargas." Then he stacked the photos together and asked, "What the hell was Amado Fortuna's cousin doing in New Mexico with a ten-year-old kid?"

"Moving fast? *No sé.*" Victor shook his head. "So Paco Fortuna is your guy?"

Matt thought about the dead man whose body was now tagged and stored at the O.M.I. in Albuquerque. The face and hands of the corpse had been badly decomposed. Positive identification could take weeks— and that was assuming Mexican authorities cooperated. "Maybe."

"A lot of people will be interested in your maybe. He was a . . . how do you say, a right-hand man?"

"To Amado?"

"*Sí.*" Victor pursed his lips. "Your questions will make people nervous—What was he doing in Los Estados Unidos; What was he doing in *Nuevo* Mexico?—they make *me* nervous." His eyes narrowed to slits. "You ever heard of Snow White?"

"Yeah. She ate the poisoned apple."

Victor shrugged. "Is it true the child may be the daughter of a condemned murderer?"

"It's true. What's the deal with the taxi?"

"Amado Fortuna wants to kill me." Victor noticed Matt's expression and flashed a macabre smile. *"No problema, Señor Norteamericano."*

SEEN THROUGH A hard plastic security barrier in the Penitentiary of New Mexico's Maximum Facility, Cash Wheeler's face appeared oddly out of focus. The drab prison-issue clothes hung off his body and made his white skin look even paler. His hair and eyes were washed to a dull gray by fluorescent lights and malnutrition. His shoulders were pressed open, and he sat stiffly upright at the table in the visitors' booth. He didn't move his head, but his eyes searched out detail. When he made no move to communicate, Sylvia picked up the telephone on her side of the barrier and waited. Almost a minute elapsed before the death row inmate responded by lifting the receiver on his phone.

Sylvia spoke first; to her own ear, her voice sounded pinched and tinny. "Thanks for the drawing," she said. She held up the piece of white paper the C.O. had given her when she arrived. By phone, she had requested a pencil drawing from Cash Wheeler. "Just sketch a man—a self-portrait if you want. Nothing fancy, a stick figure or whatever. Don't sign your name; just print your initials."

He'd agreed, asking only: "Is it some kind of psychologist thing?"

"Yeah. That's what it is."

On the other side of the barrier, Wheeler blinked. A

look at him but pressed on quietly. "The first time I saw her, Serena had bruises from the accident; they've pretty much healed now. She's leggy for a ten-year-old. She weighs eighty-eight pounds. Her hair is long and dark, and she likes it in a ponytail."

Sylvia gave a quick laugh, adding, "There's a little gap between her front teeth." She looked directly at the inmate. She wanted to personalize Serena—in name, physically, emotionally—to make the child real for Cash.

She pressed her fingers together and leaned forward toward the barrier. "Her eyes are huge. They're so dark they're almost black."

Wheeler dropped his gaze, but still he held the phone to his ear.

Afraid she was losing him, Sylvia said, "She's an artist. Her drawings are amazing—"

"Why tell me?" He shrugged, apparently uninterested.

"Do you understand your daughter might be alive?"

The inmate leaned forward until his forehead touched the security barrier—the gesture was subtle, oblique, and threatening—and the psychologist knew she was back in the con game: a world of antisocial, predatory personalities.

Wheeler said, "Here's what you should understand: I want out of here. If the kid can get me out, great."

Sylvia pushed a loose strand of hair from her face. For a moment, Wheeler's expression had revealed something unintended—the hollow bravado of a teenager. She was reminded of the blind psych screens done in prisons where inmates consistently scored below average for their age group. Almost to a man, you could take the chronological age and subtract the number of years spent behind bars. Incarceration stunted most inmates—emotionally, intellectually. In many ways, Wheeler was still a brash, angry, and pathetic nineteen-year-old.

She knew he would hate her if she allowed pity to show in her face. Speaking in a hard voice, she said, "You're not making this easy."

"Nobody made it easy for me." His tone was harsh, but he had relaxed just slightly. Resentment was a comfortable and familiar refuge.

"How can I make it easier for you now, Cash?" She didn't try to keep the edge of sarcasm from her voice.

Cash looked away, tapping his fingers on the plastic table.

Sylvia spoke softly. "I know this must open up feelings from all those years ago—"

"No." Wheeler swallowed and his Adam's apple bobbed. He spoke in a flat voice. "It doesn't open anything."

Sylvia bit her lip, then frowned. "What if Serena *is* your daughter, Cash? What do you want her life to be like? What would you *dream* for her?"

No response.

Suddenly, the inmate's sharp eyes caught and held Sylvia in their gaze. There was nothing hidden, nothing masked or challenging in his stare. His face looked naked, his innermost feelings painfully exposed. Sylvia swallowed, almost flinching at the hopelessness played out on his features. The man sitting five feet away had spent the last decade locked in a prison cell for the murder of the woman he loved. If he was guilty, remorse had eaten away at his soul. If he was innocent . . . Sylvia could only imagine what his pain must be.

But there was a faint flame in his eye, a candle flickering at the end of a long, dark tunnel—his humanity had not withered completely.

Sylvia leaned forward in her chair, the plastic digging uncomfortably into her butt. Her muscles were suddenly trembling. She clenched the phone. "If you are Serena's father, she's waited ten years and traveled five hundred miles to find you. Don't turn her away without giving her a chance."

Then it struck her like a bolt of electricity—she felt incredibly dense that she hadn't figured it out sooner. Noelle Harding's words about Serena replayed in her mind: "She *is* Elena."

"You don't believe you were the father of Elena's baby—is that it?"

She caught her lip between her teeth and shook her head slowly. She tried to remember every word the inmate had spoken in the last five minutes. He was staring at her, his eyes boring oppressively into her face. But Sylvia saw the warring emotions beneath the mask—anger, frustration, and shame.

"Cash, if you weren't the baby's father, then who?" He didn't answer. She pushed: "Did Elena tell you she'd slept with someone else? Or did you guess? Did Elena love another boy?"

In Sylvia's mind, a name swam to consciousness; early this morning, bleary-eyed, she'd watched Matt leave for the airport and Mexico. Then she'd returned to her kitchen, and over strong, black coffee she'd read more of Jim Teague's case files. All the time her curiosity had grown—who was the boy who had disappeared? Who was Jesús?

She slapped her palm gently on the table. "Cash, was

Jesús the father? Was that why you never helped Elena name the baby?"

Wheeler stood, dropping the phone to the tabletop. He swayed, then recovered. For an instant, his face revealed nothing but pain and fear—but just as quickly his expression softened. He clasped the phone one last time, held it to his mouth, and whispered, "Tell Serena the drawing's from me."

Then he turned his back on Sylvia. Within seconds he was gone. Alone, she pressed the inmate's drawing against the hard tabletop.

. . . sketch a man—a self-portrait if you want.

He'd sketched a forlorn little man—almost a stick figure—trapped inside a rectangle. Arms and legs were extended, and they pressed against each of the four corners. The face had only two features—wide black eyes. There was no mouth at all. He'd initialed it as requested: C.W.

INFRASTRUCTURE IN JUÁREZ was crumbling in comparison with its sister city, El Paso. Streets were scarred with potholes, reconstruction projects slow or nonexistent, traffic patterns chaotic. The primary colors of Mexico— red, yellow, magenta, cyan—were splashed across buildings, clothing, and billboards like an endless rainbow. The sounds this side of the border were cacophonous—horns, engines without mufflers, bells and whistles, music and voices. The smells were a rich brew of pollution, raw sewage, grease and food, and whatever else the heat cooked out.

Matt winced when Victor swerved sharply to avoid a bus pulling into traffic from a frontage lane. Victor didn't seem to notice his passenger's distress; he waved a

Jesús the father? Was that why you never helped Elena name the baby?"

Wheeler stood, dropping the phone to the tabletop. He swayed, then recovered. For an instant, his face revealed nothing but pain and fear—but just as quickly his expression softened. He clasped the phone one last time, held it to his mouth, and whispered, "Tell Serena the drawing's from me."

Then he turned his back on Sylvia. Within seconds he was gone. Alone, she pressed the inmate's drawing against the hard tabletop.

. . . *sketch a man—a self-portrait if you want.*

He'd sketched a forlorn little man—almost a stick figure—trapped inside a rectangle. Arms and legs were extended, and they pressed against each of the four corners. The face had only two features—wide black eyes. There was no mouth at all. He'd initialed it as requested: C.W.

INFRASTRUCTURE IN JUÁREZ was crumbling in comparison with its sister city, El Paso. Streets were scarred with potholes, reconstruction projects slow or nonexistent, traffic patterns chaotic. The primary colors of Mexico— red, yellow, magenta, cyan—were splashed across buildings, clothing, and billboards like an endless rainbow. The sounds this side of the border were cacophonous—horns, engines without mufflers, bells and whistles, music and voices. The smells were a rich brew of pollution, raw sewage, grease and food, and whatever else the heat cooked out.

Matt winced when Victor swerved sharply to avoid a bus pulling into traffic from a frontage lane. Victor didn't seem to notice his passenger's distress; he waved a cautionary hand at the bus driver and then sped ahead. At the intersection, he turned onto another boulevard— Avenida Abraham Lincoln—passing a massive ten-story skeleton of steel beams that rose into the skyline like the hulk of a neoteric dinosaur watching over the city.

"Monument to the drug lords," Victor said. As Matt studied the naked structure from his window, Victor explained: "Construction started in the mideighties. It was a project to launder drug money. That particular *patrón* got busted, died, or just disappeared."

"No more *dinero?*"

"A waste of perfectly good steel. There are others like it in this city." Victor braked for a red light. "If your dead man is Paco Fortuna, then Amado ordered the hit on his own cousin."

Matt massaged the base of his neck with one hand. "I can think of plenty of reasons to shut up a runaway bookkeeper."

The light changed, but Victor was caught up in his thoughts. Behind the taxi, horns blared. Victor shifted into gear, and the car crept slowly forward. He asked, "So what did Paco have on Amado? Political payoffs? New distributors in the U.S.? A second set of books? They all keep them because the *chingados* can't trust each other as far as they can spit."

"A money trail?" Matt leaned forward in the seat as if his body would propel the vehicle through the intersection. He realized that Victor Vargas was testing him.

Victor raised his eyebrows. "A money trail would be helpful," he said mildly. "We've never been able to follow his cash." The speedometer hovered at fifteen kilometers per mile. A massive truck careened past, and the trucker mouthed something unpleasant.

Matt spoke casually. "Paco Fortuna's carotid artery was sliced, and he was left to drain out."

"¿*Sí?*" Victor nodded.

"Does that sound like one of Amado's hits?" Matt watched the other man; from the corner of his eyes he saw the outside world moving by. They were on a wide boulevard lined with modest shops and apartments. The city was a socioeconomic jigsaw puzzle with barrios, middle-class neighborhoods, and mansions side by side.

Vargas's eyes were suspended in the rearview mirror. "What does E.P.I.C. say?"

Matt took a guess. "The killer is a cop."

"Why do you say that?" Vargas's voice was icy.

"That's not what I say; it's what *you* say. You don't trust me as far as you can throw me." Matt laughed uneasily. "Come on, Victor, you're not dead yet."

"I'm not worried about dying by your hand, but I am concerned about stories getting into the wrong ears." Victor's frown was cryptic. He turned the taxi down a series of winding streets, passing cul-de-sacs, parks, and houses that gained square footage with each block.

Matt turned, gazing out the passenger window. Here the houses were massive and set close together, most with adjoining walls, all with metal grillwork or thick security walls. Huge satellite dishes glared over walls. Driveways and garages were stocked with Mercedes, Porsches, and fun buggies. Four prime British roadsters were parked behind iron gates at the end of one cobblestone drive. As Victor slowed to navigate a sharp corner, the screech of mynah birds and parrots echoed from within a glass atrium. Security increased with each block: six-foot-high walls embedded with broken glass gave way to twelve-foot-high walls topped with deadly razor ribbon. Armed guards leaned languorously against grilled gates. They watched the taxi through half-shut eyelids.

Victor said, "I wouldn't mind this so much except these people have robbed my country blind."

Matt shook his head and murmured, "Damn, that wall must've cost a year of my salary." Two rancheros caught his eye; they were wearing dirty, misshapen clothes, smoking small black cigarillos, and walking a groomed and pedigreed miniature poodle.

Victor turned another corner, and Matt saw the greenish-brown sea of a golf course visible behind ornate mansions. "Want to test your handicap?" Victor asked, pointing a finger at an impressive blue-glassed skyscraper in the distance that seemed to loom over the golf course. "Amado Fortuna keeps an office in the penthouse. That way he can watch over his home turf from behind a desk." Victor guided the taxi left as the road forked.

"So we're in Amado's neighborhood?"

"Look up, my friend."

The wall was at least eighteen feet high. It was constructed of plaster in places, stone in others, and it went on and on, curving around acres of land. Twenty acres? Twenty-five? After about a quarter mile, massive wooden gates interrupted the wall. The gates were open, revealing a ten-inch crack of space. Through the opening, Matt saw an old ranchero with a shotgun eyeballing him. Behind the ranchero, a naked gravel yard seemed to stretch for miles. In the distance, low buildings ran parallel to the wall. A stable, maybe? A garage?

"Paco lived here, too?"

"No. He just worked here. At his cousin's city estate. That's the barracks for Amado's private army. He lands his helicopter inside." Victor spoke in a low voice. He kept the taxi moving at a crawl, his eyes locked on the road. "And he's touchy about sightseers." Two minutes later he pulled up at a stop sign. The wall was still to their left. The main boulevard was directly in front of them, and beyond the road an empty lot shimmered with broken glass.

Victor raised the dark muzzle of an automatic and pointed it discreetly at Matt. He said, "Get out."

"Are you fucking crazy?" Matt saw that the curious ranchero was on his way out to the street, drawn toward the idling taxicab.

Victor ordered Matt out of the taxi a second time—in Spanish. "*Ya salte o te mato.*" Get out now, or I'll kill you.

Matt believed Victor Vargas; he didn't know the man well enough to disbelieve him. He opened the door of the taxi and stepped into the street. The ranchero was outside the gates now, standing hesitantly with a cigarillo dangling from between his lips, watching.

Matt stared at the drug lord's fortress. From this vantage point, the wall continued into infinity in either direction. Every three hundred feet, turrets rose into the sky. And now he could see the rooftops of the main house—Moorish domes, finished in turquoise, white shell, and gold mosaic. Above a chapel roof, a gold cross stabbed the sky.

Here lived a man so rich and powerful he could own his own private path to God.

Matt tried to absorb what he was seeing—a billion-dollar fortune, another monument to total corruption. A flash of light caught his eye.

He said, "Those are gun turrets."

Victor Vargas glanced out the driver's window of the taxi. "*Sí*. I'd say an AK-47 has a bead on you right this minute. *Adiós, amigo*." He slammed the sedan into gear and accelerated down the street and around the corner.

The ranchero watched the taxi disappear. Then he tossed his cigarillo to the ground, wrapped his fingers around the stock of the shotgun, and began striding slowly toward Matt.

"Fuck," Matt whispered.

CHAPTER TWENTY-FOUR

SYLVIA WAS TALL, but she had to lift her chin to address the turbaned security guard who occupied the hospital hallway just outside Serena's room. "Who are you?"

"Khalsa."

Sylvia reached for the doorknob located somewhere behind the guard's substantial waist. He didn't budge. His dark blue uniform was equipped with various clip-ons: radio, beeper, cellular phone. A holster—with gun—hung off his belt. Sylvia set her hands on her hips.

"Are you keeping me out, Khalsa? Who put you here?"

"You first, ma'am. May I see some I.D.?"

Sylvia shrugged and pulled her hospital badge from her pocket. She clipped it to her cotton sweater. "I'm her doctor."

"I know about you, Dr. Strange." The guard shifted from the door.

"What am I, *famous*?"

He laughed. "No, ma'am."

Sylvia said, "Noelle Harding, right?" She walked past him without waiting for a response.

Serena was seated in a chair by the window. Cool blue sunlight washed over her face and shoulders, coating her hair with a blue-black sheen, bringing out the olive tones in her brown skin. Her head was bowed, hands clasped in her lap. Her narrow shoulders hunched forward expectantly. She looked scrawny in the new turquoise T-shirt Sylvia had purchased for her. She also looked much older than ten.

The child glanced up at Sylvia, her eyes flickering with recognition. Then she returned her attention to her vigil. Was she waiting for the dark-haired attacker to return and finish what he'd started?

Sylvia remembered an earlier vigil—only four days ago?—when she had found Serena perched in her study window. That night, the tension had been palpably brittle. At this moment, there was a stillness to the child, a concentration that belied fear.

Was she praying? Sylvia suspected Serena's spiritual leaning bordered on the fanatical. It made sense that a child who wasn't talking to humans would establish an intimate dialogue with an archetypal figure—a saint, a goddess, someone who would act as a channel for her emotional energy.

Sylvia supported that dialogue—as long as it didn't overwhelm Serena. From a therapist's standpoint, that was the kicker—judging whether a spiritual experience crossed the line of "normalcy" to become delusional or psychotic.

Sylvia's muscles gave an involuntary shiver. Outside

the glass, the Santa Fe sun shone hot and cold; the burning orange globe disappeared behind a blanket of gray clouds. She positioned the only other chair in the room so it was about three feet from Serena and the window.

It would be best to stay in the room for the morning session. The child didn't seem to be bothered by the guard's presence; most likely, she welcomed the protection.

Sylvia had known Serena for one week. Without the benefit of verbal clarification, the child's actions had sometimes appeared bizarre. But in retrospect, Serena had demonstrated irrefutable logic—she had hidden like a hunted animal, she had attempted to bury her trail at Nellie Trujillo's home, she had stowed away in Sylvia's truck—all the while very probably eluding a flesh-and-blood predator.

And, finally, she had led Sylvia to Paco's body—and the photograph of Cash Wheeler and Elena Cruz.

It was only logical to accept a guard outside the door.

Sylvia spoke softly to the child. "Are you praying? Do you have someone you talk to?"

A quick look of acknowledgment crossed the child's features.

"Can you show me who it is?" Sylvia asked. "Can you draw me a picture?"

Seemingly unsure, Serena shook her head.

Sylvia didn't appear fazed. She simply said, "Someday, if you feel like sharing that with me . . . I'd like to know."

She opened her briefcase and pulled out Cash Wheeler's initialed stick-figure drawing. Without offering any explanation, she set the page on the window ledge, directly in the child's view. Serena glanced at the paper but she showed no visible reaction. Sylvia hid any disappointment—what had she expected?—reaching once again into the briefcase to produce her father's copy of Grimms as well as a small tape recorder.

When Sylvia pressed PLAY, the tape began to roll, the whine of gears barely audible. She set the machine on the floor by her feet. And she opened the book. Over several days, Serena had heard the tale of the Six Swans several times. Now they were once again at the story's last act.

The king married the girl, but he had a wicked mother who warned him against his new bride because she was jealous. When the girl gave birth to a son, the king's mother stole the baby away. She smeared blood on the girl's mute mouth, calling the girl "one who eats the flesh of her own." But the young queen did not say a word in her own defense.

As Sylvia read the text, she was startled by a very faint sing-song noise. Could it be the child? She looked over—Serena was silent. The only audible sound was the whir of the tape recorder's small gears. After a moment, Sylvia picked up where she had left off.

And she kept silent when her second baby was stolen by the old woman. When the king's third child was also stolen, the grieving king believed his wife must be a murderess, and he sentenced her to die by fire.

There was the sing-song noise again. Sylvia stopped speaking.

Not a sound.

Again, she began to read.

> *The day of her execution happened to fall on the last day of her sentence of silence. With her, she took six shirts of wildflowers to the wooden pyre.*

Sylvia felt her heart gallop. This time, the sing-song noise clearly came from Serena. Sylvia absorbed feelings of amazement and wonder while her mouth kept opening and closing around words. Some part of her continued to read as if nothing out of the ordinary had occurred. But now her voice was accompanied by another voice—small, sweet, and musical.

> *There, she cried out in joy when she saw six swans; they flew so close to her, she tossed the shirts over their feathers . . . her brothers stood . . . as men . . .*

Sylvia let her voice fade in and out, ever so gradually.

> *in their human form once more . . .*

Until only Serena's soft voice was audible:

> *The spell was . . . broken and . . . her brothers gathered . . . around her.*

If Serena's face was shining and alert, her voice was matter-of-fact. As she picked up the drawing on the window ledge, she pointed to the initials "C.W."

Then, meticulously, she printed out words in crayon: "I want to see my dad."

*   *   *

MATT SQUINTED AGAINST the harsh sun. Dust stung his skin. He saw the ranchero approaching, perhaps thirty feet away, and then he noticed a second man. This one wore a sombrero with a brim as floppy as a massive tortilla. A holster rode low on his hips. He walked with a low, sloping stride like a movie bandito.

Matt held his hands in clear view and nodded to the closest man as he weighed his options. Should he try to communicate in Spanish or in English? In Mexico his fluent New Mexican Spanish would not blend in—and neither would a six-foot-two-inch Anglo. Too late to think . . .

He kept his eyes straight ahead, walking, calling out, *"Voy a la casa de Carmen Miranda."*

The ranchero eyed the norteamericano blankly.

Sweat was running off Matt's back, it was beading on his lip. He shook his head—*Thanks anyway, I don't need your help*—and waved one hand casually.

The ranchero shifted his shotgun.

Matt began rattling off Spanglish. His feet kept pace with his motormouth, moving him in the direction of the main boulevard. All the while he said something like: I can flag a taxi at the corner, you know, never mind, but thanks anyway for your trouble—

The ranchero was following him, dogging him a few paces back. The skin on Matt's back seemed to roll—pyloerection is what scientists call that animal reaction to challenge. If the criminal investigator had fur, it would have been standing on end.

He thought he heard the snap of a shotgun—had the Mexican just checked the load?

Shit. I'm dead.

Now the ranchero began challenging him in rapid Spanish. Who was he? What did he want? Matt thought he could feel the gun aimed between his shoulders. He knew street murders in quiet residential neighborhoods were not unusual in Juárez.

I'm fucking dead.

Anger coursed up Matt's spine—who was the cop here? This was a family neighborhood, and this god-damn little punk wanted to take him out? He wheeled around, took a deep breath, and thought *mean and big.* Pulled to his full height, he topped the Mexican by six or eight inches, and he outweighed him by seventy-five pounds.

The distant man called out to his buddy—"Hey, Flaco ¿Qué pasa?"

Matt felt the blood pumping behind his eyes. *If I'm dead—you're dead, too, motherfucker.* He stood his ground, watching Flaco's shotgun waver like a hard snake.

Finally, the Mexican shrugged and tipped the gun dismissively.

Matt was almost to the corner when he saw the taxi—driven by Vargas—pull up at the curb. He scuttled forward, moving in some hybrid lope-lunge. He grabbed the door handle, heaved himself inside, and was thrown halfway across the seat as Vargas accelerated, burning rubber. They were already out on the boulevard by the time Matt got the door shut.

He couldn't speak normally until Amado Fortuna's estate was no longer visible in the distance—his heart kept ramming itself against his ribs. Vargas pulled a pack of Delicados from one pocket and tossed a cigarette over the seat. Matt had given up smoking years earlier. He lit the cigarette anyway, ignoring the tremor in his hands.

Vargas spoke as if they had been in the middle of a conversation—in a way, they had. "Paco's killer is a *madrina*—a godmother."

"A hit man?"

"More or less—except he works for the *federales*."

"In addition to working for Amado Fortuna?"

"And he works for Amado. *Sí*." Vargas accelerated, catching the last gasp of a yellow traffic signal.

"How do you know?"

The only response was a raised eyebrow.

"If you try another trick like that . . ." Matt inhaled cigarette smoke gratefully.

A grin split the cop's face. "Out there on the street, you looked honest."

"I need a drink before I kill you." Matt didn't smile.

"First we'll get you settled at your hotel. Then I've got someone I want you to meet—an important man. Tonight, we'll find him at his office . . . in the blue grass of . . ."

THE KENTUCKY CLUB sat like a grand old lady way past her prime and surrounded by riffraff on Avenida Juárez. Her name—displayed in black deco type lined with a gold pinstripe—was the first hint of her style. Inside, the year was 1940, and regulars sipped spirits, unwinding to the mellow recorded horns of the Glen Miller Band. A gleaming mahogany bar ran the length of the narrow-waisted room—a spitting trough skirted the bar—and patrons occupied most of the eighteen red velvet stools. Behind the rich wood, arched mirrors smoky from age reflected faces. Carved wooden beams braced the high ceiling, and brass-lantern chandeliers lit the room, which was accented with a touch of pink and green neon. Between two beams, a massive Budweiser clock hung like the Sword of Damocles. A wooden eagle the size of half a man—wings unfurled—loomed over it all.

Matt and Victor Vargas took a fading red-leather booth against the wall, away from the entrance; Vargas kept his back to the corner. A man with a long, dark face and a mustache appeared from the shadows to take their order. His tie was neatly tucked into a white shirt. His black slacks disappeared behind a starched white apron.

Victor ordered a whiskey and soda. Matt ordered a *cerveza*—a Superior on Victor's recommendation. "It comes from my home state," Victor said with pride. "It's one of Mexico's best beers."

Matt glanced past a *viejo* asleep in one of several upholstered armchairs to the peeling wallpaper behind the old man's head. Over the decades, photographs had faded behind their frames—baseball teams sponsored by the bar's owner, a onetime sports promoter; boxers shaking hands in front of the referee; and above those photographs, hand-painted pictures of matadors draped in embroidered red satin muletas.

The waiter arrived with their drinks. Victor sipped whiskey, dabbed his lips with a napkin, and said, "Tell me about this child who turned up in your state."

Matt pressed his body against the padded leather seat and nodded. That was an appropriate place to start; he was sitting in a bar in Juárez because heavy hitters were after Sylvia's kid. He knew guys like Amado Fortuna didn't go away—ever. Even if you were smart, all you could do was stay one step ahead of them. And pray.

But Matt responded with a question of his own. "Do you remember anything about a torture-murder in Loving, New Mexico—ten years ago—an El Paso kid named Wheeler did his common-law wife?"

Vargas shrugged, and Matt continued: "A jury put him on death row. At the time, the guy's infant daughter disappeared—presumed murdered. Now a ten-year-old girl turns up with the inmate's photograph in her purse."

Vargas gazed fondly at the amber liquid in his glass while whiskey trickled warmly down his throat. "You mean Noelle Harding's brother? Everybody remembers that case." He ran his tongue neatly over his lips, reminding Matt of a cat. A sly cat.

Vargas said, "Anybody who reads *Texas Monthly* knows the story. Two dirt-poor, unwanted kids grow up in an El Paso charity school. Ten years later, she's one of the most powerful women in Texas; her brother's on death row. It's a Texas-style tall tale."

Matt sat up straighter. "This kid—Serena—connects some interesting people. Noelle Harding, Cash Wheeler, Bobby Dowd . . . maybe even Amado Fortuna."

The glass door of the Kentucky Club swung open, and Vargas stiffened. The *federale* watched while a man in a rumpled three-piece suit walked to the bar and straddled a stool.

For a moment Matt had wondered if the man was Victor's important contact. He wasn't sure who to expect. Vargas sure as hell didn't trust his law-enforcement compadres. Corruption had contaminated all branches of the Mexican police; now the national military was in charge. Matt had some idea what that meant to a country like Mexico—a few of her southern neighbors had turned to soldiers in a desperate reach for reform. That solved one problem but created another: once military forces took hold, they didn't like to let go.

And even generals were on the take.

"Bobby Dowd was a good cop—but unrealistic. He believed he could play the undercover game, that he could step in shit without getting it on his shoes."

Matt refocused on Vargas, took in the thought. He said, "The El Paso cops seem to believe Dowd's gone off the deep end—that he's just a cop with a junkie's problem. I get the feeling they're treating his disappearance like an embarrassment."

"They're wrong. The kid's got a habit, but he's still got a code." Vargas shook his head. "He got popped because he knows something."

"How can you be sure?"

"Bobby called me just before he disappeared—he wanted a meeting."

"About Snow White?"

Vargas tensed. Matt caught the reaction and smiled. "So I lied," he said. "You left me in the middle of a fucking street war back there, friend."

"Tell me what you know."

"It was a quiet little project set up by the D.E.A. and assorted feds a few years back. Objective: the arbitrageurs." Matt took a long sip of beer. "The feds wanted to persuade some of the biggest money movers to flip snitch."

Matt knew about the project because he was a privileged member of New Mexico's law-enforcement community. New Mexico was the favorite stomping ground for arbitrageurs. They came in various flavors: retired real estate moguls from California, art dealers, former actors who'd been in three or four movies, has-been sports stars. Where better to launder drug money than in a state almost devoid of disclosure laws? Even the feds were powerless to probe too deeply when no state laws were violated.

Snow White had definitely been interesting—a project Matt might have enjoyed working. The arbitrageurs were the elite of the drug world. They were the guys who made drug money fly around the planet like a high-tech gaggle of geese. They moved billions of dollars, and their tools were laptops, satellite uplinks, money chips, dirty bankers—and brains. To stay in business, they had to be smart.

He closed one eye and turned to Vargas. "Dowd?"

"Bobby was part of the project. He was a straight shooter, hungry to climb, a regular mini G-man in a starched white shirt." Vargas sipped whiskey, nodding. "There was a lot of talk back then about the diaries—"

Matt shook his head and snorted. "Not the Tuna Diaries *again*. This has got to be the third time this week that old b.s. story's come up."

Vargas didn't move. "Maybe it's not bullshit. Maybe the diaries were part of Snow White. It's possible the feds had a source who was willing to trade. They couldn't ask for better leverage to use on the arbitrageurs. How else would they flip those guys?"

Matt finished his beer in one swallow, almost choking. "You know that for a fact?"

Vargas took too long to answer, and Matt groaned. "Let me guess, your fountain of information is none other than Bobby Dowd?"

"What I heard was Tuna destroyed the diaries." Vargas gazed up at the ceiling. "They had transaction numbers, dates, accounts—your money trail."

Matt gave another derisive snort. "What, no names?"

Victor shrugged. "I don't think Tuna is that stupid. But if somebody knew the game, eventually they would figure out the players, no?"

"Someone like Bobby Dowd?"

Victor's smile was cool. "That project was shut down tight. If you mention Snow White, don't expect so much as a fart from the feds."

Matt narrowed his eyes, thinking, unable to avoid inhaling the dense smoke that filled the bar like a toxic cloud. He didn't buy the story of the diaries—it was too fantastic. But he knew one thing for a fact: the feds would go to great lengths to protect a high-level snitch.

Victor motioned to the server for *la cuenta* just as the door to the Kentucky Club opened again. A group of young American girls entered. They weren't more than eighteen years old; freshmen from the University of Texas. With his eye on the giggling girls, Matt hardly noticed the tiny, dark-haired man who appeared at his elbow.

At a quick glance he looked seventy, but he wasn't a man, he was a boy; a street urchin, maybe eleven or twelve years old—scrawny because he'd been chronically malnourished. His hair stood up on his head in thatches. He was barefoot, grubby, missing several teeth, and his T-shirt displayed a monstrous creature with dripping fangs over a caption: I WAS BITTEN BY THE CHUPACABRA!

Before Matt had a chance to react, Vargas spoke in formal Spanish—Matt, the very important man I wanted you to meet—introducing the boy as Chupey. Vargas stood, scattering Mexican bills on the table. "Time to go."

*   *   *

RINGED WITH GLOWING torches, the disk-shaped Pottery House had the unearthly aura of a spaceship hovering over the foothills of New Mexico's Sangre de Cristo Mountains. Sylvia had heard about the house, but as she pulled up in the passenger seat of Rosie Sanchez's Camaro she had her first view of the Frank Lloyd Wright design. She was impressed, but she had other things on her mind.

She clutched a copy of the *Albuquerque Journal* in her lap; the front-page headline read: GIRL MAY FIND FATHER ON DEATH ROW. The article spanned six columns and contained information that could only have been released through Jim Teague or Noelle Harding. It read like a hybrid soap opera and political campaign, meticulously constructed to buy Wheeler a stay of execution. Without identifying the child, the story painted a tear-jerking picture of an orphaned and psychologically traumatized girl.

> *The mute girl is under the care of a prominent local psychologist and has been hospitalized for her own protection. According to a hospital source, the child's condition is ". . . psychologically based . . . a rare childhood-onset disorder." Harding's lawyer, the celebrated Texan "Big Jim" Teague, described the child as ". . . a fragile waif. Your classic story-book orphan." He acknowledged that it will take weeks before paternity test results are known. A sample of Cash Wheeler's blood was taken while the inmate was still behind the bars of his death row cell. A private laboratory in Texas will perform the test.*

Sylvia curled the paper and slapped it against her other hand. "Why aren't we moving?"

"What is this *lambe* doing?" Rosie shifted into neutral and let the Camaro idle behind the stretch limousine that hogged the driveway. "Why don't rich people drive short cars?" She honked her horn at the limo driver, a cocky kid who'd emerged from the oversized vehicle.

"Go around." Sylvia stretched out an arm, motioning in the direction she hoped to move. "Valet parking straight ahead."

"We should have brought Matt's *troque*," Rosie said. "How can you drive that monster?"

"Very slowly." Sylvia jammed the newspaper back inside her briefcase. "I want to leave my case in your trunk—don't let me forget it."

Rosie clucked her tongue as she nosed her car past the limousine toward a row of gleaming torches and young men in valet uniform. She muttered, "If they so much as scratch my paint..." She pulled the car to a stop, shifted to neutral, and set the parking brake. A teenaged valet was already eyeing the cherry-metallic Camaro greedily, as if he planned to take it for a spin.

Rosie climbed out, smoothed her skirt so it was only two inches above her knees, and took the claim ticket from the valet. She popped the car's trunk, smiling sweetly. "Scratch it and I'll sue."

Sylvia dropped her briefcase inside the trunk and slammed the lid shut. She shot the kid a sympathetic smile. As she passed him, she whispered, "She's got the best attorney in the state—a total *cojone*-buster."

Several golf carts were shuttling guests the three hundred yards uphill to the main house, but Sylvia and

Rosie elected to walk. Both women were breathless by the time they reached Pottery House. The main entrance began with a trellis-shaded gate and a brick path through an enclosed courtyard that served as the eye of the building's elliptical design.

Guests had spilled from the living area onto the courtyard's softly illuminated lawn. The muffled hum of social interaction hung in the air. Rosie accepted a glass of wine from a passing waiter. She pointed out the rose petals floating in the ornamental reflecting pool, then stopped to warm her hands at a massive outdoor Kiva fireplace. Sylvia entered the living room, stepped down brick levels, and found herself on the other side of the indoor-outdoor fireplace, where a second fire burned hospitably.

The space was at least thirty feet long, with latias and molded walls bare of ornaments. Across the room, outside one of three glassed arches, Sylvia thought she caught a glimpse of Noelle Harding. She felt someone tap her arm, realized Rosie had joined her, then looked back. Noelle had already disappeared.

Rosie's voice was abnormally subdued. She said, "Someone told me the house is almost five thousand square feet, they used about thirty thousand adobes, there's an underground garage, and a swimming pool out back that you can swim into from the house—"

A tall, slender man with gray hair and a clipped beard stopped gracefully in his tracks to say, "And we're not in El Paso."

"What?" Rosie looked intrigued.

The man's eyes sparkled. "Wright designed this house in 1941 for an El Paso couple. Some people say Frank was inspired by Stonehenge—"

Sylvia left Rosie and her talkative acquaintance and caught up with another wandering waiter. He held out a tray of wineglasses: "We're offering a plummy burgundy or a light, woodsy chardonnay."

"Woodsy chardonnay with Frank Lloyd Wright." She accepted the drink, then crossed the room to the glassed arches, which opened onto a walled verandah. The view was all deep canyon and distant lights. Sylvia moved to the opposite end of the verandah to avoid a romantic couple. The sound of laughter and faint music from an orchestra danced on the night air.

"If I have to convince one more rich banker to give a few dollars to charity, I'll jump off this balcony."

Sylvia turned to see her hostess standing on the threshold. Noelle was dressed in simple, light-colored silk, and her blond hair hung loose just below her slender shoulders. In silhouette she appeared thin to the point of fragility, but her voice was deep and mocking.

"Was the article part of your fund-raising drive?" Sylvia asked quietly.

Noelle stepped forward to stand next to Sylvia. She looked out at the canyon. "The story was necessary. I've been fielding calls from reporters since Sunday. Teague handled the interview. *After* he had a talk with the division head at the attorney general's office of appeals. The A.G.'s attitude is refreshingly cooperative."

"And the governor?" Sylvia remembered that Noelle Harding had strong supporters in the Land of Enchantment.

"You can ask him yourself. He's my guest this evening." She turned toward Sylvia suddenly. "Did we offend you with our crassness?"

"I took you to see Serena; I talked with you openly

about her progress. Two days later, I open a newspaper and see my words attributed to a hospital source."

Harding's voice warmed with emotion. "I used you, *yes*. But public sympathy is shifting. There are whispers of possible commutation to life." She touched Sylvia's arm gently, then swung around as if the subject were settled. "I'd like to introduce you to some special people." She forged a path through the living and dining area, past an industrial-sized kitchen, and finally into an even larger room that opened on the swimming pool and deck. The pool lights gave off a soft blue glow. Sylvia followed, passing clusters of guests as they approached a busy freestanding bar. Arranged around the pool, musicians were playing soft Latin music.

As she walked, Sylvia caught snippets of party conversation.

"—according to you, Senator?"

"I heard she leases the house—"

"Peanuts or almonds?"

"*That's* Robert Redford? He's soooooo short."

Finally, Noelle entered another wing of the house. As they passed through a glassed hallway, she said, "I've been wanting to show you my work."

The sunken room was dimly lit and spacious enough to accommodate two dozen people with ease. Even in shadow, Sylvia recognized a senator, the governor, and Jim Teague's bulky frame. Teague was part of a group arranged in chairs around a nine-foot-high screen—the screening room.

Video images—professionally rendered—flashed across the screen: small children, undernourished, dirty, ill, or injured. Noelle Harding's voice narrated on tape: "This isn't some distant land, Asia, India, Africa; these children live along the border of Mexico and the United States of America. They survive in squalor, they go hungry, and they are deprived of basic educational services and medical care. Prosperity is just miles away, but they take no part in it."

The images changed: four young boys raced out of the shadows, chasing a train as it slowed on its tracks. The narration continued, "These children are forced to find income where they can—unfortunately, desperation may lead them to commit illegal acts. Many are recruited at an early age by members of the drug cartels. Once inducted, they owe lifetime allegiance to the drug lords."

The picture changed again; a man who looked like a politician spoke into a microphone: "We are fighting the drug armies with seismic sensors, cameras, infrared scopes, and always more money. But we're losing the war, my friends. And our foremost victims are our children, our future."

Sylvia felt breath on her neck, then she heard Jim Teague's voice: "I know you've looked over the case files. Are you always such a go-getter? So gung ho?"

Sylvia looked at Teague, and alcohol fumes hit her square in the face. "I'm sorry about last night's phone call."

He waved away her apology. "Find anything enlightening besides Jesús?" His laugh was short and caustic.

"I ran an on-line search of Children's Rescue Fund. That was enlightening."

Teague crossed his arms and turned so his body was square with hers. "Last year the Rescue Fund had an operating budget of one hundred and fifty million. If you throw in Harding Enterprises, it all adds up to more than a billion a year. That's not a monster to cross. I hope your search told you that much." He turned away.

Sylvia didn't answer. She pretended to return her attention to the video, glad for dim light. The lawyer had made her blush.

But now the video image grabbed her—Jim Teague in a group shot with Noelle Harding and two other men. She heard the voice-over: "In 1988, four citizens of El Paso formed the International Children's Rescue Fund. Their goal: to fight the exploitation of children—"

Sylvia turned to speak to Teague again, but he had moved back to his seat. In the flickering projected light, she felt his eye on her; she quickly glanced away. She had never considered that Teague might have been in El Paso with Noelle Harding.

She was startled when she felt fingers slide around her forearm. Rosie whispered, "Follow me."

Sylvia let her friend lead her out of the screening room—apparently undetected—and along a short hall-way. As she stepped through a doorway, Sylvia protested, "Rosie, this is Noelle's room."

"I found out she and Deck Harding—her billionaire husband—are estranged, but don't worry, they worked out the money thing." Rosie's speech was loud and loos-ened by wine. "I think she's bopping Teague."

"Bopping?"

"Doing the nasty thang! Whatever. Look what I found!" Rosie scurried to a freestanding museum-sized glass case; small pieces of sculpture and folk art were on display.

She pointed to a figurine occupying the prominent space. It was roughly three feet high, cast in dark metal, a gruesome goddess: her skirt was made of snakes, a necklace of human hearts and hands encircled her shoulders, a skull's pendant hung from the necklace; blood gushed from her headless neck, spouting upward to form double rattlesnake heads.

"Coatlicue." Noelle Harding had quietly entered the room. "She's Aztec. As you can see, she has a thirst for blood."

Sylvia was embarrassed and startled, but she hoped her question sounded casual. "Did you find her in Mexico?"

"I didn't. She was a gift from Jim. And yes, I believe he picked her up on one of his junkets to Mexico City."

VICTOR VARGAS GUIDED the taxi along the river-frontage road, heading west. Matt occupied the backseat, posing as a fare. Chupey was invisible in the front seat; his head didn't top the dash. The paved road gave way to dirt, the glow of the city lights dimmed, and the air was uncomfortably warm, even at ten-forty P.M. As they drove deeper into Anapra, the sprawling barrio that grew like a cancer on the western edge of Juárez, the dirt side streets were represented by numerals instead of names, then they were only eroded trails and, finally, ruts. Power lines ended abruptly with the main road; raw sewage flowed along rough acequias. The reflected haze of downtown softly illuminated the barren hills and the shanties that perched along their steep sides. The sounds of music, voices, and traffic drifted like a mist over the jumbled landscape. Children and dogs wandered the streets. Scrawny chickens roosted on abandoned vehicles. Every few blocks the taxi passed a local grocery or liquor store. Here the crowds were denser, as people had gathered to drink and pass the time.

Chupey sat high enough to guide Vargas along the maze of streets. His small dirty fingers pointed right, then left. After twenty minutes of winding, twisting navigation, the boy sat rigidly upright in his seat. "*¡Aquí! La niña vivió aquí!*"

Victor let the taxi roll past the house, braking to a stop about two hundred feet downhill. Matt got out of the car and rested his butt against the warm hood. The bad air, the border conditions, the trappings of poverty were all manifesting in a vague headache.

He looked up, across the street, to the residence Chupey had selected. It was set off the road, riding the edge of a ruined hillside maybe fifty feet above street level. A yard light set on a twenty-foot pole illuminated a section of the crumbling earthen wall and its foundation—hundreds of old tires. They were stacked like poker chips, jammed into the side of the hill, supporting however many tons of disintegrating clay.

A multiple-story structure—part adobe, part cinder block—occupied the space behind the adobe wall. Although the property was a ruin by middle-class standards, it appeared almost luxurious in the half darkness of the primitive surroundings. The wall probably enclosed more than an acre of property. Matt guessed it had been a prosperous villa many years ago, before the slums had overtaken it like a deadly virus.

Two *portals*—ground-level and second-story—ran the length of the main residence. Each verandah was enclosed by ten- or twelve-foot-high grillwork. A grilled exterior stairway descended the southeast wall from the second story. Another high fence enclosed the rooftop.

From the street, the residence resembled a cage, a walled fortress, a broken-down castle. Something that would wash away with the next wave. If this had been Serena's home in Juárez, the child had lived in prison.

Victor and Chupey were already making their way up a rough foot trail cut into the hillside. Matt followed. As they drew closer, he saw that a satellite dish was attached to the edge of the roof. Just below the dish, a small bare bulb burned from the upper portal, and the hot buzz of insect wings hummed on the night air.

Matt swung around abruptly at the sound of footsteps. A group of small, dirt-smeared faces stared up at him. The arrival of Victor's taxi had attracted street urchins, just as the bare lightbulb attracted moths. There was no discouraging the underage entourage. Five of the boldest children followed Matt, Victor, and Chupey to the high metal gates. While Victor dealt with the padlock, Matt tried to banter with the children. They all responded with the same good-natured shrug. The big gringo's New Mexican Spanish was sadly indecipherable.

When the men were inside the gates—followed now by at least eight street kids—Chupey led the way under the branches of a dying elm tree to double wooden doors. These opened into the main house. This time, there was no problem with the locks—they had been pried open by other hands. Matt pushed the doors wide and entered a kitchen. He used the small light on his belt, while Vargas produced a full-sized flashlight. Beams glanced off walls painted turquoise, modest furnishings, and a confusion of pots, pans, cutlery, towels strewn across the floor.

The small living room, a bathroom minus running water, and a bedroom were all in similar condition—someone had made a thorough search of the ground floor.

Victor and Matt both questioned the children.

Who lived here? *A little girl.*

Who took care of her? *Maids.*

Where was the girl? *Gone away.*

How long had she lived here? *Forever.*

Did anyone come to visit the girl? *No. Yes. An old man came to visit every week. And sometimes the children were allowed inside to watch TV.*

Did the girl go outside the house? *Never. Well, almost never. Sometimes the man who visited took her for rides.*

What was her name? *Serena.*

While Matt was searching the residence, he noticed a small cupboard set in a dark corner of the living room. It was so narrow, he had to hunch down and turn sideways to look inside. But it wasn't a cupboard, it was a door.

He knelt down and crawled into a pitch-black space. Just past the wooden doorway, he cautiously stood and shone his light off the close walls. It was a small shrine; hundreds of unlit candles had been placed on an altar. Each wall was adorned with a framed picture of the Virgin of Guadalupe. With his head bowed to avoid the ceiling, Matt approached the altar. His flashlight sent eerie shadows dancing in the gloomy room. He stepped carefully to avoid the fresh piles of rodent shit littering the floor. The altar was wooden, hand-painted, simultaneously rustic and ornate. A small framed photograph had been placed midpoint on the altar. Matt recognized the subject of the first portrait. It was the child, Serena.

Under the portrait, stacked neatly, were dozens of yellowing newspaper articles following the trial and incarceration of Cash Wheeler.

*   *   *

MATT FOLLOWED VARGAS and the children outside the house and up the exterior stairway. They entered through a room—a second bedroom—which had been searched in the same manner as the rooms below. Clothes spilled from a discarded dresser drawer. A pair of rubber boots, stockings, a T-shirt lay near a large television set. A few toys were scattered about the room as well. A stuffed giraffe lay prone on the tiled floor. One of the children, a small boy, squatted next to the stuffed animal; he gazed at it longingly.

There was one additional door. Matt pushed it open, Vargas at his side. Simultaneously their flashlight beams illuminated a long, narrow room. Both men stared, speechless. Victor whistled.

It was Chupey, nudging his way past the adults, who exclaimed, "¡Milagro!"

Miracle.

CHAPTER TWENTY-FIVE

RENZO SANTOS GAZED at his seminaked reflection in the mirror as he tossed the hotel key into the air. He saw the fingers of his gloved left hand snap at metal, pluck the key from its gravitational fall, secret it safely in the pocket of his black jacket. His next breath was one of approval; those particular reflexes were functional. The stitches along his thigh tugged uncomfortably at the damaged, swollen tissue. He flexed his gloved right hand, pain traveling from wrist to forearm to the injured shoulder. Not so good. He had limited ambidexterity; he would have to rely on his left arm for strength.

As he slipped out of the jacket, there was a short knock at the door of the hotel casita. He knew the DO NOT DISTURB sign was attached to the knob. Still wearing the gloves, he stepped naked from the bathroom and called out: "I'm in the shower; please slide it under the door." A single folded receipt appeared between door and carpet. Renzo collected his room receipt—or, more accurately, the receipt belonging to the gentleman known as Mr. Eric Sandoval.

Next, he walked to the bed and gazed down at the collection of equipment neatly laid out on the spread: modified cell phone, shortwave radio and police scanner, handcuffs, mace, numbered badge, .22-caliber semiautomatic and silencer, nine-inch switchblade. Each item was polished. Even the body armor was free of visible lint or soil. He reached down and plucked an eighth-inch strand of thread from the vest, which was imprinted with the words SPECIAL AGENT.

Renzo returned to the bathroom, where he slowly unzipped his alligator case. He measured out a small amount of powder, liquefied the drug, and filled a sterile disposable hypodermic needle. As he proceeded methodically with work he had repeated hundreds of times, a strand of saliva glistened on his lip. He chose to inject the drug into his uninjured thigh, near his genitals.

The tingling itch of warmth flowed into him almost instantly, and unlike even the purest heroin, this synthetic drug's euphoria wasn't measured by experience and repetition like everything else in Renzo's life—this white powder kept pushing him far beyond the edge to a place where he could walk on air and dance on water. It was so much better than orgasm.

When he checked his watch, the digital face showed ten minutes after eleven P.M. He dressed carefully in the dark uniform. He donned his field jacket and then the vest. The loaded .22 went into a holster, the switchblade slid into his left pocket. The gold badge with its registration number clipped onto the vest. He checked himself in the mirror. The layers had added fifteen pounds to his frame. The dark blue baseball cap rode low enough to touch his eyebrows and change the shape of his face. The bruise on his cheek was fading to yellow. In the center of the bruise, the single fang mark from *el lobo* had dried to a black scab.

He was almost ready. But first, the room. Earlier he had collected all the bloody towels, had compressed them into three plastic laundry bags, courtesy of the hotel. That same morning, the city had collected trash from its Dumpsters; the bags had been among the hotel's other waste.

He had refused maid service for three days—murmuring through the door that he had a twenty-four-hour flu. The bloodstained sheets and the mattress pad from his bed had been disposed of along with the towels. He had stolen clean sheets from a maid's cart and remade the bed himself. The mattress bore only the faintest ghost of his blood. Nothing that would arouse suspicion.

He had to ignore the traces of blood on the throw rug. Even if he scrubbed all night, evidence of the blood would remain for years.

The bathroom had been washed down, the room surfaces meticulously wiped with Windex, purloined from hotel supplies. Although he knew it was impossible to erase every trace of his existence, Renzo had come close to accomplishing that aim within the casita's twenty square feet. He had worn gloves for the last seven hours.

He left the room. A gleaming black car—a Cadillac Seville registered to a nonexistent man named Martin Diaz and supplied by a local associate—was parked fifty feet from his casita. As he covered the distance, he heard women's voices drifting across the parking lot, but he saw no one as he unlocked the Cadillac and climbed inside. On Palace Avenue he turned left, heading for Mesa Verde Hospital. The traffic lights turned green as he approached—one after the other—and he crossed town within minutes. The trip went smoothly, but why not? He had already practiced his final route to the girl they called Serena.

SYLVIA ISOLATED THE staff key on her ring as she walked up the long, shadowy path to the hospital. She glanced back at the street expecting to see a patrol car; the Santa Fe P.D. was supposed to send a car past the hospital every hour. No sign of the cops, but several vehicles were parked along the residential street. The illuminated face of her watch showed eleven-thirty. Five minutes earlier, Rosie Sanchez had dropped Sylvia off at Matt's pickup truck, which was parked in the hospital lot. Sylvia had planned to check on Serena before heading home, where she would stay up late reading more of the files on Cash Wheeler's case. She'd limited her alcohol intake at Noelle Harding's party to a glass of wine, and she felt energized.

It was only after Rosie had driven away that Sylvia realized she'd left her briefcase—and Teague's files—in the trunk of the Camaro. The briefcase contained her cell phone and Day-Timer, not to mention hundreds of confidential documents detailing Cash Wheeler's murder defense. At least she still had her purse. But shit—now she was wide awake with nothing to read. Change of plan—she would hang out longer with the sleeping child. She was feeling very protective of Serena these days.

It took two tries with her key to unlock the street door of the hospital.

A young man, barely twenty, on graveyard duty, was slumped over the admissions desk. His body was so limp, he looked dead. Sylvia called out to him. When he didn't answer, she felt a tug of misgiving and walked to the desk. His face was pressed against a logbook. His arms hung loosely at his sides. Misgiving turned to alarm.

"Hey!" Sylvia slapped the desk. "Wake up." She heard the padding of soft footfalls behind her, and she swung around. Noelle Harding's security guard—Khalsa—gave her an oddly penetrating look.

"Are you here twenty-four hours a day?" she asked.

"The shifts are twenty-four on, twenty-four off—my relief called in sick." He reached past her and brought his baton sharply down on the desk.

The attendant's head jerked twice, then he wrenched his shoulders back in a motion that could only hurt. He focused warily on the security guard, blinked, and offered Sylvia a too casual greeting. She leaned over the counter to whisper: "I think you should call somebody to cover your shift tonight."

He rubbed his eyes like a child, then mumbled, "I'll get some coffee."

"Do that. What's your name?"

"Theo."

"Theo, I don't suppose you'd know if the cops have been by?"

The security guard answered for the young man. "It's been over an hour; they're due any minute."

When Sylvia left the lobby, the guard followed. The hospital was quiet, the main hallway dimly lit. The locked ward would be slightly eerie—it always was at night. Sylvia was approaching the security door to the ward when a psychiatric nurse stepped out of a stockroom. Sylvia greeted the woman. "Hey, Peggy."

The woman lifted her finger in a small wave and moved briskly in the opposite direction down the hall, back toward the reception area. As the nurse walked, she called over her shoulder, "I'm taking a coffee break in thirty minutes. Fresh pot of java in the lounge if you drop by."

"Maybe." Sylvia entered the locked ward with the security guard on her heels. As the psychologist passed the private rooms, she heard an occasional whimper or sigh from a restless occupant. She rose slightly on tiptoe, keeping her heels above ground to muffle the sound her shoes would make on linoleum.

She reached the child's room—Khalsa took up his position guarding the door—and she entered quietly, alone. Serena was in bed asleep. Her breathing was shallow and even. The covers were twisted around her small body; her arms clutched the pillow to her cheek. Sylvia sat on the edge of the bed. The glow of a street lamp rinsed the child's skin of its warmth and made her look unnaturally pale. Her mouth was pursed, lips just slightly parted, eyes closed and fringed with lashes. Her fingers clutched fabric. Her face—sweet and sad— reminded Sylvia of an angel.

Sylvia pressed the palm of her hand to the child's forehead, felt skin that was warm and moist. Serena didn't wake, but she turned, a sigh escaping her lips. Sylvia knew she could tell herself she didn't love this child. But that would be a lie. She wasn't sure when curiosity, duty, fascination had turned to love. Had it happened when Serena tamed Nikki? Or when the child wrapped her arms around the psychologist's legs, attaching herself permanently? Or when they slept side by side?

Sylvia sat still, letting her breathing soften, allowing herself to slide into that space between sleep and waking. She felt hyperalert, but her mind drifted, floating on each breath. No insistent thoughts rattled through her consciousness. In her brain pictures appeared and disappeared just as quickly. The child. Her own face as a child. Cash Wheeler behind the prison barrier. Her father, Daniel Strange.

She held the image of her father's face. Held it without pain. Without recrimination, for the first time in years. Until that image dissolved with all the others.

Time didn't stand still, but it didn't seem to pass either. It simply balanced between the life-and-death decision of each inhalation, exhalation. Sylvia slid out of the space as gently as she had entered it. The first thing she saw was the sleeping child.

So that's what the good part of meditation was all about. All these months of sitting, straining her back, aware of every distraction, every ache and pain—all the while her mind revving like a motor. But this was a completely different state: clarity, simplicity, light. Perhaps Serena experienced something similar when she prayed?

She stirred, then gazed out the window, searching for a moon. If it was up there, it wasn't visible; it would have already moved along its path of orbit beyond the limited view offered by the east-facing window. When she stood to leave, her hand grazed the pocket of her silk jacket, and she felt something hard.

The medallion.

She'd forgotten to return it to the child. She took the silver chain and guided it gently over Serena's head.

"I promise, I'll always look out for you," she whispered. Then she kissed the child's cheek. Serena stirred without waking, twisting her body on the bed, and her small fingers found the medallion.

When Sylvia left the room, Khalsa was at his post outside the door. She said, "Keep an eye on her for me."

He nodded, and a ghost of a smile played over his rough features.

As she approached the lobby, Theo the Sleepy appeared from another hallway with a cup of steaming coffee. He lifted the cup and said, "*This* will keep me awake. Peggy made it fresh."

"You sure you don't want to get someone to cover for you?"

"Too late now. Anyway, I've got an astronomy midterm to study for." He slipped behind the desk, dropped into his chair, and faced an open textbook.

"I'll be right back." Sylvia heard the lock engage as the front doors closed behind her. She moved quickly down the walkway and stepped over to an idling vehicle. "Hey, wondered where you guys were."

A red-haired police officer smiled at her. "McDonald's. This is our dinner break. Aren't you here kind of late?"

"My third trip today. Might as well bring my suitcase and move in." Sylvia pulled a cigarette from her pocket and smiled. "Coffee break. Just wanted to say hi."

The cop handed her matches. She shivered as she lit the cigarette. The November air was cold, and she was dressed for a cocktail party. As she inhaled smoke, she lifted her face to gaze at the night sky. Yes, the moon was floating above the western horizon. Liquid yellow, it was somewhere between phases: gibbous and quarter.

She allowed herself three hits of nicotine, then she dropped the cigarette and ground it with fierce energy into the sidewalk. She waved to the cops. "Bye, guys."

Briskly, she retraced her steps to the hospital door where Theo the Sleepy let her inside. When she glanced back at the street, the cop flashed his lights.

RENZO WATCHED THE cop's headlights flash—once, twice—as the woman returned to the hospital. Was it the shrink? From this distance, he couldn't tell for certain. He'd parked the Seville one block south of Mesa Verde Hospital. At the moment, he could see Santa Fe P.D.'s finest, engine idling, in front of the building. His mouth tightened; they should have responded to a radio 10 code by now: burglary in progress. His decoys were late.

But even with the delay, Renzo felt as if his body were encased, safe from emotion, shrouded in calm. He didn't blink when the cops activated their flashing lights. They accelerated down to the end of the block, away from where Renzo was parked. As they turned the corner, they sounded the vehicle siren, one short *whoop.*

THEO WAS FAST asleep at his post behind the reception desk at Mesa Verde Hospital when the police siren sounded. He was still asleep forty-five seconds later, when someone rapped hard on the glass doors.

Khalsa had left his post in front of Room 21 to walk to the lobby; he'd heard a faint siren—one short wail—and he wanted to investigate. Two feds had come by the hospital earlier in the day—asking questions, looking at the girl. The combination of the feds and the regular cop patrols had him spooked. Everybody was interested in the half-pint occupant of Room 21. He'd read the newspapers today. He'd known right away—they were writing about her. Why else would a woman like Noelle Harding hire him to stand outside a hospital door all night?

In the lobby, when he heard the rap on glass, his blood pressure jumped. The sight of the man startled him—black pants, shirt, vest, and cap, gun in holster, badge, insignia. The uniform wasn't anything he recognized right off. It wasn't a D.E.A. or police SWAT uniform.

He tried to make sense of the picture: Was the man in black one of the *good guys*? If so, let him prove it. Khalsa approached the door cautiously. As he moved, his right hand dusted the weapon riding his hip. Through glass he studied the man's badge and I.D. According to that, the man was a cop, all right—a *Mexican* cop. A *federal.* What the hell, didn't he know *New* Mexico had declared independence a hundred years ago?

Warily, Khalsa retreated to the admissions desk, where Theo was snoring like a warthog, dead to the world, facedown in his astronomy textbook. The security guard jabbed at the young man, but Theo didn't stir. Khalsa found the main key ring on the desk. He shook the ring, picked out the key labeled MAIN, and returned to the door to unlock the dead bolt.

Khalsa blocked the open door with his substantial body mass. "What's going on?"

"Someone's coming after the girl. You're going to need backup. Radio your Dispatch." The Mexican cop stared down the security guard. "I'll patch you through to the feds."

"You're with the Mexican *federales*, you're not D.E.A.—"

"We're working with the D.E.A. and F.B.I." The Mexican set one hand on the guard's shoulder. He didn't push, but he said, "We're running out of time."

Khalsa gave way grudgingly, and the man brushed past him.

"DID YOU HEAR something?" Sylvia froze, listening. Peggy had the radio playing in the hospital's staff lounge—the oldies station—and it was hard to hear anything except the chorus of "Under the Boardwalk."

Peggy shrugged, filling a coffee mug to the brim. "I heard a fire siren. I hear them every shift because the station's so close."

Sylvia stepped to the door of the lounge and strained her ears, listening closely. The only audible sound was the mundane white noise of the hospital—and Peggy's radio.

The nurse handed Sylvia the coffee mug with a smile. "You're kind of jumpy tonight, huh?"

Sylvia nodded; she kept expecting a tall, dark demon to appear around every corner.

Peggy sat down at the small Formica-topped table, humming the 1960s tune. She patted the chair next to hers. "I get that way sometimes."

Sylvia sat in the designated chair, sipping gingerly at the scalding coffee.

The nurse touched Sylvia's arm. "I read the papers today. That story was about your little girl in Twenty-one, wasn't it?" She interpreted the psychologist's silence as confirmation and continued, "What's wrong with her? Why doesn't she speak?"

Sylvia suddenly felt weary. She really enjoyed Peggy, but she didn't feel like discussing Serena with anyone tonight.

"Is it psychological?" Peggy pressed.

"Ummmm." Steam wafted into Sylvia's nostrils.

"She could join the Carmelites." Peggy rolled her eyes at her own joke.

"What did you say?"

"I was joking." Peggy looked sheepish. "The Carmelites—the nuns who live up by St. John's College? Don't they take a vow of silence to God?"

ONCE RENZO HAD gained access to the hospital lobby, he said, "Call your dispatcher—I'll give you the number to verify my involvement—"

As the security guard activated his radio, Renzo lifted the .22 to the base of the man's neck. He said, "But first, let's go see the girl."

Khalsa stiffened and glanced toward the young man behind the desk; there would be no help from that quarter: Theo's snores rose and fell with stubborn consistency. Still, Khalsa hesitated. He could yell for help—but he'd be shot along with Theo and whoever responded to his summons. Best to keep silent, to play along and wait for a moment to catch the other man off guard. He yielded to the persuasive prod of a cool metal gun barrel.

The two men moved as one down the hallway—the guard in the lead, Renzo close behind—past private rooms. Renzo scanned glassed doors for curious faces. But apparently, the inhabitants of Mesa Verde Hospital slept through the night. Maybe it had something to do with the drugs doctors gave crazy people.

He was prepared for any encounter with additional staff. He knew the hospital kept two nurses on night shift; at this moment, they were probably in the acute-care wing. That was only a few hundred feet away, but the building wings were separated by soundproofed walls and metal designed to keep agitated patients in check.

Mesa Verde's resident security—separate from Khalsa—was an elderly man who spent most of his time prowling the rear exit of the building.

When the two men reached the end of the hall, Khalsa paused at the door to the locked ward. Renzo knew that behind this metal-and-glass barrier he would find Serena. He detected a slight increase in his heart-beat—that was all. He prodded his hostage with gunmetal.

To Khalsa, the smack of the gun echoed in his ear like an explosion. The key ring was clutched in his trembling hands, and when he didn't recognize the metal shapes he suffered a wave of nausea. The sickness passed, and then he remembered that this door opened with a punch-pad code. He entered the code and pushed open the heavy door. Both men entered the locked ward.

As Renzo approached Room 21, he felt the security guard slow.

Renzo spoke hoarsely. "Open the door."

"I don't have the key." Khalsa shook his head, lying badly.

"Open the fucking door." Renzo's voice dropped to a lethal whisper.

The guard's fingers shifted over the ring of keys.

Before he had a chance to speak, Renzo fired the .22. The explosion, muffled by the silencer, sounded like a very noisily popped top on a beer can. The guard dropped. Renzo stepped over him, stared down. The bullet's exit trajectory had done severe damage to the guard's face. Blood pooled under the dying man's head.

Renzo dragged the body away from the door to Room 21. The effort awakened new pain in his injured arm. He tried several keys before he found the correct master. Fortunately, the facility hadn't switched over fully to punch pads; he'd still be struggling to find the code. He opened the door. The child was asleep on the bed.

Renzo kept his eye on her sleeping form as he dragged Khalsa's body into the room. Dead, the man seemed to have gained twice his living mass. A few feet inside the room, Renzo released his grip.

The child had twisted her body and the sheet into knots. Street lights and shadow added to the confusing effect. Renzo crossed the space in three strides, grabbed bedding—but nothing more.

There was a soft rustling noise, like the sound of nesting mice. Renzo whirled around just as a shadow darted across the room toward the open doorway. He followed.

He stepped out of the darkened room, his eyes reacting to the lighted hallway. If he was stunned by the soft glow of fluorescence, the child must be blinded. She hurled her body down the hall toward the ward's exit door. She was barefoot, clad in green pajamas. Her dark hair was loose, flying over her shoulders as she ran.

She slammed herself against the locked door. Her small body vibrated, her ribs expanding with quickened breath. She responded to the sound of Renzo's approaching footfalls by stiffening. When he had almost reached her, she turned.

Something fell from her fingers and skidded a few feet across the slick tile—a child's coloring book. The cover was made of cracked blue vinyl decorated with cartoon dogs. Renzo recognized it instantly. Amado Fortuna's first efforts at record keeping.

Tuna's Diary.

Renzo bent down to retrieve the small book. He kept his eyes on the child.

She stared back at him with the face of a little goddess. Silent. Stunned. Huge eyes filled with sorrow and reproach. And fear. There was so much fear, Renzo wondered how she was still able to stand. Abruptly her features went slack, and she seemed to be focused on some floating point above Renzo's head. She was staring that way, trancelike, when he reached for her. His hands closed around her body; he was immediately surprised by how light she felt. He cut off the blood supply to her brain, and she went limp in his arms.

Then he pressed the snout of the .22 caliber to the back of her skull, and his trigger finger began to contract, slowly, steadily.

CHAPTER TWENTY-SIX

DIANA ROSS WAS belting out "Stop! In the Name of Love" when Sylvia stood abruptly.

Peggy looked startled. "What's wrong?"

"This time I *know* I heard something." Sylvia tossed the half-empty cup in the trash can and headed for the door of the staff lounge. As she strode along the hallway toward the main lobby, she told herself she was overreacting. But hell, there was no law against harmless compulsive behavior.

As she approached the lobby, she heard the front door swing closed. The sound was wrong—there was almost no traffic this time of night. She broke into a half run, reaching the reception area just in time to see a shadowy shape disappearing down the lighted hospital walkway, then cutting across the lawn.

Sylvia pushed open the door and stepped outside. There was no one in sight, but she heard the soft sounds of a car door opening. She turned, staring across the lawn past the parking area. The big American car was parked beyond the full arc of a streetlight's glow; but Sylvia saw the man, and she recognized Serena as he shoved the child's limp body into the vehicle's back-seat.

SHE CALLED OUT, but the man was already behind the wheel. Her voice faded on the air just as the engine caught with a deep rumble. The Cadillac pulled away from the curb, and Sylvia turned on her heel and raced back to the hospital.

The door had locked behind her. She smacked her palm hard against the glass, yelling for help. Her eyes saw a dark smear marring the thick pane—her brain registered *blood*. Through the door, she could see Peggy half running into the lobby. The nurse's face froze in alarm when she saw Sylvia pounding her fist against glass. Within seconds Peggy had the door open. "What's wrong?"

Sylvia lunged into the lobby shouting out commands: "Call nine-one-one, tell them there's been a kidnapping—the child in Room Twenty-one!"

Peggy moved back to the admissions counter just as Theo's head appeared above the desktop—eyes glazed, skin swollen from sleep. The nurse slapped him hard across the face—either to shock him into a fully alert state or to punish him because the child was gone.

Theo stumbled out of his chair, a blank look on his face, puzzlement in his eyes, and he bumped into Sylvia. She grabbed him by the T-shirt and jerked him hard. She spit out the question—"Did you see anyone?"

When Theo shook his head dully, Sylvia directed her final words to Peggy. "Tell Dispatch—Serena was taken by an adult male. I'm going to follow the car—it's a Cadillac or an Oldsmobile, dark color, new."

She shoved Theo backward and yanked car keys from her pocket. "Theo, find out what happened to Khalsa. *Now!*"

The last view Sylvia had of the hospital was of Peggy talking into the phone. Then the psychologist was running across the grass toward Matt's battered pickup.

SHE APOLOGIZED SILENTLY to Matt as she jammed the standard shift into reverse. There was the harsh groan of tortured gears. She backed out of the parking place, rammed the stick into first, then revved out of the lot. She didn't have to worry about keeping distance between vehicles; the other car had disappeared. She prayed he would head east toward the main thoroughfare, St. Francis Drive. She pressed down on the gas, hurtling along the residential streets. Her hands were shaking on the wheel. Automatically, she reached for her cell phone. It was in her briefcase—the one she'd left in Rosie's Camaro. *Fuck.*

As she approached the blinking lights of the St. Francis intersection, she saw taillights turning right—south—*yes!* Sylvia hunkered down in the seat and guided Matt's pickup in the same direction. A station wagon cut into the lane in front of her, and she hit the brakes too fast. The pickup stuttered, then smoothed out. She didn't want to get too close to the kidnapper's car. She could see now it was a Cadillac.

The car was moving as if the driver didn't know anyone was following. Get too close, he'd see her—or *feel* her on his tail. She knew instinctively he wouldn't hesitate to kill the child.

Or maybe Serena was already dead.

Sylvia stared at the upcoming traffic signal at St. Francis Drive and Cerrillos Road. The Cadillac passed through the intersection just as the light danced blearily from green to yellow to red. She braked to a stop, narrowly avoiding a collision with a single car that was crossing the intersection. She watched its slow progress from the idling pickup; the engine missed, the vehicle vibrated, and she could see smoke trailing behind the Ford. She didn't wait for the light to turn green—she checked lanes and then crept on through the intersection.

Now she passed state buildings, parks, office complexes. She knew he would continue to the interstate. It was less than a minute away. There was one more gas station before the highway entrance ramp. Ahead, the station's lights were glowing like fluorescent islands in a dark urban sea.

If she pulled off, could she convince a clerk to notify state police? She imagined the conversation—urgent shorthand, minus subtlety. *"Call nine-one-one, tell Dispatch it's about the child who was kidnapped from Mesa Verde Hospital. Tell them the kidnapper's headed for the interstate."*

In her mind, the gas-station attendant stared back at her dumbly. Her imagined words were gobbledygook. She could make the call herself—did she have a quarter? She wasn't close enough to read the license plate on the Cadillac.

A quarter mile ahead, the dark vehicle was accelerating—past the gas station. Her foot refused to ease up on the accelerator. The Cadillac—and Serena—were moving quickly out of reach.

She couldn't risk stopping. If she lost him, she lost the child. From the corner of her eye, she saw the Shell station pass in a blur of lights. Then there was the darkness of a high-desert evening at the edge of civilization.

She guided the old pickup onto the interstate, following.

He was headed north, not south.

TONIGHT—EXCLUDING THIS brief cut over to Highway 285—Renzo Santos would stay off the main highways. While I-25 dove down in a semistraight line all the way to Mexico, cops would be swarming the interstate. He figured he had thirty minutes maximum before the security guard's body—and the child's absence—were discovered. Maybe the cops had already been alerted. The trip from Santa Fe to the Mexican border took almost five hours on the fastest roads. His plan meant traveling on two-lanes, gravel, even dirt; back roads would take longer, but they had an advantage—he would make it to the border. He kept one eye on the exit signs as he followed the interstate toward the Lamy turnoff.

The child was in the backseat under a blanket. If they were stopped by the highway patrol, she was just a sleeping kid.

He glanced at his wrist—his gaze flicked to the blood staining his glove—then steadied on the watch face: 12:50 A.M. Seven minutes later, he eased the Cadillac off the highway at the exit to Lamy. This was the same road he had followed days before when he was pursuing the shrink and the child. But he would not stop again at the godforsaken spot where Paco died, where he had been attacked by *lobo loco*.

Renzo had finally cornered his prey. It was his job to find targets—to kill them if necessary—or to make them give information and then leave them dead.

This time, his prey had proved a surprisingly worthy opponent. Renzo grunted at the thought of the child's efforts at evasion and resistance—her final fight. He felt something that might just be grudging admiration. She would stay alive—as long as she was useful as his hostage.

All this time, she'd possessed the one thing that could destroy Tuna—and others as well. But she had delivered the diary straight into his hands.

Renzo pressed one palm against the pocket of his jacket. He felt the small bulge of the book.

He'd known the bookkeeper for years, but only days ago had Renzo discovered Paco's secret home in Anapra. The home where the girl had been hidden away for a decade.

Renzo's thoughts slid back to a hot, sultry afternoon ten years earlier. The first part of the journey was clearest in his mind—the shocking discovery that Elena had fled with the baby. She had run back to Cash, deserting Renzo even after his anguished confession, his vow to change his life for her, his declaration of devotion.

The shame still burned in Renzo's gut. It had driven him north after Elena. He had wanted to travel alone, but Amado had insisted that Paco go along: "My cousin needs to prove his loyalty to me. Let him get blood on his hands. Let him learn he can't afford a heart."

For three hundred miles—and ten years—Paco had remained silent. The bookkeeper had never spoken of that day. But he had watched as Renzo injected liquid courage into his own veins. And he had witnessed what

Renzo knew only as a fractured memory of blood, rage, and murder—and, finally, when it was all over—a dark sleep that lasted two days and nights until he regained consciousness.

Renzo was not aware that his lids had slid down over his yellowed eyeballs—but he blinked—twice.

"Let him get blood on his hands. Let him learn he can't afford a heart."

Renzo's thoughts stubbornly refused to let go of Paco, who had stolen the baby in front of them all. Paco, who dropped a bundle of rags in the river. For a fleeting instant, Renzo felt envy for the dead bookkeeper—Paco had died for love.

But it was over now, and Renzo had won. A picture caught in his mind: the last moments at the hospital, the child's dead weight in his arms.

Frowning, he guided the Cadillac toward Lamy, accelerating rapidly onto blacktop divided by faded white dashes—they licked under the belly of the big car. The three-hundred-horsepower engine throbbed under his thighs and butt. Nothing in the rearview mirror; no sign of company.

SYLVIA KEPT SO much distance between vehicles, she almost lost her quarry. She was slowing, navigating the exit to Lamy when she noticed the absence of lights. Headlights. Taillights. Any lights. There was no sign of a car in either direction. The engine whined as she braked hard.

He was headed south—*he had to be.*

She gave the truck gas and picked up speed.

Matt's Ford had no accurate speedometer. No gas gauge. No radio. No heater. The front end was out of alignment. The engine desperately needed a tune-up. The wheel play was loose, frighteningly flabby. The headlamps were skewed, allowing for claustrophobically narrow illumination of the highway ahead.

Ten miles southeast of Santa Fe the glow of city lights had dimmed. The moon was waning, hanging now like a yellow petal in the black sky.

She accelerated, trying to close the distance on the Cadillac—just to be sure it was ahead, not behind her. She believed the child was alive. Why steal a *dead* body from the hospital? The man—whoever he was—needed Serena alive. The child was his ticket out of the U.S. Sylvia focused hard on that thought as she pushed the Ford.

There. She caught sight of taillights. She couldn't see a license plate, couldn't even make out the general shape of the vehicle. She had to assume it was the Cadillac.

Her breath caught when the lights disappeared yet again. Had he pulled off? Had he turned? She slowed, searching for a side road, trying to remember what was out here in all this space.

There. She saw headlamps illuminating a grade. How the hell had he gained so much distance? He must be traveling ninety-five, a hundred miles per hour. At that speed, he would leave her in the dust.

Matt's truck had a maximum speed of somewhere around seventy-five, and even that was pushing it. He'd warned her the engine could blow if it was stressed for a long period. How fast was she going? She gritted her teeth, ignoring the whine of the hot engine. Glancing down, she thought it would be nice to have a seat belt. She was cold—dressed in silk for a party, not long-distance pursuit. She was hungry. There might just be half a Snickers in her small purse. And a credit card. What else? Lipstick, powder. A hairbrush in the glove compartment.

Great. She could give herself a makeover. If she only had her briefcase, her phone, and a map ... but wishful thinking would not ward off the horrible fear that the child would disappear forever into darkness.

"Oh, God." Sylvia's voice was barely a whisper inside the cold, dark truck.

Serena, I'm with you.

SHE WAS DEAD. All that was left was a blanket of darkness. A foggy quiet.

This time, Serena knew it was really true. But she felt something stirring from the ground up. Something was rumbling. Was it the death rattle old people talked about? A dark bee buzzing and buzzing. A *slap, slap, slap*ping sound. The vague feeling of moving through space.

Where had she been before dying? Mexico? The hospital? Through the fog she remembered only twilight snatches—a word, a voice, a face. The effort of remembering made her head hurt. Great waves of pain flowed through her small body. The pain made her shiver.

She tried to move, to clasp the medallion, but her arm stayed rigid—her wrists were wedged together. Her ankles, too. Pinpricks shot along her limbs, a million tingling messages exploding in muscles and nerves. Her teeth were clacking like a wind-up skeleton jaw.

Would your teeth chatter after you died?

Maybe.

She felt a rush of joy—Paco had flown down from heaven to take her hand. Elena—her own mother—

must be missing her up above, in God's world. Serena sighed. Heaven would be warm, misty, and soft.

But if you were truly dead, would you hurt so much your body felt like it was breaking? If you were on your way to heaven, the Blessed Virgin would not allow you to suffer. Not even a little bit.

A new thought made the child tremble again.

What if she weren't going to heaven? What if this was that other place?

But immediately, she knew the thought was unworthy. The Virgin was so kind, so loving, she took all her children by the hand. She said, "If you love me, I am here . . ."

> *If you need me, I am with you.*
> *If you help the poor, I am with you.*
> *If you are kind, I am with you.*
> *If you are loving, I walk with you.*
> *I am with you.*

Serena rested a moment, nestled in the comfort of those prayers. The Virgin's presence helped her find the courage to return to that place between heaven and hell—earth.

She was not dying. She was not in safe hands. It was the faint scent of medicine, the rusty smell of blood, that dashed her down from the clouds.

¡El demonio! He had come for her. And this time, even Sylvia had failed to protect her. Tears of fright, of desolation, streaked the child's cheeks. She had been abandoned by her mother, by Paco, and finally, by Sylvia.

Once again, she was all alone in the dark.

CHAPTER TWENTY-SEVEN

FIVE MILES NORTH of Clines Corners, Sylvia began to pray. Between mumbled invocations, she stared numbly at the Ford's gas gauge. The needle was resting solidly at the half-tank mark. It had stayed in that exact spot for the last forty miles. For that matter, the needle had been at the same mark for the last four thousand miles. The gauge was broken.

Clines Corners marked the intersection of 285 and I-40. Café, souvenir shop, gas station, truck stop—if the Cadillac had pulled off at Clines Corners, Sylvia knew she had to risk stopping for gas. The Ford's tank could run dry within the next fifty miles—or the next five miles. She tried to remember what Matt had told her about its capacity. But all she heard was his admonition: "Don't push the engine . . . don't drive it out of town."

So here she was, pedal to the metal, forty miles from Santa Fe and counting.

If she came face-to-face with the kidnapper at Clines

Corners, at least it would be in a public place. Not that the presence of other people would save her life—or Serena's.

The truck stop was three miles away.

She tried to track his logic in her own mind: in his eyes, she might be a pesky fly. Irritating, but not dangerous.

She posed no real threat; she carried no weapon, no telephone, no radio—*but he didn't know that.*

Would he consider her a risk?

Or would he believe that as long as he had Serena, he held all the power?

And what about Serena? How would she survive this latest trauma on top of everything else? Faith might anchor her to sanity—it might also tempt her over the edge into madness.

Then Sylvia remembered the blood on the hospital door, and she prayed the child wasn't already dead.

When the Ford was roughly a half mile from Clines Corners, Sylvia began scanning for the black Cadillac.

One-third mile. She squinted through darkness, trying to focus on the lighted parking lot. As far as she could see, it was occupied by a half dozen cars and two or three big rigs.

What if she missed the Cadillac because it was parked around the corner near the cafeteria? What if he'd pulled onto I-40? He could head west, then south on I-25. Or he might continue on the back roads.

She had to turn right or left or continue straight ahead. She had to decide.

She pressed down on the gas pedal, and the truck rumbled onto the overpass. She was betting on straight.

＊　　　＊　　　＊

IN SANTA FE, the desk clerk named Theo had been talking nervously to the special agent from the Federal Bureau of Investigation. The lobby of Mesa Verde Hospital was swimming with investigators and forensic technicians from state and federal agencies. They were investigating a murder and a kidnapping. And Theo was a witness. His astronomy textbook lay open and forgotten on the floor. From his chair behind the desk, he eagerly watched all the comings and goings. An avid fan of reality-based TV, he watched *Cops* and *Emergency!* every week.

As a female state police officer approached, he reluctantly turned his bug-eyed gaze back to the F.B.I. agent. "Dr. Sylvia Strange—the psychologist who was treating the girl—she told me to call you guys, yes sir."

The agent nodded. "She gave you a description of the kidnapper's vehicle. Did you see the vehicle yourself?"

"No, sir." Theo wagged his head woefully. He'd missed his big opportunity. If he'd saved the girl, he'd be a hero. A wise voice in his head reminded him: *You'd be a dead hero, dipshit. Just like Khalsa.*

The state police officer had come to a standstill behind the F.B.I. agent's left shoulder. She smiled encouragingly at Theo.

The F.B.I. man looked impatient. "Dr. Strange took her own vehicle in pursuit of this man?"

Theo nodded. "Yes, sir."

"Can you describe her vehicle?"

"No, sir."

The federal agent contained his frustration. "Did you watch her drive off?"

"I was calling you guys." Theo's voice wavered to a stop.

"You were on duty when she arrived tonight, weren't you?"

Theo nodded mutely. He was afraid to open his mouth.

"Did you see her vehicle at that time?"

"Ummm, she parked off to the side, in that lot over there."

"What kind of vehicle does she normally drive?"

Theo had turned bright pink, and he was about to break out crying when a woman spoke up. "I know Dr. Strange. She drives a Toyota pickup with a camper shell."

The federal agent scribbled on his notepad, then looked up at the woman. Her face was familiar. She was blond, thin, intense. "You are?"

"Noelle Harding. The girl who was kidnapped is my niece." Harding intentionally trespassed on the federal agent's personal space; her manner was direct, her expression all business. "Special Agent . . . Carter. I'm sure the kidnapper is headed to Mexico. I want all relevant law-enforcement personnel alerted. I expect helicopter transport."

"Ma'am?"

"Don't 'ma'am' me, Mr. Carter—I've already spoken to the governor of my home state. He has expressed his support."

"Yes, ma'am."

FIVE MILES OUTSIDE the pit stop named Corona, Renzo passed a cop. He didn't even bother to slow down. He was going ninety-eight miles per hour. If the cop had clocked him, it was over. Even without radar, the cop had to be an idiot to miss that kind of speed.

But the cop didn't follow. That made Renzo even

more nervous. He'd been listening to the scanners—so far nothing. Nobody knew what kind of car he was driving. But he couldn't assume that. Someone in the hospital might have seen him leave. In that case, there would be a network of cops up and down the state with one thing on their minds: tracking Renzo.

The cops might be using a scrambled radio frequency—especially if the feds were already in on it.

He drove through the darkness—his mind racing—for the next thirty miles. He watched the moon disappear. He felt the miles stretch out behind the Cadillac. His wounds were beginning to burn, the stitches itched—but he felt no pain, no fatigue. It was as if a barrier existed between his body and his mind. The drugs? But they were wearing off—he felt their diminishing power as if his blood were thinning. He would need to dose himself again. Maybe in Carrizozo.

And what about the girl? If the feds were tracking him—and he increasingly suspected they might be—then he needed her more than ever. She was his only insurance. But once he reached the border of Mexico, she would die.

For an instant, he thought he heard Elena's soft voice. It sent shivers through his body. He remembered his fevered dream from a few nights ago—when the poison from the *lobo loco* had tainted his body. Elena had come to him that night—she had reached out from her grave.

He lifted his wrist to his lips and kissed his silver bracelet—the face of Coatlicue. Was the fever returning to weaken his mind? Why else would he think of Elena?

And then, fifteen miles north of Carrizozo, Renzo *felt* the child.

She was staring at him. Her eyes bored into the back

of his neck like twin metal screws. He refused to look at her, keeping his gaze on the road ahead. On the gray strip of asphalt, the yellow center line had faded out to sorry, intermittent dashes. Otherwise, just before sunrise, the world was wide open. Potholes and ruts jarred the Cadillac's thirty-thousand-dollar suspension system. He'd hit a rabbit a few miles back. Bad luck.

He found himself counting the power poles that loomed out of darkness. He looked everywhere but at the child. After a few minutes his mouth tasted like wood. He realized his reaction was foolish. Why should he be spooked by some girl? Even if she was Elena's child, she wasn't a ghost.

He swallowed painfully, licked his lips. Finally, he tipped his head, pulling his eyes to the mirror to verify his gut instinct.

She was sitting up, staring with those big black eyes. She met his gaze.

His eyes slid away. She made no sound, not even a moan. By now, the tape on her wrists and ankles had certainly cut off her circulation. Her hands and feet had to be numb. But she didn't whine, didn't cry out or complain. She just kept staring. He adjusted the rearview mirror so the ghost disappeared.

He drove like that for another ten miles. He readjusted the mirror. Their gazes met, locked, did not waver. It spooked him.

His mother-the-*puta* had dragged him to visit the Virgin when he was a boy. The church had been filled with women, with cripples, with children, with the poor, the infirm, and the sick. The crowds had smelled of sweat and misery and pain—they had frightened a boy of five.

He'd seen women and girls overcome with the Holy Mother's blessing. They had fallen to their knees, palms up, tears streaming down their dusty cheeks. For hours, for a whole day, they would stay kneeling on bruised and bloodied knees. But they felt no pain, and their faces glowed with radiant peace.

The Mother's Blessing, they said, Spanish prayers rolling off their tongues.

She is the Holy Mother. She is always with us. She is Everything, Everywhere.

She is here.

His mother, too, had knelt in front of the statues, the paintings, the pictures. She had knelt with the other women, and she had wept. And now Renzo remembered who his mother had prayed for so fervently—her son.

He gasped. In the darkness of the Cadillac, ghosts fluttered around his face like pecking birds.

He felt for his gun, his fingers tightening around the butt of the .22 caliber. The cold gunmetal made him feel powerful. With his fingers on steel, he summoned the courage to look in the rearview mirror one more time. And then he knew what had been haunting him.

The Blessed mother at the shrine . . . Serena looked just like *La Virgen.*

CHAPTER TWENTY-EIGHT

MATT ENGLAND HAD been asleep for less than ten minutes when the phone rang in the hotel room of the Juárez Holiday Inn. Must be Vargas, he thought groggily.

But it was Dale Pitkin at E.P.I.C.—the only other person who knew where to reach the two men. Pitkin's voice was hard. "Bad news," he said. "The girl was kidnapped from Santa Fe. Sylvia went after the guy."

"Jesus," Matt said. In an instant, he was awake. "The cops know what to look for? Her license plate is . . . T-S-X-three-one-one."

"Matt, they know."

"A Toyota truck, green, 1996—"

"They *know*. They're cops. You're a cop. Pour yourself a shot of something strong and get dressed—"

"Give me what you've got." Matt gripped the phone hard.

"The details are sketchy. They're expecting the kidnapper to hit the border within the next two hours."

"Who is he?"

"The Cadillac's registered to a Martin Díaz. A nice upstanding citizen who died two years ago. It's all phony."

"No description."

"Just from Sylvia and then the cops along the way. White or Hispanic adult male."

"It's got to be the same guy who jumped Sylvia and the kid in Santa Fe." Matt gritted his teeth. "Vargas knows who he is—an assassin on the *federales'* payroll. What do they call them, godmothers?"

"A *madrina.*" A beat went by before Pitkin said, "You and Victor better get your asses across the border."

Matt slapped the side of his head. "Shit! Sylvia's in my truck, not the Toyota. She borrowed my Ford. The damn thing doesn't go faster than seventy-five."

"It does now." Dale Pitkin cleared his throat. "The last report they got was five minutes ago from the high-way patrol north of Carrizozo. The Cadillac was clocked doing ninety-nine miles per hour."

"There's no way she could keep up."

"When the cops didn't see your gal's Toyota truck, they started noticing a funky pickup. She's only fifteen miles behind him—he keeps slowing down when he hits the towns along Fifty-four."

"Goddammit, the cops move in, they'll freak the bastard."

"They know that. They're keeping a distance."

"What about the feds?"

"They've got air backup, a SWAT team ready to truck at the border, agents along the way. By now they've probably got a procession going behind the perp."

"He'll do the kid without blinking."

"At the moment she's his only bargaining chip."

"Sylvia?"

"In the meantime, your lady's stayed with him." Pitkin laughed. "She's a true American hero, amigo. If I were you, I'd get ready for a rendezvous. I'll keep you informed."

Matt's last words were, "Shit, she doesn't know how to switch to the second gas tank."

WITH THE VALLEY of Fire lava flow visible in predawn light, Sylvia saw the highway sign—CARRIZOZO 8 MI.—just as the truck's engine began to sputter. It coughed, caught, held another hundred yards, then coughed again. She swayed the steering wheel from side to side, sloshing the last of the gasoline around the tank. That might coax another two or three miles out of the engine. After that, the Ford would be running on fumes.

The sun was just beginning to tint a heavy gray sky. Intermittent rain splattered the Ford's grimy, bug-spattered windshield. Thick smoke spewed from the rear of the truck. Hazy-eyed and sleep-deprived, Sylvia shifted in the seat, stretched aching muscles. The fact that she was about to roll to a stop had kicked adrenaline into her veins. It worked better than coffee.

Facts—meaningless in her present circumstances—raced through her overamped mind: Carrizozo; the town sat smack in the middle of the junction of U.S. 54 and 380, in a corner of Lincoln County; Billy the psychopathic Kid country. Hadn't the town grown up in the late 1800s because of the railroad? There'd been a gold rush around here somewhere . . . near Carrizo Mountain . . . placer gold discovered in the 1880s.

Something else drifted in and out of her consciousness. It seemed like ages since she'd read through Jim Teague's files, rather than mere hours. Obsessively, she'd gone over the coroner's report on the murders of Elena Cruz and the motel manager. All the time something had nagged at her—some similarity between their murders and the murder of the man Matt called Paco.

A name kept running through her brain: *Jesús* . . .

The weird boy the investigators had never been able to track down. The boy Cash Wheeler claimed had openly admired Elena Cruz. If he was still alive, he'd be in his late twenties, early thirties by now.

Sylvia gunned the engine, gaining as much roll as she could. Then she shifted into neutral, took her foot off the pedal, and sat back for the ride as two tons of metal coasted into town.

ON THE OUTSKIRTS OF Carrizozo, Renzo had slowed the Cadillac to twenty-five miles per hour. For the last twenty minutes, he'd watched the battered Ford pickup on his tail. He'd seen its distinctively skewed headlights earlier—but only when he slowed. The truck couldn't keep up speed.

It could belong to a farmer heading to Carrizozo.

It could belong to someone who was on his tail.

He maintained a sedate speed through the small town, unsuccessfully attempting to ignore the rumble of his stomach. He was famished. A job always made him hungry. And he had his health to consider; he was still recovering from the run-in with *el lobo*.

When he was drifting on the drug, he could go for days without eating. But when his hunger finally caught up with him, he couldn't ignore the voracious craving.

The Cadillac needed gas anyway. One fill-up and he would make it all the way to the border.

He drove conservatively, his head swaying left, then right, until he pulled into the parking lot of the last truck stop at the edge of the small town.

His stomach growled again. He pulled up at a bank of gas pumps.

When he leaned over the seat and prodded the girl, she didn't move. He spoke to her quietly: "If you make any noise, I'll kill you." He left her locked in the car.

Inside the truck stop's orange-and-yellow café, he used the bathroom. WASH YOUR HANDS, the sign above the sink ordered.

While Renzo was busy at one sink, a food server emerged from one of the stalls. A kid. Pimply. Oily. He was still zipping up his grungy pants. The kid had started toward the door when Renzo called out softly. "Wash your hands."

The kid stopped, glaring defiantly at the intrusive stranger. But he saw something in the man's eyes that made him pull back. The fight went out of him like a puff of air. He washed his hands. With soap.

At the register, Renzo asked for a box to carry out five burgers, two orders of fries, and three Cokes. The pimply-faced kid watched him leave. It had been a mistake to speak up, but Renzo hated germs.

The girl was almost invisible through the tinted windows. He set the box on the warm hood of the Cadillac and unlocked the door. She hadn't moved. *But her eyes followed every move he made.*

Frustrated but trying not to show it, he unwrapped a burger and tossed it into the backseat. Maybe she was hungry. Let her eat with her mouth like a dog.

He turned—moving toward the gas pump—but stopped in his tracks with a shudder. Elena's floating head appeared in front of his eyes, and she screamed at him: *If you murder my child, you'll be cursed.*

The vision evaporated like a faint mist. But Renzo couldn't erase Elena's words. Was her screaming voice the result of the drugs in his body? Was his blood poisoned? Or had he seen a dead woman?

SYLVIA HAD LOST the Cadillac. He was out of reach. Serena was out of reach. Her only chance now was to pull over, find a phone, and notify law enforcement. Unless her hunch was right, and various agencies were already tracking their progress. She'd noticed more than one police car in the past fifty miles.

The truck sputtered out, and Sylvia guided the coasting vehicle into the brightly lit truck stop. She rolled up next to a row of pumps behind a massive tractor-trailer. She was in the trucker's lane. Tough; she was driving a truck, too. And it was out of gas.

She climbed wearily from behind the wheel. She felt like shit—sore, stiff, exhausted, hungry, with a massive headache. The thought of losing the child made her physically ill. She fell back against the truck's faded fender, energy draining from her muscles like water.

A man said, "Lady, you all right?"

Did she fucking *look* all right? She clutched her purse, ready to talk a quarter out of the guy—a cheap price to pay for asking stupid questions.

Her first priority was to call State Dispatch to alert them to her location. The Cadillac had to be within twenty or thirty miles.

She turned, pushing herself toward the station's

minimart. She stopped in her tracks. She was staring at a black Cadillac Seville.

Sylvia strode toward the car. She didn't take time to think—to worry about danger. If Serena was inside, she might be able to grab her before he—

The kidnapper was standing at the rear of the big black car. He looked up, saw her, and his face went slack.

Seconds passed, maybe a minute. Sylvia lost any true sense of time. But she gave a soft cry when she saw the shadow of Serena's face pressed to the car's tinted rear window. She brought her hand to her mouth, bit down hard on her lip.

She wanted to call out, to cry for help. There were people around. But she'd seen something else—she'd seen the man slide his hand under his jacket, his hand grazing the butt of his weapon.

He watched her—waiting to see how she would react.

She could cry for help—he would shoot the child. He could kill her—but he'd still have to get out of town, away from witnesses. He couldn't shoot *everybody*.

She took a step toward the Cadillac.

He took a step toward her.

Checkmate. They stared at each other, exhausted.

Sylvia shook her head and spoke softly. "I won't do anything stupid." She reached out her right hand and pressed her palm to the window of the car. On the other side of glass, Serena reached out two fingers.

The man spoke in English with the voice Sylvia remembered. But it was smoother, more refined. He said, "I'm going to drive out of here, and you're going to stay right behind me. In sight. If you do what I say, she lives."

Sylvia nodded. Her mouth had gone dry as dust. She licked her lips and tried to swallow.

"Do you need some help, lady?"

Sylvia almost jumped at the sound of a new voice. That same stupid trucker was asking stupid questions. She barely looked at him. "I'm fine."

"You sure you're okay?"

"I'm *fine*." Sylvia's voice cracked on the second word. Cutting her eyes away, she saw the kidnapper's fingers close around the butt of his weapon. She turned toward the trucker and forced herself to flash him a wide smile. "Hey, I'm really fine. *Really*. But thanks for asking."

The trucker nodded, hips jutting forward aggressively. He shot the other man an ominous look, then walked away with a swagger.

Sylvia felt like she was going to melt into the ground. She said, "I need to fill up the Ford."

He nodded. "I'll be watching." He shielded his eyes with his hand—a bracelet gleamed on his wrist—and he looked up. The air moved with the sound of heavy blades.

Sylvia stared up at the sky. A helicopter dipped low over the station. She felt her stomach drop. The troops had arrived.

MATT CAUGHT THE phone before the first ring was even a bleat. "Talk to me."

Dale Pitkin said, "They picked up your truck and the Cadillac at Alamogordo."

"Sylvia—"

"Seems to be fine. But Matt—"

"What?"

"It's turning into an O.J."

"Shit."

"Noelle Harding threw her weight around—called the governor of Texas, the governor called the regional head of the F.B.I. They've got snipers in the air, feds on the ground, at the border. All they're missing is the damn army. These guys get trigger-happy real easily."

"What route is he taking?"

"He's cutting from Alamogordo straight down Fifty-four to El Paso. By now he should have about ten cops on his tail. He should reach the Rio Grande at oh-six hundred hours."

"With the sunrise. We're ready to go on this end." Matt lowered his voice. "Run Renzo Santos Portrillo through your computer. See what you get."

"That him?"

"Looks like it. That information is courtesy of our mutual friend."

"This Renzo—if that's who he is—he's calling himself Jesús."

"How the hell do you know that?"

"As soon as he saw the choppers in the sky, he made contact with the feds. He's been on his cell with the F.B.I. hostage negotiators."

"What's his deal?"

"He says he wants to bargain."

"He's a goddamn professional assassin for the *federales*. He's probably killed ten, fifteen, twenty men easy. He's not going to fucking bargain unless the chips are on his side." Matt paused, imagining the scene on the highway. He said, "Can the snipers get a bead on him in the vehicle?"

"Tinted windows. He says the kid's in his lap."

"I believe him."

"The command point is I-Ten near the bridge."
Pitkin paused a moment. Then he added, "Matt? Your
lady's going to need all the help she can get."

RENZO FOLLOWED I-10 as far as Sunland Park's
urban sprawl where highways diverged and U.S. 85 cut
south below the interstate. The Ford pickup was thirty
feet behind him; behind the Ford, a half dozen cop cars
kept rush-hour traffic at bay. A space of maybe fifty feet
in front of the Cadillac was clear; cops were funneling
traffic to the sides of the interstate. A mile or so ahead,
the interstate followed a rise, and from there all the way
through El Paso, it was bumper-to-bumper.

An El Paso P.D. car was parked at the head of the off
ramp to U.S. 85. Renzo almost tore paint off the vehicle
when he took the ramp. Glancing quickly at his rearview
mirror, he watched the Ford swerve—scrape past the
police unit taking paint *and* metal—following the
Cadillac's lead.

Now he was on U.S. 85—divided highway, two lanes
each way. Almost immediately, two cop cars passed him
on the left, pressing ahead. Renzo kept the space tight.
He glanced over and saw the light on his cell phone
blinking—hostage negotiators.

He held the phone to his mouth, switched it on, and
barked, "I changed my mind." He hung up before any of
the feds had a chance to reply.

The cops slowed in front of him, not responding to
orders from the helicopters but because they had no
choice; commuter traffic was stacking up. Renzo knew
he had two and a half, three miles or so before he
reached the heart of El Paso. He'd just passed a small
cemetery, and then the industrial waste of Smeltertown

north of the highway. This was the triangulated intersection of three states—New Mexico, Texas, and Chihuahua—all rubbing shoulders under the shadow of Cristo Rey Monument, the white cross crowning the Mexican peak. It was territorial hell for law enforcement: city and state cops, *federales*, I.N.S. and border patrol, U.S. Customs, the D.E.A. and the F.B.I., not to mention E.P.I.C.'s U.S. military reinforcements and Mexico's army.

Renzo took in the lay of the land: the train tracks running on both sides of the highway met and flowed together on 85's northern flank; the Rio Grande/Río Bravo edged the highway's south side. The highway itself was a chain-link, concrete, and asphalt canyon between river and railroad.

One mile to go.

The child moaned—maybe she was whispering. Her eyes were half closed. She crouched on the front seat beside him, praying—she reminded him of a crushed flower.

Renzo checked his rearview mirror. The Ford was still with him, gaining a few feet perhaps. He tapped his foot on the brake pedal twice in quick succession. The truck backed off, heeding the brake lights. Renzo imagined the woman must be dazed from exhaustion by now—in Carrizozo, he hadn't allowed her to buy food or drinks. He hadn't let her use the rest room.

Now he watched the terrain vigilantly. He was coming up on the location where U.S. 85 ran closest to the Rio Grande. It was the last dip before the highway cut north again. The stretch of several hundred feet was a favored location for border jumping. The chain-link fence was continually trespassed by illegals using wire cutters to slice through the metal barrier. The fence was accessed in at least three or four locations on a given week.

Cop cars still pushed fitfully against the solid lanes of traffic seventy feet ahead of Renzo. Behind, more cop cars regulated the heavy traffic to a slow-running stream. The Cadillac and the Ford were two ships isolated in a small two-hundred-foot sea of calm.

He saw a gap in the fence, passed it, slowing. Forty feet along the road, another gap. He spotted the three-foot-high split when he was thirty feet away. As he lifted his foot from the gas pedal, he heard a roar overhead. A helicopter appeared, swaying, chopping air with its massive rotors. The child's eyes shot open, and she gasped. He reached over a restraining hand as the helicopter disappeared over the roof of the Cadillac. He heard it traveling away from the highway, the roar receding like a wave.

Renzo braked. As the Cadillac rolled quietly to a stop, he cut the engine. In a chain reaction, the Ford jerked to a standstill. Then the cops ahead realized what had happened, and they cut sideways and braked. Finally, the cops in the rear sounded sirens, and two lanes of traffic, hundreds of cars and trucks, came to a grinding halt.

CHAPTER TWENTY-NINE

IN THE MIDDLE of U.S. 85, Sylvia cut the Ford's engine. Waves of heat rolled off the hood of the truck. The smell of burning rubber and exhaust stung her eyes. She sat immobile in the heavy air, sweat slick on her arms and face. Her window was rolled down, but there was not even a hint of breeze; every other vehicle within her immediate view was enclosed, air-conditioned. Through the windshield, just beyond the divided highway's northern bank, the stacks of an industrial mill belched black smoke into the already hazy sky. Looming in front of the mill, the railroad trestle had cut north, skirting Mexico, bridging New Mexico and Texas. A truncated freight train idled on the tracks.

Directly behind the Ford, the highway was clear for several car lengths; beyond the clearing, traffic backed up for miles. Where a trooper on a motorcycle had muscled his way between the two eastbound lanes, Sylvia had a view of asphalt.

To the south, she could see a battered and torn chain-link fence bounding the highway and the Rio Grande. Somewhere in the middle of that filthy river, the world became Mexico. On the opposite bank, a small, stooped woman dressed in red and white followed a river path. Behind the woman, slums crawled up the sides of the desiccated mountains.

Where the kidnapper was headed.

She swallowed—her parched throat aching—as she watched the driver's door on the black Cadillac swing slowly open. The vehicles were so close, the Ford nudged the Seville's bumper. When the Cadillac shifted on its shocks, the Ford rocked sympathetically.

No one stepped out of the Seville. Sylvia swallowed again; this time, her dehydrated tongue refused to relax, and she fought off the panic that she would choke to death stalled in traffic at the end of the world.

Ten miles in either direction, U.S. 85 was a solid metal zipper of cars, vans, buses, and trucks. The Cadillac and the Ford were wedged together in the eye of a gigantic urban storm. But the road might have been empty; all Sylvia could see was the open door in front of her. Nothing moved.

Finally, he emerged—*they* emerged—like a shy blind creature reluctantly stepping from the dark of a cave. The man seemed to be squatting behind Serena—using her as a belly shield; the child's legs hung limply against his thighs. Somehow, he must have tied her over his chest—a blanket was draped over both their heads serape-style so they melded into one amorphous body. There was no way to tell if she was injured or unconscious, alive or dead. Behind a fold of colorful fabric, Sylvia saw a shape that might've been his hand holding a gun.

The silence surprised her. She had expected to hear the F.B.I. announce its presence, assert its authority. Instead, she was startled by a shrill ring; it came from the interior of the Cadillac—the kidnapper's cell phone. Sylvia guessed it must be the F.B.I.'s hostage negotiators, who would be working to establish and maintain rapport. The last thing they wanted to do was spook a desperate perp.

She realized the Ford's steering wheel had dug an angry welt into her thigh. She took a breath and released her muscles. Without moving her head she could see at least four law-enforcement officers— shielded behind official cars, squatting between the stationary lanes of rush-hour traffic. She heard the roar of the helicopter—more than one; the news crews had smelled the scent of blood—but the noise of the engines faded quickly.

Along U.S. 85, a hundred faces peered out from behind windshields: parents driving children to school, men and women headed for the office, Mexican citizens who had just crossed the border for a day's work. They were all frozen together in this surreal montage: kidnapper, child, cops.

Sylvia's skin itched, pain shot along the back of her neck. She imagined she could feel the bead of a sniper's rifle, and she knew Serena's kidnapper felt it, too.

Reluctantly, she moved, hefting a thousand pounds just to press down on the latch, push the Ford's door open. White light stung her unprotected eyes when she stepped out of the truck. She felt the shift of weapons in the world, the kinetic force of action, reaction. Sights repositioned on a moving target. She licked her lips, inched her arms upward until her palms were level with her face; she pictured the ridiculous image of a mime pressing against an invisible windowpane.

She took a first step toward the man and Serena, her knees shaking so badly she thought they might actually knock. She had to pee; that urgent realization hit her, but all she could do was contract her muscles.

She took a second step, and a voice boomed out from the heavens: "This is the F.B.I. Stay where you are. Get down on your knees. Put your hands behind your head."

Fuck. Did the idiots believe *she* was a kidnapper? Well, she goddamn hadn't driven five hundred miles to end up on her hands and knees. She took another step forward, and the disembodied voice seemed to explode overhead.

"Down on your knees! I repeat, this is the F.B.I."

"Sylvia, do what they say!"

Sylvia sobbed with relief when she recognized Matt's amplified voice coming from somewhere close by. She yelled as loudly as she could, "Tell them to back off. We can talk this over." Sweat trickled along her ribs while she waited for a response. The silence seemed to last forever—what the hell were they doing, calling the president?

Finally, Matt's voice echoed again: "Go ahead, talk. But don't move any closer."

Sylvia nodded. Her shoulders were aching, but she didn't dare lower her arms. She faced the man and the child, what she could see of them. They were roughly eight or ten feet away. She tried to sound calm. She said, "Serena, I'm here." As far as she could tell, there was no reaction from the child.

When she spoke to the man, her tone took on an intentional edge of intimacy. "What should I call you?"

Seconds passed. She finally sighed. "I could really use a cigarette."

"Do you know who I am?"

She was startled by the sound of his voice. "I don't know what you call yourself now. Your name used to be Jesús."

He stood silent for such a long time, Sylvia began to think she'd destroyed any chance of negotiation. But eventually he spoke again. "Once I get into Mexico, I'll give you the girl."

"I can't negotiate for the F.B.I."

"You can tell them I don't want to kill her, but I will if they force the situation." He bit off the last word.

Sylvia wasn't sure if she saw the child move or not. She called out sharply, "Serena?" *There*—she thought she saw the slightest movement. She steadied herself and refocused on the man.

He said, "If I die, so does the girl."

"Look around." Very slowly, Sylvia lowered her hands to her sides; her muscles were putty. She said, "Give me Serena, and I'll tell them to cooperate."

He laughed but stopped suddenly when the child called out in a soft voice: "Sylvia."

Relief flowed through Sylvia. "I'm here. I'm right here, Serena." She glanced around—at the cops, at the helicopter hovering beyond the smokestacks, at the traffic. He had stopped here because the river—and Mexico—were so close. The Rio Grande was shallow, running twenty or thirty feet across. Beyond the link fence, the banks were dirt, rough, screened by shrubs, weeds, scraggy trees, the kind of scrub vegetation that survived even on a diet of chemical waste. Curious onlookers had gathered on the opposite bank. Mexico was just a hop, skip, and a jump away. Once you got past the cops, the hardware, the high-powered rifles . . .

She murmured, "Shit." Then she turned to address the man. She said, "Tell me how you want to do this—this exchange. I'll talk to them. I *swear* I'll try to get you a deal."

She thought he started to step forward, to bend down, so the child could reach the ground with her feet. Sylvia's body contracted automatically—but she jerked back when she heard the sharp crack. The sound was unmistakable—a rifle shot. Someone screamed—voices exploded in confusion. In the distance to her left she saw cops, stooped over, moving fast across the asphalt.

Under the jumble of blanket, man and child stumbled two paces toward Sylvia. As the man collapsed to his knees on the hard road surface, she saw Serena twist out from under his body, but she was still tangled in the blanket.

Sylvia put it together—gunshot—blood on the ground, on the child. He'd been shot—had Serena? *Oh, God.* Heart racing, she scrambled forward on her knees, reaching out for the child, calling her name.

She touched Serena just as the man lurched up. Instantly, she heard another crack. A second shot.

The blanket slid to the man's shoulders, and he stared at Sylvia with glazed eyes. His face was contorted in pain—and fury. Blood had smeared the side of his head—it flowed now from his shoulder.

He reached out one hand—his bracelet flashing on his wrist—and something fell to the ground. Sylvia thought it must be his gun.

He opened his mouth and glared straight at her, spitting out the words—"Double-crossing bitch!"—and then he thrust his body away, rolling under the Cadillac.

A cop was bellowing—"Get out of the way!"—over and over. Sylvia stumbled forward on her knees.

The voice coming from the bullhorn blurred to nonsense.

She was suddenly aware of a sharp, repetitive noise. The helicopter. It loomed over the highway like a giant predatory bird, sending waves of heat bouncing down on the asphalt. Sylvia's hair was blown back from her face. She sheltered Serena in her arms.

Gunfire broke out all around her—she cried out. Amid the chaos, she saw with unforgettable clarity the kidnapper's face when he cursed her. It was a second in time that had no meaning, but all Sylvia could think was, *I didn't betray you.*

RENZO FELT SOMEBODY punch in the side of his head. He heard the explosion—knew it was a long-range weapon.

Sniper.

Red bombs went off behind his eyes. His body jerked forward, and the girl went down with him.

Another sharp sound—the second shot. *Shoulder!* The blanket was wrenched forward where he and the girl fell.

"Double-crossing bitch!"

The diary hit the ground, skittering out of reach. Renzo used the last of his strength to thrust his body under the Cadillac.

He kept rolling—a man started shouting commands—and gunshots broke out. Renzo hit the fence, and somehow he wedged his feet, his knees, his body through the jagged metal slit. He fell, his hip slamming painfully against concrete, and he hit muddy water. The Rio Grande was boiling. Water popping and snarling like a living thing as bullets broke its filthy surface.

Leaking a thick trail of blood, he slithered through weeds, yellow mud, trash—the stench was poisonous. When he was fifteen or twenty feet downriver, he dove under the rank oily surface—the liquid border. Bullets fell on either side of his wounded body. His lungs were bursting, eyes burning, but he swam blindly ahead. The river was less than four or five feet deep, and he scraped the bottom.

SOMEONE KEPT HOUNDING Sylvia—a cop. He was shouting, "Are you injured?"

She would not let go of Serena.

"Ma'am, is the child injured?"

She clutched Serena in her arms, felt small hands grip her tight.

"F.B.I.—*are you all right?*"

She gazed down into dark eyes, saw sparks of life. She touched the child, searching for injury. While her hands grazed Serena's small frame, she felt something pressing against her knee. She looked down, saw the familiar coloring book—Serena's prized possession. It lay open, spine broken, two pages exposed: colors, scribbles, crude figures—too rough to be the child's work—and faint rows of penciled numbers and letters running underneath the rainbow colors like a subterranean stream.

A large hand reached for the book; startled, Sylvia looked up into Matt's face. He was staring at Serena's book as if he'd heard it speak.

Just as the child's small fingers grasped the pages, a voice said, "That's federal evidence."

Sylvia shaded her eyes, barely aware of the severe visage of a young, uptight federal agent. She heard Matt growl in frustration—he was out of his territory—but he didn't resist the agent who took possession of the book.

Then Matt had his arms around Sylvia—holding her and Serena so tightly they could hardly breathe.

For thirty minutes, everything occurred in a haze. Sylvia vaguely heard Matt arguing with the feds. Their response: "You're way out of your jurisdiction."

Then Matt whispering in her ear: "We've got to talk."

She thought she heard a familiar Texas twang. Big Jim Teague, fringed in leather, tossing his formidable weight around.

From a great distance someone announced, "They've got a floater two hundred yards downriver. A crew's going down."

And another voice: "... shooter on the Mexican side."

Sylvia felt the sting as something was injected into her arm. She was too exhausted to argue with the E.M.T. Wrapped in blankets, sipping fruit juice from straws, psychologist and child were finally stowed inside the comfortably dim interior ... of an ambulance? Or was it a limo-van?

CHAPTER THIRTY

THIRTY FLOORS ABOVE the city of El Paso, Texas, the Harding Building rose to a needle point, its microwave antenna piercing a smoggy sky. The building housed a bank, law offices, AeroChihuahua, a private tourism bureau, and the regional headquarters of the International Children's Rescue Fund. Noelle Harding maintained a five-thousand-square-foot suite on the top floor. Service staff privately referred to it as the Eagle's Nest.

The exterior walls were floor-to-ceiling glass, affording a view of a rusty sun as it set behind Comanche Peak and the Franklin Mountains. At the foot of the mountains—and as far as the eye could see in any direction—the urban sprawl of El Paso and Juárez spread out like a massive living, breathing, crazy quilt.

The view awaited Sylvia when she opened her eyes after six hours of solid sleep. The sleep had come only after an interminable session spent answering repetitive questions for the F.B.I. At the end of the debriefing session, she had demanded that she be taken to Serena. She'd expected to find her in a hospital.

But a quiet woman with a starched blue uniform and a lilting Mexican accent had explained: "This is the home of Señora Harding."

A wide verandah rimmed the suite's south and southwestern flanks. So far, Sylvia had discovered six rooms—living, dining, kitchen, library, and bedrooms—all very large. There were at least twice that many.

A hospital bed had been moved into the bedroom where Serena now slept. The space was immaculate and cheerful. The woven rug was patterned with rainbows, the wallpaper was decorated with Disney characters—Bambi, Dumbo, Mickey Mouse and Minnie, Snow White and the Seven Dwarfs. A nursery, ready and waiting.

A private nurse sat in a stiff-backed chair watching over the child. The woman was crisp, efficient, uncommunicative.

Sylvia had stayed with Serena for thirty minutes; she just wanted to be close to the sleeping child, to reassure herself the ordeal was over. But even that short amount of time had been difficult. Whatever sedative the E.M.T. had shot into her arm was quickly wearing off. In its place, emotional overload was setting in; the aftermath of shock.

The main living area of the penthouse was a multi-level expanse of creams, tawny golds, and icy blues. The filtered air was cool and fresh. The carpet felt like an overgrown lawn—four full inches overgrown. Sylvia opened handcrafted cupboards until she found what she was searching for: a fully stocked wet bar. She poured herself a long shot of vodka, fell back into a vanilla linen chair, and stared numbly out at the sister cities—two nations joined together by a watery seam of river.

She knew she'd never fully take in what she'd witnessed this morning on the highway. That would be impossible. Her mind would break the events into fragments, allowing regulated and select recall. For the immediate future, any loud noise, any abrupt flash of light was gunfire. Back in Santa Fe, she'd need her own shrink.

But there was one instant she would never forget— the shockingly intimate moment when the man had been shot—and when he'd cursed Sylvia.

She'd seen that bracelet on his arm—inlaid with Noelle Harding's snake-woman.

Over the past hours, the dangerous memory had battered her like a shark slamming repeatedly into the hull of a boat. Eventually, the shark had broken through her defenses—with a slow and clumsy realization—before it finally plunged her into deep waters.

She raised the glass to her lips, closing both eyes as she swallowed the icy, oily alcohol. It wasn't Sylvia who was the double-crossing bitch. She wasn't the one who had shot the kidnapper in the back—it was Noelle Harding.

Once that door opened in her consciousness—connecting a kidnapper known as Jesús to Noelle Harding— door after door swung wide. The possible scenarios were endless—and awful.

She fingered the card in her wallet. Matt had given it to her this morning. He said she could reach him with a phone call; that he'd be close by, but he had some business that couldn't wait.

Screw the F.B.I. and the D.E.A. and the cops in El Paso and Mexico—Sylvia needed Matt. *Now.*

The private elevator door opened. But it wasn't Noelle Harding or Matt England. Jim Teague greeted her somberly. "Are you all right?"

She shook her head, and he glanced at her drink, then proceeded to pour himself a shot of eighteen-year-old cognac. He foamed the golden alcohol with a blast of soda. Then he walked over to her, his fringed bulk oddly compatible with all the stark modern whiteness, the arctic decor. He touched her shoulder, sat on a couch, and downed two thirds of his drink. "Back in Texas, Grandma Teague used to say, Shit and fall back in it."

Sylvia raised one eyebrow. She realized she was tucked deep into the egg-shaped chair, legs crossed, arms wrapped around her body. Her eyes seemed trapped by the flickering gold and silver light display; sunset over urban landscape.

"The show's amazing when the sun hits the mountain above Juárez." Teague's voice broke like a choirboy's. He coughed, finishing the last of the cognac with a grunt. He heaved himself off the couch, walked unsteadily to the bar, and refilled his snifter. As a snack, he popped a handful of stuffed green olives between his lips.

Sylvia forced herself to make eye contact with the lawyer, noticing for the first time how his graying hair curled around his ears. His skin was tanned with a ruddy cast. Beneath his trademark bead-trimmed leather jacket, his white shirt was missing a button. His bolo tie had slipped askew. She unwrapped her arms and leaned toward him.

She said, "The snake-woman." She slurred the word, and he looked puzzled. She tried again. "Your tie. The Aztec goddess . . ."

He nodded. "You mean Coatlicue? The bloodthirsty

lady herself. When the Spaniards conquered Mexico, they really did a job on the Indians. They wiped out the old temples, but"—he overemphasized the conjunction—"they didn't wipe out the beliefs."

"Where did you get it—your tie?"

He shrugged. "A knickknack from Noelle. She's crazy about Coatlicue." He took another pull on his cognac, and a glint flashed in his eye. "Want to go to bed?"

Her eyebrows shot skyward.

He was humoring a tired child. "How long has it been since you've slept, Sylvia?"

She blinked, spoke too brightly. "I just slept for six hours straight."

"Excellent. And before that?"

"Yesterday. No. Two days ago."

"Shouldn't you get horizontal?"

"I *am* horizontal." She gripped the chair that threatened to swallow her up.

"Try your bed. One thing about the Eagle's Nest—guest accommodations are first-class."

Sylvia stood, swaying in a nonexistent breeze. She turned her back on Teague and carried her glass to the bar. With a flourish, she poured herself a second shot of vodka, then she added another dash. Using silver tongs, she collected two cubes of ice from a sweating silver bucket. It *looked* like silver. It probably was silver.

Sylvia leaned her hips against the bar. "How the hell do you stand it?"

Teague didn't answer, and she pushed. "How can you work for her?"

"Time to eighty-six you on the martinis."

She sipped vodka, shrugged.

"Right. I'll make this short. Noelle has been granted temporary status as Serena's foster parent."

Sylvia didn't even blink. "That was fast."

"Until the paternity issue is resolved, it's the most logical solution—"

"Is it?" She let her gaze travel the room. She was surrounded by all the trappings of civilized power—aesthetic grace, stateliness, wealth. And absolute control.

Noelle Harding controlled Serena's destiny. The Harding empire was a billion-dollar enterprise. If Noelle wanted press coverage, she got press coverage. If she wanted to take a young, innocent child under her wing—a child who might be her own long-lost niece—then who would stop her?

Teague frowned at her. "Certainly you agree this will serve the child's needs."

"No." Sylvia stood, suddenly rigid. "I don't agree. But Noelle gets what she wants." She turned her back on Teague.

Behind glass, the city was aflame. Beneath the darkening sky, buildings shimmered in dying sunlight. The Rio Grande was a golden ribbon wrapped around El Paso and Juárez and its neighboring barrio of Anapra.

Sylvia's tone bit the evening air. "What's the deal, Big Jim? How does it all work? It's something to do with the drug trade, isn't it? Did Noelle get pulled in when she was too young to know better?"

Teague said, "I can't answer that."

But he *knew* the answer—Sylvia could hear that admission in his voice. The fight went out of her.

The lawyer watched her for a few moments. Then he walked across the room, stopping only when he was inches from Sylvia. She looked up to see his eyes, and she could smell the cognac on his breath, feel his breath on her cheeks. He leaned down, even closer, and murmured, "Does arbitrage ring a bell?"

"What?" Sylvia knew she'd disappointed him because he shook his head and pulled away abruptly.

He said, "Maybe I'll see you up in Santa Fe one of these days."

She closed her eyes. When she opened them again, Big Jim Teague was gone.

SYLVIA SLEPT FOR two more hours. She awoke, stretched on the white couch, in darkness. Her body had stiffened painfully. Her neck ached. She stood unsteadily. Night had closed around the Harding Building. Groggily, she made her way to Serena's room. The nurse greeted her with a finger to moued lips. Sylvia nodded, stood over the sleeping child for several minutes, then retreated to her guest room.

She sat on the bed and studied the telephone's myriad buttons. At the moment Line 2 was blinking; she chose Line 4 and dialed the number Matt had given her. A man answered, "Pitkin here."

Sylvia said, "Dale? This is Sylvia Strange. Matt told me—"

Pitkin interrupted her with anxious questions: Was she hanging in okay? Was the child all right? Did she need anything? After only seconds of his sympathetic inquiries, Sylvia felt better. She asked for news.

Pitkin said, "You didn't hear this from me, but the latest word is the Mexican cops got your guy—Lorenzo Santos Portrillo—Renzo. He's got a hundred aliases."

A.k.a. Jesús. "Who did he work for?"

Pitkin hesitated—just for an instant. Then he said,

"Yeah?"

"Out there today—you did good."

She thought he'd hung up, but she still had the phone to her ear when she heard Dale Pitkin ask, "Do you remember Snow White?"

"The wicked stepmother." She held her breath. Pitkin wasn't talking about fairy tales.

"That's her. The one with the looking glass. If you don't watch out, you might miss the poisoned apple."

SYLVIA HUNG UP the telephone, reluctant to let go of Dale Pitkin. She'd never met the man, but she was already attached to him. He seemed decent and smart. Matt believed he was honest. And hadn't he given her what she needed—veiled confirmation that Noelle Harding was connected to the kidnapper? From the sound of Pitkin's voice, she knew he'd put himself at risk. And he'd warned her that she was at risk, too.

Maybe she was too exhausted to react properly to the warning; or maybe she just needed to think everything through—the complications and the consequences for the child and for herself. Noelle Harding wasn't going to throw her off the roof of the penthouse. But she could cause Sylvia enormous injury—all she had to do was bar her from Serena.

Sylvia lay back on the bed, then immediately pushed herself up. She felt sick to her stomach—and she was starving. She'd seen a massive refrigerator in the kitchen; she was craving a bologna sandwich. As she moved toward the door, she caught a whiff of her own sweat. She walked to a full-length mirror and stood with her hands by her sides. She looked like something the cat wouldn't bother to drag in—kitty would leave her out on the doorstep.

"Yeah?"

"Out there today—you did good."

She thought he'd hung up, but she still had the phone to her ear when she heard Dale Pitkin ask, "Do you remember Snow White?"

"The wicked stepmother." She held her breath. Pitkin wasn't talking about fairy tales.

"That's her. The one with the looking glass. If you don't watch out, you might miss the poisoned apple."

SYLVIA HUNG UP the telephone, reluctant to let go of Dale Pitkin. She'd never met the man, but she was already attached to him. He seemed decent and smart. Matt believed he was honest. And hadn't he given her what she needed—veiled confirmation that Noelle Harding was connected to the kidnapper? From the sound of Pitkin's voice, she knew he'd put himself at risk. And he'd warned her that she was at risk, too.

Maybe she was too exhausted to react properly to the warning; or maybe she just needed to think everything through—the complications and the consequences for the child and for herself. Noelle Harding wasn't going to throw her off the roof of the penthouse. But she could cause Sylvia enormous injury—all she had to do was bar her from Serena.

Sylvia lay back on the bed, then immediately pushed herself up. She felt sick to her stomach—and she was starving. She'd seen a massive refrigerator in the kitchen; she was craving a bologna sandwich. As she moved toward the door, she caught a whiff of her own sweat. She walked to a full-length mirror and stood with her hands by her sides. She looked like something the cat wouldn't bother to drag in—kitty would leave her out on the doorstep.

Ignoring the rumblings of her stomach—and a dim panic—she detoured into what looked like the bathroom. It was a small mirrored anteroom with three additional doors; she smacked her forehead on a mirror. She found the first door: sauna. Door number two opened onto what looked like a Japanese bathhouse. The Jacuzzi was humming. Soft blue lights glowed from a lap pool.

The third door offered access to a shower that was larger than Sylvia's office. She turned the jets to hot, stripped off her soiled clothes, and stayed under pulsing water streams until her muscles melted. Then she borrowed one of a half dozen swimsuits and dove into the salt-treated water.

As she began a series of laps, she let her thoughts dissolve like the liquid her body glided through. One lap, two, three . . . one breath, two, three . . .

Eventually, with her muscles measuring each familiar stroke, each kick, her mind settled into balance. What came to her was the ghostly image of swimming neck and neck with Noelle Harding. She was sleeping in the other woman's penthouse, wearing her clothes, swimming in her pool; as fatigue set in—and the laps surged past—it seemed only natural to imagine her life.

Noelle Wheeler had begun her existence as an abandoned child, an orphan whose only relative was a younger brother named Cash. She'd kept her family together—through years of deprivation, through the orphanage in El Paso, through loneliness and shame, through her own rise to power.

She'd done only what was necessary—what other lost children did: she'd put her knowledge of the streets to work. She'd hustled, she'd manipulated, she'd stolen—

and she'd gotten herself noticed by Amado Fortuna or someone just like him.

And when her brother was accused of murdering the woman he loved, she had stood by him—becoming in his reflection a heroine, a savior, a martyr. For ten years playing the role of her lifetime. And why not? She'd sacrificed everything to keep her brother from following in her footsteps. She had been tough enough and ruthless enough so that he could remain innocent . . . so he could fall in love with a sweet young girl.

So he could pay back all her sacrifices by betraying her with Elena Cruz.

But that was something Noelle could never allow. It would have been easy to enlist the help of someone like Jesús—to manipulate him so he would eliminate the competition. The fact that her brother was convicted of the murder must have come as a shock. But with her brother on death row, she became a crusader—and she had Cash all to herself.

So where had Paco figured into the equation? Had he been involved in the murder of Serena's mother?

Sylvia broke the rhythm of her strokes, and she gulped air. She felt sick, shaky.

She remembered the lighthearted psych lecture she'd given Tomás Sanchez a lifetime ago about the narcissistic personality, about a soulless vampire who exists only by feeding on the lifeblood of the people around him . . . or her.

Trembling, she pulled herself from the water. She found a thick white terry robe draped over a hook and put it on.

Barefoot, she padded down the softly lit hallway toward the living room. She was halfway there when she caught a glimpse of shoulder-length hair and pale skin in the glass. For a moment, she thought she was viewing her own reflection—but the hair was too light, the body too rigid.

Noelle Harding was waiting for her on the verandah. Sylvia opened the sliding glass door and stepped out onto the wide balcony. Thirty stories above the city, the soft, warm wind had begun to clear away the worst of the smog. The bristling heat of the desert was finally backing off. Shimmering strands of light stretched for miles, alive like a million winking eyes. When she looked back at the penthouse, she saw she was almost directly outside the bedroom where Serena slept. The nurse was sitting stiffly in her straight-backed chair, reading a magazine with a small book-light clamped to the pages.

In the room beyond Serena's, a desk lamp illuminated books and papers on a large desk. Big Jim Teague was ensconced in the swivel chair; while Sylvia watched, he stood and walked from the office.

Noelle Harding turned her back on the city. She gazed calmly at Sylvia. Muted ambient light caught the angles and planes of her face. Wisps of her blond hair danced in the breeze.

Sylvia clutched the robe tightly around her body as she walked toward Noelle. When she stood only inches from the other woman, she asked, "Was it worth it?"

"You would never understand." Harding spoke with icy calm.

"I've been trying to put the picture together . . . the orphanage, the drugs, the charity, the money, the access to power . . ." Sylvia held out her hands. "But none of that really matters, does it?"

Noelle didn't respond. She didn't speak, didn't move.

She just stared passively, as if waiting for a tiresome child to finish a tantrum.

Sylvia had stopped shaking—she was angry enough to regain control. She caught sight of Serena through the glass. The glow of the night-light washed her small form with a rosy tint. Calm flowed into Sylvia's body.

She took a breath. "Did Elena Cruz find out you were dealing drugs? Is that why she was killed? Or was it just that you couldn't bear to see your brother in love with another woman?"

Noelle Harding gave a small, impatient shake of her head. Sylvia reached out a restraining hand but stopped short of touching the other woman. "You knew your brother was innocent. You let him rot in a twelve-by-eight-foot cell. You'd let him die."

The rumble of a jet taking off from El Paso International Airport reverberated across the night sky. Sylvia wrapped her arms tightly around her torso. "Your money won't buy the child's love. Your connections won't bring back Elena. They won't save your brother."

"Eventually, with patience," Noelle said, "Serena will come to love me."

CHAPTER THIRTY-ONE

MATT ENGLAND KICKED open the door of Room 13 at the Buenas Noches Motel. He crouched, gun raised, aimed at an empty room. A tattered table lamp cast a ring of light, not much, but enough to see that the bad guys had come and gone.

Matt stepped inside and moved quickly to check behind closed doors. Except for a few twisted hangers the closet was empty. The bathroom stank of urine. It looked as though the toilet hadn't been flushed for weeks; the bowl was wadded with toilet paper and more toxic material. Blood was smeared around the sink, and droplets had spattered the floor. A soiled towel blocked the shower drain. No curtain. One very small frosted window.

Matt caught sight of his reflection. The guy in the mirror fit right in with the rest of the decor—tired, beat, grim. When he moved back into the bedroom, he saw Victor Vargas standing by the rumpled bed staring down at a mess of food containers, pornographic magazines, and a filthy hypodermic needle.

With a grim countenance, Vargas said, "Looks like they threw a party."

Both men swung around abruptly toward the door when they heard the crunch of glass underfoot. The face staring in at them was barely level with Matt's belt.

"Hace treinta minutos que se fueron." He raised his small arms, elbows tucked into his waist, and shrugged. "We jus' mees 'em."

Matt stepped over to Chupey; he hunkered down to the boy's level, questioning him in Spanish. Chupey sputtered something too quick and too regional for Matt to catch.

Victor filled in the missing information. "A friend of his runs numbers, booze, whores—whatever they want. Amado's men use the Buenas Noches as a home away from home."

Vargas went back to poking through the trash on and around the bed. He was reluctant to touch anything, so he used his pen to prod and move various pieces. He reached for the used syringe, then shook his head. "Un-uh. Not with that needle—*está sucio.*"

Matt was talking to Chupey. In Spanish he asked, "Your friend, will he talk to us?"

Chupey shook his head. His eyes were big and much too old for his face; right now they were focused on the fifty-dollar fountain pen in Matt's breast pocket. The yellow frosted pen was a rebuilt, vintage 1948.

Jeepers creepers, where'd you get those peepers . . . The old tune ran through Matt's head. He moved his hand to his pocket, fingers stroking the smooth surface of the writing instrument, and he repeated his question to Chupey.

This time, the little-old-man-of-a-boy nodded.

BOBBY DOWD HIT the cement headfirst, and that's where Amado Fortuna's boys left him while they went outside to smoke. He was so stoned, so sick, he didn't feel a thing. He thought his eyes must be open, but it was dark inside . . . wherever he was. He saw the dim shadow of walls surrounding him. High walls, very close. He shoved himself over onto one elbow, and he kept rolling until he hit something solid. While he recovered—on his back on the floor—he rested his hand against plaster. No, not plaster. This wall was peeling away under his fingers.

Bobby decided he would try to sit up and clear his head. He leveraged himself with a knee and an elbow, hoisted his body, and promptly fell flat.

He knew Fortuna's men were going to kill him tonight. They'd lost interest in him. He'd deciphered enough of their whispered tête-à-têtes to know it was time to say good night.

The stuff they'd injected into his veins had made him swear off contraband for life. If, by some miracle, he lived through this, he vowed to himself he would get clean. It made him feel better just to know he meant it. He hoped his old man, Smoky Joe Dowd, was watching from the Big Ranch in the sky.

He hadn't given up any useful information—he was certain of that—not even when he'd been drugged crazy. Not even when they'd cut him, burned him, broken his insides.

That was small consolation for the way he'd failed

Paco. The last act of Bobby's Paco dream had finally come clear in his fevered brain.

Paco had stood over the table at Rosa's, their usual meeting place, nailing the cop with his myopic stare. In his impeccable English, he'd whispered something ... Bobby couldn't quite hear ... something about a *straw* house, which got the cop thinking about three little pigs.

Then, like a condemned man, Paco had warned Bobby that time was running out. The bookkeeper had one chance left to bring down Amado Fortuna: Arb. 37—arbitrageur *numero uno* ... the only person powerful enough to beat the Tuna at his game.

Arb. 37 would help Paco settle the score with his *primo*. And after Paco was gone, Arb. 37 could protect a "dwarf" and offer her a future ... and her true father.

All in trade for the Tuna Diaries.

Paco had disappeared before Bobby had a chance to chin himself out of the dope haze and warn the bookkeeper—Arb. 37 was a "girlfriend," a snitch who was sleeping with the feds and playing all sides against the middle. Arb. 37 was poison. She was Snow White.

VICTOR VARGAS DROVE the taxi. Chupey rode in the front seat—his habit these days. Matt was in the back with Chupey's friend, Delora.

Delora was fourteen years old, she stood five-feet-three inches tall, and she wore red-hot skintight Lycra leggings with a sequined crop top. She had thick frosted hair that brushed the cheeks of her tiny butt. She wore a crust of makeup, and her lips glowed with a lipstick so red Matt feared it might have a half-life.

But under all the trimmings, Delora was a *he*. A transvestite.

Now, the teenager powdered his/her nose. The trip had cost Matt fifty dollars cash, his prized 1948 fountain pen, his new underwater sport watch, and the promise of a portable CD player. Delora granted credit only because Chupey vouched for the big gringo cop.

Victor Vargas was guiding the taxi along the route Sylvia had followed this morning. Except he was on the other side of the river, and he was headed downstream, not upstream. He skirted the barrio of Anapra, and when the dirt road became a narrow track of ruts—a challenge even for an off-road vehicle—he slowed to less than ten miles per hour.

When Vargas braked the taxi to a stop, Matt could see Smeltertown across the river. Here, Mexico's border cut directly west, adjoining New Mexico. The trail skirted Cristo Rey—the white cross riding the high point on the rough mountain.

The barrio of Anapra had continued to creep and sprawl over these mountains although this area wasn't officially marked on any map. Victor maneuvered them past shanties and tents. Matt was reminded of the nomads who lived in the great deserts and moved with the winds. He knew that just over the crest of the next hill, U.S. border-patrol vehicles were parked in U.S. territory waiting for jumpers.

It was another twenty minutes before they came to the old Mexico–New Mexico border crossing near the railroad tracks of the Pacific Transportation Company. Delora had painted her face twice during the final leg of the journey.

In between blotting lips and powdering cheeks, she waved glossy red fingernails. *Aquí. Allí.* This way . . . no, that way, to the norteamericano.

Matt hoped Delora was right. More than that, he hoped they weren't too late.

Victor braked the taxi when he reached the end of the trail. He shut down the engine and tipped his head to signal they would have to walk from here. The vehicle had barely made it to this point. Matt climbed out quietly, then tensed when Delora slammed the door.

The night air was stale, warm, and dense. Only one or two of the brightest stars were visible in the sky. The moon had just begun to crest the mountain, providing milky light.

Delora's sandals quickly filled with dirt; the teenager cried out when she cut a painted toe on a broken bottle. Matt finally took Delora's arm to help her over the rough terrain—shooting Chupey a withering look when he caught the boy grinning.

Delora led the group downhill to the fence. There she pointed to a warehouse roughly three hundred yards away. It was long and narrow, with a sloping corrugated roof. A windmill creaked nearby.

The warehouse was within easy striking distance except for one problem.

"It's in *New* Mexico," Matt whispered, shaking his head.

"*Sí.*"

The two cops stared at each other. They knew the border patrol was parked within a quarter mile. They usually set up numerous patrols along this stretch because crossing was a relatively easy prospect—and people regularly paced the hillside waiting for their chance.

Whether you were a felon, a civilian, or a member of law enforcement, border jumping was illegal.

But the cops were going to cross, and they were going to do it now. They'd just seen three men moving from a parked car toward the entrance to the warehouse.

MATT TORE HIS pants crawling under the fence break. He almost didn't make it through, but Delora and Chupey pushed from the Mexico side. He carried at least a hundred pounds more than most border jumpers. Vargas followed. They warned the boys to stay away from the fence—and to watch for border patrol.

Matt crouched low, following Victor's lead down the sloping hillside. He stumbled once, straining something in his ankle, but he didn't slow his stride. They split off from each other when they were a few hundred feet from the warehouse. Matt could hear fractured Spanish phrases drifting on night air.

Two of the men were still outside, talking. The other one had disappeared carrying a metal gas can.

Matt found cover behind a thicket of high weeds; the thorny, scratchy stalks were probably the by-product of cesspool drainage.

He caught a flash of Victor's white shirt disappearing behind a rusted-out junker. He could tell that the two men had been drinking, and one mumbled something about taking a leak. When the shorter man stepped five paces toward Matt, his buddy turned away to light a cigarette.

Victor got the smoker; Matt got the pisser.

Victor made his move, darting out from behind the vehicle and scrambling across dirt. He caught the smoker on the side of his head with a bat—no, a goddamn two-by-four.

Matt lunged for the other guy, who was busy nosing

his penis from his pants. The criminal investigator caught his target around the knees, felt something wet against his elbow, and took the guy down.

BOBBY DOWD HEARD the door open as someone entered the warehouse. Amado Fortuna's boys had finished their bullshit session. They'd probably killed a bottle of tequila. Now it was time to kill a cop.

Screw you, little pig!

That was it. The "straw house" fell out of some cubbyhole in Bobby's brain, and he remembered. Paco had told him the *straw* house was made of cash.

Bobby heard the sound of footsteps. He was still braced in the corner—still in darkness.

One set of shoes approached, leisurely, accompanied by a mediocre whistle. Bobby identified his soon-to-be-assassin—the kicker with the big feet. The ugly runt who'd taken great pleasure inflicting severe pain.

Bobby hoisted himself halfway up. One barely functional hand contracted into a fist—a half-assed fist that hurt like hell—but better than nothing. He wasn't going down without a fight.

The feet came closer—five steps away, four—and then there was the sound of splashing liquid, the reek of gasoline.

Just when Bobby Dowd took a final breath and shot his fist out hoping for full body contact, something pushed him and he went down.

More footsteps sounded, furtive, darting across the rough floor. His tormentor was gone—or keeping very still. Bobby reached out blindly. Orange and white spots danced in his retina. He saw a shape, then it dissolved.

In the midst of his body's own light show, he heard

the sound of scuffling. Then a painful crunching—definitely bones breaking—and a loud groan.

A deep male voice—an Anglo—mumbled, "Got you, motherfucker!"

And then the lights went on.

When his vision cleared, Bobby Dowd brought his bloodied, swollen fingers to his nose. He widened his eyes. He stared blankly, focused, refocused.

He was so crazy he thought he was holding the edge of a hundred-dollar bill. A greenback.

He ran his fingers over that wall that was holding him up. Paper. Bills. That green color everywhere. Stacks and stacks and stacks.

Aisles and aisles.

A Wal-Mart of money.

It was dry and dusty—now doused with gasoline. And it had probably been stashed here for years. Stuck in a warehouse in the thick of U.S. border territory. Merely another one of Amado Fortuna's stash houses.

It was dry as straw.

Then Bobby Dowd saw two angels appear. He recognized one. The other was a new face. But pleasing to view. He opened his mouth—*Hey, guys, happy to see you. If you give me a hand, we can talk about Snow White and Tuna's Diary, or we could just sit here a minute—*

What he actually managed to say was, "Hey, Vargas. Beep beep," before he passed out cold.

CHAPTER THIRTY-TWO

SERENA'S EYES SHOT wide open. She sat up in bed and cried out, blinking repeatedly. The room was unfamiliar. Where was she? There was glass along one wall. She saw a glowing nighttime sky. An airplane was streaking across the top of the world.

Memory returned, stunning her with its force. Yesterday—the demon—her terrible journey. Pain... heat and thirst... the horrible sound of guns... and people everywhere.

She heard Paco calling to her, *Fresa, no puedo descansar, no puedo dormir.* Strawberry, I can't rest, I can't sleep.

¡Ven aquí, Fresa! Come here.

Don't stay in that place! Cross the river. Keep your promise.

And then the room turned white with radiant light. Warmth flowed through the child's body as she gazed up at a face filled with sorrow and comfort... green mantle

...stars exploding...a musical voice whispering: *Cruza el río, Angelita*... *Cumple con tu manda.* Cross the river. Keep your vow.

The stars exploded, and a wave of heat washed over the child, almost drowning her with its power. She gasped for air. Then the world grew dark.

Serena heard a soft rustling sound, blinked her way up from the shadows, and saw a nurse standing over the bed. Worry creased the woman's face as she pressed her palm against the child's forehead.

Serena pulled away, eyes wide with shock. She spoke one word insistently: "Sylvia."

IN THE BEDROOM next door, Sylvia stumbled from the bed. She'd fallen asleep on top of the spread. It took her seconds to reach Serena. The child clung to her. The dam burst and a flood of tears broke through; great sobs wracked her small body.

Then came words.

Serena raised her tear-streaked face to Sylvia. Her eyes were somber, but her pupils were dilated and she was trembling. She spoke haltingly at first. Her voice was high and soft. She whispered, "They're calling me, Sylvia."

Her words gained strength and speed, breaking into fragments. She was rattling off Spanish and English, mixing up her speech, hiccupping, breathless—as if everything she had been holding inside had to escape at once.

"I go...you take me now...cross the river... *me voy a México ahorita*...I can't stay here...we go now... *a México*...to Anapra...home...I must go now ...She's calling me—"

Urgently, Sylvia questioned the child over her raving monologue. "*Who's* calling you, Serena? *Who* do you see? Is it Paco? Is it God?"

"—cross the river . . . *prometí* . . . *She's* calling to me—"

Sylvia gripped Serena's shoulders. "You see the Virgin—"

Serena nodded wildly, words still tumbling from her lips: "She's calling . . . *¡prometí!* . . . can't stay . . . go home . . . I must . . . *ahorita mismo me voy* . . . Anapra—" The flow went on and on for minutes until the child was exhausted by the effort of communication and Sylvia was exhausted by the work of listening.

And then—as suddenly as it had begun—Serena's speech slowed to a numbing repetition of two words: *home, Anapra, home, Anapra.*

Her brow was feverish-hot, and her skin had broken a sweat. Sylvia tried to lie down beside her on the mattress, but Serena scooted out from under the covers. Her narrow frame almost disappeared beneath too large, brand-new cotton pajamas. Woman and girl were alone in the room; the nurse had retreated to the hallway.

Sylvia sat on the edge of the bed—fascinated and alarmed—watching while the child went tenaciously about the business of dressing herself in pants, blouse, shoes. Sylvia recognized the behavior—it was an echo of the morning in Santa Fe when Serena had directed her to Paco's body. Then too, the child had been on a trajectory, motivated to reach a specific point in time.

Sylvia also recognized behavior that was on the brink—the child had pushed outward, exposing secrets, opening herself to terrible vulnerability. She had broken through her silent prison to reach a turning point: move ahead, open even farther. Or step back—and close up again, perhaps forever.

Sylvia took a deep breath. Serena was still trying to button her shirt when she parked herself in front of Sylvia. She set both her hands on Sylvia's thighs. She leaned forward, and she said, "Home."

Sylvia couldn't quite get used to the child's lilting voice, which reminded her of a finch's song. She tilted her head and said, "We'll go to Anapra, Serena, but not now."

Serena shook her head, and her thumb fluttered to her mouth. "Anapra. *Home.*"

Sylvia held Serena by the shoulders. "We can't go to Mexico tonight. I'm sorry, sweetheart."

"Anapra, *sí.*" Serena's eyes filled with desperate pleading.

"It's not possible." Sylvia took the child in her arms and rocked her gently. Minutes passed, and Serena didn't move. When a half hour had passed, Sylvia's muscles began to cramp. Still, she didn't shift her body. But the pain became excruciating. When she eased Serena down on the mattress, she saw the child's face—and she flushed with fear. She was looking at a listless shrunken body, an infant with thumb in mouth. The child had regressed abruptly, closing in on herself like the petals of a dying flower.

SYLVIA FOUND A small blanket in the closet and wrapped it around Serena as if she were a baby. She groaned when she hefted the child—eighty pounds was pushing it. She stared at the doorway. The nurse was probably standing directly outside, making the hallway impassable. Breathlessly, Sylvia slid the bolt in place.

Then she carried Serena out the sliding glass door to the verandah.

It was deserted. And the door to her room was open. With a sigh of relief, she entered the room and set Serena on her bed. She was already dressed—like the child, in borrowed clothes—but she put on her shoes and grabbed her small purse.

This time, when she lifted Serena, she saw that her eyes were open. She whispered in the child's ear, "Anapra, home." She steadied herself for the rest of the journey.

With the child in her arms, she made her way back across the verandah, through the living room, and into the penthouse elevator. It glided all the way to the ground floor without stopping. Express.

As the elevator doors opened, Sylvia pressed her back against the wall. The high marble security station was visible just beyond a thick pillar. Bright lights illuminated several video monitors. The station faced the main ground-floor entrance and exit.

Stepping out of the elevator, Sylvia tightened her hold on the child. From here, she had a clear view across the lobby. The security station was deserted.

Tentatively at first, then gaining speed, she moved toward the main doors. As she passed the desk, she saw a cigarette burning in an ashtray. For an instant, she could taste the snaking plume of smoke.

Her hand was already on the massive door handle when she heard echoing footsteps. She pushed her weight against glass, imagining the security guard's approach. The door didn't budge. Panic made her shaky, and she almost dropped the child. She staggered, hip pressing the release bar, and the door swung open with a low, smooth hiss.

* * *

OUTSIDE THE HARDING Building, the street was quiet—it was still an hour shy of dawn. The air was warm and stale, but it felt wonderful. Sylvia kept moving in the direction of downtown and the river. For two blocks, she didn't stop, didn't look back. She turned a sharp corner and collapsed against the side of an old stone building. The child landed on both feet.

Sylvia said, "I can't carry you the whole way."

Serena stared numbly forward, her thumb thrust deep in her mouth.

"If we're going to Anapra, you have to help me. You have to show me the way, Serena. That's part of the deal."

Still, the child did not respond.

They managed another few blocks, and then Sylvia saw a dilapidated taxicab turn in their direction.

THE CABDRIVER SHOWED no interest in his fare, and the drive through downtown El Paso took minutes; traffic signals flashed yellow. They passed impressive and historic stone buildings, a few modest high-rises, and the usual nondescript jumble of a border city. The Santa Fe bridge—to Mexico—was almost deserted. Except for a few pedestrians, a few cars . . . and the customs official who waved the taxi to pull over and stop.

The cabbie was mumbling angrily, and he shot Sylvia an accusing look. She felt her heart sink. It dropped even further when a black Mercedes pulled up and parked next to the taxi. Three men occupied the German-made car—the Harding insignia was discreetly embossed on the driver-side door. Sylvia guessed they were Noelle's employees—members of her private security force?

A second Mercedes rolled to a stop on the other side of the cab. The driver—heavily armed and very silent—climbed slowly out. He was big. He opened Sylvia's door.

She sat for a moment, frozen, trying to figure out an escape route. But there was none. The customs official had turned his back and walked away. The cabdriver was pleading for everyone to leave him alone.

Sylvia refused the big man's assistance; she carried Serena to the car. Noelle Harding was in the backseat. "Get in," she ordered quietly.

They didn't turn back toward the U.S.; instead the Mercedes sailed past the border crossing like a ship passing over the ocean. They entered Mexico.

AND NOW THE child began to point the way home. Even in the kindness of predawn light, Anapra looked like a world out of hell. Paved streets gave way to ruts that climbed the devastated hillsides. It seemed as if a giant beast had traveled each eroding peak, tearing the last remnants of life from the parched dirt. The hills were literally falling in on the homes below. For the most part, the houses were shacks. Some actually had walls and trees. Many were bare of paint, lacking adequate roofs. The worst were cardboard and tire hovels, with plastic and paper for windows, blankets for doors. Chickens scratched earth, eroding it to dust; those scrawny animals wouldn't survive long in Anapra. Starving dogs roamed the streets nosing trash beside the open sewers. Children followed the dogs.

Sylvia tried to imagine Serena's lifetime, spent on

these streets. But it was the child's presence that reminded her that it wasn't so—she had been sheltered above the streets in an adobe fortress. Returning home, Serena was coming back to life. She fidgeted in the seat, silently guiding the car, her mouth set in an anxious frown around her small thumb.

During the journey, Noelle Harding spoke only once. She turned toward Sylvia, trapping her with piercing blue eyes. "For Serena's sake, I hope you've made the right decision."

Sylvia swallowed painfully. *Had she?* Would this journey to Anapra help free Serena from a violent past? Or would it push her past the point of return, triggering an ecstatic experience that verged on madness? Numbly, Sylvia stared out at the desolate landscape.

At the child's insistence, the Mercedes stopped in front of a corner *tienda*, a neighborhood store. Signs in the dusty windows advertised LOTTO and PEÑACOLA. The driver of Harding's car stayed put, and the three other men led the way toward the crumbling hacienda; they negotiated the footpath behind the store.

She saw the house from Serena's first drawing— it rode the cleft of a naked hill in the shadow of the Cristo Rey Monument. It was supported by stacks of tires and rotting wood. The surrounding wall was eroding just like the earth it rested upon. The structure was two stories high, grilled and impenetrable—at least for a child. On the highest roof was a small caged turret—a widow's walk. As Matt had described, the entire structure was an evolution of adobe to cinder blocks to woodwork.

The child had watched the world from that prison. She would have looked out at Anapra, the river border, and El Paso. At night, she would have seen the lights of Los Estados Unidos. And she would have seen neighbor children playing on the streets below.

Sylvia took in the child's world as she moved—almost breathed it in, trying to absorb every detail. Colors, smells, sounds. It was all part of the puzzle. The satellite dish meant that Serena had learned English with the help of U.S. broadcasting; microwaves crossed borders with impunity.

Sylvia noticed several small scruffy boys standing off to one side watching the procession, scared off by the men in dark clothes who packed weapons.

Serena didn't seem aware of the other children; she was too caught up in the drama of this moment. A moment Sylvia believed must be filled with ghosts.

The sun hadn't climbed over the hills, but the air was already uncomfortably warm. Perspiration trickled down Sylvia's neck, back, and under her arms. She could only imagine what it would be like in the full heat of the day. The trail led past rotting trash, withered cactus, the glitter of broken glass. They reached the main gate, which hung open on rusty hinges. On the other side of the wall, the courtyard was more night than day, shaded by a massive cottonwood.

One man stationed himself in the courtyard near a dilapidated well. He pulled cigarettes from his pocket and settled in to keep watch. The taller of the two remaining men entered the house. When Noelle stepped through the double wooden doors, Serena went into action.

Gripping Sylvia's hand, she pulled with a force that belied a ten-year-old's diminutive mass. The psychologist caught a fleeting glimpse of the living area before she realized that Serena was headed around the front of the house to the exterior stairway.

As Sylvia climbed higher, she gazed out at the emerging view of slum, river, and the endless city sprawl. With each step, she felt more isolated, more imprisoned.

Matt had tried to tell her what she would find upstairs.

SYLVIA STEPPED THROUGH the doorway and stopped in her tracks. She heard footsteps, felt Noelle Harding's presence, but her attention was riveted on the vision directly before her.

An explosion of color—vibrant reds, yellows, greens, purples, blues . . .

Trees, faces, landscapes familiar and exotic . . .

"My God." It was Noelle who spoke. "What *is* this?"

. . . house paint, watercolors, crayons, pastels . . . murals covering smooth plaster . . . rainbows, sunsets . . . paint spattered on the floors . . . broken crayons, paint cans . . . charcoal . . .

Sylvia's whisper was hoarse. "Serena's story."

The child was swaying, dancing around the room—arms spread wide, head back. The energy of the work seemed to flow into her delicate body. She was in a state of possession, of trancelike ecstasy.

Sylvia moved into the center of the room. Her eyes raced from image to image—from face to figure to building to landscape. And slowly, the mural began to come into focus. The work had been divided into sections—scenes—but the divisions were stylistic, rather than actual borders. The artistic technique grew more sophisticated and skilled as the eye moved clockwise, south to west to north—because the child had grown.

When Sylvia had turned almost a full circle to her starting point, she saw that the work abruptly stopped. Serena's story in Anapra was not quite finished.

When her eyes settled on the child, she caught her breath.

SERENA LET THE light and the color flow into her arms and legs. Heat made her skin tingle, almost burning—she was surrounded by her history. *Her story.* As Paco had told it to her—with words and pictures and pieces of the past. Just as Serena had let it flow into her skin and out again—from her fingers to the blank walls.

Trembling, she ran to the first panel. She let her fingers trail along the cool plaster, gazing up at the story of her beginning: her mother—angel pretty—cradling a baby to her breast.

Tears began to stream from the child's eyes as she stood on tiptoe and kissed Elena's face. For a horrible instant, the room spun around, pulling her toward its swirling center. She gasped for breath, stumbling toward the second panel.

El demonio, a dark blade of fury racing toward her mother. The demon had stolen Elena's life.

A cry of pure grief escaped the child. Through tears, she could barely see the third panel—a man trapped behind bars: her father, dying because she wasn't with him.

Sobs wracked her small body as she traced the image with her fingers.

She had painted Paco almost flying—with a baby bundled in his arms. He had told her the story so many times. And she had grown up in those arms—this home.

Then she began to race around the room crying all their names.

Breathless, from the center of the floor, Serena cried out, "Good-bye, home! Good-bye."

THE PAINTED VISIONS filled Sylvia with awe. They expressed a level of passionate intensity that was almost frightening. Everything came together on these walls—the child's trances, her prayers, her drawings, her incredible strength of will, her vibrant life-energy. And her isolation.

Sylvia had almost reached Serena when she stopped abruptly, her gaze on the farthest mural. She saw a very small child, a girl who knelt on bare knees, face raised toward the Virgin. A beam of light arced from goddess to child.

The child in this story had been *chosen.*

SYLVIA FELT A small hand clasp hers. She knelt down and kissed Serena's forehead, wiping tears from the child's face.

In a voice that cracked with emotion, the child whispered, "Anapra."

"Home?"

"*Old* home. Good-bye, old home."

Sylvia looked deep into the child's eyes, and she could believe Serena had been chosen; she had been touched by something extraordinary.

She whispered to the child. "Oh, Serena, you kept your vow of silence."

Serena blinked, nodding slowly, as if she had just awakened from a dream. "It's time to get my daddy," she said softly.

CHAPTER THIRTY-THREE

"*PERDÓNAME, PADRE.*" Forgive me, Father. Renzo Santos appeared from his nest beneath a fraying blanket. He crept out from behind the wooden pew, leaving a trail of blood as he crawled across the chapel floor.

His sweat- and blood-soaked clothes clung to his body. His dark hair was slick as sealskin. Blood still oozed from his shoulder, although his vessels should have dried to dust. White powder stained his nose and face. He'd snorted the last of his drug, and the chemicals were galloping horses trampling his brain.

He crawled past rough wooden pews, approaching the altar and its nimbus of a hundred votive candles, most burned out by now, each flame representing the suffering of man, woman, or child. It took all Renzo's strength to cover two feet, three, four . . .

He moved through light and dark, hampered only by his half death. The first bullet was poisoning his body. The second bullet was eating away his power like a rat gnaws through cheese. Was he hours or minutes from dying? It was dawn, the time of day when even churches and cathedrals are abandoned except by the truly wretched. Renzo was terrified to leave this earth.

Death was bad enough—but if he left with a black moon and no confession . . .

Sacrament . . . absolution . . . blood sacrifice . . .

He slid his knife from the sheath strapped to his ankle. He flipped the blade; in candlelight it shimmered, alive. He pressed the cutting edge to his left forearm—he pushed down through flesh. He lifted the now bloody blade and moved it down his arm almost an inch, cutting. Finally, he set the blade to his wrist and cut again.

As he watched the swell of thick red fluid, he hungered for the taste of lifeblood.

But Renzo let the blood run freely from his arm to the chapel floor, where it soaked darkly into the rough adobe mud.

His blood offering . . .

It was a miracle he was alive. He had barely escaped across the river. Once out of the stinking water, he found refuge in a massive concrete pipe that dripped raw sewage into the Río Bravo. Bloodied, weak, shivering, he had crawled up the pipe like a suckling crawling back into the womb to undo his own birth.

Now time was moving backward, and he had no idea how long it had taken to reach the other end of the pipe. But eventually, he had fallen back down into the world. And when he landed, he found himself deep inside the barrio of Anapra. His mother-the-*puta*'s womb was a miserable slum where each and every man was invisible.

Renzo Santos Portrillo was only one among millions of miserable human beings.

From there, he made his way to sanctuary.

A violent tremor wracked Renzo's ruined body. He fell to his side, knees clutched protectively to belly. He lay still, his breathing shallow. Even in the haze of blood loss, the fevered dementia, the drug delusions, he knew that certain factions within the *federales* would work to protect him. After all, he was one of their own. He had tortured and murdered on assignment; he had been paid with federal currency; perhaps the very same money that Amado Fortuna had paid to the *federales* in bribes.

His was a world of favors bought and sold—coercion, terrorism, torture, death.

Other members of the federal judicial police would refuse to admit their failure to apprehend an international criminal. They would refuse to lose face in front of Los Estados Unidos and the F.B.I.

Which gave him time . . .

Was someone there? Or was his mind playing tricks? What did the priest say? Renzo could not hear, so he whispered, "*Venga del oscuro, Padre.*" Come out of the dark, Father.

The tendons in his neck stood out like thick cords as he lifted his head. He gazed upward, expecting to see the face of the priest. Instead, it was a woman who looked down upon him. Sweet face, brown skin, lips kissed by rose petals. Her boundless, deep-lidded eyes sent out rays of light, beams so powerful they froze Renzo where he huddled on hands and knees.

"*La Virgen . . .*" Her eyes closed, light fading, and only in her soft glow could he move again. He reached out one trembling arm, fingers straining to touch the hem of her green cloak. Now he saw she radiated sun rays.

Renzo did not know if his lips moved when he said his prayer. Was he thinking or speaking? It did not matter, because the Virgin heard his every word.

He felt her hand like a ray of fire scalding his brow. She was burning away his mortal sins. As she leaned down, he heard the rustling of her green cloak. She whispered to him, giving him permission to do what he must do. She warmed him in her boundless light.

Agonized and weeping, Renzo Santos began the endless walk of absolution.

When he reached the chapel door, he inched his way through. He thought he wouldn't be able to stand again. Muscles shivered violently.

The drug state would reach its zenith soon—and then it would fade, the last of his strength draining away with the chemicals.

Voices brought him back to the world.

The voice of the child.

And the voice of Coatlicue—*his* destroyer.

He shut his eyes, his body shuddering as a spasm overwhelmed him. He used his fingers as claws. Slick and wet, they found purchase. He stood upright. And now he gripped his knife in one hand.

Renzo saw the first man standing near the open doors; he was facing the courtyard, speaking quietly to his friend, who must be outside.

Renzo moved across dirt floors. Twelve, maybe fifteen feet to the kitchen—an ocean to a dying man. Without a sound, he took up position against the wall. And then he brushed the toe of his shoe against newspaper that had fallen to the floor. The rustle was barely audible, faint.

But it was enough to draw the man. When he

stepped into the kitchen, Renzo gripped him from behind, left arm across the throat, right hand thrusting deep and swift with the blade.

WHEN SYLVIA STOOD, she found herself looking straight into Noelle Harding's impassive face. For an instant, she saw nothing—then the emptiness was replaced with a convincing expression of concern.

Noelle shifted her focus to Serena and smiled warmly. "You're a brave girl, and we need to get you home."

Serena refused to relax her grip on Sylvia.

Noelle turned toward the man who had appeared at the doorway. "I think we're finished here," she said.

He nodded, then froze at the sound of a heavy thump. It came from outside, the ground floor.

"What was that?" Noelle snapped.

With a low, urgent whisper the man spoke into his radio. At first the only response was silence, then a male voice: *I'm here.*

What was that?

I'll check it out—

But almost simultaneously, the sound of a single gunshot reverberated in the air. The man moved quickly back along the portal, out of Sylvia's sight.

She reached for the child, but Serena was gone.

Both women ran toward the door—and Sylvia gave a startled cry at a second explosion of gunfire. She heard a man yell out—and something clattered down the stairs.

Sylvia reached the doorway first—she stepped through only to be pushed out of the way by Noelle Harding. Serena was nowhere in sight.

Harding was calling out for help when the apparition

appeared twenty feet away at the top of the stairway. He was no longer the smooth, dangerous man who had stolen Serena across an entire state.

This *thing* had just stepped out of the mouth of hell. Bleeding, filthy, crazy written all over his face. He took a step forward, then another, weaving as he moved.

Noelle was rooted in place. Sylvia called out to the other woman, then she backed away. She hit the wall behind her and felt cool metal against her skin. A hand ladder, ten rungs leading to the rooftop.

The man was only a few yards from Noelle Harding. He mumbled phrases in Spanish. Prayers? Denials? Sylvia didn't understand the words. But she heard Noelle's response.

She spit out words as if they were burning her mouth. "You were supposed to kill them both, you bastard!"

Lorenzo Santos Portrillo blinked as he pulled the trigger. The first bullet went wide. The second hit Noelle in the forehead. The woman's mouth jerked open as her head was forced sharply backward.

SYLVIA GRABBED THE metal handrail and pulled her body toward the roof. Her foot slipped from the rung, her sweaty hands almost lost their hold. She chinned herself the final two feet. Just out of reach, enclosed by grillwork, Serena was huddled in the farthest corner of the widow's walk.

When the child saw Sylvia, she skittered forward, reaching out to help.

Sylvia blinked. The dawn sunlight was brilliant and blinding, draining the color from the world that fell away below. Her fingers clutched at the grill. She hung on, her eyes locked on the child. Her breath tore in and out of her throat, her heart hammering against her chest. She needed one more burst of strength to lift herself up onto the roof—

Serena screamed, "He's coming!"

At the same instant, Sylvia heard harsh, labored breathing.

She twisted just in time to see the demon reaching for her with one bloody hand. She swung her body out, thrusting her legs forward. He dodged impact, and his fingers caught one of her ankles.

His weight pulled her down, and her hands were quickly losing their grip on the metal grill. She cried out, a soft sound that grew to a growl. When Serena's fingers closed around her wrists, she almost didn't register their warmth. She managed to lift her chin, just enough to see the fierce look on the child's face.

The demon's fingernails cut through Sylvia's skin, and he tugged like a shark yanking dumbly at its prey.

Strength fading, Sylvia kicked at him with her free leg.

I'll never let you have this child—she wasn't sure if she spoke the thought aloud.

At that moment, she heard Serena cry out.

"You killed my *mamá!*"

Adrenaline ripped through Sylvia—she wasn't going to let the demon hurt Serena again. She managed a last jarring twist, wrenching her body away from the wall. He was forced off balance, and her foot hit him dead on.

He grunted—a look of surprise crossed his face—then he fell back with arms spread wide, almost flying.

The fence gave way on impact, and his body dropped over the wall, bouncing off the adobe base, off rocks, then rolling down the cliff to land at the feet of four street urchins who were trailed by a small mangy dog.

The children had been drawn by the sound of gunfire. While three of them kept their distance, the fourth—who was bolder than his *compañeros*—raised the sharp stick he used as a cane and prodded the battered body, once, twice, just to make sure the demon was dead.

CHAPTER THIRTY-FOUR

THE SUN WAS SHINING when Cash Wheeler left North Facility for the last time. The man walked with an odd hitch to his left leg, eyes squinting in the bright light. He looked pale and naked as a newborn mouse. His arms were held tightly to his sides, as if accustomed to limited space. For an instant, Sylvia saw panic flare in his eyes; she held her breath. The hitch grew more pronounced for a few steps as he regained self-control.

An hour earlier, in a borrowed office in North Facility, Sylvia had taken a seat next to Cash. She had waited quietly while he pulled himself together. Several times, when the tremors became so intense his teeth chattered, she gripped his arm. Without looking up, he nodded his thanks. It took him minutes, but at last he forced himself to meet her eyes.

He found his voice, hoarse and half broken. "I can't face her now."

Sylvia nodded. "Take your time."

"I threw up this morning." Cash hunched into himself. "I don't know how to be a father . . ."

"You can learn. Your daughter will help you."

When the inmate looked up at Sylvia, the pain cleared for a moment, and he took a deep breath.

After Noelle Harding's death—and the events that followed—Big Jim Teague had worked twenty hours a day to gain Cash's release. In the end, it was granted by a governor who was on his way out—and who had socialized with Noelle Harding.

DNA had proved Wheeler's paternity of Serena—and an agreement was reached with Child Protective Services. Sylvia would have custody of the child until Wheeler adjusted to freedom and fatherhood.

Outside, they walked side by side, Sylvia silently counting the paces until they would reach Rosie and Serena. Matt stood off by himself, obviously caught up by the drama, and looking both vulnerable *and* satisfied.

She recognized the look on Serena's face. Love. And wonderment. And a touch of terror.

When less than ten feet separated father and daughter, Cash slowed. Sylvia followed his lead, coming to a standstill. A cold wind scattered dust, grass, feathers from a bird across asphalt. In the distance, a perimeter-patrol vehicle slowly skirted the high metal fence. The C.O. behind the steering wheel had his arm dangling out the window. The regulation shotgun—visible even from sixty feet—was mounted beside him. A jackrabbit dashed past the vehicle, flushed from its lair.

Serena made the first move. She took four paces forward until she was directly in front of her father. Then she looked up, smiled tentatively, and took the last two fingers of his left hand in hers. Cash moved

forward to keep pace beside his daughter, headed anywhere and nowhere in particular. They crossed the
parking lot, the big man and his little girl. The other
three watched them go.

At last, when Cash and Serena had almost reached
the beginning of the road, the man knelt down, then sat
on a rock that had been painted white by prison crews.
The child sat next to him—on another rock. He bent his
head, his shoulders beginning to shake. Silently, Serena
wrapped her arms around her father.

CHAPTER THIRTY-FIVE

AT EIGHT-FIFTEEN on a Wednesday night, the Bar-B was deserted except for the bartender and a lone customer who lounged in one of the faux leopard-skin chairs. After a three-month relationship conducted via E-mail and long-distance telephone calls, Sylvia had a firm picture in her mind of Joshua Harold, private investigator: six feet, 185 pounds, fifty-five, gray-blond hair—Crocodile Dundee without the Australian accent.

The Harry who now stood before her in the bar was in his midthirties, five-eight, two hundred pounds—most of it muscle—and skin with the sheen of dark chocolate.

The man made Sylvia crave a candy bar.

She shook his hand and sat at his table. He was drinking a Santa Fe Pale Ale, and he'd worked an inch off a hand-rolled stogie. Sylvia smiled broadly.

"What?" Harry's question was friendly.

"I had you pegged as a natural blonde."

Harry's laugh was a loose, rumbling baritone.

Sylvia ordered a French martini from the bartender, and then she focused on Harry. "You have any more of those?"

The cigar did a three-sixty rotation between his lips, and his eyebrows flicked up, then down. "Sure. I don't let them go to waste." When she didn't retreat, he pulled a cellophane package from his breast pocket. As he gently worked the wrapping loose, the single gold band on his right middle finger caught the light. He was dressed in a dark jacket, light-colored shirt, black jeans.

The bartender brought Sylvia's martini to the table. She tested the drink—made with premium vodka and Cointreau—and the alcohol brought slow heat to her belly.

"Good?" Harry nipped the end of the cigar with his pocketknife. He flicked his lighter, and Sylvia drew the blue flame in the direction of her mouth, igniting sharply pungent tobacco. The strong fumes made her skin tingle; she felt the rush—the brief flash of wooziness. She exhaled and washed the taste down her throat with a sip of martini.

Harry tugged on his beer, all the while watching the psychologist. His smile was just beginning to wear lines around his mouth, his chin had sprouted a few days of beard, and his eyes worked with his face to communicate an almost indecent level of acumen.

Feeling his assessment, Sylvia was suddenly self-conscious, aware of this stranger who seemed like a friend—a man she hardly knew but who knew more about her family than she did.

Harry smiled again, glancing away, perhaps to give her time to collect herself without scrutiny. After a few moments, he said, "You called your mother."

"Yeah." Sylvia hid behind the martini glass. "We had a good talk. She's coming to visit for a week."

"Bonnie's quite a woman." Smoke escaped his lips; it swirled in oily patterns through the air. "She says you're a foster mom. A little girl?"

"It's a long story." Sylvia smiled, nodding slowly.

"Congratulations. How's it going?"

"Hard. Terrific. Really hard and really terrific."

"I've got a son," Harry said. "An eight-year-old."

"Great age."

"Special age."

They talked for a few minutes—about kids, music, food, Santa Fe, and L.A., where Harry was based. Any subject but the business that had brought them together at a ridiculously chichi cigar bar in northern New Mexico.

Sylvia worked her way through most of the martini, all the while puffing on the cigar and suffering occasional flashes of queasiness.

Finally, Harry asked, "Ready to get down to it?"

She nodded, suddenly numb. He set a thick manila envelope on the table in front of her.

"Summarize," she said.

"Only if you're sitting down."

Her eyes widened.

Harry said, "Your father left Santa Fe when you were thirteen. He traveled through Arizona and Nevada under the name of Gristina."

"His mother's maiden name."

"After ten months on the road, he was arrested in

California for vagrancy—spent a few nights in a San Bernardino hoosegow."

Sylvia swallowed; her finger traced the stem of the cocktail glass.

"When Daniel Gristina reached L.A., he talked to the folks at the V.A. hospital. While he was there, he met a woman named Cora Tate. She worked in administration for the V.A." Harry tilted his head, and his eyes settled on the psychologist. "Cora helped your father acquire a new identity. He became James or Jim Rule."

Sylvia finished the martini, took a drag on the cigar, then automatically tipped the now empty glass to her lips.

"You want another drink?" Harry signaled the bartender.

Sylvia found enough voice to ask, "My father and this woman had a relationship?"

"A bit more than that."

She bit down on the cigar and waved her fingers at the P.I. in a gesture that clearly meant, *Spill it.*

"Almost two years to the day your father left Santa Fe, he and Cora were married in Los Angeles."

She deposited the cigar in an ashtray and took a deep breath, holding herself in check while the bartender set a second round of drinks on the table. When they were alone again, Sylvia lifted her glass. "To my dad, the polygamist." She drank, then said with mock cheer, "Hey, it could be worse."

"It is," Harry said. "You've got a sister."

"Shit." Sylvia began to laugh while tears overflowed her eyes. "Give me a minute," she sputtered.

He did; he gave her several, and then said, "You're green."

"I think I'm going to be sick."

Harry twisted in his faux leopard-skin chair. "Where's the toilet? I'll help you."

Sylvia held up both hands, eyes closed. "Wait . . . it's passing." She wiped her hair from her face and mumbled, "It's the cigar."

"Yeah, right." Harry produced a clean white handkerchief from a pocket.

Sylvia accepted the offering and blew her nose. When she had recovered, she looked the investigator in his lovely face and said, "Thank you. I mean it."

"You want to hear about your sister?"

"Whoa. Don't think so." She shook her head and held up her glass. "Not until I have *another* drink. My editor will be happy." When she saw the bemused look on Joshua Harold's face, she explained. "I've got the last chapter of my book. *El fin.* That's all she wrote, folks." She expelled air in a great huffing sigh. "Well, that wasn't so bad."

Harry said, "It's usually better to know the truth than to let your imagination fill in the blanks."

Sylvia nodded. She sat up straighter, readying herself to ask the next question that had popped into her head. "When did he die?" When Harry didn't respond, Sylvia leaned forward anxiously. Her elbows dug into the hard surface. "He *is* dead."

"Not officially." Harry took one of her hands in his and patted it gently, a grandfatherly gesture. "About eight years ago, Daniel Strange, a.k.a. Daniel Gristina, a.k.a. Jim Rule disappeared."

"He walked out on his second family, too?" Sylvia began to laugh, a deep, snorting guffaw. The bartender and two new customers turned to stare.

Harry had witnessed a hundred people take the news about lost family members. As he watched the striking woman across the table, hearing the slightly wild sound of her laughter, he smiled. He recognized her laughter as a healthy noise.

POCKET BOOKS
PROUDLY PRESENTS

THE
DR. SYLVIA STRANGE
NOVELS

SARAH LOVETT

DANGEROUS ATTACHMENTS

ACQUIRED MOTIVES

DANTES' INFERNO

Available in paperback from Pocket Books

and

DARK ALCHEMY

Available in hardcover from Simon & Schuster

Turn the page for a preview. . . .

DANGEROUS ATTACHMENTS

*Hunted by the escaped killer known as the Jackal,
Sylvia must stay one step ahead or become the
madman's next prey.*

El chacal, the Jackal, stood on the second tier of cell block one
and stared down at the activity on the floor below. In the
common area, four inmates were playing a round of bridge. A
fifth inmate sat rigid in front of the TV and whispered to
Brooke, a regular on *The Bold and the Beautiful.* The Jackal
sighed; an honest day's labor was rare in this world.

He closed his eyes and silently recited the words of St.
Ignatius Loyola. "Teach us, good Lord, to serve Thee . . . to toil
and not to seek for rest; to labour and not ask for any reward
save that of knowing that we do Thy will."

It was a lesson most of the occupants of CB-1 had not yet
learned. And there were other lessons: thou shalt not steal . . .
thou shalt not kill.

He turned back to gaze into an open cell. The small square
window was already charcoal gray. Each day another two
minutes of daylight were lost. It would keep on that way—
getting darker and darker—until the winter solstice.

Day and night, just like his own two selves. He'd grown so
used to them, he hardly noticed the transformation anymore.
Day getting shorter. Night, longer and longer, ready to take its
due.

It was the killing that made him split apart in the beginning. Or maybe the split was the reason he had begun to kill.

Thou shalt not kill. Finally, after doing so many bad, hurt-
ful things, he had learned: thou shalt not kill.

Unless you are doing His will.

*To labour and not ask for any reward
Save that of knowing that we do Thy will.*

The Jackal had been offered a task, but had not even considered it, until the Lord intervened. The Lord said, "Accept the task, Jackal, and be rewarded." *His will be done.*

The task was to kill. Not a senseless, selfish kill like some of the men had done, like he himself had done a long time ago. This kill was part of the Lord's divine plan.

On earth as it is in heaven.

The reward was great: it would become the crowning glory of his work for the Lord.

He sighed and gazed down at the sheet of paper he'd been clutching in his right hand. Things had been going so well.

But then, a snafu. Somebody was nosy.

And now, he had twice the work.

One hit had become two hits.

The second name was written in pencil, faint but legible. His own handwriting. Over and over. Just the way the nuns had taught him to write *Be sure your sin will find you out*—on the blackboard one hundred times.

The second name covered the page ninety-seven times. The Jackal thought it was an odd name. He took the stub of pencil from his pocket, licked the tip, and smoothed the sheet of paper over the rail. In minute script he added the last three repetitions: Sylvia Strange Sylvia Strange Sylvia Strange.

ACQUIRED MOTIVES

*When Sylvia's wish for lethal justice comes true in
the form of a serial killer who targets rapists, she
must find the means to stop him—before he turns
on her.*

Anthony Randall didn't look like a self-confessed sadistic
rapist. His large blue eyes were free of guile, his cheeks were
tinged pink, his lips habitually worked themselves into a soft
frown. He looked younger than his twenty-two years.

He looked like an altar boy.

Sylvia Strange shifted in the hardwood chair where she had
been poised for more than thirty minutes. The glare of the
fluorescent lights made her head ache. Her navy silk skirt was
creased. She hoped dark circles of perspiration weren't visible
under the arms of her suit jacket. It was her job to maintain
the illusion of control even when the courtroom resembled
the inside of a pressure cooker.

Sylvia noticed sweat easing down Judge Nathaniel
Howzer's throat to the collar of his black robes. The judge had
summoned opposing counsel to the bench three times during
the past fifteen minutes. Clearly, he wasn't pleased with the
most recent turn of events.

Just days earlier, Erin Tulley, an officer with the New Mexico
State Police, had admitted that Anthony Randall had been reeling under the effects of drugs and alcohol when he confessed to
rape. The law demanded that confessions be knowing and vol-
untary—tricky when the confessor's system was toxic.

Immediately following Tulley's turnaround, the defense
had filed a motion to suppress the confession. If granted,
there would be no trial, and the defendant would walk. The
judge had refused to render a decision on the motion until he
heard the testimony of the evaluating forensic psychologist:
Sylvia Strange.

As Judge Howzer conferred yet again with defense and prosecuting attorneys, the bailiff fanned himself with both hands. It had to be pushing ninety degrees in the courtroom. A female journalist in the gallery lifted a ponytail of graying hair above her neck and strained forward to catch the breeze from a portable fan. The nose and mouth of another reporter were covered with a white mask to filter out environmental impurities.

Behind the press row, the family members of the rape victim were huddled together. The victim's mother looked as if she was shell-shocked. Sylvia could hardly bear to glance at the woman.

Judge Howzer finished his murmured consultation with the attorneys. Sylvia took a deep breath to regain her focus as Tony Klavin, the defendant's attorney, approached the witness stand. Klavin was thirty-five, athletic, and aggressive; he committed every ounce of energy to this examination.

"Dr. Strange, at any time during the fifteen hours you spent with the defendant Anthony Randall, did you discuss his family history?"

Sylvia saw Randall seated at the defense table, his blond head held perfectly still. She said, "During the examining interview I obtained a clinical history to establish the individuality of the defendant's background, his family, education, and life experiences."

Tony Klavin nodded sagely and the dark curl that licked his forehead bounced ever so gently. He'd earned a reputation as a cunning and oily defense attorney by taking on offensive clients and winning their high-profile cases. He jammed both hands into his pants pockets and hunkered down. "Did Anthony Randall have a tragic childhood?"

"Objection." The prosecutor, Jack O'Dell, was on his feet. He shook his head in disgust. "Dr. Strange has not been qualified by this court as a dramaturge, Your Honor."

"Mr. Klavin, rephrase the question in less theatrical language."

Tony Klavin touched the tips of his fingers together; his hands formed a triangle. "Dr. Strange, did Anthony Randall become a substance abuser when he was eleven years old?"

For a split second she locked eyes with the defendant; it was like looking into the eyes of something dead. Six weeks ago, during the final clinical interview at the jail, Randall had been cocky, convinced that his ability to manipulate would get him whatever the hell he wanted. He wasn't sophisticated enough to be cognizant of the MMPI-2 validity scales, which detected "fake bad" crazies—those hard-core cases who wanted the world to think they were too sick to take responsibility for their crimes. But he had a good handle on his sociopathic skills: deceit, control, exploitation.

To hear Anthony Randall tell it, *he* was the victim.

Sylvia felt the dampness between her shoulder blades, and one droplet of sweat slowly traveled down her spine. She ran her tongue over her lips and willed herself to speak. "Anthony Randall was hospitalized for alcohol abuse when he was twelve."

"At what age did he begin to drink?"

"Between the ages of ten and eleven."

"And did he also begin sniffing glue?"

Jack O'Dell interjected, "Your Honor—"

While the attorneys argued another point of admissibility, Sylvia took a breath and centered her mind on the business at hand. In this case, she was a witness for the defense. As a forensic psychologist, she worked for prosecution, defense, or the court—whoever requested her services. Impartiality was a professional requirement.

Sylvia had evaluated hundreds of criminal offenders. She had heard enough truly horrific life stories to fill volumes. And most of the time, she felt empathy for the defendants. But Anthony Randall left her cold. He enjoyed inflicting pain.

Sylvia continued to answer Tony Klavin's questions, to build a case for Anthony Randall, the conduct-disordered child who had grown into a dysfunctional, antisocial adult. With each response, Sylvia felt her stomach muscles clench. Months ago, when she first read the police crime reports, she'd wept. Anthony Randall had beaten and raped a fourteen-year-old girl with a metal pipe. And then he'd left her for dead.

Flora Escudero had survived—just barely. But she had been unable to identify her masked attacker.

Sylvia was no proponent of the death penalty. It was an archaic, unjust system—racially and economically biased, outrageously expensive, imperfect, and inhumane.

But she couldn't deny the intensity of the primitive emotion that welled up inside her: she wanted Anthony Randall to die.

DANTES' INFERNO

The clock is ticking as Dr. Strange tracks a serial bomber—her only lead, notorious killer John Dantes.

April 23, 2000—11:14 A.M. Los Angeles was wearing her April best: cerulean sky, whipping cream clouds, rain-washed air that whispered promises of orange blossoms and money. An LA day of sweet nothings.

Wanda Davenport, schoolteacher and amateur painter, expertly gripped the T-shirt of ten-year-old Jason Redding just as he was about to poke a grimy finger between the sculptured buttocks of a 2,500-year-old Icarus. Antiquities were the thing at the Getty Center. And so were toilets. The lack of toilets. Four of her fifth-graders needed to pee, and her assistant was nowhere in sight.

"Line up, guys," Wanda barked with practiced authority. "Jason, you get to hold my hand."

The boy moaned and rolled his eyes, but his face was glowing with excitement. Her class had been planning this trip for six months. Given a choice between Universal Studios and the Getty, they'd gone with art. Fifth-graders! Who woulda thunk?

But then again, Wanda Davenport wasn't your everyday teacher. She was so passionate about Art a wee bit of her passion rubbed off on just about anyone who spent a few weeks under her tutelage. She loved the realists, the impressionists, the dadaists—from the classical artists to the graffiti artists, she was a devoted fan.

She smiled to herself as she gave the command to march. Jason caused her a lot of grief, but secretly he was one of her favorites. He was smart, hyper, and creative. One of these days he could be a famous artist, architect, inventor, physicist, whatever.

"Turn right!" Wanda should've had a night job as a drill sergeant.

Jason nearly tripped over his own two feet, which were audaciously encased in neon green athletic sneakers, one size too big. Wanda knew that his mother, Molly Redding, was a recovering substance abuser; she was also a single mom supporting her only child by waiting tables. These were rough times in the Redding household, but there was love and hope, and Jason was a terrific kid.

"Turn left!" Wanda ordered her students, watching as Maria Hernandez accepted a fireball from Suzie Brown; the bright pink candy disappeared between white teeth.

Twenty minutes earlier, Wanda had herded her troop of ten- and eleven-year-olds onto the white tram car for transport to the hilltop. The 1.4-mile drive had provided a startling view of Los Angeles and the Pacific Ocean. The moneyed view. The new J. Paul Getty Center was situated in Brentwood, nuzzled by Santa Monica, nosed in by mountains.

From the tram and the marble terrace fronting the museum at the hilltop, Wanda had called out city names for her children: Ocean Park, Venice, LA proper (the downtown heart of the metropolitan monster, with its constant halo of smog), San Pedro's south-end industrial shipyards, a tail in the distance . . . then back to Santa Monica and the ocean pier extending like a neon leg into blue waters . . . and last but not least, up the coast to movie-star Malibu, which had incorporated just as mud slides devoured great bites of earth and forest fires grazed the landscape down to bare, charred skin.

With that lesson in geographic and economic boundaries, the kids had marched into the reception building; Wanda barely had time to glance at the program provided for the tour; her students demanded 110 percent of her energy. No matter—she knew this place by heart. In her mind the architectural design was Greek temple married to art deco ocean liner. She'd wandered Robert Irwin's chameleon gardens for hours; each season offered new colors, new scents, new shapes and shades. Santa Monica's Big Blue Bus ran straight to the grounds. She'd lost count of her visits. Nobody had believed Culture could draw a crowd in LA. Well, just look at her kids!

With one expert swipe, Wanda removed a wad of gum from behind the ear of one of her oldest charges while simultaneously comforting the youngest, who was complaining of a stomachache. She couldn't wait to get them into the garden, her very favorite part of the facility. They began the trek across the first exterior courtyard. Water ran like glass between slabs of marble. The children shuffled and slid their shoes across the smooth stones.

"Hey, guys, remember the name of the architect? We covered this in class."

She barely caught Jason's mumbled response: "Meier."

"Richard Meier. That's correct, Mr. Redding."

They were almost to the stairway leading to the museum café and the outdoor dining deck. Within seconds, the central garden would rush into view. Lush with primary color and geometric form (chaos and pattern all at once), it overflowed the space between the multilevel museum and the institutes.

Wanda felt a tug at her sleeve and turned in surprise, looking down at the agitated face of another of her kids.

"Please, Miss Davenport, I have to go," a small voice announced.

"Break time, guys," Wanda called out cheerfully. "When we reach the bottom of these stairs, we'll use the rest rooms and regroup for the garden. Carla, hands to yourself. Thank you. No running, Hector."

They turned the corner, only to be welcomed by the sight of bougainvillea, jacaranda, orchid, daisy, iris, wild grasses, each as lovely and as ephemeral as a butterfly.

Wanda Davenport's last view in life consisted of the gardens she loved so much.

Jason Redding discovered the treasure chest beneath the stairwell. He opened it curiously, saw an intricate, whimsical, handmade collage—an infernal machine constructed of polished wood, ivory, colored wire, and spiked metal pipe filled with black powder.

The puzzled child heard a hissing sound, saw smoke and soft petals, twisting and turning, floating upward: initiation.

One neon green sneaker survived unscathed.

DARK ALCHEMY

Dr. Sylvia Strange finds herself playing cat one moment and mouse the next when she must profile a prominent scientist so brilliant she leaves no evidence of her murders.

"One of the most problematic aspects of the case is the longitudinal factor; the deaths have occurred over a span of at least a decade," Edmond Sweetheart said. He was standing at the window of his room at the Eldorado Hotel. Behind him, the New Mexico sky was the color of raw turquoise and quartzite, metallic cirrus clouds highlighting a blue-green scrim.

"Why did it take so long to put it together?" Dr. Sylvia Strange had chosen to sit at one end of a cream-colored suede sofa in front of a polished burl table, the room's centerpiece. For the moment, she would keep her distance—from Sweetheart, from this new case. Her slender fingers slid over the black frame of the sunglasses that still shaded her eyes. Her shoulder-length hair was slightly damp from the shower she'd taken after a harder-than-usual workout at the gym. She studied the simple arrangement of flowers on the table: pale lavender orchids blooming from a slender vase the color of moss. Late afternoon sun highlighted the moist, fleshlike texture of the blossoms. The air was laced with a heavy, sweet scent. "Why didn't anybody link the deaths?"

"They were written off as unfortunate accidents." Sweetheart frowned. "Everyone missed the connection—the CID, FBI, Dutch investigators—until a young, biochemistry grad assistant was poisoned in London six months ago. Her name was Samantha Grayson. Her fiancé happened to be an analyst with M.I.6—the Brit's intelligence service responsible for foreign intelligence. He didn't buy the idea that his girlfriend had accidentally contaminated herself with high doses of an experimental neurotoxin. Samantha Grayson died a bad death, but her fiancé had some consolation—he zeroed in on a suspect."

"But M.I.6 chases spies, not serial poisoners." Sylvia stretched both arms along the crest of the couch, settling in. "And this is a criminal matter."

She was aware that Sweetheart was impatient. He reminded her of a parent irritated with a sassing child. "So who gets to play Sherlock Holmes, the FBI?"

"As of the last week, the case belongs to the FBI, yes."

She nodded. Although the FBI handled most of its investigations on home turf, in complex international criminal cases the feds were often called upon to head up investigations, to integrate information from all involved local law enforcement agencies—and to ward off the inevitable territorial battles that could destroy any chance of justice and the successful apprehension and prosecution of the guilty party or parties.

"And the FBI is using you—?"

"To gather a profile on the suspect."

Sylvia shrugged. "Correct me if I'm wrong, but the last time I looked, you were a counterterrorist expert. Is there something you're leaving out of your narration?"

"There are unusual facets to this case."

"For instance."

"The suspect deals with particularly lethal neurotoxins classified as biological weapons. As far as we know, at this moment, there's no active terrorist agenda; nevertheless, more than one agency is seeking swift closure."

Sweetheart had his weight pressed against the window frame. The carved wood looked too delicate to support his 280 pounds. "The suspect is female, caucasian, forty-four, never-married, although she's had a series of lovers. She's American, a research toxicologist and molecular biochemist with an I.Q. that's off the charts."

"You've got my attention."

"She received her B.S. from Harvard, then went on to complete her graduate work at Berkeley, top of her class, then medical school, and a one-year fellowship at MIT—by then she was all of twenty-six. She rose swiftly in her career, she cut her teeth on the big shows—Rajneesh, Aum Shinrykyo, the Ventro extortion; she had access to the anthrax samples after nine-eleven—worked for all the big players, including

Lawrence Livermore, the CDC, WHO, USAMRID, DOD. As a consultant she's worked in the private sector as well." Sweetheart knew the facts, reciting them succinctly, steadily, until he paused for emphasis. "Two, maybe three people in the world know as much about exotic neurotoxins and their antidotes as this woman. No one knows more."

Sylvia set her sunglasses on the table next the moss-colored vase. She rubbed the two tiny contact triangles that marked the bridge of her nose. "How many people has she killed? Who were they?"

"It appears the victims were colleagues, fellow researchers, grad assistants. How many? Three? Five? A half dozen?" Sweetheart shrugged. "The investigation has been a challenge; five days ago the target was put under surveillance; we both know it's a trick to gather forensic evidence in a serial case without tipping off the bad guy. Add to that the fact that she doesn't use mundane, easily detectable compounds like arsenic or cyanide. Bodies still need to be exhumed; after years, compounds degrade, pathologists come up with inconclusive data. Think Donald Harvey: he was convicted of 39 poisonings, his count was 86. We may never know how many people she's poisoned."

"Who is she?"

"Her name is Christine Palmer."

"Fielding Palmer's daughter?" Sylvia was visibly surprised. Sweetheart nodded. "What do you know about her?"

"What everybody knows. There was a short profile in *Time* or *Newsweek* a year ago—tied to that outbreak of environmental fish toxin and the rumors it was some government plot to cover up research in biological weapons. The slant of the profile was 'daughter follows in famous father's footsteps.'" Sylvia shifted position, settling deeper into the couch, crossing her ankles. She toyed restlessly with the diamond and ruby ring on the third finger of her left hand. "That can't have been easy. Fielding Palmer was amazing. Immunologist, biologist, pioneer AIDS researcher, writer."

"Did you read his book?"

Sylvia nodded. Fielding Palmer had died of brain cancer in the early 1990s, at the height of his fame and just after the publication of his classic, *A Life of Small Reflections*. The book was a series of essays exploring the ethical complexities, the moral dilemmas of scientific research at the close of the 20th century. He'd been a prescient writer, anticipating the ever deepening moral and ethical quicksand of a world that embraced the science of gene therapy, cloning, and the bio-engineering of new organisms.

Sylvia frowned. It jarred and disturbed—this idea that his only daughter might be a serial poisoner. The thought had an obscene quality.

She saw that Sweetheart had his eyes on her again—he was reading her, gleaning information like some biochemically sensitive scanner. Well, let him wait; she signaled time out as she left the couch, heading for the dark oak cabinet that accommodated the room's mini-bar. She squatted down in front of the cabinet, rifling the refrigerator for a miniature of Stolichnaya and a can of tonic. From the selection of exorbitantly priced junk food she selected a bag of Cheetos.

"Join me?" she asked, as she poured vodka into a tumbler.

"Maybe later."

Sylvia swirled the liquid in the glass, and the tiny bubbles of tonic seemed to bounce off the oily vodka. She turned, holding the glass in front of her face, staring at Sweetheart, her left eye magnified through a watery lens. She said, "That's the beauty of poison—invisibility."

Visit the
Simon & Schuster Web site:
www.SimonSays.com

and sign up for our
mystery e-mail updates!

Keep up on the latest
new releases, author appearances,
news, chats, special offers, and more!

We'll deliver the information
right to your inbox — if it's new,
you'll know about it.

SIMON & SCHUSTER
A VIACOM COMPANY
www.SimonSays.com

POCKET BOOKS   POCKET STAR BOOKS

2350-01